THE QUEEN OF THE DAWN

ALSO BY S. M. GAITHER

The Shadows & Crowns series:

The Song of the Marked
A Twist of the Blade
The Call of the Void
A Crown of the Gods

The Serpents & Kings series

The Shift Chronicles

The Drowning Empire series

SHADOWS & CROWNS
BOOK FIVE

S. M. GAITHER

PENGUIN BOOKS

PENGUIN BOOKS

UK | USA | Canada | Ireland | Australia
India | New Zealand | South Africa

Penguin Books is part of the Penguin Random House group of companies
whose addresses can be found at global.penguinrandomhouse.com

First published by S. M. Gaither/Yellow Door Publishing, INC in 2022
First published in the UK by Del Rey in 2022
Published in Penguin Books 2024
001

Map illustrations by S. M. Gaither

Ensemble character art by Grace Callaway & Silverfoot art by Natalie Bernard

Typeset in 9.89/16pt CrimsonText by Jouve (UK), Milton Keynes
Printed and bound in Great Britain by Clays Ltd, Elcograf S.p.A.

The authorised representative in the EEA is Penguin Random House Ireland,
Morrison Chambers, 32 Nassau Street, Dublin D02 YH68

A CIP catalogue record for this book is available from the British Library

ISBN: 978–1–804–94589–6

www.greenpenguin.co.uk

To Rachel—

For refusing to let me run away

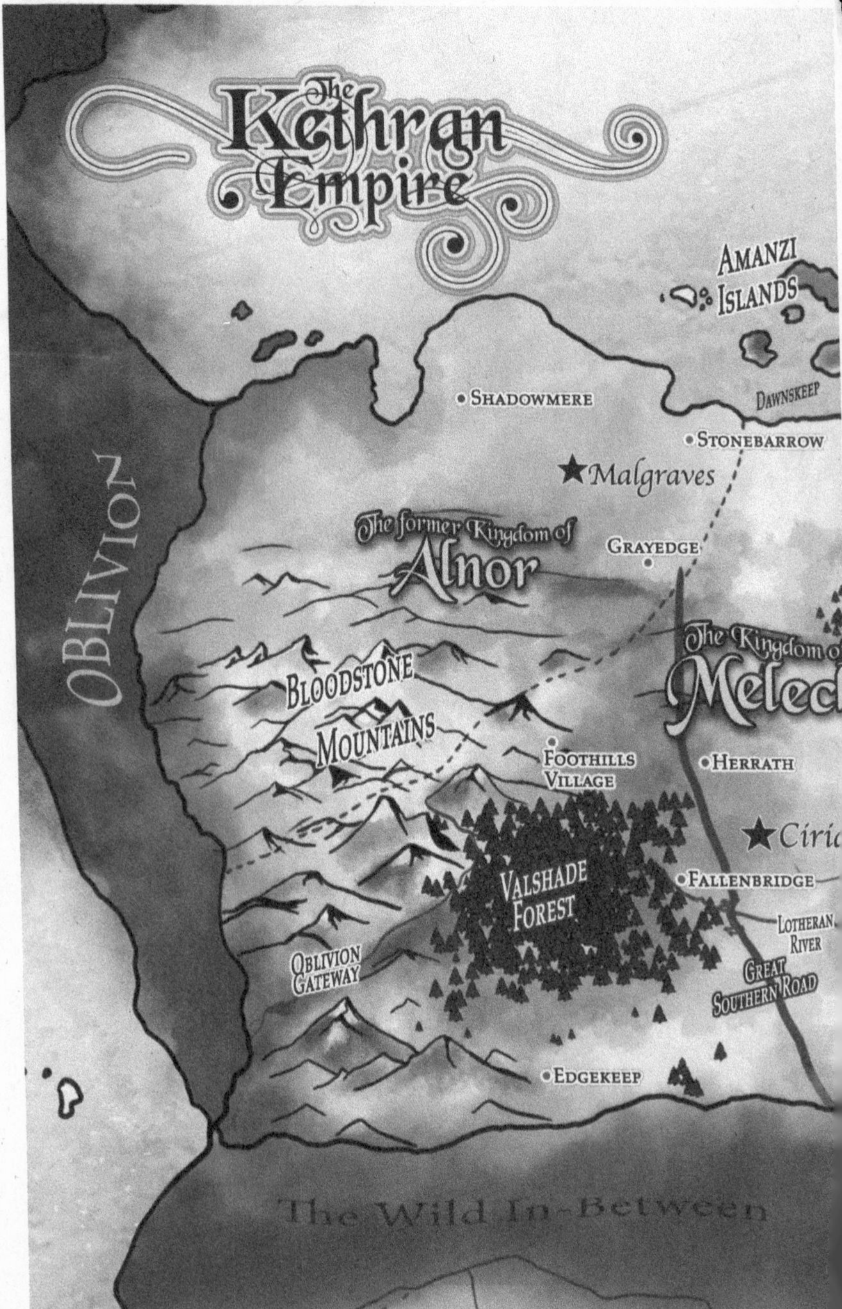

The Kethran Empire

Amanzi Islands
Shadowmere
Dawnskeep
Stonebarrow
Malgraves
Oblivion
The former Kingdom of
Alnor
Grayedge
The Kingdom of
Melec
Bloodstone Mountains
Foothills Village
Herrath
Ciri
Valshade Forest
Fallenbridge
Lotheran River
Great Southern Road
Oblivion Gateway
Edgekeep
The Wild In-Between

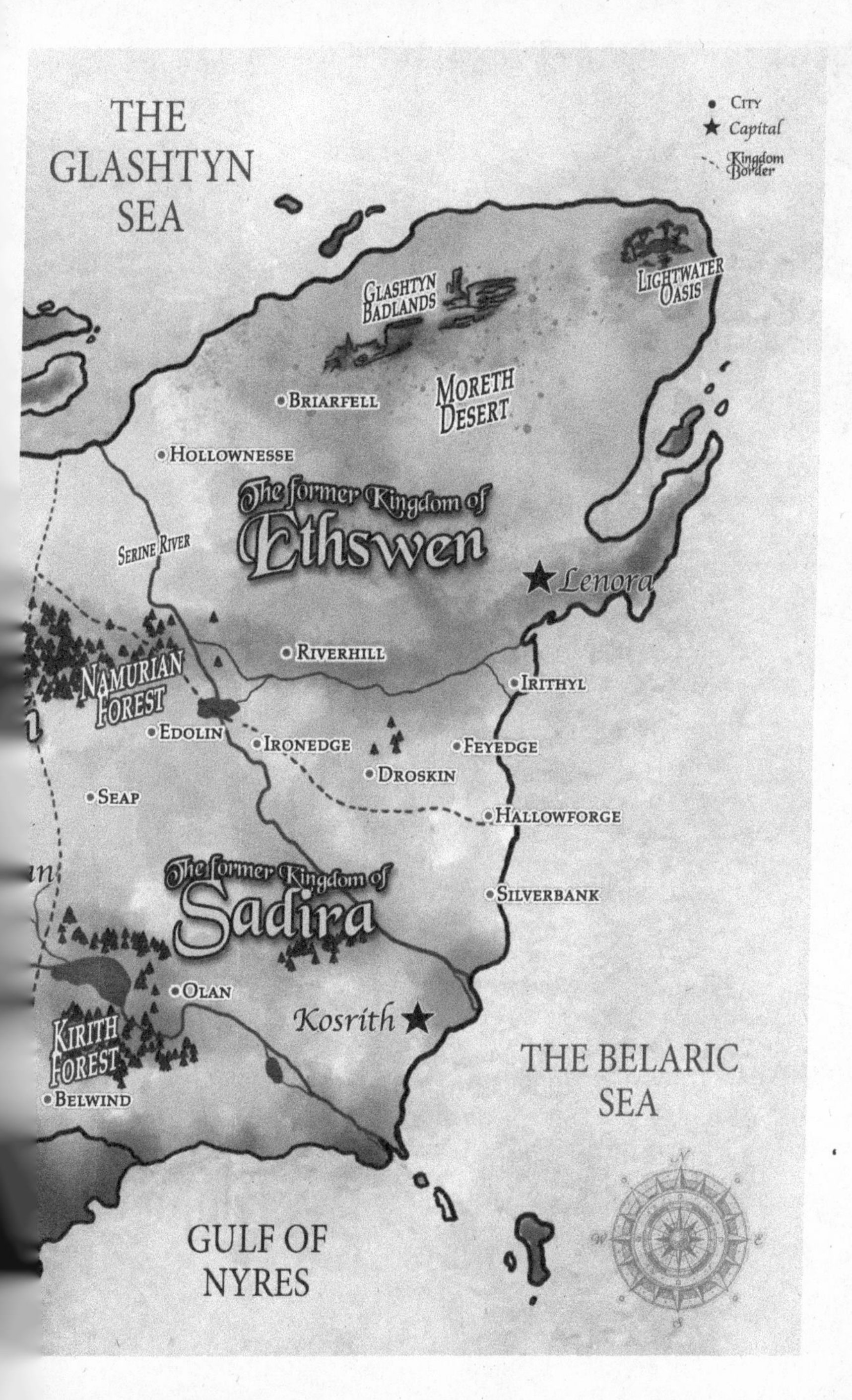
THE GLASHTYN SEA
City
Capital
Kingdom Border
GLASHTYN BADLANDS
LIGHTWATER OASIS
BRIARFELL
MORETH DESERT
HOLLOWNESSE
The former Kingdom of
Ethswen
SERINE RIVER
Lenora
RIVERHILL
NAMURIAN FOREST
IRITHYL
EDOLIN
IRONEDGE
FEYEDGE
DROSKIN
SEAP
HALLOWFORGE
The former Kingdom of
Sadira
SILVERBANK
OLAN
Kosrith
KIRITH FOREST
BELWIND
THE BELARIC SEA
GULF OF NYRES

City
Capital
Kingdom Border
The Kethran Empire
GLASHTYN SEA
Amanzi Islands
Glashtyn Badlands
Lightwater Oasis
Moreth Desert
Briarfell
Dawnskeep
Shadowmere
Hollownesse
Stonebarrow
Malgraves
Oblivion
The former Kingdom of Alnor
Grayedge
The former Kingdom of Ethswen
Lenora
Riverhill
Irithyl
The Kingdom of Melech
Namurian Forest
Edolin
Ironedge
Feyedge
Droskin
Bloodstone Mountains
Foothills Village
Herrath
Seap
Hallowforge
Ciridan
The former Kingdom of Sadira
Silverbank
Valshade Forest
Fallenbridge
Oblivion Gateway
Great Southern Road
Olan
Kirith Forest
Kosrith
Belwind
Edgekeep
The Wild in Between
GULF OF NYRES
Kavus
Ostedge
Cobos Desert
Glasker
Eriden
Rykarra
Kingdom of Valin
Hollowforge
THE BELARIC SEA
BAY OF SINKING SOULS
Kingdom of Galasea
Antier Jungle
Vanish
Termarth
Gateway of the Sun
Greybank Penisula
Idalia
Sinhara Mountains
Sora
Belhurst
Vespera
Kingdom of Lumeria
Indres River
Nephele Dustfields
Verlore Forest
Amara (the gateway to the Middle Heavens)
The Sundolian Empire
N
W
E
S

THE HIERARCHY OF GODS

THE QUEEN OF THE DAWN

CHAPTER I

Within the murky water, Casia heard no sound.

There had been sound in the beginning. Too much of it. The roar of the current, the thunder of her own heartbeat, the sloshing of waves that had accompanied her initial descent into the frigid river—all together a beastly symphony trying to drive her down, down, and deeper down into a chaos she thought she'd never surface from.

Now it was silent.

Each passing moment felt longer than the one before it.

The space around her appeared to stretch into infinite grey waves, yet she felt trapped. Tight. Bricked in. Encased in stone, heavy and sinking, and it was only a matter of time, she was certain, before she hit the bed of the river and the sands buried her. Drowned her. *Erased her.*

Her lips formed a silent word at this last thought—*no.*

That wasn't right.

Somewhere, far in the back of her mind, she remembered the warning the Goddess of Time had given her. Those sacrificed to the River Drow's waves did not drown among them; they merely treaded water. Forever.

So there was no bed below, waiting to take her in.

Was there a surface above?

She closed her eyes.

It should have brought darkness. Instead, it brought *brightness*—a dozen flashing memories of surfacing, emerging from a murkiness not unlike the one she currently tumbled within. She saw the brilliant faces of her friends; the sparkling dwellings of gods she'd walked alongside; the promising glow of her kingdom and her crown and everything she had been trying to save. She heard a voice…

Her own?

Yes—a far-off memory of it, a quiet whisper of a promise she had made to herself what felt like years ago now.

No matter what dark waters await us, I will keep fighting my way back to the surface.

Magic unfurled in her. Her eyes blinked open as her power sparked within the grey waters, embers of light swirling first from the tips of her fingers before lifting from the veins of her arms. Her heart pounded as the brilliance diffused around her—as she waited for another light to answer it. Across miles, across worlds, across lifetimes… she had gotten used to Elander's magic responding, joining hers.

Would he be able to feel her now?

She just wanted him to know—wanted *all* the ones she'd left behind to know—that she was still fighting.

She summoned and sent another burst of magic surging forth.

Another, another, another.

Then finally, a response—an answering surge of magic. She had not created this surge, but it belonged to her all the same; it thundered through her as surely as the beat of her own heart.

Elander.

A light inside the darkness, leading her home.

She just had to keep reaching for it.

She kept summoning until she could no longer separate herself from her power—from him—and there, within the bright silence, she waited and hoped.

CHAPTER 2

Elander spun around as another section of the Ciridan Palace crumbled.

A bridge between two of the towers had been compromised—struck and cracked by a wayward blast of magic—and now those towers were tilting toward one another, their sides buckling under the weight of their own impending collapse, their bricks shifting free and clattering to the ground with rapidly increasing frequency.

He fought the urge to sprint for safety, instead searching the space below the towers for anyone who might be in harm's way.

All of the bodies he saw appeared dead.

No one left to save.

The violent *tinging* and *cracking* of shattering glass and the thunder of falling stone vibrated through him, rattling his bones and making his balance sway. He gripped the sword in his hand more tightly and backed swiftly away from the towers.

The air sizzled with magic and shivered with unnatural

breezes. The scent of blood and other bodily fluids mingled with dust and fire, making his stomach turn and his eyes water. The sound of shouting and clashing weapons pounded into his skull, reverberating through it without mercy.

There were too many enemies to count.

The initial attack had been largely made up of the familiar, faceless monstrosities they'd fought in the past, the *namtar*—servants of the Dark God with an ability to shift and negate energy. But as the hours pressed on, more nightmarish beings had slid into the ranks. Elander recognized deadly creatures he had not seen in decades; the servants of divine enemies who hadn't walked this mortal plane in at least as long.

To his right, a birdlike creature with glowing eyes and curved, claw-tipped wings resembling scythes ripped the flesh from a fallen soldier.

To his left, another beast encircled a trio of palace guards. Flames sprung up wherever its paws stepped, fanned further to life as it unhinged its jaw and exhaled a roar of breath laced with smoke. Before the guards disappeared behind the wall of flames, Elander caught a glimpse of them dropping to their knees and starting to beg for mercy.

So much chaos.

He desperately wanted to stop it all. To turn away from the devastation and focus only on the single most devastating thing to him—

Casia was gone.

She had vanished into the air only minutes ago, whisked away by use of a magical hourglass the Goddess of Time had given her. He only wanted to think of her in that moment—*where had she gone? how could he reach her?*—but before he could answer these questions, he first had to survive the battle directly in front of him.

A sudden howl made him spin around, drawing his gaze to the orchestrator of this battle.

Malaphar, the Dark God of Chaos himself, had been contained by magic—by a combined effort from Casia and the Goddess of the Moon.

His cage had splintered.

He was breaking free, his body more shadow than solid flesh as it expanded and blotted out the scenery behind him.

The first definite parts to reform were his wings, unfolding and stretching out from his confines with violent twitches. Each snapping twitch sent bits of magic peeling into the air with a sound like chains popping, breaking off link by link.

Once the powerful wings had broken free, it took only a single mighty flap to lift him entirely up and out of his prison. He hovered for a moment, a terrifying cloud of darkness surveying the death and destruction he'd caused.

The ground shook as the god touched down upon it. The dark armor covering him glistened like inky feathers in the moonlight as he twisted toward Elander while simultaneously reaching for the weapon at his hip.

He withdrew an obsidian blade that crackled with whitish-blue light and swung it in a wild arc. A wave of shadowy energy swept outward with the motion, flattening everything around him—people and trees and manmade structures alike.

As the energy washed over Elander, his own magic ignited—the magic of a guardian, a *vitali,* rising to form armor made of golden light, pulsing like stars emerging against a deepening twilight.

He managed to stay on his feet even as others collapsed around him.

Soon he was the only thing still standing within the god's path, and he was the one Malaphar's burning eyes narrowed on.

Behind him, Elander heard the sound of countless pounding boots, all growing fainter—running away.

He gave no thought to escaping. He would die where he stood before he turned away from this monster who had taken so much from him.

"All of these most *powerful* humans gathered to plot my demise," said the god with a chuckle, his fiery eyes scanning the chaos and landing on the closest pile of debris—a jumble of broken furniture pieces and shards of dishes. "What a waste of good food and wine this evening has been."

Elander did not reply as he readjusted his hold on the sword in his hand. *Shadowslayer*. It was Casia's sword, but he'd used it in the past—had picked it up and carried on for her when her hold on it had faltered.

He thought he could feel her energy radiating from it even now, whenever he squeezed the grip.

"And the *queen* herself seems to have fled the party," Malaphar added, a smile splitting his features, his sharp white teeth nearly lost against his ashen complexion.

The words were splinters gouging their way under Elander's skin, but in the raw spaces they left behind, a stubborn thought settled in—*she's not gone*.

"Pity she couldn't stick around for the ending."

"This is not the ending." Elander lifted Shadowslayer, pointing the tip at Malaphar's chest. "And she's closer than you think." Along with the threat in his voice came strands of magic, lifting from Shadowslayer's edge and twisting together until they were a near-solid extension of the blade.

The god's smile disappeared.

In the span of a breath, another wave of darkness rose at Malaphar's back.

With no more warning than this, he was upon Elander, his black sword drawn and slicing forward, pulling that dark wave as he came.

Elander ducked the first swing, but the shadows following in the sword's wake blinded him to Malaphar's second strike. A vicious spin brought the obsidian blade back toward Elander, and he caught only a last-second glimmer of steel before it struck his arm, leaving behind a shallow gash and a searing pain that nearly made him lose his balance.

Another spin, another strike—

Elander managed to parry the second. Their blades collided, releasing sparks of light and swirls of shadow. He leapt back. Forward again. Again and again they collided, until the air was filled with so much magical residue that Elander was forced to retreat in search of air he could breathe.

He caught his breath, but the foggy residue of their powers still hung heavily around him, making it difficult to see and keep track of his target.

But *something* was cutting clearly through the murky air; Elander glanced down at his bloodied sleeve, and then beyond that...the sword he held was *glowing*. The etched symbols of the Sun Goddess and her court were burning brightly along the blade.

He felt it again as he clenched the grip—the familiar heartbeat of Casia's magic weaving through the empty spaces of his own, building and fortifying his power.

End this battle so I can focus on finding her.

The weapon seemed eager to obey, warming and humming beneath his touch. The symbols blazed even more brightly upon its steel edge. As they did, he spotted something strange out of the corner of his eye—a light the same color as the symbols on the sword. It was spreading from a crack in the ground close to where he'd last seen Casia.

The light bled through this fissure, spilling out and flooding the battlefield. The closer Elander came to it, the harder the sword in his hand vibrated, and the bolder the markings on the blade became.

He stepped more fully into the light, lowering his eyes against the overwhelming brightness.

The Dark God reappeared, another wall of darkness rising up behind him as he came. When he slammed to a stop—mere inches from Elander—that wall continued onward, washing over Elander like a storm-thrown wave. It eclipsed the light and reduced everything to a terrifying, silent void.

Elander dropped to one knee, stabbing the sword into the cracked ground. One hand remained tightly wrapped around the weapon's grip while he used the other to brace himself against the dirt.

The dark continued to press in, still absorbing all brightness and sound. Elander heard nothing but the thundering beat of his own heart, his pulse pounding in his ears, until—

A second heartbeat.

He held tighter to Shadowslayer.

He didn't know where Casia had gone, or how far she might have been, but there was no mistaking the pulse of her, nor the warmth starting to flood through his body. And he could only think one thought, over and over.

Come back to me.

The hammering beat grew faster, almost violent, and the light expanded with the same rhythm. Faster, louder, *brighter*—bright enough to drive away every wave of darkness that Malaphar summoned.

It was blisteringly hot for a moment, noise roaring all around Elander, and then…

Cold silence.

He exhaled slowly.

The radiance faded, revealing a battlefield now emptied of the Dark God and his minions.

"Impossible," he heard himself whisper.

Because it was. It *should* have been. Not only was the Dark God missing, but so too were all the remnants of his power. All the beasts that served his court, all the shadowy threads of his personal magic, all the void archers whose ranks had been a hundred strong *at least*…

All of it.

Gone.

Elander knelt for a moment in the center of the sudden emptiness, head tucked toward his chest, vision spinning.

He heard footsteps followed by a familiar voice—Nephele, Goddess of Storms. "It felt like…*her* for a moment there, didn't it?"

A second familiar voice—Inya, Goddess of the Moon—answered. "Solatis…" She sounded overwhelmed. Awed, almost.

"Could she still have a hold on this world after all?"

"It didn't feel like Solatis." Elander slowly rose back to his feet. He looked in the same direction they were staring in, toward the edge of the palace grounds where a barrier—a newly reinforced version of one they'd put in place earlier that day—glistened brightly. He felt the goddesses gazes slowly turning toward him, expectant, but he kept his eyes on that distant barrier. "It felt like Casia. Like she was weaving her power into my own, same as we've been doing for weeks."

Out of the corner of his vision, Elander thought he saw them exchange a concerned look.

Inya spoke first. "That necklace she had…the power it radiated…it was the Time Goddess's, wasn't it?"

Elander kept his eyes averted.

Nephele gave an irritable snort. "So she could be anywhere across the reaches of space and time at this point. Knowing Santi, she—"

"*Hush,*" Inya said. "Wherever she is, at least we're protected for the moment—long enough to make our next plan."

For the moment.

Elander doubted it would last. He needed to move, to search, to do *something* before that glimmering barrier around the palace failed once more and the darkness returned. "It seems unlikely that Santi's servant is still lingering around here," he thought aloud. "But perhaps if we could find her…"

"We'll spread out and search," Inya offered.

Nephele started to speak—an objection of some sort, most likely—but Elander had already started to walk away, and he didn't look back.

Fallen bodies from both sides littered the ground. His eyes glazed over as he moved, but he couldn't help noticing a scarf of fine silk to his right, snaked across the ground, drenched in blood. He wondered briefly about who it had belonged to. There had been so many nobles present, such a successful meeting of dozens of the empire's most powerful people...

It had turned so disastrous, so quickly, that all of these things felt like they had been nothing more than a dream—and now they had woken up.

He kept moving. Through the blood and brokenness, stepping over shattered glass and still bodies splayed out in odd positions; maneuvering around the healers darting about and trying to find bodies that still moved and cried out to them for help.

He wasn't entirely sure where he was going. He was simply trying to get to a place where he could focus better.

He eventually reached it—in the shadow of a tower that still stood completely intact. Flowering white trees dotted the space, their fallen blossoms carpeting the ground, their heady scent stronger than all the blood and ruin he'd walked away from. It was eerie how normal everything seemed when he stood within those trees.

He squeezed Shadowslayer once more. And he sensed it again: a warmth that felt like *her*. The air hummed with faint power, stirring enough to make the branches sway and shed more of their flowers.

What did it mean?

He wanted to believe Casia was on the other side of it. That she was reaching out to him. That their connection was as strong as it had ever been, regardless of where she was, and that their magic had combined—as it had been doing so often these past weeks—to create the powerful shield now surrounding the palace and its grounds.

But another, far more devastating thought had also occurred to him.

When the Goddess of the Sun—the deity he and Casia

ultimately owed their magic to—had been sealed away weeks ago, some of her excess power had spilled out over the mortal lands.

Was that what had happened with Casia and her power, too? What if…

What if she had left this plane for good, and he had been left behind, nothing but a vessel to catch what he could of her fading light?

The world reeled around him at the thought. It couldn't be true. This empire needed more than just her light. It needed *her*.

And so did he.

He moved closer to the intact tower and walked along it, pausing to steady his balance against the cold stone every so often. That warmth and power of Casia followed him. He occasionally thought he heard her voice among the fluttering. But when he tried to focus on it, it disappeared. He could scarcely even picture her face, for some reason; he saw only grey waves whenever he tried.

Someone shouted for him—Zev. He turned toward the noise, happy for the distraction even if the Fire-kind did get on his nerves. Whatever foolish squabbles they'd had in the past seemed irrelevant at the moment.

The last time he'd seen Zev, he'd been helping Laurent escape with…

Nessa.

The Feather-kind girl had been stabbed by Malaphar. Elander had not seen all of it unfolding, only the immediate aftermath, and now he remembered the awful *after* moments with nauseating clarity: the way everything had seemed to collapse all around them; the frightened but determined look in Casia's eyes before she'd vanished; the words she'd said…

I love you, I love you, I love you.

If Casia had been here, finding out what happened to Nessa would have been her first priority. So until he figured out how to reach Casia, he decided he would carry her sword and trace the steps he knew she'd take; it was all he could think to do.

He took one last look at the dust swirling and settling over the eerie, emptying battlefield, and then he turned and hurried after Zev, hoping he'd lead the way to Nessa.

CHAPTER 3

Zev ran across the yard, heading for the small stone house that had once served as the master groundskeeper's dwelling.

Elander followed closely behind. His thoughts were still distracted, his eyes drawn over and over again to the still-faintly pulsing sword in his hand rather than on the path they were taking—he nearly collided with Zev when he came to a sudden halt several feet away from the door of the house.

Zev swept a wary glance at the desolation around them before opening that door and beckoning Elander inside. "This is why I was trying to get your attention," he quietly said. "Because I need you to tell me what *that* is."

Elander looked to where Zev pointed.

A creature floated in the center of the room, its long arms and legs dangling out from underneath a cocooning cape of ivory and gold feathers. Its head was oval in shape, two antlers that resembled tree branches creeping out from the back of it, and its mouth was wide, curved and beak-like.

Orias, the Feather spirit—the divine being associated with calmness and clarity.

Beyond the spirit, beyond the soft golden glow she emitted, a makeshift bed had been made of what appeared to be chair cushions and various linens and articles of clothing piled together in the corner.

The person resting there was mostly swallowed up by the pile, but Elander recognized the honey waves of Nessa's hair cascading over the side of the cushion.

He watched carefully for a moment, until he saw movement from Nessa—a subtle tilt of her head toward the spirit.

Not dead quite yet.

He allowed himself a small sigh of relief.

Silverfoot's paws rested on the same cushion as Nessa's head, lifting the fox's lanky body up so he could occasionally sniff and whine at her still form, while Rhea paced at a distance, twisting and untwisting a handkerchief.

The spirit hovered perhaps ten feet away from the bed, her yellow eyes fixed on Nessa.

A certain half-elf was standing between the two of them, blocking the spirit from moving any closer than this.

Laurent was flanked on either side by two soldiers, all with weapons drawn and glowing with the divine magic they had been infused with. There was something feral about the half-elf's appearance, and it brought to mind every story Elander had ever heard about the elves of Moreth and their viciousness. Laurent's father—the former king of that realm—had been among the most vicious. And it was far from Laurent's usual demeanor, but in that moment, he looked every bit that dangerous king's successor.

The spirit stopped her hovering, soundlessly dropping to

the wooden plank floor. A ring of pale yellow light encircled the spot where she touched down.

The soldiers flanking Laurent shifted into more ready stances.

The spirit flared her wings, and a symbol appeared between her shoulder blades—the same delicate feather pattern that graced Nessa's skin. The mark flashed brightly upon the spirit's back before the spirit refolded her wings, covering it. Elander thought he could see Nessa's hand lighting beneath a cloth that had been tossed over her, glowing as if in answer.

Zev shuffled uncertainly beside him. "So, is that..."

"The Feather spirit," Elander confirmed. "Servant of the Goddess of Healing."

Zev studied the creature for a moment, arms folding against his chest, before he muttered, "Nice of that goddess to decide to send help *now*."

Elander secretly felt a similar stab of irritation; they had petitioned that deity to more fully join their cause several times over the past weeks. She'd staunchly refused each time, as was typical of the pacifistic goddess.

"She already saved your reckless, sorry hide once before, don't forget," Rhea reminded Zev, grimly, as she came to stand beside her brother. "And at least she's sending more help now—better late than never."

Elander nodded. He steadied himself and stepped cautiously between Laurent and Orias. He studied the spirit for a moment—he couldn't remember the last time he'd seen her in person—and then he moved to Laurent and laid a hand on his shoulder. "Let her pass," he said, nodding back at the spirit, who was now watching him with a curious look. "She can help."

She's on our side, he wanted to add—because he couldn't imagine the Goddess of Healing or her servants ever joining Malaphar's ranks. But he couldn't find the confidence to say this out loud.

How could they be certain about *any* of the divine beings at this point?

Then again, Orias had managed to breach the enclosing walls of Sun magic that had driven Malaphar and his followers away.

That had to mean something, didn't it?

He frowned. There were too many things he didn't understand. All he was certain of right then was that this spirit was connected to Nessa, and it could help keep her calm until they could find the means to heal her, if nothing else. He explained as much to Laurent—several times—until the half-elf finally relented and stepped aside.

The tension in the room coiled tightly as Orias approached the makeshift bed, but it released just as quickly as the spirit's feathers ruffled and magic bloomed around her.

It was the same calming magic Nessa possessed, only magnified several times over. The soldiers around Laurent were instantly overcome by it; two of them leaned so heavily against the wall they ended up sliding down it and staying there, eyes fluttering shut as they landed, while the other two remained standing, closing their eyes and bowing their heads as if overcome by the sudden urge to meditate.

As the magic sank over Nessa, Elander heard her take a deep, if somewhat rattling, breath.

Laurent's body had grown less stiff within the falling net of the spirit's magic, but his gaze remained as alert as ever as he followed every move Orias made. The hand on his sword never relaxed, even after the spirit stepped away from Nessa and stopped summoning magic.

Orias made no sound aside from the soft ruffling of feathers as she moved, sweeping away from the bed and disappearing into the air, leaving nothing but a shimmer of pale gold where she'd last stood.

The calmness she'd created lingered. The air teemed with her power. She hadn't gone far, Elander didn't think. But why had she gone away at all? All these shifting energies and the divine coming and going...it was making it hard to find his balance.

He watched Nessa's weak form, waiting again for her to show some sign of life. And finally, there it was—a slight rise and fall of the linens she was buried beneath. *Still breathing.*

Barely.

Laurent moved to kneel beside her. Rhea drifted closer as well, kneeling on the other side and feeling her way toward Nessa's hand, which she clasped tightly.

Zev watched them for a moment before giving his head a little shake—as if trying to rid it of the warm and fuzzy feeling caused by the spirit's magic. He moved to the window behind Elander and stood with his arms braced against the sill, his expression as dark as the night he was staring out into.

After a few minutes he spoke, low enough for only Elander to hear. "Where did Cas go?"

"I wish I knew."

Zev didn't take his eyes away from the window.

"That necklace she had was a gift from the Time Goddess," Elander explained. "It could conceivably have taken her to anywhere...or any *when*."

Zev let out a soft curse. One of his hands was clenched

into a fist, and he seemed to be fighting the urge to put it through the glass pane in front of him.

It didn't seem like the *worst* idea to Elander, given their current options.

A few more minutes passed before Zev turned and started to speak again—only to be interrupted by a sharp bark.

Rhea stood quickly, her attention shifting toward the door as Silverfoot bounded toward it, his barking growing more frantic.

The Goddess of Storms appeared a moment later, dragging the lesser-spirit of Air, Velia, behind her. A rope of lightning encircled the spirit, keeping her from managing more than a few stiff steps and unnatural twitches.

Elander strode furiously toward them, Zev right behind him. The Storm Goddess tightened her lasso of magic and forced the spirit to stand up straighter as Elander reached her.

"The goddess you serve gave Casia a necklace weeks ago, didn't she?"

The spirit's large eyes flashed with understanding—and fear—at Elander's question.

"Do you know where Cas is?" Zev demanded.

Velia attempted to twist free of Nephele's magic, writhing and yowling like a wounded cat.

Elander closed the remaining space between them with inhuman speed, snatching the spirit by the throat. The movement was so violent that it even startled the Goddess of Storms—though not enough to make her magic loosen its hold. The current of it tingled through Elander's arm as he squeezed more tightly, his hand nearly large enough to encircle the spirit's thin neck.

One of the spirit's long antennae twitched. It made no more sound or attempts to wriggle free, but Elander felt a new magic coursing through him—the spirit's own as she tried to use her divine power to disappear.

Nephele's magic was stronger, paralyzing the spirit's powers and causing her body to go partially limp.

"Tell us where Casia is," Elander growled.

"Let me go first." The spirit's voice was breathy and weak.

Elander held her more tightly.

"I can't think of where she is when I can't *breathe*," wailed the spirit.

"Maybe we should let her speak," Rhea said uncertainly.

Elander hesitated. Slowly, reluctantly, he uncurled his fingers and took a step back. He looked to the Storm Goddess.

Nephele's nose wrinkled in displeasure, but she eventually conceded and the ropes of lightning loosened, releasing the Air spirit, though the air still crackled with her magic. There were flames flickering to life in the edge of Elander's vision, as well; Zev, trying and failing to keep his temper under control.

The spirit watched each threatening crackle and flicker with increasingly wide eyes, head shifting side to side as she cowered beneath Elander. She seemed to be calculating something.

"Speak," Elander commanded.

Velia didn't speak.

"You are playing a dangerous game."

Still no response.

"I have already killed one divine spirit tonight," he snapped, catching the spirit once more by the throat and lifting her gaze to his, "and I will not hesitate to kill a second if you do not *tell me where my queen is.*"

The fresh memory of his own sword cutting Caden down burned in his mind, making his breath hitch violently and his grip on Velia tighten.

He *wanted* to kill something in that moment. *Anything.* And this writhing creature in his grasp made the perfect target.

A spirit for a spirit.

It only seemed fair.

He resisted only because he needed Velia to answer his questions.

And after another threatening squeeze, the spirit finally choked out a word: "*Kantrum.*"

A chill raced through Elander, numbing him so brutally quickly that his grip faltered. The spirit wrenched herself free and bounded away, putting several feet between them before twisting back, lowering her head, and blinking her large eyes up at Elander.

"I didn't witness it," said Velia, panting. "I only know what my goddess had planned to do."

The sparks of lightning and swirls of flame faded from the air. He could feel Nephele and Zev staring at him, their shock and confusion a palpable thing, a weight settling heavily on his shoulders.

Elander could not bring himself to speak over the lump forming in his throat. *Kantrum.* That was the last place he'd expected to hear—the last place he *wanted* to hear.

The realm outside of time and space.

What had Casia been *thinking*?

The vision he'd had earlier—the grey waves washing

through his thoughts whenever he'd tried to picture her face... Now it made sense.

"She's in the river," he whispered.

No.

The Air spirit took several steps back.

Elander clenched his hands into fists, focusing on the feel of his nails digging into his palms. He needed the biting pain. This was a nightmare, but he was wide awake, and he had to *stay* awake. To make a plan of some sort.

The spirit continued cautiously putting space between them.

Elander closed in on her again with a few long strides. "The Goddess of Time walks in and out of that place at will. Can you do the same?"

Velia froze. She trembled and fidgeted, but didn't take another step.

Yes, in other words.

"Take me there. Now."

The spirit lowered her gaze. Shook her head. Tried to speak several times without managing it.

It was Nephele who eventually cleared her throat and said, "Casia is not divine. Neither are you. That place could end you both. The river there..."

Elander ignored her and took another step toward the Air spirit, who had sunk even lower to the ground.

"My goddess gave her to that river," said the spirit without lifting her head, "and the Storm Goddess speaks the truth—that river does not give back."

He knew that already.

He didn't care.

"She will not resurface." The spirit's words came out in a hoarse whisper. "Neither would you, if you were to—"

"Take me there," he repeated.

The spirit's trembling grew more intense.

Hopeless. He was tempted to make good on his earlier threat, to take the life of this stupid creature. But something stayed his hand—the spirit hadn't disappeared, even after Nephele released her, even though she had the power to whisk herself to essentially anywhere else.

"Why are you still here?" he asked.

No answer.

"You feel regret for what you've done, don't you? You must want to fix it, or else you would have fled by now."

The spirit slowly lifted her head. The shivering continued, but her gaze focused on his without blinking.

"*Fix it,* spirit. If you take me to that river's edge, perhaps then you won't be remembered as nothing more than a sniveling, cowardly servant on what will eventually be the losing side of this divine war."

The room went very quiet.

Nephele seemed to be holding back another argument.

Silverfoot sat between the goddess and Rhea, his tail twitching uncertainly and a soft whine escaping him every time he glanced up at Nephele.

Rhea still held the handkerchief from earlier, still working it nervously between her hands. "Maybe we should come up with a less dangerous plan—"

"What *isn't* fucking dangerous at this point?" her brother interrupted. "We don't have time to debate this. Cas is in trouble. And without her, this world, this war, it's *all* in trouble. We..." He trailed off. Looked to Elander. Took a deep breath that only partly settled the restless flickers of fire swirling around his hands. "You have to bring her back."

Elander narrowed his gaze on the spirit. "Face what

you've done and help make it right—or flee like the coward you seem to be. Which is it?"

The air rippled again with the spirit's gathering power.

Preparing to flee? A snarl of disgust twisted Elander's lips, fully expecting that to be the choice the creature made.

But then, without saying another word, the spirit stretched a slender hand toward him.

CHAPTER 4

Elander reached back.

A single touch was all it took. The world reduced to waves of the Air spirit's power pressing in, wrapping around, pulling him off his feet.

His senses completely left him. For how long, he wasn't sure, but when they returned, he was kneeling on a beach covered in grey sand and countless small pebbles, and he was alone. He searched for Velia, but there was no living creature on this beach aside from himself.

That could be a problem when it's time to go back to the mortal realm.

He stood slowly, brushing the grit from his knees. A river stretched before him, the color of dense fog, churning viciously. It was oddly quiet in spite of the turbulent waters —like it might have been an incomplete illusion created by magic.

But it wasn't an illusion.

He could feel Casia's life-force pulsing somewhere far

below the waves—that was real—and the sword in his hand glowed more brightly than ever.

He removed that sword, along with his belt, his coat, and his boots, and he piled them on a large, flat rock. The blade continued to glow. A beacon to lead him back to the shore once he found what he was looking for within the waves…

He hoped.

That river does not give back.

"We'll see about that," he muttered to no one.

He knelt beside the river in question and ran his fingers through the grey water. It felt thicker than water. More like blood. Months ago, he would have felt nothing but hopelessness as he stared at the strange liquid dripping slowly from his fingertips…

But he wouldn't let that despair overtake him now.

Casia was still fighting somewhere down in the depths. Whether she had any hope of winning wouldn't matter to her, so it didn't matter to him; he knew he might not resurface, and he didn't care.

Going on without her would be worse. It was the same thought he'd had earlier, pounding over and over in his head: the world needed her.

He needed her.

So he took a deep breath, and he dove.

He expected more resistance from the waves. To feel the thick water collecting, congealing like blood against his skin. Instead, it felt like diving through air. He moved too quickly, twisting and turning, almost free-falling downward.

He was dozens—perhaps hundreds—of feet below the surface in what felt like only seconds. He only suspected the depth because of how dark it had become; otherwise he was so disoriented that he might not have realized where he was at all.

It was peaceful, the way the water slid over him as he sank. A smooth caress calling him to surrender. Oddly, he found that he could breathe—though each inhale brought increased heaviness against his chest, as if he was inhaling muck that clung to his lungs and weighed them down a little more with every breath.

The pressure became so intense that he lost the pulse of Casia's magic somewhere beneath the crushing weight. Without the beat of her pounding through him, the weight pushing him down seemed less bearable, harder to fight against. He again felt the urge to surrender to the caressing waves, and this time he gave into it, letting his eyes flutter shut.

This was a mistake.

As soon as his eyes closed, it was as if something had latched onto his shoulders and yanked, pulling him down. He slipped so quickly through the water it made his stomach flip. All his muscles tensed, preparing for a collision with the riverbed.

His head broke through the rough surface of the river instead.

He managed to open his eyes again, and only then did he understand how truly disoriented he had been. *Not down*, he realized. Something had been pulling him *up*.

He blinked, and then he was inexplicably on the shore again, stretched out on his side, coughing up river water and digging his fingers into the gritty ground, trying to stop the world from spinning around him, trying to understand what was happening.

How?

The River Drow did not give back, and yet it had spat him out—empty-handed but still alive. He sat up.

Light.

His vision was suddenly filled with it, such brilliance reflecting off the river's surface that he had to shield his eyes. This warmth, this brightness, it felt familiar…

But it wasn't Casia.

He rubbed his watering eyes, and a figure began to take shape, standing in the middle of the river. On top of the water. She was *standing* on top of the water, with no need for the wings folded against her back. The golden patterns on her dark skin were the only bright spots among the dismal landscape; the glow surrounding her the only light that seemed warm and true.

Solatis.

The Goddess of Life.

He stared for what felt like a very long time, trying to make sense of her. She was gone from the mortal world, but this was not the mortal world—humans did not tread in Kantrum. But the gods rarely did either…so why was she here?

The questions continued to tumble as restlessly as the river before him. Where had Casia gone? What had she done to catch the attention of this goddess and bring her here?

He gave his head a shake. He could ask her all of those things when he found her again. Right now, he needed to focus on the finding.

Rising to his feet, he walked back to the river, pacing its edge. It churned even more violently than before, its waves rising up and curling in unnatural ways—almost as if beckoning him, daring him to try again.

The goddess watched him without speaking. Waiting.

Expectant. He understood what she asked for, and he was determined to answer. He would not fail her. He would not fail Casia.

They exchanged no words, but the goddess nodded in an approving sort of way, as though she had heard his last thoughts. Her hand reached out over the water. A drop of light fell from it, sinking into the river and illuminating a path down into its depths.

She was gone in the next instant, disappearing so quickly, so easily, that it was hard to believe she'd been there at all. But the light she'd shared remained.

Elander kept his eyes on it as he dove.

He moved as swiftly as before, twisting and tumbling ever downward. The trail of light faded after a few moments, sweeping fear over him along with darkness. His lungs burned. He remembered he had been able to breathe before, and he chanced it again, inhaling deeply. With renewed vigor, he swam on, drawing upon the magic inside of him as he went, sending out waves of it and seeking Casia's answering power.

After a few moments—after he had nearly given up hope—he felt a faint pulse in response. Hardly daring to believe it, he sent another burst of energy radiating outward.

Another responding pulse.

He fought to keep breathing, to keep steady, to keep searching, until…

There.

Casia was suspended in a pool of light just below him, her hair and clothing floating around her, her eyes closed and head bowed in concentration.

He felt wide awake suddenly, and struck by the same sense of awe he'd had so many times before whenever he looked at her—that she was still here, still fighting, even among the dark waves that should have long ago claimed her.

Her eyes clenched more tightly shut. Concentrating, maybe? Could she sense him approaching? He kicked his way toward her, summoning more magic as he went.

The pool of light around her answered his power, expanding and brightening until it surrounded him as well. As it did, he became suspended as she was, floating without any real effort, oblivious to the river pressing in around them. The urge to calmly surrender to the water was back again, lulling him into a false sense of security. He *knew* it was false, and yet he still found himself wanting to stay.

Casia's eyes remained closed, but her chin lifted. Her furrowed brow relaxed. He thought he saw her lips curving, a small smile of recognition—*there you are.*

Then she went limp, and her body began to sink, nearly falling out of Elander's reach before he came to his senses. He caught her around the middle and pulled her close.

The light around them faded.

The water was churning, sliding over them again, pulling them down. Elander willed himself not to panic, thinking instead of the immense light he'd managed to summon back on the battlefield in Ciridan. Of all the light the two of them had carried together in the past. Of the goddess walking on water, and the sword he'd left on the shore...

The sword.

He couldn't see it, or its glow, but he could still *sense* it. Faintly—very faintly—but it was enough to let him know which way was up.

He started toward it. It no longer felt like swimming through air. It felt as if they were rising through thick mud, his hands clawing and pulling them up inch by painstaking inch.

It might have been only seconds, or minutes, but it *felt* like hours before he finally saw a weak beam of the sword's light, and then another hour before he broke through the surface.

He staggered from the river, every ounce of strength he had left focused on keeping his balance, on keeping Casia secured in his arms and carrying her away from the grey waves.

Once they reached soft grass rather than rough pebbles, he knelt and placed her on the ground. His entire body ached. His eyes were damp—not entirely the river's doing—and his chest heaved in one painful breath after the other as Casia's body remained still. Lifeless. Cold. He cupped her cheek and studied her pale complexion, feeling the color and life draining from his own body as the seconds ticked by without any response from her.

"Wake up," he pleaded. "*Wake up.*"

Out of the corner of his eye, he spotted the sword he'd left at the riverside. Its light had gone out. Still, he crawled toward it, fumbled to grip it, and then carried it back and laid it across Casia's chest. He draped her cold hand over the hilt. Squeezed his own hand over hers, trying to infuse it with warmth, with strength, with...*something*.

Nothing happened right away.

But then he saw light—a faint flickering as the symbols at the base of the blade started to wake up.

He reached toward those symbols and summoned every bit of magic he could, pouring himself into them until they flared more violently to life, wrapping Casia in a cocoon so bright and searing that he instinctively started to take a step away from it.

He stopped as he saw Casia moving within the brightness. She had taken a breath, deep and filling, and now her head was lifting, and he no longer thought of backing away from the burning light—only of reaching her and holding her through it.

After a moment of him holding her, she slowly leaned back. Her eyes blinked open.

They didn't speak at first.

There were no words in any tongue that he recalled from any lifetime that could have captured precisely what he was feeling as he watched the life coming back to her eyes, as he felt her hand moving upon his chest, her fingers shaking but determined to wrap themselves into his damp shirt and hold on to him.

A soft note, something between a sigh and a weak, overwhelmed laugh, escaped her. "You found me."

He held her more tightly, cradling her head to his chest. "Nowhere you could go," he reminded her.

Her eyes shimmered with unshed tears as she inhaled deeply and gripped the front of his shirt with more strength than before.

He rose, pulling her up and steadying her against him, and then called for the Air spirit. They needed to get away from this place as soon as possible.

But it wasn't the spirit who answered him.

"How did you get out of the river?" The voice slid over him like a soft, cold breeze. He fought off a shiver as he and Casia turned to find the Goddess of Time approaching them, her gaze narrowed and her fingers clenched around a small golden dagger.

How did you get out of the river?

Elander remained unsure. Solatis still felt as if she had been a dream. And the way he'd been able to feel Casia's magic, even through the Drow's nightmarish waves...

The Time Goddess looked between the two of them, lips curling in a snarl.

"There is more magic between the two of us than you could ever hope to understand," he snarled back. "Whatever schemes you devised never had any hope of succeeding."

"Is that so?"

He said nothing else. If he had anything else to say to this horrid goddess, it would be with the sword still faintly emitting that light.

He crouched, without taking his gaze off Santi, and picked up the sword.

The goddess's eyes glinted like metal in the sun as she watched him. She sheathed her dagger against her back, her mouth twitched, and Elander thought he caught a flash of emerging fangs. She had a favored beastly form, like so many of the Marr—a winged lioness, in her case. He didn't like their odds if she shifted into that form.

Casia steeled herself and stepped away from his steadying grip. Elander still held her sword, but her power was awakening further, even without the blade's help. He could sense it building, and soon he could *see* it—pale light rising around her, making her skin shimmer and the strands of her hair float as they had in the river.

There was something...*different* about the way it felt. Whatever she'd done, wherever she'd gone, it had changed her magic. Made it more powerful. He was almost certain of it.

The goddess regarded them with a nasty scowl, her hand

lifting, preparing to counter their attack. But in the depths of her eyes, Elander saw a flicker of fear—and he saw that alarm swell whenever her gaze fell upon Casia.

She notices the change, too.

He chanced a longer look at Casia, and he saw the pale light around her gathering into something bolder, clearer, forming an outline of another being...

Before it fully took shape, the Goddess of Time gave a wild cry and swept forward, her fingers shifting into lioness claws as she came.

Elander darted between them, sword colliding with her claws in a shower of sparks. The goddess bounded to the right before twisting and preparing to strike once more. Elander lifted Shadowslayer for a second parry—

Something else countered before he could.

A blur of wings and antennae wrapped in a pale green glow barreled its way between him and the goddess, throwing the goddess off balance and knocking her backward.

Velia.

Elander caught only a quick glimpse of the spirit before powerful waves of her magic had wrapped around him and Casia, pressing swiftly in, dropping them both to their knees. The world pinched in so quickly that it disoriented them both; they were at the mercy of the magic as it swept them off their feet.

The last clear image Elander had of Kantrum was of the goddess swooping down upon her servant, claws outstretched and aiming for the creature's heart.

A wet, ripping sound followed, along with a guttural cry that was swiftly silenced as Elander and Casia twisted and tumbled back toward the mortal realm. The terrible sounds echoed in Elander's mind as they touched back down on Kethran soil.

They knelt together for a long moment, braced against one another, while they waited for their surroundings to stop spinning.

Casia moved first. Her eyes were wide as she found her balance and lifted her gaze to his. "Velia helped you reach Kantrum, didn't she?"

He nodded.

"What will happen to her now?"

The question caused a sharp pang of guilt in his stomach.

Fix it, spirit.

She had done as he'd commanded. But the cost…

He slowly rose to his feet, shaking his head. "I don't know. But we can't dwell on it." Casia started to protest, but he mentioned Nessa, and her focus predictably shifted. "The Feather spirit has visited and comforted her, but that spirit doesn't have the same healing abilities as the goddess she serves."

"But she's still alive—still okay—right?"

"…We should hurry back to her."

Casia fixed him with a hard look; he hadn't answered her question.

Because he didn't know.

He'd once had magic that could have told him precisely what sort of state Nessa was in—the ability to sense lives fading away, preparing to leave this mortal plane for another. Now he simply had intuition, a bad feeling without any real power behind it.

He shrugged the feeling off and helped Casia up. "We should hurry," he repeated.

She didn't press him this time. They marched onward

through the palace grounds, picking their way through battle remnants and broken things, just as he had done earlier. The barrier around the grounds remained intact. He tried to explain its emergence, and the way that strange surge of magic had driven their enemies away—even though he still didn't entirely understand what had happened.

She listened without speaking, her pace growing more hurried as his explanations became increasingly complicated and uncertain, so that they were nearly running by the time they reached the house that held Nessa.

Zev was standing outside, his head tilted toward the sky, his arms braced stiffly against the brick behind him.

His expression was strange, Elander thought, his paranoia resurfacing.

Casia didn't seem to notice, or care—she sprinted to Zev's side and threw her arms around him, burying her face in his chest.

Zev didn't hug her back.

Elander's eyes trailed to the front door that had been left partially ajar. He stopped fighting off the foreboding feeling trying to overtake him, instead reaching for some thread of that darker power that once came so easily to him.

He still couldn't feel her life-force. But he felt what he thought was a hint of Nessa's magic, faint and fading, until…

It went out.

A terrible cold seized him. He stopped reaching and focused instead on closing the space Casia had put between them. He reached her just as she pulled back from Zev and looked up at him.

"Take me to Nessa." There was a question in her wavering voice, now.

Zev had to swallow several times before he could finally answer her. "You're too late."

Casia's breath hitched, audibly, and Elander stepped closer to place a steadying hand against her once more.

"You're too late." Zev tried to reach for the wall behind him, to brace against it again, but he missed and simply sank to his knees instead. "She's gone."

CHAPTER 5

Cas felt as if she had tumbled back into the River Drow, her legs sweeping out from under her, her lungs burning, her shattered heart beating as if trying to escape her chest and all the death surrounding and suffocating her.

She knelt before Zev, taking one of his hands and squeezing it. His gaze lifted toward hers but fixed on something far beyond her, haunted and unsure—the same way he'd looked at her before she'd disappeared from the battlefield earlier. She swallowed away the dryness in her throat, closing her eyes against the horrifying images of that battle, and she squeezed Zev's hand harder.

I can fix this.

That was the last thing she had said to him before her disappearance. She'd had an idea, a sudden understanding that she hadn't had time to explain—and she didn't have time to explain herself now, either. She just had to follow through and finish what she'd started.

She rose to her feet. Zev didn't; he seemed to be in a

complete trance. She sensed powerful magic approaching, and out of the corner of her eye, she saw the Goddess of Storms drawing near. Elander paused to speak with her.

So Cas stepped into the house alone.

She quickly found the room Nessa had been brought to. Laurent sat in the center of a makeshift bed, holding her limp body against him. He made no sound—nothing did. It was as quiet and dark as a crypt.

Rhea was speechless and still in the nearby corner, mirroring the position her brother had fallen into outside—kneeling with her hands braced against the ground. Even Silverfoot was silent as he caught sight of Cas, though the fox's eyes flashed brighter as she drew closer. Rhea's head lifted, her lips parting and her face twisting in a strange combination of sorrow and relief. Rhea didn't break the deathly silence, either, but Cas could still read what she was clearly thinking, the same thing her brother had said—

Too late.

Cas reached for her throat, where the hourglass the Sand Goddess had given her once hung. It was gone, but it had served its purpose, bringing her back to the point in time when she and Elander had met, the point that had triggered her existence in this lifetime, in this body of a queen—an existence that the Dark God and his servant thought they could undo. She had proven them wrong. She was still here.

And she was not too late.

She had not traversed timelines and realms to fully embrace herself and her powers only to arrive *too late.*

She would fix this.

Without any more hesitation she stepped toward Laurent and Nessa.

"Where were you?" Laurent didn't take his eyes from Nessa's face as he spoke. His voice was devoid of emotion.

Cas didn't reply. She suspected he wouldn't hear anything she said in that moment, anyway.

So instead, she closed her eyes and let her power speak for her. She willingly placed herself back in the River Drow, mentally returning to the moment when she'd felt her power surging like never before—when she'd felt Elander reaching for her across the worlds and waves. And then to the moment when the two of them had stood upon the shore, when she swore she'd felt the Goddess of the Sun's arms wrapping around her.

A gasp sounded behind her, and Cas realized there were soldiers lining the walls of the room, half-hidden in shadows that the light she was summoning had chased away. She heard what sounded like them dropping to their knees as the power around her grew brighter. She heard whispers about the queen and the goddess; ramblings of confusion and awe as they tried to make sense of what they were seeing —or *who*.

She was both, in that moment.

One intertwined with the other. A queen subjugating one of the most powerful deities of their world. She felt Solatis the same way she had on the shore—like a second body doubling around her own, protecting her. The Giver of Life. Reversing death was beyond all other deities...aside from Solatis.

So no.

She was not *too late*.

A light touch against her back told her Elander had caught up. As he drew closer, she relaxed further, letting more of the goddess overtake her. Her hands were no longer solely her own as she held them out to Laurent and encouraged him to transfer Nessa to her arms.

He hesitated for a moment, his eyes slightly wide as they trailed over her body, studying the divine glow that encased it, before he did as she asked.

Nessa felt lighter than she should have, as if she was fading away even as Cas's magic enveloped her. Cas pulled her closer. She felt her arms being steadied—by Elander or the goddess, or maybe both—and she forgot about everything outside of the cold, limp bundle she held.

So cold.

Cas pressed her forehead to Nessa's and directed her thoughts toward warmth. She was speaking, though she didn't know where the words were coming from, or even what they meant—the goddess was overtaking more and more of her. It would have made her panic months ago, but now she was not afraid. She could do this. She was strong enough to channel this power into existence.

And she was not alone. Every time she started to lose focus, she heard a soft voice calling her name, calling her back—Solatis. Every time she felt her body threatening to crumple under the weight of it all, she felt strong hands steadying her again—Elander.

The air was warming. Little flecks of golden light floated around them, bursting occasionally. With each burst, another wave of warmth cascaded down. Several of those shimmering flecks settled on Nessa's skin, and soon, Cas thought she saw color coming back to that cold skin.

The warmth became sweltering. Cas fought the urge to blink as her eyes watered. The room hummed with power, and everything seemed to be tensing, bracing for—

Movement.

Only the tiniest twitch behind Nessa's eyelids at first. But then she sucked in a tiny breath of the shimmering air, followed by a deeper inhale, and her head shifted closer to Cas's chest, burrowing deeper into the light and warmth.

Cas held her for a moment—long enough to make sure these movements didn't cease—and then she placed her back into Laurent's waiting arms.

She took a deep breath, overcome by sudden dizziness. Her exhale seemed to release all the power she had summoned. As the last wisps of it left her, the room shifted and spun faster. Her knees buckled.

Elander caught her before she hit the ground, and as soon as his protective embrace closed around her, she stopped fighting and let her exhaustion take her away.

CHAPTER 6

Cas opened her eyes to find herself curled up on a stiff mattress. The room around her was intact—untouched by all their battles—and it was high in a tower of some sort, judging by the sliver of distant ground she could see through a small part in the curtains.

Elander's hand was wrapped tightly around her own. He was doubled over the bed in an awkward position that suggested he'd fought sleep for as long as he could before it took him anyway—and he could usually last for days without sleeping.

How long had she been out for?

She sat up. The blankets shifting and falling off her made only a soft rustling, but this was all it took to make Elander's eyes pop open.

"Good morning," she said.

"Is it?" He massaged the space between his eyes before looking to the window, to the curtains glowing with the sunrise, to confirm it for himself.

She clenched the blanket in her hands, rubbing its silk

edge between her fingers in a soothing, repetitive motion. "How long have I been asleep?"

He took a moment to calculate. "Three days, before I fell asleep myself," he finally settled on, looking back to the window. "The longest three days of my existence."

She stilled her hands, bracing herself against the mattress before she said, "And Nessa..."

"Getting stronger every day."

Cas leaned back into the pillows, the weight of her relief unbalancing her.

Elander regarded her with a solemn look as he ran a hand through his sleep-mussed hair. "Though now we're all wondering what sort of strength it took from *you*, to do what you did."

She rubbed a chill from the back of her neck as the images of her latest trials with magic came flooding back. "I'm sorry. I didn't mean to worry you, to not explain things before I did them, I just..." A sudden influx of energy made her pause, pulling her gaze toward the door.

It was different from her and Elander's magic, and she was too groggy to place it immediately. The hairs on her arms rose—only to relax just as quickly. Because although this power was foreign, it didn't feel hostile. Quite the opposite.

"Namu, I think," said Elander.

The Goddess of Healing appeared in the doorway a moment later.

Cas stiffened and sat up straighter.

Without so much as a curt greeting, the goddess moved to the window and threw the curtains completely open. She seemed to be taking inventory of everything outside, her ruddy skin appearing warmer in the sunlight and her long, elegant fingers tapping the sill in a steady rhythm.

Cas and Elander watched her as she watched the world outside, until finally Cas grew impatient and cleared her throat. "Why are you here? We sent for you weeks ago, and you seemed to have no—"

The goddess turned and fixed her piercing green eyes on Cas, cutting her off.

Cas's head was still spinning from exhaustion; she couldn't find her words again before the goddess spoke.

"My servant told me what you did. I was intrigued. It seems Solatis still left a bit of herself in this world, and she's channeling it through you." She turned her face back toward the window.

Cas frowned but held her tongue.

Better late than never, perhaps.

The goddess was late, and unexpected, but at least there was nothing hostile in her demeanor, she decided—and Elander seemed to agree.

"I'll be right back," he told her, kissing her forehead before getting to his feet. "I promised I'd let the others know when you woke up. We'll sort things out together."

He left, and Cas sat cross-legged on the bed and continued to watch the Healing Goddess without a word, soaking in the warm power she effortlessly gave off. It was like sitting in a steamy bath, complete with therapeutic scents of jasmine and spice that drifted from the goddess with every move she made. Cas started slipping back toward sleep—until the goddess's blunt voice broke the silence.

"Have you figured out the answer to my question yet, Shadowslayer?"

Cas tried to remember the details of their last encounter, all the questions they'd asked one another…

Her head only continued to spin.

Namu fixed another intimidating gaze on her. "I once asked you what you would make of the things that had been given to you. Both the good and the bad." She moved directly before Cas with only a few long strides. "You've come a long way since that moment. Your empire now faces the full wrath of the gods themselves…but you've grown stronger, too, haven't you?"

Cas let her eyes trail to a patch of sunlight on the floor—long and narrow and tapered at one end, it made her think of a sword. She focused until she felt the pulse of the blade Solatis had granted her, and her gaze shifted to where it had been propped up in a nearby chair.

"So now I find myself even more curious about the answer," continued the goddess. "What mark will you leave behind? What will you do now?"

Instead of replying, Cas climbed from the bed and slowly walked to the window. She braced her arms against the sill and basked in the golden light, even warmer than the goddess's magic.

She *had* grown stronger. Yet she was exhausted as she stared out over the palace grounds, watching the soldiers and servants still picking up the pieces from their latest battle, thinking of all that had been destroyed, and all that still could be before the end. Her tiredness would pass soon enough—it always did—but in that moment, every part of her rebelled at the thought of picking up her sword. She wanted to go back to sleep.

But perhaps strength was not always about grabbing a sword and brandishing it tirelessly against monsters. Maybe, sometimes, it was standing amongst the rubble. Breathing it in. Being tired but still deciding to take another step, despite not knowing what awaited you on the other side.

That was what she would do, she thought, turning back to the goddess.

"The doubt that was in your eyes back then isn't there any longer," said Namu. "Good."

You must be certain, or the waters won't carry you—they'll drown you.

That was what the Time Goddess had told Cas about the River Drow. And even though she'd survived that river, the weight of its waters still seemed to hover over her.

Nothing but certainty was allowed now, or else she might still lose herself among the waves.

She fully met Namu's intimidating gaze. "I have no doubt about what needs to be done. I can't rest until Malaphar and his magic are sealed away." She walked over to the chair that held her sword, her eyes falling to the jeweled emblem embedded in its hilt.

Before they could finish their conversation, Elander reappeared, followed swiftly by Rhea. Zev appeared soon after his sister, but Laurent remained with Nessa, Cas was told.

Rhea quickly wrapped Cas in a bone-crushing hug. "Explain yourself," she demanded as she leaned away. "Where in the world did you *go*?"

Cas found herself searching for the Healing Goddess. As intimidating as she was, there was a quiet strength about her that was easy to draw from.

The goddess nodded encouragingly as their eyes met. Cas felt warmer, more confident. "I had to go back to the beginning."

"The beginning?" Rhea repeated.

"To when Elander and I met—a *breaking point* in the history of this world, the Goddess of Stars called it."

"But why there?"

"It was something Solatis said when I met her face-to-face at Dawnskeep...something about *choice.* My choice to love and to live, to embrace it all in spite of the darkness, is part of why she saved me and asked me to carry her sword. So when the Dark God and his court cornered me and told me I'd made the wrong choice, that I needed to undo it, I knew better. I heard Solatis's voice in my head, and I think I finally understood what she meant that day at Dawnskeep... That the full power she wanted to grant me was only waiting on me to embrace it. To stop being afraid of my past. Obsessed with it. To stop running away. So that is where I went—back to my past, where I chose to set into motion everything that eventually led up to this moment."

A hush settled over the group. Even Zev was quiet, contemplating. Elander was watching her closely, a hint of a soft, awed little smile on his lips. Their gazes met, and she found herself unable to look away from him.

"I had been so afraid that we broke the world," she said, quietly, "but I had a feeling you and I would be able to put things back together, too. I'm still not sure which—"

"Both," the Healing Goddess interjected.

Everyone tilted their face toward her.

"For that is the true, dual nature of love, isn't it?" she said. "A terrible, wonderful force. Nothing can break things so completely. Nothing can heal things so fully. And Solatis and her magic have a duality about them as well—life itself is both a beautiful and a terrible thing."

Cas nodded. "If I had not gone back to the past, then this

present—this very moment—would not exist…for better or worse."

Zev looked around. "And you're sure *this* particular lifetime was worth securing through time-travel? Could you not have done some strategic editing while you were bouncing around in that past life?"

Cas did not hesitate. "*Choice.* That's the thing," she repeated. "It seems impossible for us to carry on after everything that's happened, I know. That is precisely what Malaphar and the ones that serve him wanted me to believe. If I'd fallen for it, this would all be over—but at what cost? I wouldn't be here to stand against his evil." She shook her head to rid it of the grim thought. "We're here. We're still alive. And now we have the chance to keep going. To make *this* present—this lifetime —better. No matter how he and his followers try to erase us, we *must* keep coming back, stronger than before."

She felt the Healing Goddess staring. Out of the corner of her eye, she could see the beginning of a pleased smile spreading across the deity's face, and a new feeling buzzed in Cas's chest. Confidence—or pride, even.

She had finally given a full answer to the question that goddess had posed.

She picked up her sword and twisted it about as she considered her next words. The blade felt lighter than ever.

"A word of caution, if I could…" said the goddess, back to her usual matter-of-fact demeanor. "You may be more powerful than ever at the moment, but that power will only take you so far. It is a finite source now that the Sun Goddess is sealed out of this world."

"Is there no way to expand this source?" Rhea asked.

"Casia can channel Solatis's power better than any being in existence, and with Elander's help—"

"But they cannot *create* it. Not even the Marr can do that. It will be a gradual decline as time goes by, now that the initial chaos of the Sun Goddess's sealing has passed. Granted, Solatis scattered points of her power around before she left—in pieces, such as Casia and the sword she carries—so she is still able to reach us through those as well. But I wouldn't count on those things lasting, either."

The already somber mood in the room grew deeper. Cas could hardly breathe beneath the weight settling on her shoulders.

"I've been dealing with it myself over the past decade," continued the goddess, "ever since my own upper-god was weakened and violently ousted from this realm. Every time I use my magic here, I feel the well of it draining. It no longer refills. It's only a matter of time before it's gone completely."

"Is the same thing not happening to the other Marr in your court?" Zev asked.

"It was." Her nose scrunched in disgust. "But they have found other sources to supplement their existence in this realm as of late."

A quiet confusion settled over them for a long moment, until Elander's gaze snapped toward the goddess, realization lighting in his eyes. "Malaphar is offering them more magic in exchange for service, isn't he?"

Zev breathed out a curse. "Can he actually do that?"

"It will mean a corrupted, unpredictable form of their original magic, won't it?" Elander looked to the Healing Goddess for confirmation.

She nodded solemnly. "Santi was offered such a deal, I suspect. And it must have been an extraordinary amount of power he offered, because I would not have expected her to take his side, otherwise."

Cas went back to twisting her sword around with small, expert movements. Focusing on keeping those movements smooth kept her hands steady, preventing them from shaking even as her heart raced faster and faster.

"As more of my court joins him, my power disappears even more swiftly," said the goddess. "The flow of our magic is disrupted beyond repair. And I fear the same fate awaits the Sun Court and those with magic ultimately derived from Solatis. So use what power you have smartly, as I said—there's no way of knowing when it might run out."

"So much for a limitless, Sun-magic fueled killing spree, then?" muttered Zev.

Cas stopped twisting the sword and took a deep breath. "This only validates our original plan even further," she said. "We have to finish what my father and brother started with the Antaeum Points—to seal off the source of Malaphar's power and weaken him to the point that we can finish him off with a calculated attack."

The room grew quiet, almost suffocatingly so, as the weight of their task settled over them.

A new voice eventually broke the silence—Laurent's. "To Mistwilde, then?"

Cas turned, preparing to reply, but froze as she saw that he wasn't alone.

Nessa was beside him, holding tightly to his arm.

A choked sound—something between a sob of disbelief and laughter—escaped Cas. Her feet were carrying her to Nessa without another thought, her arms closing around her so enthusiastically that the two of them would likely have tumbled to the floor if Laurent hadn't placed a strong hand against Nessa's back to catch her.

Nessa smelled of lavender and chamomile and other healing plants, and she radiated warmth—so much warmth that Cas wondered if the Goddess of Healing had wrapped her in some sort of lasting protection. Cas held her tighter, sinking more fully into that warmth, until Nessa eked out a cough.

"I love you, Cas, but I can't breathe."

With quiet laughter bubbling up and eyes shimmering with tears, Cas leaned back, taking Nessa's hands in hers and squeezing those instead. It all still felt impossible, and she couldn't help but whisper, "You were dead."

Nessa squeezed back. "How lucky I am, then, to have a friend who seems to outsmart and defeat death at every turn." She gripped Cas's hands tighter for a moment before clearing her throat and nodding toward the rest of the room.

Cas remembered where they were—what they'd been discussing—and turned and found everyone looking expectantly at her.

"...To Mistwilde," she agreed as her eyes fell again on Laurent. "But we're all going together, this time."

No one objected. Not that Cas would have listened if they had. She would not stay behind this time; she had a clear feeling—a vision, almost—that they were all meant to go together, to march side-by-side toward whatever ending awaited them.

"We were starting to make some headway with the king of that realm," Elander said. "Enough that we aren't likely to be murdered on sight when we all show up at his door, at least."

"Not likely," repeated Zev, "but you're saying there's a chance."

Elander shrugged. "Always a chance."

"What of this palace and city in the meantime?" asked Laurent.

Cas looked expectantly to Silverfoot, and then to Rhea, who had been taking care of many of their large-scale operations since they'd arrived in Ciridan.

"Over the past few days, I've met with many of the people who were attending the banquet," said Rhea.

"They've actually stayed?" asked Cas.

"Some. And I believe they all understand the scope of things now. Several have asked how they might be able to help recover things here, and where they can otherwise help. There's also a small group of the loyal palace workers we already had sticking around. Between them all, I believe order can be maintained for a few weeks, at least." She hesitated. "And it might be easier on them if we drew the eye of the gods elsewhere."

Cas nodded, a grim but indisputable thought overtaking her—it was time to move again.

This palace and city would be safer if she wasn't in it.

HOURS LATER, Cas stood in the room she'd started to think of as *hers* over the past weeks.

It was still relatively undamaged. A few windows had been broken, one of the walls scorched by some sort of magic, but the foundations of it remained. Her bed was perfectly intact, and neatly made, even—though it was currently covered in a messy assortment of clothing and supplies, as she was busy packing.

She paused as her hand fell upon a bracelet with beads of white and silver.

Queen Soryn had given it to her.

Between Cas and the elven realm of Mistwilde stretched the realm that queen was valiantly trying to return to its former glory—the fallen Kingdom of Sadira. Partly for this reason, Cas had insisted they travel on horseback rather than trying to arrange magic of some sort, which was in short supply, anyhow; she intended to go through Sadira and see its queen face-to-face along the way.

Soryn had declined the invitation to the disastrous banquet. Maybe for the best, in hindsight—but Cas feared their short-lived but solid alliance might have been coming to an end.

They had stood together in battles in the past—bloody clashes with her brother and divine beasts alike—but so much had changed in the months since they'd last been together...Cas's goals included. She had never imagined the possibility of entirely sealing away the gods and their magic. And Sadira had always been more reliant on magic than any of the other Kethran kingdoms. What would such an act do to that kingdom?

They were rewriting the entire structure of their world. And though she now had no doubts that it was for the best, that didn't mean it would come without devastating sacrifices.

And maybe those sacrifices had already started elsewhere —such as the draining of magic the Healing Goddess had warned about. Cas hadn't grown weaker—perhaps because of her greater connection to Solatis—but there was a chance

Soryn and her magic-reliant soldiers had already experienced loss...

Was that why the Sadiran Queen had denied the invitation to the banquet?

Cas rubbed the bracelet between her fingers, focusing on the feel of one bead at a time and trying to keep her fears from spiraling.

A soft knock on her partially-ajar door, followed by Elander's voice, jostled her from her thoughts. "Finished packing?"

"Almost." Cas continued rifling through her belongings, avoiding looking directly into his eyes.

Avoiding them did no good; he sensed her fear anyway.

"That's the bracelet Soryn gave you, isn't it?"

She nodded.

He took it, studying it for a moment before slipping it onto her wrist. "You know...she may be angry and concerned about the way the war and magic has shifted, but Soryn is not a fool. She'll listen to you. We'll be able to come to some sort of understanding about the future and what's really at stake."

She closed her hand into a fist to keep from anxiously plucking at the beads, and she met his eyes, willingly losing herself in the comforting depths of them for a moment. "I hope you're right."

He flashed a smirk. "I usually am."

She gave an amused snort and managed to roll some of the tension from her shoulders, letting her fears about Soryn fall away. Her focus returned to the bags spread across her bed. "It feels strange to be heading out on the road once more."

"It does," Elander agreed, shifting closer to help her organize those overflowing bags.

His hand brushed hers as they both reached for a leather canteen, one etched with a tiger similar to the one that featured on the Solasen family crest. Cas paused, a flood of emotions overcoming her—the good, the bad, the complicated.

"What's wrong?"

"I don't know." She smiled weakly, glancing around at the room she'd soon be leaving behind. "It almost felt like we had it for a moment there, didn't it?"

He gave her a curious look.

"As though we were a proper king and queen in a proper palace. Or something like that."

A concerned frown pulled at the corners of his mouth.

"It's just that... I was able to see it, almost." She averted her eyes again, fidgeting with the bracelet as she spoke. "A sun setting on a quiet, peaceful ceremony. Everyone there to celebrate. And everything after."

He went back to organizing her supplies, trying to find a suitable place to put the canteen, but after a moment he looked up from this task and asked, "And what does *everything after* entail?"

There was a slight smile dancing in his eyes, the kind she hadn't seen in what felt like weeks. It drew a more earnest grin from her. It made her want to dream. To hope for things—and in that moment that hope felt more defiant than anything they'd ever done. She grabbed hold of it as though it was a blade she could defend them with, and she kept defying the darkness threatening them, thinking instead of the future she wanted.

"We'll need heirs, of course," she said, matter-of-factly.

Elander dropped the canteen, but recovered quickly, snatching it in mid-air before it hit the bed.

She grinned more brightly, amused that she could still unbalance him—if only for an instant—and then she moved closer, unable to resist the look he was regarding her with.

"A few, at least." She ran her hands up and down the edges of his unfastened traveling coat, pausing to finger the buttons of it and smooth the collar. "Unless you have any objections?"

"None come to mind." He took one of her wandering hands and held it still, pressing it over his heart. "In fact, I'm very interested in hearing more about this future you've been envisioning."

"Well." Her cheeks warmed. Her throat felt dry. He could still unbalance her, too, it seemed—and she didn't mind it. She hoped that feeling would never completely go away. "I can see the palace overrun with children, actually," she told him. "And dogs and music and messes, and all of the *good* kinds of chaos we can find. The celebrations and casual gatherings, alike; the endless chatter and laughter."

He listened closely, his smile lifting a bit more with every word she spoke.

"And then you, old and grey—"

"But still handsome."

"Obviously."

"And you will be as stunning as ever, too."

"We must remain equals, yes."

"You far surpass me now," he insisted, "but whatever you say."

"If you keep saying things like that, I am going to end up the most vain queen in history before it's all said and done."

"You can't keep me from speaking the truth."

Her blush deepened, and she started to playfully shove him away, but he held tight to her hand and used it to twirl her in a small circle. She gave in to the dance, and they were gone for a moment, waltzing away from the preparations that had overtaken the palace.

But she soon brought them both to a halt and her head started to turn, her eyes trailing back toward her waiting bags.

He caught her chin and held it. "To everything after," he said, lifting the canteen before taking a sip and then offering it to her.

As she sipped from it, she swore she felt the edges of her heart fluttering as if it were trying to sprout wings. She had been trying to harden it, to steel it in preparation for the tasks ahead...but he always managed to crack that stone casing, somehow.

There is no use steeling it, she decided—even if it meant it ended up broken before the end.

Her frown gave way to another soft smile. "I love you."

His hand slipped under her chin again, tilting her mouth up to meet his. The kiss was soft and slow, as though they had all the time in the world. She knew better, of course.

She kissed him back as if she didn't.

His tongue slipped between her lips and danced against her own. She sighed softly into his mouth. He deepened the kiss, reaching for her other hand as he did, and he guided both of her arms around his neck.

Once she had latched on to him, he lifted her onto the nearest piece of furniture—a chest of drawers against the back wall. This brought her closer to his height, allowing him to easily reach the sensitive pulse of her throat. That pulse skipped faster as he pressed closer, just warm breaths and the tip of his nose brushing teasingly against her at first.

Her head tilted back and her fingers tangled through his hair, pulling him closer, pressing his mouth more firmly to her skin and causing dark laughter to spill out of him.

"I believe you've been thinking about making heirs too much," he teased, each word vibrating deliciously against her skin.

"It's part of my job as queen."

"Maybe not the *most* pressing part at the moment."

"That doesn't mean we can't practice for when it *is*."

She felt his lips inching upward as he brought them to the curve of her shoulder. He kissed a trail up along her neck, slipping his hand beneath her shirt and around to the small of her back, his fingers splaying against her skin as she shivered and shifted beneath him. She leaned closer to the dresser's top, nearly flat against it. She wanted him to keep coming, to climb on top of her completely. It was not a particularly large dresser—but she felt confident they could make this work.

His hips pressed against her and his hands slid along her arms, pushing them up on either side of her head, pinning her even more tightly to the polished wood.

Her heart hammered faster as his head dipped toward her neck once more.

"So much I want to do to you," he whispered, warm breath brushing her earlobe, "so little time."

"We could work on our efficiency," she suggested, which drew more laughter from him.

"So insistent."

"You should know this about me by now."

"Yes." He leaned back, smiling. "But still, *efficient* is not really the word I want you to associate with me and moments like these."

"There are worse things you could be."

"True," he murmured, curling a lock of her hair that had slipped free of her braid. "But I prefer to savor you as much as possible."

The sound of voices drawing closer to the room made Cas reluctantly nod in agreement. "I suppose I should finish packing, anyway."

Elander took a step back, straightening his coat and shirt that her hands had rumpled. While he went to the hallway to see who the voices belonged to, Cas circled her room one last time, searching for anything she might have missed, before she closed up and latched her bags.

Elander returned as she was securing Shadowslayer in its sheath and double-checking her other weapons. He didn't speak right away, but she felt his gaze on her.

"There's one thing you need to know before we leave."

She tilted her face toward him.

"We still have *it*, even if you can't see it at the moment. Even if the scenery changes, nothing else does. I knew precisely what I was getting into when I asked you to marry me. Even if it's months from now, or years, or another lifetime before it's all settled."

There it was again—that fluttering in her chest.

She took his hand, drawing it against the rapid beating of her heart, holding it tightly as she stood up on her tiptoes and planted a quick kiss on his lips.

"We should get going," she said as she pulled away.

Because a sinking feeling in her stomach told her there was still a long way between them and everything after.

CHAPTER 7

The air smelled of apples and rain. Grey clouds had been stretching over them for the last several miles, ominous and occasionally plopping a fat raindrop onto their heads.

A small grove of trees stood in the distance. Cas and Zev trotted down to it, going as far as they could on their mounts —until the trees tangled too closely to ride between—and then they slid from their horses' backs and crept deeper into the trees, noting the trampled undergrowth, the copious amount of broken branches, and the fallen, squashed apples.

They paused as they came to a small clearing. Within it, the scent of blood and burned things overwhelmed the thickly sweet haze of ripened fruit. The air tingled; it felt like Storm-kind energy. Cas scanned the area, searching for the source of the bloody scent but not finding it—though she did notice that a few of the trees bore burn marks.

"Magical residue." She wrinkled her nose. "And I think it's fresh."

Zev finished inspecting a scorched trunk before slowly

backing away from it. "I have a bad feeling about this place. I don't think we should stay anywhere near here." He looked over his shoulder. Through the spindly clutches of trees, a slash of flower-dotted hill was still visible, and on the other side of it their small army was waiting, planning to start setting up camp—barring a negative scouting report.

Cas nudged a rotten apple with the toe of her boot. She didn't disagree with Zev's ominous feeling, but this was the third potential camping spot they'd scouted this evening. They had been riding for two days now, with only brief periods of rotating rest—they had yet to stop and set up a full camp, and it was still another two days' ride to Sadira's capital city and its queen. The incoming storms could potentially double those days.

"The horses aren't going to hold out much longer," she pointed out. "Nor are their riders."

Zev rapped his knuckles together in frustration, letting little puffs of smoke and flame fly up from them. "Would be nice if we had some sort of magic that could create protection, or reveal better paths...or, you know, if we had *the actual goddesses* who control such things. Damn divine beings, coming and going as they please..."

Cas smiled meekly as he muttered on about their lack of divine company.

They both knew the real reason those goddesses hadn't traveled with them—because it was getting harder for them to do so.

Just as the Healing Goddess had warned, the well of their power was not refilling as it once had. Even Nephele had admitted to feeling more drained than usual. They were also missing one of their court; the Star Goddess had not been seen in weeks. They didn't suspect her of disloyalty, as in the case of the Time and Mountain deities—but she was clearly gone.

She had always been aloof, and now it seemed she had vacated the mortal realm entirely. And one less goddess meant one more disruption in the flow of the Sun Court's power.

So the remaining goddesses were storing their power, waiting for the most opportune moments to strike against their enemies, knowing they might only have limited opportunities.

"We have a few human magic-users among us," Cas said, trying to remain optimistic. "And Elander and I, too—we can all spare something, surely…enough to create a shield to give us a brief rest."

"Too risky, isn't it?"

"Since when have you been overly concerned with risk?" She knelt and picked up a fallen apple that appeared to be mostly intact.

"Since our potential failing now means the end of the world, rather than us just missing out on a payday?"

"Well, for what it's worth," she continued, polishing the apple with her coat sleeve, "*I* still don't feel any limits on my magic. I still feel more powerful than ever." It was so much power that it was making her feel somewhat restless, honestly—but she didn't say this part out loud. She had grown beyond the anxiety surrounding her powers.

Or that's what she needed everyone following her to believe, at least.

Zev didn't look convinced about her plan, but Cas turned and started back to the horses before he could argue.

They returned to their company and briefed them on what they'd found. Cas went first to Laurent, who seemed even less enthusiastic than Zev about her plan to test the limits of their group's collective magic. They debated for a moment. Nessa arrived to mediate, and Laurent soon after bowed out of the fight and went to speak with some of their soldiers, grumbling to himself as he went.

Cas watched him go, holding in a sigh. She gave the apple to Nessa, and then went searching for Elander.

It took several minutes, but she finally found him sitting alone on the side of a hill, hidden from most of their party, his horse tethered to a tree at the base of the sloping ground.

Odd that he isn't storming through our ranks and shouting orders. He so loves shouting orders...

But he'd been somewhat odd for most of the past day—quieter than usual, even when she prodded and teased him. Concern ate a pit into her stomach, and she forgot about her camping and risky magic plans and picked her way down the steep hillside to him.

She slowed as she caught sight of the haunted look on his face.

He was leaning forward with his elbows on his knees, balancing a sword on upturned palms, studying the white stones in its hilt. He didn't take his eyes off the weapon until she was standing right next to him.

She had seen that sword before, she realized. "Caden's, wasn't it?"

He nodded. "Surprised I found it among the wreckage at the palace. I wasn't going to carry it with me, but it's elven made—so I thought it would be too useful against magic to leave behind. I was thinking of what the Healing Goddess said, about our need to ration our own magic. So I've been trying to get used to the feel of this blade whenever I have a spare moment like this, so that I can wield it instead."

She settled down beside him. She doubted he'd kept it solely because of its usefulness, but she didn't say so.

She picked a small purple flower, plucked its petals off one by one before holding her palm out and letting the rising wind carry them away. Quietly, she said, "I'm sorry."

"For what?"

"That we couldn't save him. That I brought Nessa back—but I only have so much power, and it wasn't enough to..." She trailed off as he shook his head at her, glancing her way—just for a moment—before he went back to studying the blade.

Cas drew her knees toward her chest and rested her head upon them. Images of the battlefield at Ciridan, of the palace crumbling and littered with fallen bodies, flickered mercilessly through her thoughts. So many people she hadn't been able to save...

She buried her face into her knees and fought the urge to rock back and forth, to let her hands tap against her boots, to find some other motion that could carry her away from everything. She didn't want to be carried away just then; she wanted to stay here in the quiet wreck of it all with him.

"You don't need to apologize," Elander said. "And that's a dangerous line of thinking."

The Healing Goddess had told her the same thing—because Cas had asked, of course. Had asked if there was some way her full, newly-embraced magic might undo the losses they'd suffered that night. If it could undo *all* the loss and pain that wrapped like a choking fist around her lifetimes.

The goddess had seemed uncharacteristically sympathetic as she'd shaken her head and told her *no*. *Magic has limits. The evidence of that is around you, even if you'd like to ignore it.*

"Queen or not, you are not responsible for saving everyone," Elander said—which was, again, essentially what the goddess had told her.

Try to save them all, and you'll end up saving no one.

Cas lifted her heavy head and watched Elander for a moment. The wind was picking up in earnest now, whipping her hair wildly about. She tucked a strand behind her ear and looked to the sword he held, and then back up to his face.

"You're not responsible for that, either," she told him.

He looked as though he wanted to argue, but ultimately couldn't come up with anything to say, so he just gave her a small, grateful smile instead.

They were quiet for several moments, until Cas suddenly remembered why she had sought him out in the first place. She started to tell him of the signs of magic they'd spotted nearby—

An explosion in the distance interrupted her, causing them both to jump to their feet.

Cas took a few cautious steps toward the sound, squinting at the distant, gloomy sky, searching it for signs of smoke, streaks of magical energy...

She saw nothing.

"Whatever that was, it sounds like it's directly on the path we'd planned to travel," Elander muttered. "Good thing we stopped when we did and didn't charge right into the middle of it."

A moment later, Cas saw Laurent on horseback in the distance, leading a group of riders away from the rest of their party. Scouting out a safer route? Her stomach clenched as she lost sight of him against the grey horizon.

"I want to see what's going on," she said.

Elander nodded and started toward his horse, beckoning her to follow. He gave her a leg up, climbed up behind her, and then they set off in the same direction as Laurent and the others.

They rode for a half-mile, their pace cautious as they continued to study their surroundings. No more explosive sounds reached them, but there were other sounds to be concerned with. As they drew closer, Cas began to pick out individual notes—people shouting, horses frantically braying and snorting, and heavy, hurried footsteps.

They spotted a ridge lined with trees and rode toward it, using the cover of foliage to get closer and closer to the sounds. Stopping in the center of the narrow grove, tall pines standing like sentinels around them, Cas peered through branches and instantly caught a flash of movement—a woman in light armor scampered over the rocky terrain below them, casting wary looks over her shoulder as she went.

That armor, the emblem stitched in teal and silver across the leather breastplate...

A Sadiran soldier?

Cas followed the woman's line of sight and spotted people following her. A strange parade of people—some were running toward that Sadiran woman without looking back, some were engaged in sword combat as they came, some sought bushes and other hiding places and crouched within them.

Her gaze snapped back to the Sadiran woman just as she veered wildly, barely avoiding an arrow, and nearly collided with a twisting grey tree. The woman limped for a few steps before finding her balance, and then spun around and withdrew a sword—just in time to meet another soldier who exploded from seemingly nowhere.

Cas saw the flash of steel as their blades met, but she didn't see what happened to the woman beyond this, as her attention was yanked toward a trio of men running dangerously near to where she and Elander hid.

Elander's arm slid protectively around her waist, drawing her closer to him. His horse shivered beneath them, stamping her foot and tossing her head. Cas ran a soothing hand along the mare's neck, willing the creature to be still for just another moment.

Another soldier had caught up to the trio. The three men made quick work of killing him—though the pursuant did manage to strike one of the men's arms, splattering the rocky ground with drops of violent red. The cry he bellowed made Elander's horse stomp and snort more insistently.

Cas's eyes were drawn to the bloodied sleeve of the soldier's jacket, and she saw a patch that featured what appeared to be clouds swirling around a sword pointing upward.

"That's the emblem of Sadira's army, isn't it?" The red darkening it made it difficult to see, but she was almost certain of what she saw.

Elander steadied the horse before he looked for himself. "Yes, it is."

Cas frowned. Sadiran soldiers...their *allies*. She hoped.

They couldn't just ignore whatever was happening to them, could they?

At first, it had appeared to be a relatively small skirmish —not worth mixing themselves up in, maybe. But a realization struck her as she continued to watch, noting the way the Sadiran soldiers didn't stop running, even after they finished off their enemies. "They look like they're trying to retreat, don't they?"

Elander watched the scene below them for another moment."But from where?"

He was already seeking the answer to his own question, even as he asked it, nudging his horse back into a quick trot. There was energy in the air—more magic than they had felt since leaving Ciridan. Cas didn't have to ask to know what Elander was thinking.

A larger battle is looming nearby.

They followed the energy, moving in the direction those soldiers all seemed to have been running away from. The trees grew more sparse as they rode on, but a fine mist had started to fall, and fog was rolling in thick waves, providing further cover. Still, they eventually reached an open stretch where that cover was not enough to conceal them; it would have been dangerous—foolish—to go farther.

But they didn't *need* to go any farther.

Her back was pressed tightly to Elander's chest, so she felt his heartbeat speed up; the sharp intake of his breath; the rumble of his magic coming to life as he wrapped his arm tightly around her once more. It was difficult to keep her own magic from rising, from seeking and folding into the protective waves of his.

They couldn't let that magic rage indiscriminately. They had to be careful. Strategic. That was what they had decided. Cas had adamantly agreed to this.

But an exception might have to be made tonight.

Because below them, they had found the larger battle, and there were…

Bodies.

So many *bodies*.

CHAPTER 8

The bodies lined the banks of a slow-moving, winding river and dotted the rocky hills that stretched up from either side of that river, their numbers so great that Cas witnessed several people tripping over them.

Even at a distance, the scent of magic and metal and blood enveloped her and Elander, made heavier by the damp air. Her stomach rolled and the haunting images of the Ciridan battle tried again to resurface, but she forced them away and kept scanning the area.

She saw Sadiran banners and horses dressed in the kingdom's colors of grey and turquoise. A shimmering barrier was taking shape around a group of soldiers close to the river—Sky magic. Which fully confirmed things; such magic was the specialty of Soryn and many of her followers. Even after so much magic had been purged from the Kethran Empire, they had continued to worship the goddess who granted that magic—another deity whom Cas had actually *met*.

That deity—Indre—was the sister of Nephele, and before leaving Ciridan, Cas had asked the Goddess of Storms to reach out on her behalf, to try and convince the Sky Goddess to help her win Soryn over.

It was likely a fool's hope, and she knew it; the Sky Goddess had only begrudgingly helped them back in Ciridan. She hadn't fled the mortal world yet, according to Nephele, but Cas was not counting on her being any more useful than the Star Goddess who *had* fully abandoned them.

Just another annoying, finicky divine being.

An arrow struck the ground uncomfortably close to where they stood, and Cas quickly forgot about the goddesses.

Elander's hand squeezed her shoulder and nudged her attention toward something behind them—Laurent and his riders were in the distance, again disappearing into the bleak landscape.

Just before they turned to follow him, Cas caught sight of another banner fluttering in the wind—this one a bold crimson with a golden tree in its center, which belonged to the Kingdom of Ethswen. She had met the beautiful but terrifying princess of that kingdom months ago, during her brief stay in the elven realm of Moreth. They had not gotten along, to say the least—the meeting had ended with Cas accidentally electrocuting one of the princess's guards.

And suddenly it wasn't only that latest battle in Ciridan haunting her thoughts, but *all* the battles that seemed to build and swallow her up everywhere she went. All the dark and dead things she'd left in her wake, the number of fallen bodies so great she'd lost count at this point…

They caught up to Laurent, and Cas desperately tried to

focus on his face rather than on all the dead faces in her memories.

"Seems we've stumbled across a battlefield," Elander said.

"But one that's avoidable, at least," said Laurent. "We can sweep wide and go around it, but we need to be quick, before either side catches wind of us and decides to drag us into things."

"The cover of rain and fog should help," Elander said, glancing up at the swollen clouds.

"Casia?"

Cas started to meet Laurent's gaze, to agree with the plan they were discussing. But then her eyes fell upon another Sadiran banner, this one damp and trampled so thoroughly into the muddy ground that she'd nearly overlooked it. "There's a chance Soryn is here somewhere. Even if she isn't, she's almost certainly aware of this battle—or will be."

Laurent hesitated. "What are you suggesting?"

"That if we want her to honor our alliance, we could first prove that we plan to do the same. It will be harder for her to decline an audience with me after I've helped lead her army to a victory."

A pained cry sounded close to them—too close—and their circle of riders shifted nervously.

Laurent's voice remained calm despite the escalating situation. "We don't have the numbers to tip them toward a victory."

"There are other ways to win battles, aside from numbers." She tore her eyes from the banner and met his. "We can be strategic."

They stared one another down for a moment, Cas's gaze stubborn and unblinking, Laurent's as steady and intimidating as always.

It was Elander who spoke next, ending their standoff. "We knew the road through Sadira was likely to be paved with battles," he pointed out. "We won't be able to outrun them all."

"And you personally selected most of the ones traveling with us, knowing we would need to fight such battles, didn't you?" Cas added.

After loosing a slow, strained breath, Laurent finally agreed.

"We'll send someone back to rally the rest of our company," Cas said, "while we find somewhere safer to make a plan for when they catch up to us."

Elander volunteered to be the rallying messenger. As he galloped away, Cas hoisted herself into the saddle behind Laurent, and together with a handful of their soldiers they made their way to a distant stretch of the river, wading through shallow waters to reach a large grouping of rocks and trees on the other side. The rest of their riders went to further scout the battlefield and spy for more useful information.

Cas dismounted, found a large boulder, and settled down behind it. She lasted several minutes before her anxiety managed to wrap itself around her, slinking down her arm, tingling across her skin and making her fingers twitch and tap against the rocks around her.

The movements were quiet, more subtle than they'd once been—she had gotten better at hiding this side of herself when in the company of her soldiers—but Laurent's hearing was better than most; he stood several feet away, but his head still tilted toward her tapping fingers, though he never looked directly at them.

"It shouldn't take long for the rest of our group to catch

up," he assured her, his gaze fixing on something in the distance.

She stilled her hands and sank deeper into her hiding place, deeper into herself. She wasn't there long before the clip-clopping of hooves drew her back upright, sending her creeping toward the sound to try and get a closer look.

Across the river, trotting along a path half-shrouded in trees and fog, was a small host of riders wearing cloaks that waved between shades of deep purple and navy. The air simmered with power—not the same energy that divine magic gave off, but a clear change in the atmosphere. It was difficult to tell from a distance, but Cas suspected these riders' ears were tapered, that their eyes reflected an unnatural amount of the muted sunlight. She grew more certain of this when she noticed the flag attached to the saddle of the last rider, fluttering in the wind.

"That flag..."

It was a deep shade of navy, with silver thread weaving briars along its edges and crossed swords in its center, and it represented neither Sadira nor Ethswen.

"The Morethian banner." Laurent's voice finally betrayed a bit of emotion—though it was still difficult to read it. Anger? Fear? Disgust?

Cas felt all of these and more. Her hands were sweating, her skin burning at the memory of sharp metal carving into it.

Her hands traveled over the scars that remained from the torture she'd suffered at the hands of the Morethian Queen, lingering the longest over a particularly large gash on her shoulder. She started to tap it, but resisted, digging her fingernails into the raised flesh instead. It hurt badly enough to snap her back to her senses, and once she had them, she kept moving so she wouldn't lose them again.

She stole her way to another grouping of boulders, remaining out of sight but watching the riders as closely as she could to determine their destination. They were heading toward the main battlefield, she was almost certain.

Nine of them were in this group, but they rode loudly and confidently, as if there were a great deal more of them. Were more coming from other directions? She swept a gaze all around, searching—but all she saw was a lone Sadiran soldier, wounded and heaving for breath, leaning against a tree.

The group of nine saw him as well.

They trotted over to him.

Cas pressed a hand to her mouth to keep sound from escaping. Her own group numbered only five now that they'd split up—and three of them were plain, magicless humans. It would be foolish to give themselves away.

She could do nothing except watch as three of the riders dismounted and strode toward the injured man.

One lifted him by the front of his bloodied coat, and the other two withdrew swords, waving them casually, tauntingly around as they drew closer.

The first slice cut part of the man's right arm cleanly from his body, sending it to the ground with a sickening *thump*. The man's scream was piercing but short-lived as another slice nearly severed the opposite arm and shock overtook him. His face turned a terrifying shade of mottled purple and white. His body slumped in the elf's hold.

The six on horseback looked on, jeering and laughing as though this was the greatest sport they had ever witnessed.

The three who had dismounted held back none of their

inhuman strength, severing the rest of the limbs from the man's body before lopping his head cleanly from his neck. They tossed the head to one of the riders, who snatched it by the hair—a trophy, or maybe a morbid warning to throw at the feet of their waiting enemies—and then they wiped their blades on the glass and sheathed them before leaping back onto their horses and riding onward.

What was left of the Sadiran man lay in a jumbled, bloody pile that Cas couldn't seem to look away from. She swallowed the bile rising in the back of her throat as Laurent caught up with her.

"Are you all right?" he whispered.

She blinked. She still couldn't make herself look away from the slaughter, but she closed her eyes, and that helped her find her center again. "Those were Morethian soldiers... have they come to aid Ethswen?"

"They certainly aren't here to aid Sadira."

"But Moreth and Ethswen have been at odds for *years*, haven't they?"

He averted his gaze from the slaughtered man. "Sarith has been giving the Mistwilde king trouble for weeks now. She's been exiled from that realm—her own homeland—and she hasn't taken it well." His tone remained even, though it seemed as if he was struggling to manage it now. "And the easiest way to Mistwilde is also through Sadira...so it's not a stretch to think Sarith will have reached out to the Ethswenian Queens and tried to make a deal with them, despite their history. Those queens get help crushing Sadira. Sarith gets help making a pathway into Mistwilde. I doubt their alliance is anything more than that."

"Do you think Sarith knows of the Antaeum Point that lies in Mistwilde?" The horrifying thought had crossed Cas's mind before now—she'd just been hoping it wasn't true. "She helped my brother seal the one near Dawnskeep. Even if she didn't fully understand what she was doing at the time, there's a chance she's figured it out—that she's realized what sort of power and influence she could wield if she could overtake the last point and exploit it."

Laurent didn't tell her what he was thinking, as per usual, but his grim face was enough of an answer. "Let's just focus on getting to the other side of this battle."

On to the other side.

Cas's gaze tracked toward the direction the riders had disappeared into. "If Morethian forces are funneling in as well, we may be even more outnumbered than we originally thought."

Laurent nodded. "Yes. But I do think you were right about staying and helping. We just need a plan."

Their scouts returned a few minutes later, bringing information about numbers, positions, and the landscape they'd be contending with. The river was shallow, wide, and slow-moving for as far as they'd been able to see, they told her, and Cas wondered if there was some way they could use it to their advantage.

She was about to suggest this when the thunder of pounding hooves drew their attention.

Two Sadiran soldiers were running down the hill beside them, two riders pursuing them on beastly black horses—more elves.

A cold sweat broke over Cas's skin as she pictured these two soldiers scattered into pieces like the one from before. She and her group were not outnumbered this time. They had to do *something*.

Laurent was already running.

He was halfway to the Sadiran men before Cas realized he had moved, and even then she was stunned in place for a moment, not believing what she was seeing. It wasn't like him to rush recklessly into battle.

It was the Morethian symbols lining the horses tack that had spurred him on, she suspected. However much he resisted his claim to that symbol and all it represented, he seemed determined not to let anyone else die at the hands of it.

He snatched up a large stone and flung it into the chest of the closest horse, causing the creature to rear wildly.

Its rider dangled precariously from the saddle for a moment before abandoning his attempts to stay upright. He leapt to the ground, grabbing a sword from the sheath attached to the saddle and drawing it out as he fell. The movement was stunningly, terrifyingly graceful, as were his next movements as he landed in a crouch and then sprung instantly toward Laurent.

He and Laurent circled one another for a moment before exploding into a dizzying battle of swords, darting about so quickly that Cas could not keep track of them.

She was used to seeing Laurent move with this sort of speed and grace, but she had rarely seen him meet his match in one-on-one combat.

The second rider was still chasing the Sadiran soldiers, she realized.

She ran to help, shouting orders to her own soldiers as she went. Several followed her, three of them catching the Sadiran soldiers and pulling them clear of their pursuer. Two more went to help Laurent, while Cas moved into the path of the rider and withdrew her sword. The simple motion of lifting it created a sparking shower of Storm magic without any effort from her.

The sparks caught the rider's attention, slowing him to a trot.

Cas chanced a quick glance at her soldiers. They had circled the Sadiran men, one of whom appeared to have collapsed from exhaustion. Cas called forth more sparks—a relatively conservative spell—as she swept away from the circle, drawing the elf farther away as well.

His horse plodded after her with heavy, deliberate steps. The elf's eyes were wild and hungry, two pits of devouring fire burning bright among the dreariness.

She lifted her sword.

He laughed at her boldness.

Then he charged.

She summoned a quick bolt of lightning and sent it hurtling toward the horse's feet. Electricity wrapped its ankles, making the creature buck wildly. Its rider attempted to force calm with several rough jerks of the reins and then kicked the creature forward, leaping over the fence of lightning and landing with a thud that shook the earth and sent chills shooting down Cas's spine.

Her enemy continued his charge.

But the horse remained skittish, throwing off the rider's balance. It was easy enough to duck and roll to avoid both the horse and the wayward swipe of its rider's sword. The horse continued to buck and protest, so the elf leapt from its back as gracefully as his companion had—except his sword didn't make the leap with him.

But he had another weapon—a dagger. He whipped it from the sheath at his back and slashed forward in the next motion, sending Cas into an awkward tumble as she spun away. She dropped in time to avoid the blade, but only just caught herself among an outcropping of rocks. Her chin scraped the largest of the boulders and a hiss of pain escaped her.

She snatched up a handful of loose pebbles and flung it toward the elf's eyes. It confused him more than anything—which gave her an opportunity to get around behind him, to swing her sword for his legs.

He was too quick.

He jumped, spun around, and nearly caught her neck with his dagger; she avoided it only because the ground was uneven and she stumbled down an abrupt drop-off in the same instant he stabbed.

The near-miss made her pulse race. Her magic raced in tandem, preparing to rise up and fight. She knew it was risky to waste it, but she was physically outmatched; she had no choice.

He kicked a loose stone at her. As she sidestepped to avoid it, he rushed her, curving around her outstretched sword and colliding with her chest, knocking her onto her back. The jarring motion seemed to press more of her magic free. She didn't fight its rise this time, letting it spill from her and fold around her enemy.

He lifted his sword, which glowed with a pale green light. Like most elven-made weapons, it resisted divine magic, absorbing most of it before sending it scattering in all directions.

He laughed at her again, then taunted her in an elven tongue she didn't understand.

She had to resist the urge to finish him off in a blaze of stronger magic.

Stay calm. Strategize.

He shook the last of the electric sparks from his blade and started toward her—

An arrow struck his arm, courtesy of one of her soldiers.

While he was distracted, she scrambled to her feet. Her eyes fell on a puddle between them, which still crackled with remnants of her magic.

She had an idea.

She flung more rocks at his face before backing toward the river behind her, taunting him as she went. She was loud and obnoxious, using every elvish slur Laurent had ever taught her, until her target finally tore his gaze from the man who had shot him and followed her.

Once they were both knee-deep in the water, Cas scrambled to the shore and then immediately turned back and flung two small orbs of Storm-kind magic into the waves. The water did most of the work after this, conducting her magic and turning her subdued summoning into a brilliant display of power.

It didn't drop him instantly, as it would have done to a human. But it made his body twitch and convulse out of his control, making it essentially impossible for him to leave the water.

So Cas only had to be patient, to continue feeding small amounts of magic to the river to keep the electric current flowing.

Moments later his body sank—only to float back to the surface just downstream, face down and unmoving.

Cas fell back against the sloped bank, clutching Shadowslayer tightly as she caught her breath. The instant she caught it, she looked to the battle on the other side, searching for Laurent. She spotted him quickly—in one piece and in the midst of sheathing his sword, thankfully. The one he'd been fighting was splayed on the ground, unmoving, behind him.

"Still all right over there?" Laurent called as their eyes met.

"Yes, but how about giving me a signal next time?" she huffed as she pushed back to her feet.

He regarded her with a smirk. "Says the woman who has been charging into one battle after the other—without signaling—since the day I met her."

Cas grinned, regretting it instantly as the motion pulled uncomfortably at her scraped chin. "That's a fair point, I suppose."

They turned their attention to the two Sadiran men being held by their soldiers. As Cas made her way toward them, their eyes grew wild with a mixture of shock and fear.

Her hair, her eyes, her magic...her reputation preceded her, and they clearly recognized her.

But what had they heard?

"We're here to help," she assured them.

It took a bit more coaxing, but they eventually trusted their saviors enough to stop trying to wiggle their way free and keep running. After being subjected to a polite yet firm interrogation, they informed Cas and the others that the battle they'd witnessed had started as an ambush. The Sadiran forces were attempting to establish a strategic stronghold at the village of Ironedge and the areas surrounding it—with more of those forces due to arrive as the day went on.

"So we'll just have to help them hold out until the main army arrives," said Laurent.

"And hopefully Soryn will be somewhere in the ranks of that army."

Cas ordered for water and medical care to be given to the Sadiran soldiers, and as the men recovered and their nerves subsided, they grew more compliant—helpful, even, as Cas and Laurent continued to scheme their next moves.

They were in the middle of this scheming when the soldiers' eyes again grew wide at the sight of someone approaching, and Cas turned to find Elander galloping toward them.

He pointed back to his left as he reached them. "The rest of our company are waiting just beyond those hills," he said, "where they have trees and more cover. They're ready for whatever command you have to give them." He dismounted, giving his exhausted mare a quick rubdown before he turned to face Cas more fully.

He saw the cut across her chin, and he frowned, reaching to brush aside a lock of hair that had stuck itself to the scraped skin. "Why is it that every time I go away, I come back to find you bloodier than you were when I left you?"

"I didn't start it this time. He did." She pointed a finger in Laurent's direction. "I wasn't the reckless one for once."

A corner of his mouth lifted. "First time for everything, I suppose." His half-smile quickly fell. "I sensed your magic, too."

She looked back to the river. The dead elf had floated far out of sight by this point. "Not much of it," she told Elander. "And we won't need much more to help the Sadiran army until their reinforcements arrive."

He gave her a curious look, as did their followers who were crowding closer.

Cas met each of their anxious gazes in turn. "Because I have a plan."

CHAPTER 9

Beads of nervous sweat trickled down the back of Cas's neck, mixing with the rain falling faster and faster, as she surveyed the battlefield before her.

Over two hours had passed, and the fighting was subdued and scattered compared to before, each side drawing back to reorganize and regroup.

Perfect.

But there was no telling how long it would last.

Cas lifted her hand and brought forth a single spark of Storm energy, signaling.

The two men they'd helped had found the courage to return to their regiment now that Cas and her followers were behind them. These two were the ones who answered her signal, slipping down among the bands of Sadiran soldiers, making their way through the ranks and bringing word of Cas and her army—and the plan she'd told them to share. As that word spread, Cas sent some of her own army closer, letting them integrate and speak directly with their allies.

Elander caught up to her after questioning several of these allies. His expression was grave, his body tense. "Two of their commanding officers were killed early this morning," he told her. "They've been largely rudderless for most of the day because of it. Most of them seem moments away from surrendering."

Cas withdrew her sword, letting magic dance upon the blade and draw eyes toward her. "We're not surrendering," she said, as much to herself as to Elander, as she strode toward the largest group of Sadiran soldiers she saw, her sword sparking more brightly.

She welcomed the gazes that followed her in a way she never had before. Like those of the fleeing men she'd helped save, many of the eyes that fell upon her now widened in some combination of disbelief and uncertainty. Equally dubious whispers started to rise—but she silenced them quickly, drowning the chatter out with a barrage of orders.

They needed the bulk of their forces to gather—enough to draw the attention of their enemy.

And then they were all going to run away.

They weren't going far, only across the river, while the strongest of the Sky-kind among them erected barriers to help funnel their foes after them—and into that river.

She directed Zev to lead that gathered mass of their soldiers, making use of his loud mouth and bright magic to catch their enemy's attention.

While he led the charge to infuriate and draw those enemies in, Nessa weaved in and out of the Sadiran forces, using her magic to keep them calm enough to hold their ground until it was time to move.

Rhea positioned herself out of sight but continued to

scout through Silverfoot's eyes, watching for any large groups of enemy soldiers they might have missed.

Laurent prepared to direct the staged retreat to the other side of the river, while Cas and Elander took their places along the water's edge, readying their magic.

Not everyone agreed to follow her plans—but there were enough who did.

She hoped.

She knelt at the riverside, flanked on either side by two Sky-kind who were ready to provide cover shields if necessary. She ordered them to stay alert, but to only use their magic if absolutely necessary, while she kept her eyes on Zev.

Zev was surrounded by other magic users as well—more Fire-kind. Their magic derived from the Dark God, so it burned more brightly than ever with no need to ration it yet. Zev called forth a flame, shooting it high into the cloudy sky that was growing darker as evening settled in.

Cas watched it go, holding her breath, letting its brightness fill her with more hope.

This is going to work.

This has to work.

A barrage of enemy arrows answered the flame's call.

Shields of magic went up, creating a dome around the Fire-kind and all the soldiers positioned in a ready circle just behind them.

But many of the strands of Sky magic that wove the dome together were weak, pulsing in and out like embers in a doused fire, and the arrows managed to pierce these weaker patches. When another shower of arrows swiftly followed the first, several found their way through the newly-created holes, striking three Sadiran soldiers—that Cas *saw.*

A rope of anxiety twisted through her at the sound of the

soldiers' cries, but she braced her hands into the damp ground and held her position, letting the feel of the solid earth solidify her resolve.

The enemy army was regrouped and rushing toward them in earnest, pouring in from multiple directions, drawn in by more and more crass shouting and beckoning flames. They still relied mostly on arrows, but several had appeared on the ridge above the river, swords drawn and readied.

When Cas's soldiers remained in place beneath the dome of magic, these swordbearers started to make their way down the hill.

Her soldiers then did as she had ordered them to, cowering and backing away, drawing the enemy farther down the hill, giving them a false sense of confidence that grew and grew…

Almost…

"RETREAT!" came Laurent's booming voice, and at his signal, their soldiers swiftly abandoned their dome of magic and focused instead on running, wading swiftly through the thigh-high water and making their way to the other side of the river.

The enemy saw the apparent retreat and rushed to exploit it.

Once the majority had waded into the waves, the most powerful of Sadira's magic-wielders emerged from their hiding places. Shields of magic went up along the banks on each side, trapping the enemy in the river.

Cas's gaze swept over her forces. The ones they'd hidden were the strongest shield makers they currently had, and yet, like the dome from before, the strands of magic they summoned were paler than she'd hoped they would be.

But she didn't dwell on it—she didn't have time. She

shifted her stance, making certain she was clear of the water, and readied her own magic.

Bit by bit, she let that magic jump from her command and into the water.

Strategic, she reminded herself, watching to see the way the waves picked up that power, tumbled it around, amplified it.

Elander was some distance down the river, doing the same thing. She couldn't see him through the fog swirling around the water and the haze of magical residue in the air, but she saw his light—and *felt* it—and that was enough to coax her own into something bolder. She pictured their power meeting, the bolts of it intertwining and setting the world alight.

Nothing can break things so completely.

Nothing can heal things so fully.

It seemed as though today would be full of broken things that she could only hope would put them on a path toward healing.

With a sound like the earth cracking open, more streaks of lightning shot from her hands and into the water, racing toward the center of the river.

In her peripheral vision, she saw movement on the hillside. More enemy archers coming closer, taking aim at the Sky-kind who had turned that river into a cage. An arrow felled one, and then another, and suddenly the shields were flickering, the cage in danger of breaking open.

Heart pounding in her throat, Cas ordered the ones protecting her to help secure the shields instead, and then she withdrew Shadowslayer and stabbed it down into the muddy bank. She squeezed its handle until the symbols in its steel all blazed brightly.

The mud around her bubbled up as power sizzled from the sword and snaked down toward the water. Then the water itself was bubbling, erupting, foaming and violently churning with electricity.

The sight seemed to give courage to the Sky-kind on both sides of the bank, who drew out more of their magic and weaved it more tightly, more boldly together.

A few enemies still managed to slip through some patches of the barriers, but they came slowly enough that it wasn't difficult to pick them off.

Cas and Elander's magic continued to pour into the river, which grew so bright it became blinding, the heat roiling off it hot enough to sizzle the skin of anyone who got too close.

Once the enemies slipping through ceased, Cas stopped pouring magic into the water. She soon felt Elander doing the same. The storm continued for several minutes after they'd stopped, filling the air with static and steam.

When it finally settled and cleared, there were too many floating dead to count.

The ones still living created a harrowing chorus of groans and cries as they rolled and staggered out of the water. Most of these survivors ran, tripping and stumbling, for safety. The ones who didn't run ended up regretting their choice as they met arrows and blades.

Cas averted her eyes and then closed them for just a moment, long enough to push down the sick feeling rising up from her stomach.

One of the Sadiran soldiers let out a victorious cry. Several more followed his example, their desire to surrender momentarily forgotten.

But they had scarcely caught their breath when Rhea shouted, warning them of more approaching enemies.

The battle raged on and on.

They trapped a few additional, smaller groups in the river, bringing them to an electrifying end, before all of their enemies caught on to this tactic and retreated from the water's edge, firing instead from a distance with both magic and arrows.

But by this point the numbers had been evened out, the morale of their opponents lowered by heavy losses sustained so brutally quickly.

Cas thought she saw more Sadiran soldiers—new faces—beginning to trickle in.

The reinforcements they'd been waiting for?

An arrow whizzed by Cas's head, striking an Ethswenian soldier who had been nocking his own arrow to fire at her. The soldier fell back, clutching his chest, and Cas turned to see Nessa lowering her bow, a grim but satisfied expression on her face.

Cas returned the favor a moment later, sprinting to intercept a man attempting to sneak up on Nessa. She knocked him to the ground, whipped the dagger from the sheath at Nessa's hip, and stabbed him between the shoulder blades as he was trying to stand.

He fell face-first to the ground, blood spurting from the wound as Cas withdrew the knife. He writhed about in directionless agony for several seconds before crawling for the cover of a bush. Blood continued to pour from him, a river of it trailing from under the bush and glistening in the fading daylight, clearly giving away his hiding place.

Cas left him to die in peace, grabbing Nessa's arm and pulling her away. After wiping the blood from the dagger, she handed it back to Nessa and then sent her toward a nearby patch of trees where some of their wounded were being tended to.

Cas went the opposite way, darting back toward the river to help finish off any of the more resilient enemy soldiers who had managed to fight their way out of the electrified water.

She caught sight of one of these soldiers and started toward him—but drew abruptly to a stop, gasping as she realized he wasn't an enemy, but one of Sadira's own who had gotten caught up in the trap she'd planned.

He was pulling himself from the river, dragging his body through the muddy bank, his hands slipping and sliding as they grappled for something sturdy to grab on to.

Cas raced toward him to offer help.

Her arm seized up as she reached for him.

Within seconds, the rest of her body had followed suit, her muscles tightening and contracting so violently she couldn't stay on her feet. She tumbled to her hands and knees, managing just enough control to break her fall, but once she was down she lost even this control; her limbs crumpled beneath her and her face landed in cold, pebbly muck.

The soldier managed to crawl farther away from the water and call for help.

Nessa was there a moment later, dropping to her side and lifting her head out of the mud. Cas's body had seized up during panic attacks in the past, and Nessa had witnessed it and used her power to calm and relax Cas's muscles—so she tried to do the same thing now.

But it wasn't panic that had brought Cas to her knees this time.

It was *magic*.

She tried to explain this, but it was impossible to speak. It felt like the very breath in her lungs was being controlled, pulled away from her. Her spine stiffened, and she could no longer sit upright. She collapsed against Nessa's chest.

The claws of magic around her head trapped it in place, but her eyes could still move. She raised them to the sight of a woman making her way down the sloped bank.

Cas knew this woman. She was more battle-worn than the last time they'd met, her dark hair wildly disheveled, her brown skin marred by dirt and what looked like blood along the left side of her face. Her clothes were far more plain than anything Cas had ever seen her wearing. But the Sundolian emblem on her coat, her golden eyes, the way she carried herself...it was all unmistakable. As was the mark of the coiled serpent glowing upon her hand.

This was Alaya, the Dragon Queen of the Sundolian Empire—and the wife of Soryn's cousin.

Apparently, she had traveled north to aid her family.

Cas heard someone shout her name—Elander, she thought. She could still only move her eyes, so she couldn't be certain until he was kneeling at her side in the next moment, his arm curving around her waist and helping to steady her; she could feel his touch, but she couldn't respond to it in any way.

The Dragon Queen stepped closer to them.

Elander rose back to his feet. The air shook with power, his fury made tangible and rolling off him in waves. "Release her, *you snake*!"

Laurent appeared in Cas's peripheral vision as well, bow readied and aimed at the Sundolian High Queen.

The queen ignored them both, her golden eyes locked on Cas's. She seemed to be trying to read something in the depths of Cas's gaze, despite the distance and fading daylight between them. To be searching those depths for answers about all that had happened to Cas over the past months.

Were they still allies, as they had been during their last meeting?

Doesn't seem like it at the moment.

Elander took a threatening step toward the queen. The air filled with sparks.

Don't, Cas wanted to say. *We need to save our magic for our enemies—and she isn't our enemy.*

The queen waved her hand, and Cas's lungs gave a violent shudder before tightening, making her cough. Elander's head snapped back toward her, eyes widening.

"Stay back," warned Alaya in a heavily-accented version of the Kethran common tongue. "And lower your weapons."

Laurent slowly did as she said.

Elander's hand remained on the hilt of Caden's sword for a long moment, but he ultimately let it go and followed Laurent's example. The air settled, and he backed away from the queen without taking his eyes off her, kneeling again at Cas's side.

The queen glanced over her shoulder. Wiggled her fingers. Glanced at the glowing mark on her hand, and then over her shoulder again. Waiting on someone, it seemed.

It took only moments more for that someone to arrive.

A rider crested the hill behind the Dragon Queen. She was dressed entirely in black. Her leather armor was the same shade as her massive horse's coat, making them seem like one continuous monster that was much larger and imposing than everyone standing around her.

She stayed on that horse for a moment as she surveyed the scene below her, then she leapt gracefully to the ground and handed the reins to one of the three soldiers who swept silently to her side, like ghosts from the dark fog. She removed her riding gloves, and palmed the handle of the sword at her hip—considering withdrawing it for a moment, perhaps, before deciding otherwise.

Like the queen who had arrived before her, she did all of this without taking her eyes off Cas. Then she strode forward, pulling her hood aside and letting the waves of her hair—as black as her armor and horse—tumble free.

Soryn.

Cas tried again to move, but it was useless.

The man that Cas had been trying to help from the river had found his feet without her assistance. He staggered toward his queen, arms raised in a gesture of peace.

Soryn stiffened as he approached her. Her focus remained on Cas, but her head tilted toward the man as she listened to what he had to say.

As he finished and bowed before his queen, Soryn's eyes narrowed more completely on Cas. They stayed there for several moments past the point of comfortable, searing and bright, and in her paralyzed state, Cas felt as if she was being held over an open flame.

Finally, Soryn looked over to the Sundolian Queen and nodded.

Instantly, the pressure around Cas's muscles released.

With Nessa and Elander's help, she rose to her feet. The effects of magic lingered, making her legs tingle and tremble, but she managed one step after the other until she was directly in front of her old ally.

Soryn lifted her chin. "Greetings, Your Majesty." Her tone was difficult to read—not quite mocking, but certainly not reverent or friendly.

Cas met the queen's unnervingly cold and odd, turquoise eyes without flinching. "We need to talk."

"So I've gathered." A muscle worked in Soryn's jaw. Annoyance flickered through her bright gaze. "The village of Ironedge is two miles south of here," she finally said. "It has been largely abandoned by civilians, and the remaining people stand ready to quarter our army. We'll regroup there. And we can *talk* after I've had a chance to speak with my own soldiers about all that's transpired today."

The soldiers who were answering to me just moments ago.

Cas wanted to point this out, to make some biting comment about how the two of them were on the same side, both of them queens trying to do right by their people, that she was not some *nuisance* who needed to wait her turn to speak...

But she thought better of it. Saving their conversation until some of the tension from this battle had subsided might make Soryn more receptive to what she had to say.

Hopefully.

CHAPTER 10

The village of Ironedge was eerily silent, the only sound the echoing pitter-patter of raindrops upon the empty streets.

Cas had arrived at the designated meeting spot well before Soryn—she'd been waiting for no less than an hour alongside Rhea, Silverfoot, and Nessa.

Scarcely a word passed between the group of them as they huddled together on a small porch, outside of the rain but still damp from the fog that wrapped them up along with everything else. Nessa had been using her magic to chase away the chill and their nerves alike, despite Cas's insistence that she needed to ration her power—though it was hard to argue for long about that magic use. This was a strategic calming of nerves, wasn't it? If she could not calmly handle this meeting with Soryn, the days ahead would be more difficult.

So she didn't protest as Nessa sat behind her on the porch steps, absently redoing her disheveled braid while letting warm magic flow from her fingertips, through the strands of her hair, and over her scalp.

Finally, Soryn emerged from the fog, the sides of her black steed slick and shining with sweat and rainwater and its snorts puffing clouds into the cold air.

She eyed Cas's company wearily as she dismounted. "We have no need for such a full audience, do we?"

Cas bristled, but held in her objection. She knew Soryn was trying to control her. With the Sundolian Queen's magic, with her insistence on not talking to her until after they'd left the battlefield—and now, with this.

But Cas had learned long ago that people usually reached most recklessly for control when they were afraid, and she decided once more not to stoke the embers of Soryn's fear and mistrust.

She nodded to Soryn, then looked to her friends, silencing Nessa with a pointed look.

"I'll be fine," she told them. "You all should be resting and regrouping while you can, anyhow."

"Are you sure?" Nessa's eyes darted uncertainly, covertly, toward Soryn as that queen handed off her horse to a young man who bowed so low he nearly toppled over.

"Of course."

I trust Soryn, Cas wanted to add—but couldn't.

Silverfoot let out a soft whine and Rhea silenced him with a reassuring pat between the ears. "We'll be close," she told Cas, and Silverfoot seconded the promise with a yip and a swish of his tail.

Cas followed Soryn into the small house that smelled of dust and cold, damp things. They reached a room flanked by soldiers and went inside. Another soldier awaited them in here, and he handed Soryn a bundle of papers tied together with twine. Soryn thanked and then dismissed him.

The Dragon Queen arrived shortly after, interrupting their meeting before it could start. She and Soryn spoke at length—and rapidly—in the Sundolian common tongue. It sounded like they were having an argument.

Cas understood some of what they were saying, but not all. Her skin grew hot with irritation as she was forced to wait, yet again, for her chance to have a meaningful conversation with Soryn.

Her patience quickly thinned, and she started to interrupt —when a knock at the door interrupted all of them.

Another familiar woman stood on the threshold: Sade, the second in command to Alaya. The two women exchanged a few brief words. Then, at Sade's insistent look, the Dragon Queen bade farewell to Soryn and turned to leave, her golden eyes catching briefly on Cas.

Cas felt as she had at the riverside, as though this woman's stare might peel away layers of skin and bone and reveal every thought and fear tumbling in her mind. Her hand absently reached for the back of her neck, trying to massage away the memory of the queen's magic overtaking her muscles. She was glad she was leaving.

"Tread carefully," said the Dragon Queen as she passed by, her voice low and meant only for the two of them. Her eyes softened the tiniest bit as she said it, and her voice had not sounded like the threat Cas had braced herself for.

What had she been speaking with Soryn about?

Cas watched her leave, wondering if there was a chance she'd actually been arguing on her behalf.

She forced her gaze back to Soryn and made her voice as

amicable as possible. "I'm glad you have such powerful allies close by."

"They put themselves at great risk to be here," said Soryn, offhandedly, as she untied the bundle of papers the soldier had given her and started to leaf through them.

Cas tried again to keep her voice friendly, to reawaken some feeling of the camaraderie they'd shared before. "I had forgotten how powerful that queen is."

Soryn kept searching the papers in her hands. "Her magic is derived from the Serpent Goddess, who serves the Dark One. She still has plenty of power to draw from." She paused her scanning, though she still didn't glance up. "The same, it seems, cannot be said of my own."

Cas's heart dropped at this confirmation of her fears. She chose her next words carefully. "My power is at risk, too, for what it's worth."

Soryn shook her head. Paused. Crumpled one of the papers in her hand before she realized what she was doing, and then immediately smoothed it back out. "It's true, then. The things I've heard."

Cas didn't reply, wondering, as she had earlier, about what the people in this kingdom had *heard*.

Soryn answered without her having to ask. "You *willingly* locked away the source of your own magic. Of *countless* good magic users, and I cannot understand—"

"*I* didn't do it. My brother did. This was always his ultimate goal, it turns out." Cas took a deep, bracing breath. "And now that I have had time to think over the matter, to understand *why* that was the goal...even if I don't agree with the methods he used, I believe his decision was the right one. I think what he and my father started must be finished if we want to put a stop to the endless meddling of the gods and the instability that comes from it."

Soryn laughed—a harsh sound, like glass scraping over rocks. "Your brother has finally succeeded in winning you over to his side, has he?"

"We are beyond choosing *sides* at this point. It's more complicated than simply good versus evil, or whatever other notions you've come up with—"

"*Notions,*" interrupted Soryn in that same harsh tone she'd laughed in. "What *notions* do you think I have?"

Cas dug her fingernails into her palms, focusing on the biting pain and willing her temper not to flare.

Soryn studied her for a long moment before she finally spoke again, her tone calm and hollowed out, her fingers curling tightly around the papers she still held. "I believed we were working toward the same goal. When last we parted, you were off to find a way to battle gods and kings—but not at the expense of my people. Now, it seems, you have given up on those of us with magic, and at what cost to me and my kingdom? Without magic, we have nothing. It is the only thing that has kept us from being entirely crushed these past decades."

"I didn't *give up*. Things have changed."

"Clearly."

"If there was a way to create peace without such drastic measures, do you not think I would be choosing that instead?"

Soryn averted her gaze but said nothing, as though she truly didn't know *what* to think of Cas any longer. It was a rare show of indecision from the normally stoic young leader. It disappeared quickly, replaced by her usual hard lines and cold eyes as she narrowed her gaze back on Cas.

Cas steadied herself, refusing to draw away from that steely gaze. "What's done is done. The fact is that only one of the Moraki remains, he is stronger than ever, and he is no champion of mortals. We need to level the playing field, whatever the cost, or we will not be able to rid this world of him. I know you're afraid of what comes next—of the changes this will mean to magic and to your kingdom that has relied on it for so long. But that doesn't mean we can keep going down the same path and let it take us all the way to *ruin*. Change is upon us whether you accept it or not."

Soryn placed the papers on a table by the window, folded her arms across her chest, and stayed quiet for a long time. A *very* long time.

Then, while staring out of that frost-edged window, she finally said, "I've arranged for houses to accommodate both you and at least some of your traveling party for the night."

"And tomorrow?"

"You will leave this city in the morning. Continue on to Mistwilde if you so choose—I've been told that's your destination, and I won't stand in your way of reaching it. But you will not stay within my ranks. My soldiers will not answer to you again. Sadira has fought enough battles on her own in the past, and it seems this trend is better off continuing." She turned and started for the door.

Cas didn't move. "Is it pride that's making you act like such a fool?"

Soryn paused mid-step.

"Sadira can't return to what it was before. It cannot be your mother and father's kingdom."

"Hold your tongue."

Cas closed the distance between them, stopping just short

of grabbing the queen and giving her a violent shake. "You will have to make it your own kingdom, to fight the challenges we're facing *now*, not the same battles your parents—"

"*Hold. Your. Tongue.*"

Cas breathed in deeply. She again considered snatching Soryn and trying to shake some sense into her—until she caught sight of a silent, dark figure moving into the doorway. The Sundolian Queen. She'd likely been drawn back to the room by the sound of their raised voices, and even the faint, subdued hum of her power sent a tingle of warning dancing over Cas's skin.

She held her tongue.

Soryn slowly turned and continued her march toward the door. "Now, if you'll excuse me," she said, coldly, "I need to speak with my remaining leaders and finish counting our dead and calculating our losses."

AFTER BEING USHERED from Soryn's presence by several heavily-armed soldiers, Cas made her way back outside.

Her friends had not gone to rest as she'd suggested; they were waiting for her on the same porch she'd left them on.

Nessa popped eagerly into her path, eyes wide with curiosity and concern. "How'd it go?"

Cas tried to avert her gaze, but her companions were relentless. Silverfoot let out a whine as he stared up at her, studying her intently through softly glowing eyes.

"That poorly, hm?" asked Rhea.

"Soryn is being very…stubborn," said Cas. "As I feared she might be. The Sundolian Queen seems potentially more cooperative, but I don't know how much influence she truly has here. We've been given until tomorrow morning to move on from Ironedge."

Nessa bristled, her face turning even redder than it already was in the cold air. "If Soryn is going to be so difficult, then let's just leave tonight and be done with her."

Cas sighed, wishing it was as simple as that. "And what becomes of our kingdoms after all this is over? Assuming we manage to save the world from the divine threat without her help, then we just have another war to fight with Sadira. I'm thinking of the future, and I want her on my side. Besides, when Solatis tasked me with saving this world, she said it would require an alliance of the divine *and* mortals unlike anything this world has ever known."

"I still think she's being crass," muttered Nessa. Reluctantly, she added, "Though I suppose when you're desperate for allies, even the *rude* ones count for something."

Cas managed a small smile as Rhea gave her shoulder a reassuring squeeze.

She appreciated her friends' company and steady loyalty. But she found herself not wanting to linger in their presence —she felt like she had failed them, and she just wanted to get away from everything for a while, to regroup in private before her next inevitable battle.

After sharing a more complete summary of her meeting, she slipped away and started toward the house Soryn had granted her for the night.

The rain had turned to snow, fat flakes of it swirling and dying upon her hair. She loved snow. The simple joy of catching it on her tongue, the way a fresh blanket of it made everything feel clean and new. But now she only huddled against the cold that accompanied it, drew her hood over her head, and trudged onward.

She slowed—though only for a few steps—when she heard Elander's voice behind her.

He jogged to catch up with her. "Where are you going?"

"To sleep. In preparation for what will be an early morning, it seems." She tried to speed up again, to escape his prying gaze just as she'd done with the others, but he caught her by the arm and pulled her to a stop.

She put up a half-hearted fight before giving in and burying her face against his chest. He held her for a long moment, neither of them speaking. She gripped his shirt, her frustration making her fists clench so tightly she was likely permanently ruining the cloth.

"I take it the meeting didn't go well."

She forced her hands to unclench as she explained precisely how *not well* it had gone, her face never fully leaving his chest and her words half-muffled by his shirt.

After she'd finished, he was quiet for a moment, considering. "Maybe Soryn will see things differently come morning."

She leaned back and met his eyes. "Why would she?"

He shrugged. "Because things often look different in the daylight."

She pressed her head back against his chest. She wanted to hear the steady beat of his heart again. "Let's hope so."

The snow became heavier. A fierce gust of wind spun up around them, encircling them in a flurry of white, and she felt briefly removed from everything outside of the two of them. She looked up at him again, at the snowflakes caught on his long lashes and his handsome face slightly flushed from the cold. She stood on her tiptoes to kiss him, letting the warmth from it sink through her, all the way down to the tips of her toes, before she spoke again.

"We should get out of the cold. Go warm up together, maybe."

Elander wiped a few melted snowdrops from her cheek and fixed her hood that had been knocked away by the wind. "You should go rest, as you said, and focus on the morning and what comes next with Soryn."

This was not the response she expected—he never missed an opportunity to *warm up* with her.

She stepped out of his embrace, studying the distracted look in his eyes; he was keeping something from her. "Never mind me," she said, "where were *you* going?"

He hesitated before locking his gaze on hers once more. "Laurent was speaking with some of the townspeople... They've been dealing with unrest for weeks now—Ethswen and Morethian soldiers alike causing them trouble. It's partly why so many have fled, and why Soryn herself has marched here to reclaim the area."

More hesitation. Cas fixed him with an insistent look, and he took her hand and pulled her into motion, continuing his explanation as they walked.

"There are also rumors that the attack we witnessed was very...coordinated. That the Morethian Queen herself might have been here days ago, laying the groundwork for it and for...well, we aren't sure what else. But she's clearly on the move, and we want to find out more."

Cas slowed to a stop, stomach flipping as images of the elves dismembering that Sadiran man flashed through her mind. She fought the urge to reach for the scar on her shoulder.

Elander's gaze was already fixed on it, and the darkness in his eyes sent a chill down her spine.

She swallowed hard. "Do you think Sarith is still close by?"

"I don't know." He pressed his lips to hers in a quick goodbye kiss, causing a shiver of power between them. "But I promise you I am going to find out."

CHAPTER 11

Elander crouched in the shadow of a tall pine, peering at a lake with water the color of frosted glass. The snow reached nearly to his ankles, but it was no longer falling. Breaks in the clouds allowed for occasional glimpses of the moon, and parts of the lake glowed so brightly in its light that it seemed as though the waters were holding it captive rather than merely reflecting its beams.

Laurent was directly to Elander's right, with Zev beside him. After two hours of interrogating townspeople and soldiers, the three of them had determined that the most credible sightings of their target centered around the area of the lake.

So here they were, breaths steaming, hands and feet going numb, bodies tense and expectant.

A crack of brittle branches jerked Elander's gaze upward. He stared into the dizzying circle of towering pines as powdery snow, clearly shaken free by something, drifted over him. He thought he saw an odd shadow leaping between the dense pine needles. Squinted, but…No, nothing there.

Just the wind at work.

He pulled his coat more tightly around himself and cupped a hand over his mouth, trying to warm the air cutting a sharp path down his throat with every breath. The temperature had dropped brutally quickly once the sun went down—too quickly, almost—and so he was watching for signs of the Ice Goddess or her minions in addition to signs of elves.

No shortage of things that could cause us trouble.

"What is the deal with this lake, anyway?" asked Zev in a whisper. He sounded unsettled, eager to fill the eerie silence with conversation.

Laurent took a moment to reply, as he was busy shaking snow from the collar of his coat, disgust written all over his face. He wasn't a fan of the cold or the damp. "The locals now call it Lake Haven," he said, "but the elves have a different name for it—*Ulondar*. The legend says it was the site where a warrior-elf of the same name—the eventual founder of Mistwilde—went to battle with one of the Moraki who were trying to strip the elves of their magic. He lost, of course, and the power the upper-god drove from him after his loss ate a massive hole in the ground that eventually filled with water. Water that was tainted with the lingering energies of the expelled magic."

Elander looked back to the lake. It wasn't hard to believe that magic had played a part in coloring the milky waters. Even as the moon slipped back behind the clouds, sections of the gently rippling waves kept glowing.

"The rivers flowing out from this lake supposedly contain magic as well, in various forms. One of those rivers eventually forms the Kethran-facing borders of Mistwilde, and that river—*Mirdor*—has a mind of its own they say, and a goal of keeping out anyone who might bring ill things into Mistwilde."

"You and Elander entered Mistwilde without issue, didn't you?"

Laurent nodded. "We had to cross the river—the Air spirit couldn't bring us any closer than that. But yes, we did it without any problems. Which is likely one reason why King Talos didn't immediately throw us out. The waters of Mirdor are a screening test of sorts."

"One Sarith is not likely to pass," said Elander.

"Which might be why she's here—*if* the rumors are true about that," said Laurent. "Another part of the legend claims there are rituals to be done with Ulondar's waters; spells you can create that will help you counter the tricks and treacheries of the rivers that flow from it."

Zev considered these legends for a long moment. "That all sounds a bit farfetched, doesn't it?"

Laurent cut him a sideways glance. "More farfetched than Casia traveling back in time? Or us walking alongside gods? Doing battle with them?"

Zev accepted this point with a shrug and went back to watching the lake.

Minutes passed without incident or signs of movement, and they decided to abandon their post and follow the gently sloping ground to a hiding spot closer to the lake.

They had only been in this new hiding place for a few minutes before Zev felt the need to interrupt the silence again. "You know," he said to Elander, "Cas still doesn't think we know each other well enough, even after everything we've been through."

Elander didn't take his eyes off the lake. "And...?"

"And she'll be glad we're out here together, I guess."

"This is not a get-to-know-one-another adventure. It's a rather more pressing mission than that."

"Can't it be both?"

Elander scoffed. "Yes, because getting to know you better is number three on my to-do list—right below saving the world from vengeful gods, and murdering this sadistic bitch of an elf queen we're trying to track down. So, very high priority, already…but maybe I should shuffle that list some? I could make you number one."

"I was just making conversation."

"Movement on the opposite bank, off to the right," said Laurent, focusing on the mission rather than the chatter, as per usual.

The three of them quieted again, watching for more movement.

When it didn't come, Zev grew bored of the silence and started filling it with words. Again. "She's been looking at you differently over these past weeks, I've noticed."

Elander didn't reply right away, busying himself with scanning the stretch of land to their right. The ground on this side rose steeply into a thick clutch of trees—too thick. Too easy for someone to sneak up on them.

"Everything has become different over these past weeks," he told Zev.

"I suppose I just want to know what the future holds. What the plan is once all this saving the world business is over with."

Elander knew what he was truly asking; he and Casia were fairly certain Zev had guessed at the proposal and plans they'd made. But Casia had decided not to *officially* tell any of her friends of their engagement until they could all properly celebrate the occasion—and Elander wasn't going to be the one to steal the joy of that eventual conversation from her.

Instead, he lowered his voice and said, "I'd tell you my plans for her, but they're all wildly indecent."

Zev had no response to this.

Miraculous.

Elander kept going, intending to silence him on the matter more completely. "I could go into detail, but I don't think you want to hear about the things she and I are going to do once we have more time to ourselves. All the ways we're going to fuck and—"

"Okay, never mind. You can stop."

"Are you sure?"

"Positive."

"It might be awkward, but you might learn some things, too."

"Stop."

"I meant general pointers for your own sad love life, not specific to her."

"I don't need pointers from *you*."

"I have a wealth of experience regarding such things, you know."

He snorted. "Does Cas know about all of your countless *experiences*, I wonder?"

"Oh yes, she's very aware of how experienced I am."

Zev breathed out a soft curse in his native Sundolian tongue.

"What is it? Have I made you uncomfortable?"

"I'm going to set you on fire if you don't stop talking."

"Well, let me know if you change your mind about the pointers."

Zev fumed, Laurent chuckled, and Elander returned his

full attention to scanning their surroundings until he saw more movement in the direction Laurent had indicated—and this time, the moving figure was well-illuminated by a moon that had suddenly emerged from behind the clouds. Elander watched as they crept their way along the shore, occasionally darting behind rocks and fallen logs, before ultimately disappearing into the tall, swaying grass of a flowering reed plant.

"There's a person in the grass there," he said, voice barely above a whisper.

After a moment of closing his eyes and focusing, tapered ears twitching slightly, Laurent nodded. "Two of them, I think."

The second body soon appeared just outside of the concealing reeds. He took a container from the first figure and crept down to the lake. He scooped water into the container, and it clearly glowed from within—a beacon of pale light shooting straight up into the air—before he hastily sealed it off.

Elander glanced toward Laurent. "Something for the rituals you spoke of?"

"Possibly."

"I vote we get closer and find out," said Zev.

"We agree on something for once," said Elander, already pulling Caden's sword free of its sheath and searching for the most covert way to approach their targets.

Zev led the way, fire swirling to life in his cupped palm, its light turned discreetly away from those targets. Elander followed at a short distance, while Laurent brought up the rear, his bow in his hands and his eyes scanning for any extra company in the distance.

It was impossible to truly sneak up on an elf. Once they were convinced the two in the grass were the only ones they had to deal with, they abandoned any attempts at stealth and ambushed their targets instead.

Zev set fire to the bush, then stretched that fire into a rope that encircled the first elf. The flames danced just off the elf's body, licking at his skin and clothing, tightening a little more with every movement.

He quickly stopped moving.

The fire continued to swirl around him, smoking and making him appear as though he was burning at the stake, even though Zev continued to have an impressive amount of control over the flames, keeping them from catching in earnest.

The second elf abandoned his companion and bolted for the distant trees.

Laurent was faster. He used no weapon aside from his fist, catching the runner with a powerful punch to his jaw and knocking him to the earth.

The elf bounced back to his feet almost instantly, but now Elander had closed in from the other side. He withdrew his sword, quick as a breath, and thrust it into the elf's face.

The elf drew up short, narrowly avoiding impalement. He stumbled and dropped the container of lake water—a decorative canteen of sorts—which Laurent snatched up and secured.

Elander cut off the elf's attempt to win the canteen back, pushing him against the steep riverbank. "Why don't you have a seat?" he ordered, swinging the sword toward his chest, nudging the tip of it just below the clasp of the elf's cloak.

The elf leaned away, nearly parallel to the ground but somehow keeping his balance, gracefully twisting his arms behind his back and catching himself against the slope. His eyes darted wildly from side to side in search of an escape route.

Elander pressed the sword into the hollow of his throat.

The elf sat.

Elander stepped closer, while Laurent loomed just behind him, an arrow nocked and ready.

"That's a Morethian emblem on your cloak there, isn't it?" Elander used the sword to poke said emblem, and the elf sank away from the sharp tip, falling fully back against the hill. "You're a long way from home."

His captive didn't reply.

"Tell me...what brings you to this lake?"

The elf bared his teeth. "Sightseeing."

Elander met the elf's nasty smile with one of his own.

Then he whipped the blade up across his face, expertly applying just enough pressure to leave only a shallow cut across his sharp chin—a warning.

The drops of blood bored steaming holes into the snow. A satisfying sight. *Too* satisfying. Such things usually didn't affect him one way or another—he had seen enough that he could keep his head level—but now he was thinking of *other* blood. Other scars. And he did not feel *level*. He was not thinking of anything in that moment except...

Blood for blood.

He wanted to spill every last bit of this pathetic creature's blood.

But not as badly as he wanted to spill that of the Morethian Queen, so he managed to stay focused on gathering information about her.

"Your queen," he continued, voice cutting the chill air like a knife, "has she walked this area lately?"

"The queen walks where she pleases."

"That is not what I asked." His sword did not move, but his tone was enough to make his captive flinch, to make the elf's eyes dart briefly toward the drops of red in the snow.

He seemed to be weighing the cost of silence, deciding quickly that it wasn't one he was willing to pay. "I...I do not know where she's walked," he stammered. "I am only a lowly soldier, I know nothing of—" The steel edge pressed to his jaw, biting into his flesh, cutting him off.

"So it sounds as though it won't raise any suspicion—or cause me any problems—if I paint the snow with the rest of your blood, hm?" Elander gave the blade a flick, shaking another few drops of scarlet into that snow. "No one will miss you, least of all the queen in question. Do I have that right?"

The elf closed his eyes.

"I'm growing impatient," Elander warned.

"The queen walks where she pleases," the elf repeated in between gulps for air, "but she has long been enamored with this lake and—"

An arrow whizzed past Elander, very nearly slicing his cheek open. He instinctively leapt back. Not far, but it was all the elf needed—his inhuman speed and reflexes allowed him to roll out of reach of Elander's sword, and to spring to his feet and start running without a trace of hesitation.

Several things happened in the span of only seconds.

There came a terrible, guttural howl, followed swiftly by the scent of burnt flesh—Zev had tightened the fiery rope, preventing the other elf from escaping.

A second arrow flew toward them, this one close enough that it would have struck Laurent if he'd been a slow human.

Laurent took aim at the source of the shot—at a third elf who had joined them, crouching atop one of the nearby hills

—and released a counter arrow. Laurent was one of the most accurate shots Elander had ever met, but their enemy had the high ground; he merely needed to drop down and let the hill protect him.

"Don't waste your arrows," Elander told him, breaking in front of him and sprinting after their target himself.

He made it halfway up the hill before Laurent caught him by the shoulder and yanked him back.

"I doubt that archer would have risked shooting at us so openly if he didn't have more backup somewhere close by," said Laurent. "We follow him and there's a good chance we'll be running straight into a horde of enemies."

Elander furiously jerked free of his hold. But didn't take another step—he knew Laurent was right.

Zev joined them. The elf he'd been holding captive was at the lake's edge, crawling toward the relief of cool water. Still moving—though barely. They left him alone, and the three of them cautiously scanned the area for more enemies.

The burned elf soon went silent and still, sprawled out on the shore, water lapping gently over him. His companion didn't return for him, nor did anyone else. The night settled around them, still and heavy. Even the wind grew motionless, no longer swirling the powdery snow or rippling the frosty surface of the lake.

Elander cursed under his breath as he returned his sword to its sheath.

"We have this," Laurent reminded him, holding up the canteen. Now that it was quiet, they heard what sounded like a soft humming coming from its contents. "And I believe it was clear enough that our targets were hiding information about Sarith."

Elander attempted to roll some of the tension from his neck and shoulders. "So she's close by..."

"Or was," said Laurent, more calmly. "With her sights set on Mistwilde—if her interest in this lake is any indication—our paths will inevitably cross."

Elander slowly nodded, understanding even if he didn't want to. "We should go back and inform the others that we have one more thing to plan for."

He looked to the hill the elves had disappeared over, gathering up his anger like kindling, more fuel to feed the vengeful fire burning so violently in his chest.

Soon enough.

The day of reckoning was coming, and it could not come soon enough.

CHAPTER 12

Weary and frustrated, Elander made his way to the house where Casia slept.

After a brief discussion with her guards, he slipped inside and found her asleep on a bed in the back room, tangled up in a thin blanket, her limbs hanging halfway off the mattress.

Exhausted.

He had been able to tell this earlier, but he'd still expected her to be awake, anxiously going over every word she had left to say to Soryn, every path they might take from here... but even she occasionally reached limits, he supposed. The air had an unnatural warmth to it too, and he wondered if Nessa had been there recently, if her magic had helped lull Casia to sleep. He made a mental note to thank the Featherkind woman for that.

He carefully shifted Casia back toward the center of the mattress, untangling the blanket and tucking it more securely around her. She tossed and turned for a moment before going still again, her lips softly parting, one hand outstretched toward him as though she was waiting for him to reach back even as she slept.

He leaned away, but he couldn't keep his eyes from sliding over her face and then down along the curves and dips of her body that were clearly outlined beneath the threadbare blanket. He had to brace an arm against the bed for a moment to steady himself.

No matter how many times he looked at her, her beauty still threatened his balance.

He left her to sleep in peace and moved silently to the pile of his bags in the corner, pulling out clean—and dry—clothing. But his eyes kept drifting toward Casia as he changed. At her hair spilling across the white sheets, at her hand still reaching, at the moonlight painting her into a brighter, more ethereal version of herself.

At the scars on her skin.

He still had not forgiven himself for not being there to prevent them. For not protecting her. He *wouldn't* forgive himself until he settled things with the one responsible for the worst of those marks—and maybe not even then.

Her brow furrowed and she curled tighter under the blanket. Could she sense his stare? His frustrations? He averted his eyes. He didn't want to wake her.

He was staring out of the window, absently unbuttoning his snow-dampened shirt and watching more snow that had started to fall, when the first soft cry escaped Casia. He turned to see her tossing and turning, tangling the blankets around herself once more.

Another nightmare.

He hesitated, giving her a chance to escape it on her own; he still didn't want to wake her if he didn't have to.

But the nightmare persisted until he couldn't stand back

and watch it any longer. He walked over and gently pressed a hand to the side of her face. "Casia."

She shrunk away from her name as though it was a knife he'd lifted against her. Her hand struck toward him, fingers clawing the air, trying to protect her from whatever monstrous things were filling her head. He caught her arm and held it at her side, pinning down her attempts to fight until she finally woke.

She stared up at him through hooded eyes, chest heaving and fingers clutching the sheets beneath her as if they were her only tether to the world.

"It's me," he said softly.

"...You're back."

He nodded.

She released the sheets and cupped his face with her hands. Her breath came in little stops and starts as she drew his mouth down to meet her own, pulling him into a slow kiss.

She kept his face against hers even after the kiss ended, her hands sliding into his hair, holding him close and breathing him in. "I was worried."

"Nothing to worry about," he whispered against her lips, and she nodded, even though they both knew it was a lie.

She let him go. He leaned back but stayed at her side, his hand in hers, thumb tapping a steady rhythm against her palm. Her eyes closed, then blinked open again and studied him carefully, as though she still didn't quite believe he was real. "I thought I was only dreaming of you for a moment there."

He gave her a crooked grin. "Who says you aren't dreaming? I'm very dreamy looking, aren't I?"

She slowly smiled back, eyes lighting in that mischievous

way that was going to be the death of him someday, he was certain.

"This is far too tame for one of my dreams about you and me in bed together," she said.

He inhaled a little more sharply than he'd meant to as a curl of desire went through him, making the muscles in his stomach go taut. "Well, it's only just started," he informed her. "Give it time."

She reached for his other hand and pulled him toward her, pressing his body down against hers.

And he forgot about scars and queens and things lost in the snow. There was only her. Only her hands moving along his body, sliding across his stomach, his chest, finishing unbuttoning his shirt. Only her spice and flower scent. Only her breath warm against his cheek as their noses brushed, her lips falling open at the touch of his, her tongue as soft and certain as her wandering hands as they moved together, sighed together, closed the empty spaces together.

Together, together, together.

Gods, he had never wanted anything more than the two of them together—in this way and every other—for the rest of his existence.

He buried his face into the curve of her neck because he loved the way it made her shiver when he breathed against her skin, loved the way her hair surrounded and enveloped him in her intoxicating scent. Her hands continued to roam over his body, lazily tracing ridges of muscle, pausing on his chest and lightly tapping in time to his rapidly beating heart.

He kissed a trail from her throat up to her lips before slowly dragging himself away so he could see her face. "Are we dreaming now?"

"I'm still not sure." Another of those smiles—and this time, he returned it with a mischievous look of his own.

"You could try pinching yourself," he suggested. "I've heard that sometimes helps you wake up if you're dreaming."

She ran her tongue across her lips.

Gods.

"I could," she agreed.

He found the hem of her nightdress, pushed it toward her hips, pulled away the soft undergarment beneath it. Then he took her hand and smoothed it underneath the fabric and up across the planes of her stomach, guiding it toward the peak of one of her breasts. She followed his lead, fingertips circling the fullness of one breast, then the other, before skimming over their velvety tips.

He released her hand, drawing back again so he could admire her as she worked. "There's an image I wouldn't mind having in my own dreams every night."

A corner of her mouth lifted. Her eyes fluttered shut and stayed that way, half-listening, half-lost in the feel of her own fingertips. He still had his damp shirt on, unbuttoned and hanging open, but the chill of it was long forgotten as he watched her.

A wave of lightheadedness soon drew him back toward her body in search of balance. Admiring the view was not enough; he needed to touch her, needed to feel her moving against him, needed her taste on his tongue.

His hands slid along her inner thighs, urging them apart. He followed his hands with his lips, kissing trails along her soft skin up to her navel and back down between her legs, savoring the taste of heat and salt and *her*.

His tongue brushed over her center and she let out a sigh, hands falling to the bed and clenching the sheets beside her. He took hold of one of those hands and pushed it upwards again, silently commanding it back toward her breasts before burying his face against her warmth once more. He traced her with his tongue, losing himself in the feel of her thighs clenching around him and her body trembling beneath him, until her back arched and a particularly violent shudder went through her.

"What about now?" he inquired, lifting his head so he could meet her heavy gaze. "Still asleep?"

Her response was more soft moan than words, but it sounded like *yes*.

"We could try applying pressure elsewhere, since the pinching didn't work."

The moan became a gasp of breath as he dragged a hand along the length of her body, from the hollow of her throat down between the valley of her breasts, over her stomach, curved it between her thighs. He abandoned words as well, speaking instead with his touch, his fingers taking up the job his mouth had started. She rocked slowly against his palm until he slid two of those fingers inside of her, and then her movements became wilder, hungrier, more insistent.

He slipped his free hand around to her back and pulled her upright, yanking her closer and pressing his fingers deeper with the same motion. Another pleasurable shudder rocked through her and she collapsed forward, her arms draping around his neck and her hips thrusting toward him, trying to pull him even deeper. He curled one of the fingers inside her, pressing the heel of his hand more firmly against her, and the noise she made…

He nearly lost himself at the sound of it.

He wanted to make her do it again.

But he forced himself to withdraw instead, not ready to

bring her so close to climax so soon, and he simply held her for a moment.

She lifted her head and pressed her lips to his. "This feels more like a dream than ever," she breathed, in between kissing him.

"Waking is a lost cause, it seems." He kissed her back, taking her bottom lip between his teeth and parting it from the other, slipping his tongue into her mouth and letting it brush against hers. "So we might as well finish things now that we've started," he murmured, pulling away. "I'm curious, anyhow."

"Curious?"

"About just how *untamed* your dreams about us in bed together usually are."

Her eyes found his.

And if he had not already been fully at her mercy, the look she gave him in that moment would have done it—he suspected it would have brought any man or god or king to his knees before her.

Then she was moving, reaching for his belt, undoing it and freeing his hardened length. Drawing her nightgown up and over her head. Lifting her hips into a better position. Taking hold of him and stroking, her hands working until they were slick and she could guide him easily inside of her. Her knees came to rest on either side of his hips as she sank fully onto him, pushing his cock deeper while her eyes closed briefly, blissfully.

His lips had parted—he had started to say something, but he'd forgotten *what.* She had rendered him speechless, and she was swiftly stealing away all thought and reason as her arms reached around his neck once more, steadying herself so she could move her hips in a pounding rhythm against him.

He kept one hand braced against the bed. The other couldn't resist reaching for her; he circled an arm around her waist and brought it up to the small of her back. As she moved more furiously against him, he caressed lower, his fingers splaying out in a commanding grip and pulling her harder against him with every thrust.

He let her do most of the work at first, but it was impossible not to be coaxed into motion as he watched her. His hips soon lifted to meet hers, and as their connection deepened, she gave a soft cry of pleasure and her head dipped toward her chest.

He caught her chin and kept it lifted. "You should know by now that I want to see your face whenever I'm inside you like this."

Her eyes met his more fully, heavy with desire as they drank him in, inviting him deeper.

An invitation he would never decline.

He stood, lifting her easily along with him, moving away from the bed before guiding himself back inside her. Her legs wrapped around his waist. He pushed a hand through her hair, trailed it briefly around her throat, curled it over her shoulder and shoved her down, pushed them more completely together.

Her mouth fell open as their new position allowed the full size of him to fill her. He held her tightly against him, and when her head tilted back this time, the note that escaped it was a combination of pain and pleasure. He held her still more tightly, locking her in place so she would feel every throb of him.

"Arms around my neck again," he ordered.

She obeyed, balancing herself more completely. He gripped the backs of her thighs and lifted her up, only to pull her back. Lifted her, dropped her, up and down, over and over, finding a rhythm as she had done—but he was stronger, able to control her movements while rising to meet them with his own.

He moved slowly at first, not wanting to cause her more pain. But soon she was urging him faster, rolling her hips and testing his balance and control with each seductive movement.

He brought his mouth to her ear. "Dream Casia is very eager, isn't she?"

She tightened her legs around his waist, pulling herself more flush against his body, pressing him more deeply into her. He had to steady himself against the dizzying wave of heat that shot through him.

"I'll take that as a *yes.*" His fingers dug into her thighs, spreading her legs further apart before he drove harder into her, and it wasn't long after that he felt her control slipping, her body twisting wildly, back arching in anticipation.

He shoved her against the nearest wall, using it to help keep her steady while he brought her closer to release.

Her chin started to dip again, but he caught it tightly between his fingers. "Your face," he reminded her. "I want to see it while you come for me."

The rough command—and the powerful thrust he accented it with—caused a trembling that soon overtook her completely. One of her hands braced against the wall behind her and her head tipped back. A sweet cry of surrender rose in her throat, and the sound of it vibrated through Elander's body, rousing every part of him to life, drawing him deeper, closer—he felt like he could never get close enough to her, but it didn't stop him from trying, from burying his face against her and losing himself in the waves of her sound and scent and warmth until they had both surrendered completely.

He kept her pressed to the wall until the last drop of him was spent, then held her legs around his waist as he carried her to the bed, laying her on her back before easing out of her and stretching out beside her. They faced one another without speaking for several moments while he traced patterns on her skin, smiling at the way his touch made her body shiver with little aftershocks of pleasure.

She closed her eyes and breathed a soft sigh. Her voice was a whisper, a confession meant for no one other than him, as she said, "I just want to keep dreaming."

You can. For as long as you want.

He wished he could say this; that it was a promise he could have kept. But his thoughts had already drifted back to broken kingdoms and blood-stained snow. So he only pulled her close and kissed her forehead, silently cursing the rapidly-approaching morning and the wars it would bring.

ELANDER WOKE as the first rays of dawn stretched through the house. He rolled over, searching for Casia—but she was on the other side of the room, standing by the window, watching the snow that had started to fall once more. It had fallen for the better part of the night, judging by the pile gathered along the window ledge.

He noticed Casia shivering, and he pulled on his pants and crossed the room, wrapping his arms around her from behind and holding her against his bare chest.

"Good morning."

"Good morning," she replied absently, still shivering. She could have moved away from the drafty window and been warmer, but she seemed too mesmerized by the drifting snow, which didn't surprise him—she hated the cold, but she loved snow.

Why can't we have snow when it's warm? she'd once lamented to him. *You know the Goddess of Winter, don't you? Surely she can work some sort of magic and make that possible.*

He smiled at the memory, though it was soured by thoughts of that goddess who had once been his friend. He shook the Ice Goddess's face from his mind, and he rested his chin on Casia's shoulder, gathering her closer, losing himself—as he had last night—in thoughts of the things he *had* and not the things he'd lost.

She relaxed against him. The heat of their intertwined bodies—fanned hotter by the occasional kiss he pressed to her hair and skin—soon stopped her shivering.

Her body sank even more fully against him, tempting him toward an encore performance of last night's dream. His hands moved of their own accord, smoothing their way down her body, edging toward the hem of her nightshirt, nearly finding their way to skin—

Something moved along the edge of the yard.

He tightened his arms around her, gaze narrowing. He wanted to think he'd imagined it.

But then Casia leaned away from him, pressing against the window for a closer look, and whispered, "There's something out there."

CHAPTER 13

Cas was dressed and outside moments later, Shadowslayer in her hand, Elander following closely behind her.

There was a strange scent in the air—not the usual crispness of fresh snow but of damp earth tinged with something metallic, and a taste of salt even though they were hundreds of miles from the sea. That air seemed to creep over her skin, making it itch as she stole her way toward the spot where she'd seen shadows moving. The itch grew worse the deeper she moved into the trees.

Magic.

She had thought she felt it inside, and now it was undeniable. An exceptionally powerful magic user had recently woven their way through the trees around the village. So very powerful…

A god?

She found no source of the power, and it seemed to be fading—or maybe moving away from her—as the seconds passed.

Elander called out her name. She spun back toward him, and only then did she realize how far apart they had somehow drifted—she could barely see him for the trees and piles of snow that separated them.

He had gotten distracted.

Distracted by a crowd of people that were coming closer, emerging from the fog and falling snow and materializing into a full army before them.

Cas raced toward Elander as quickly as she could—retracing her tracks but still unsteady in the deeper snow drifts—while she scanned the approaching brigade.

They looked less like an army than she'd thought from a distance. They were poorly dressed, many without armor, and most carried nothing. Where were their weapons? No less than three dozen formed messy ranks that marched toward them…but no, *marching* wasn't the right word, either.

They were *floating,* their steps unhindered by the ever-deepening snow.

Magic at work?

An uneasy tingle crept over her skull and down her back. "This is…are these more Morethian soldiers? Or from Ethswen? Or…"

"Look closer." Elander sounded confused, uncertain—a rarity for him, and that unsettled Cas even more.

She took a few steps in the direction he pointed, narrowing her gaze on the man who appeared to be leading the charge. Her breath caught.

This can't be.

Her eyes darted to the men on either side of the leader.

Those faces...

She recognized some of those faces.

"Those are some of the soldiers we lost yesterday." She

staggered backward to Elander's side, her gaze drawn once more to the man leading them. His face was divided by two gruesome slashes. A Morethian elf had caused those wounds, had slit his face open with a black and gleaming blade—Cas had watched it *happen*.

And she had watched this man die while Nessa tried desperately to calm him down with her magic.

Elander hesitated. "In a way…yes."

She looked closer at the soldier. His feet weren't touching the ground.

None of their feet were quite touching it, and their movements were more strange the longer she looked—too smooth. Like ghosts but more solid, skating along as though upon ice rather than snow.

"What are they?"

Elander answered quietly, almost as though he didn't want to say it out loud. "*Revenants*."

The first line of these revenants were upon them a moment later, pushed by a sudden howl of wind.

Cas moved even closer to Elander, ducking to avoid one of the ghostly creatures as it drifted wildly toward them, body twisting and spinning as though it had little control over its movements—which was somehow more unsettling than facing a monster who had *complete* control.

"They're harmless when they're just floating around like this," Elander said, "and they don't last long unless they find a host."

"A host?"

"They can overtake living bodies and, well…"

Her stomach clenched. "You don't need to elaborate."

"They need an opening to get in, however—a fresh wound, usually."

She placed a hand on Shadowslayer's pommel just so she could feel the comforting hum of warm power it gave off whenever she squeezed it. "This is Death magic?"

He nodded.

Cas couldn't help turning once more toward the forest behind them, her eyes automatically searching the dark places for signs of whoever was controlling this horde of creatures.

Was Varen nearby?

She shook the complicated thoughts of her brother from her mind. "We should warn Soryn and the others, and then make our way toward the places where the wounded are being tended to. They'll need to be protected, somehow."

He agreed, and they hurried to rouse the rest of their companions before racing to find the Sadiran Queen.

As they neared the center of the city, they had no trouble discerning which houses the wounded were being kept within—more revenants had gathered around them, drawn like wolves to the scent of blood.

Soryn was stomping her way in between the three houses, yelling orders and directing soldiers. She looked less composed than Cas had ever seen her. Fury and fear twisted her normally stoic features into something wild and unsettling; her skin was painted a bright shade of red from a combination of her shouting and the blisteringly cold air.

The Sundolian Queen was here as well. Her powerful magic didn't seem nearly as effective on the revenants as it did against living things, but she was still able to give orders, as was Sade, and between the three of them they had managed to direct the Sky magic wielders well enough to surround the houses in shields. The windows were reinforced, as were the doors, the chimneys—any possible opening.

But like the ones from their earlier battlefield, these shields were more thin than they had been in the past. And the revenants cared little for the natural laws that governed bodies; their shapes twisted and collapsed in impossible ways, allowing them to shrink and seep into places no human could have.

Cas had little hope of Soryn listening to her. She ran after the queen anyway, breaking into her path and forcing her to stop.

Soryn started to roar another order, but Cas cut her off. "There are more of these revenants on the outskirts of the city. If they converge toward your wounded, you won't have enough magic-users to protect everyone. These ghostly creatures will overtake the wounded, and then you'll have to fight your *own* army."

Soryn didn't reply, though she had gone very still by the end of Cas's warning.

At least she isn't ignoring me.

A gust of wind sent a revenant careening toward them. Soryn ducked to avoid the creature, bright eyes following it as it drifted onward and crashed into one of the shields. Her eyes widened slightly as she watched the revenant slide down along the shield, its pale fingers clawing and causing narrow tears that might have given it a way in, had its assault not been interrupted by a burst of Sky magic.

Soryn watched the soldier responsible for that magic for a moment before silently stepping around Cas and making her way toward another group of her magic users.

Cas grabbed her arm and held her back. "We're spread too thin," she pressed. "We need to concentrate the wounded into one place and put all our resources into protecting *that* place until we can get rid of the threat."

Soryn glanced from the grip Cas had on her sleeve to another revenant who had started clawing at the shield. She seemed to be calculating. Then she shrugged free of Cas's hold without a word.

Cas fought the urge to chase after her. Her friends converged toward her before she could move, followed swiftly by some of her own soldiers, offering thoughts and ideas about how to win Soryn over. But Cas had no patience for such things—they didn't have time to fall back and make detailed plans to win over the stubborn queen.

So she started to move on her own, shouting warnings and orders as she saw fit.

Soryn watched her doing this, a combination of gall and fury blazing in her eyes, and Cas felt a prickle of fear as she recalled their earlier conversation.

My soldiers will not answer to you again.

But despite her threat, Soryn did not interfere. She might have, if not for the sudden influx of revenants—they seemed to be pouring in from every direction now, swirling among the falling snow, creeping through the waning shields like cold breezes slipping through cracks in old houses.

Cas ignored Soryn's gaze and continued to work. She decided to gather the wounded into the center house, and she drew enough Sky-kind to her side that they were able to create two shields running parallel to each other between the left house and that center one—a protective tunnel of sorts. Once it was established, she directed every able body to help her carry the wounded ones toward the middle.

Soon the same operation was started on the house to the right.

Cas was scanning her surroundings, trying to determine what she should do next, when a group of struggling soldiers caught her eye.

They had slipped outside of the protective barriers somehow; three men, trying to keep a fourth under control. The fourth was wrapped in bandages, panicking at the chaos around him—delirious, perhaps because of the extent of his injuries and blood loss—and he managed to swing a punch that freed him from his keepers. He sprinted an impressive distance away from them before falling face-first into a snow bank.

Even from a distance, Cas could see the stark contrast of his bloody bandages against the icy white.

A group of revenants descended, and the three men who had been trying to help all stumbled back, clambering for the safety of the shields and leaving their wounded companion to his fate.

Cas ran to help the fallen man, making it to within mere feet of him before a revenant overtook her and dove for the man's back.

The ghastly creature buried its face into a bloody swath of the man's torn coat, and then it was gone in a puff of shadows, disappearing so quickly that Cas would have missed it if she'd blinked.

The wounded man twitched once.

He rose to his feet and turned to face her, his movements no longer frantic and jerky. His eyes flashed briefly to the color of moonlit snow before turning to a dark shade of blue —black, almost.

He let out a yowl like a wounded animal before lunging toward her.

His abilities seemed almost inhuman, as if the revenant

had gifted him with a small dose of divine power. He moved quickly enough to catch Cas in the shoulder as she attempted to twist out of his path. She was sent spinning toward the ground and barely caught herself, landing in an awkward crouch with one hand pressed into the bitingly cold snow. Her hand jerked away from the cold and reached instead for the warm power of her sword.

But she didn't draw it out.

She couldn't kill this man—he wasn't truly an enemy.

He let out a deep, rumbling noise that sounded almost like dark laughter, as if he was listening in on the moral dilemma raging in her mind.

She leapt to her feet.

He flung himself at her once more. Cas twisted away and hit the ground again—more gracefully this time—before immediately bouncing upright and darting around behind the possessed man.

She briefly had a clear shot at his back. She still didn't swing her sword—even though she could see no other ending to this scuffle.

If I don't kill him, then his possessed body might end up killing me.

She hesitated too long. Long enough that the possessed soldier was suddenly facing her again, diving at her in the next beat and taking her arm in a punishing grip.

He squeezed with nearly-divine strength, crushing her arm so tightly in his fist that Cas braced for the sound of her bones cracking and popping. She maneuvered as best she could in his hold, squirming and trying to stop him from grabbing her other arm. He started to reach for it as well—

Soryn seemed to materialize from the air, her sword

falling toward the revenant's shoulder and forcing him to jump back and release Cas as he did.

Soryn stepped between Cas and the stolen soldier while lifting her sword, its blade gleaming with turquoise light. *Indre's Grace*—otherwise known as Shieldmaker. The sword lived up to the moniker now, its light pulsing brighter than ever, wrapping the queen and Cas in a barrier that rippled like a sky reflected upon a stormy sea.

But the monster quickly proved too strong for the queen and her fading magic.

A deafening roar rattled the night as a white glow overtook the shield and started to leach away its color, its strength.

Death magic at work, Cas realized, *draining the Sky magic even further.*

The shield shattered and the man on the other side broke through in a flurry of sound and dead, aimless rage. He got his hands wrapped securely around Soryn's neck. She stumbled beneath the violent motion, sword flopping uselessly out beside her, unable to keep her balance as he threw his full weight against her.

She dropped to her knees, choking, hand grappling to keep a grip on Shieldmaker.

Before the man could squeeze the life from her, Cas swept around and plunged Shadowslayer into his back, directly between his shoulders. The skin around the puncture wound hissed and bubbled as the sword glowed brighter, like a healing elixir disinfecting a wound. The man staggered back, the revenant fleeing from his body with a blood-chilling scream.

The demon did not return, but the damage was done; the bleeding was too great, too rapid to stop. The man collapsed once more to the snow as it turned red and steamed all around him, and this time he didn't get up.

Soryn shook free of the dead body and got to her feet. Her face lifted to the sky. She didn't look at her dead soldier —or at Cas—as she asked, "How do we get rid of these damn ghosts?"

Cas's heart leapt at the change in her tone—from cold and furious to a kind of steeled resolve—until she realized she didn't know the answer to Soryn's question.

"We'll figure that out once we get things more secure and we can concentrate," she hedged. "Were all of the wounded here in these houses?"

"Most. But some of the less-severely wounded were gathered with the rest of our army along the edges of the city, prepared to help defend us if the need arose."

Cas's gaze shot toward Elander, who had just returned to her side after helping to direct the injured toward their designated safe house. "They don't need deep wounds to take over a host, do they?" she asked.

He shook his head. "A shallow cut is sufficient."

"And the more able-bodied wounded will be a greater threat to us," Cas thought aloud, chest squeezing with dread at the thought.

Soryn nodded in grim agreement. "We need to get this under control somehow."

Cas didn't hesitate, eager for the chance to continue regaining the queen's trust. "Stay here and help keep the shields in order. I'll focus on warning the rest of your soldiers and directing them to you."

They finished securing the center house, and then Cas and Elander each led a team through the city—toward opposite edges—seeking out the other wounded Soryn had mentioned.

Cas found groups in scattered pockets and directed them toward the center of the city as promised. She raced tirelessly up and down every street until she'd rallied more soldiers than she could count, all despite her lungs aching for want of breath and her hands and feet going numb from the cold.

The sun was rising, but it hardly mattered; fog still lingered and the wind whipped the snow about, casting the world in a grey haze that made it difficult to see beyond their immediate surroundings.

Laurent had gone with Elander while Rhea and Nessa stayed behind to help the wounded. But Zev remained at Cas's side, and his fire was useful—it cut through some of the grey murkiness, and it seemed to frighten the spirit-like revenants, allowing them to push their way through the hordes they encountered and reach the living soldiers before they could be made into hosts.

They arrived at the last street before the city gave way to the rolling hills and the forest beyond. The fog was thinner here, so they paused and regrouped while cautiously surveying their surroundings.

Despite the quiet emptiness, Cas was immediately struck with a foreboding feeling—one that proved accurate a moment later as a person emerged from the direction of the forest.

It wasn't floating, but crunching loudly through the snow. Its movements seemed unnervingly smooth, and its eyes were a gleaming shade of obsidian.

Another soldier lost to possession?

The soldier jumped toward Cas, reaching for her throat.

Zev reacted automatically—by drawing his sword, surrounding it with flames, and cutting her attacker down, protecting her as he had so many times in the past.

He only seemed to realize what he'd done after the body hit the ground, splashing into the melted snow and mud with a sickening thud.

Another soldier they couldn't bring back.

Cas's gaze whipped toward his, her words catching painfully in her throat.

Two more possessed soldiers emerged before they could exchange a word. Cas danced away from the first, leading it in circles and trying to disorient it, while Zev sheathed his sword and used his hands to meet the attack of the second.

They scuffled briefly before both Cas and Zev managed to break away into space. Zev summoned a line of fire to push the monsters back and create more of this space. The solid version of the revenants didn't seem as bothered by it as the floating versions were, but it still slowed them down enough to allow a quick escape.

Cas ran back into the city, darting into a yard fenced in by tall trees that provided some concealment. Zev caught up to her moments later.

"If we could find the source of them," said Cas, in between heaving attempts at breath, "we might be able to put a stop to all of these horrible things all at once."

"We might," Zev replied. He sounded distracted. His gaze was locked on something in the distance, and soon he was moving toward it, heading for the same battlefield they'd only just escaped.

Was he upset about that soldier he'd killed?

It wasn't like him to let this kind of emotion show. But it

had been a long few days, and perhaps the overwhelming amount of loss and blood was getting to him.

"Come on," Cas encouraged, hooking her arm through his and pulling him back toward the city. "We've sent as many soldiers back as we can; we should go check in with the others."

He said nothing to this, but he allowed himself to be pulled along.

His continued silence started to unnerve her after a few moments.

"Zev?"

A single twitch was her only response.

She drew to a stop, looking him over, and realized then that her coat sleeve was covered in blood—his.

"When did you get that cut on your arm?" She gingerly patted the drenched cloth, and her hand came away covered in more blood.

Her skin prickled with warning.

A fresh wound.

CHAPTER 14

Zev's eyes flashed white, then to that incredibly dark shade of blue, and Cas realized what had happened—

An instant too late.

Before she could let go of his arm, he had slashed upward with a knife drawn from near his hip. It caught her thigh—cutting more clothing than flesh, thankfully. As she stumbled away from him, he was already following up that first stab with a second one, this time aiming for her chest.

She fell onto her back to avoid it, letting the snow break her fall. The cold—and the sight of Zev looming over her, knife outstretched—briefly shocked her into stillness before she managed to roll out of his reach and stumble her way back to her feet.

She scrambled and slipped, leaving a slushy, muddy trail in her wake. She ran until she felt her legs starting to give out on her, her head whipping frantically back and forth, searching for someone who could help. But there was no one, the streets were jarringly empty, and soon she couldn't help chancing a look over her shoulder—

Zev was right *there.*

She ducked, narrowly avoiding his swinging fist.

"Stop!"

Could he hear her?

Was the real Zev still conscious underneath the revenant's control? She should have asked Elander more about how these creatures worked when she'd had the chance.

Zev summoned fire, guiding it to the knife still clutched in his other hand. His too-dark eyes flashed as brightly as the heated blade—with glee, as if the revenant inside of him had just realized that he had Fire magic to wield in addition to Death magic.

"*Please stop*!" Panic made her voice hoarse.

How could she reach him?

How could she stop him without hurting him?

She knew the answer almost as soon as she asked herself the question, but she wanted to find another, safer solution.

Zev swung the heated knife, and the air turned sweltering, making Cas's already labored breathing even more difficult. She winced as her eyes watered, and she fought to keep those eyes open, to stay focused on Zev without letting her rising panic overwhelm her.

She could feel them as plainly as she had before she brought Nessa back: the tendrils of Death weaving their way around Zev's body. The revenant's magic felt like it was trying to choke out Zev's life-force, same as the Dark God's power had nearly claimed Nessa's.

Cas's own power stirred at the memory of that terrifying moment. Of the horror she had only just managed to reverse.

She had the power to do it again.

She had *the answer.*

She was already overwhelmed, thinking of what came next—*there were so many of these ghosts to drive away*—but she could come up with no other solution.

Her hand lifted toward Zev's wounded arm. She closed her eyes and thought of the sun she couldn't see through the greyness, of a dawn boldly breaking and scattering the last shadows of night.

Light eclipsed them both for several blinding seconds.

Cas felt as if she was floating, and she sank to her knees to avoid losing her balance. She steadied herself among the brightness and kept summoning until finally she heard it—the telltale scream that meant the revenant had been ousted from its host.

She floated for a few more moments, lost in the bright waves of her power. When her balance settled and clear vision returned, she and Zev were curled up side-by-side on the icy ground. She didn't move. She held her breath as she waited for him to take one of his own, and she didn't move until he blinked his eyes open.

His normal, dazzlingly hazel eyes.

"You owe me a drink after that," she mumbled, pushing back to her feet.

"I'll buy you several," he replied, cringing as he sat up, rubbing his bleeding arm. "But it looks like that'll have to wait for a bit."

Cas followed his gaze and saw a row of dark-eyed soldiers moving toward them.

Zev leapt to his feet and summoned a ring of fire to protect them.

It didn't work this time.

The overtaken soldiers walked *straight through* the flames, indifferent even though it was clearly burning them, catching on their hair and clothing and filling the air with a terrible smell. Any pain it caused didn't register, didn't slow or even interrupt their smooth gaits.

"Put out the fires," Cas said frantically. "We can't let them hurt the bodies they've overtaken!"

Zev was too stunned to comprehend until she took hold of his arm and shook him from his stupor—but then he swiftly followed her orders, dousing the fires in a flash and leaving them surrounded by nothing more than rising smoke and seeping snow melt.

The line of soldiers stalked closer.

Cas clenched her hands to keep them still, to prevent them from anxiously tapping against herself. Her entire body was tingling. Her sword, still sheathed at her side, hummed, reminding her of her power…

It had worked on Zev, hadn't it?

The soldiers were nearly upon them. Her gaze froze on the one in the center of the line. Dead, lifeless eyes and an expressionless face—yet something about the tilt of his head and the slump of his shoulders suggested agony, and the sight wrenched her heart.

She had a cure, and she could not bring herself to let these people suffer any more than she could have allowed Zev to suffer.

She lifted both her hands toward the approaching line, and she repeated the same magic she'd used against Zev. She found the threads of Death, loosened them, unraveled them completely, and then surrounded the soldiers with light instead of darkness, holding her power as steady as she could while it drew the poison from her targets.

She was unable to keep her balance this time.

When the job was finished, she was kneeling in slushy snow. The feeling in her hands and feet was gone. It was several moments before she found the energy to lift her head and make certain she'd accomplished what she'd been trying to do.

Through vision still tunneled and blurred from her dizziness, she saw the revenant spirits twisting from their hosts like chimney smoke, swirling up until they were lost against the grey sky.

She exhaled slowly. As the last of the spirits slipped out and floated upward, she brought a hand to her temple, squeezing and trying to stop the pounding in it.

"You can't do that kind of magic indefinitely," Zev said as he helped her stand. "We need another solution."

Cas agreed, but she still shook her head. "I don't think there *is* any other way to end this, aside from ending the one pulling the strings. Malaphar is trying to force me to use my Sun magic as much as possible. He wants to make sure that life-giving magic is weakened before he faces us again."

"Fucking coward," Zev muttered.

Her gaze swept over the groaning soldiers as they came back to their senses and struggled to their feet. Five in total, and three of them had what looked like still-bleeding wounds—much more gruesome-looking than the ones she and Zev had sustained. She worried they would attract more trouble in no time at all.

"Help lead these wounded back to the shelter before they attract more revenants," she told Zev. "I'll be right behind you."

Zev started to question her, but a cry of pain from one of the soldiers distracted him.

While he moved to help, Cas cautiously moved away from them, her gaze narrowed on the alleyway across the street. She had sensed more revenant magic—but subdued, as if it were deeply buried in a human host. She wanted to make sure she hadn't missed one of the possessed, so she crept carefully toward the alley, summoning lightning to her palm as she went. It didn't cut through the dreariness as well as Zev's fire, but it still allowed her to see…

Nothing there.

She studied things for a few moments longer, but nothing appeared. Her curiosity sated for the moment, she turned to follow quickly after Zev.

But something else caught her eye before she could take a step—a woman stumbling her way up a distant hill. A bloody trail dotted the snow behind her.

Cas held her breath, expecting…

A revenant was following the trail, swooping and diving along behind the bleeding woman like a hawk playing with its prey.

Of course.

Cas sprinted after them, Shadowslayer withdrawn and leading the way with electricity wrapped around its blade. The heat from the sword melted a clear path through the snow, making it easier for her to catch up to the struggling woman.

The spirit was still faster. Cas lost her race against it, just as she'd lost the race against the one back in the city's center. It reached the woman and shot toward her freely-bleeding leg, its ghost-like body collapsing and disappearing, leaving behind a plume of smokey residue as it wormed its way into its new host.

Cas slid to a stop and prepared to summon her negating magic.

But before she could call forth a single spark of light, *other* magic struck the revenant's new host. That revenant was ruthlessly ejected with the strike—not coaxed out by her light, but *yanked* out as if some invisible power had lassoed it and pulled. It writhed within this new power, twisting like a violent but small, contained storm.

And then it simply…*stopped.*

It hovered above the ground for a moment, suspended. Its color began to fade, bleeding out until its ghostly body was nearly the same shade as the snow beneath it, and then drifted down, sank into that snow and remained still.

Drained by magic.

Cas spun toward a thick row of trees in the distance. She was not surprised to see a blond-haired figure emerging from between the trunks, surrounded by living shadows that made his eyes seem brighter, almost glowing with their unsettling, reddish-golden gleam.

Varen.

She started toward her brother—until the woman that had nearly lost her body to the revenant moaned softly. Cas moved swiftly to her side to look her over instead. Her gaze was glassy, her skin pale from shock. Cas took off her own coat and wrapped it around the woman, pulling her out of the deeper snow drifts and into a patch that was mostly melted. Then she tried something with her magic—a version of the same negating power that drove out the revenants, but much more subtle. Just enough to put more life back into the woman's dead eyes.

It seemed to work, at least well enough to give her a fighting chance. Her skin flushed with color and her breathing grew less labored. Cas helped steady her balance before pointing her in the direction of Zev and the others.

As the woman hurried away in search of refuge, Cas turned to face her brother.

Varen didn't speak as he drew near, eyes appraising her as he came. She had left her coat wrapped around the wounded woman, and now she fought to keep herself from shivering.

"I had a feeling you were close by." She threw a glance over her shoulder. "You summoned those revenant creatures into this realm?"

"Not because I wanted to."

A hint of regret clung to the words. It could have been an act. She no longer knew what was real and what was fake with Varen, and she didn't have the energy left to guess at it this morning.

"But you managed to deal with their little possession tricks well enough, didn't you?" he asked.

She fought off another shiver, wondering how much he'd seen—how closely he'd been watching her—without her knowing.

"Though it seems it's drained you."

She wished he was wrong. But she felt it in a way she hadn't in weeks…as if she had gotten close to the edges of her power and very nearly toppled over. And unlike nearly every time before, she didn't feel herself recovering as the minutes passed—not even after she had a chance to catch her breath.

"Yes," she snapped. "Which was what *he* hoped for, I'm certain. He thinks he can bleed us out, that he can even the odds so that he actually stands a chance against me."

Varen simply nodded. "You need to hurry and get to Mistwilde—and focus on evening out the odds yourself."

The Antaeum Point.

Frustration made her voice clipped. "Then why are you here, distracting me?"

"Patience, sister. One day you'll learn it, I hope." He smiled in that clever way of his—the way he always did when he knew something she didn't—and then he took a small bag from his pocket and tossed it to her.

Inside was a familiar sight—a smooth, carefully forged Blood crystal.

"A final gift from Caden, which he regrettably wasn't able to bring himself. For obvious reasons."

She guarded herself against the gruesome images of Caden's death, focusing instead on tracing the edges of the crystal.

"You'll need the information contained in that crystal to help you seal off the point in Mistwilde," said Varen. "It isn't a complete guide, but it should help."

She clenched her fingers around it. "You're helping, and yet you're responsible for at least several deaths in this city this morning." She breathed in a deep, steadying breath.

Not because I wanted to.

The longer she stood with him, the more she wanted to believe what he said. And she knew how the magic of the Moraki and their chosen servants worked, knew that the freedom of those servants only extended so far...so it likely *was* the truth.

It didn't make it easier to accept. She was supposed to be protecting this world, a chosen vessel of the Goddess of *Life*. But Death seemed to follow her wherever she went, clawing its way into the light she was so desperately clinging to, dimming it and making all her battles less clear.

"I don't know what I'm supposed to say to you," she

admitted. "Or how I can accept your help, or trust you, knowing the god that looms over you."

He didn't reply. He *couldn't* reply, it seemed; his body had suddenly gone rigid, his face frozen in a stoic expression. He swayed uncertainly on his feet, and Cas moved toward him without really meaning to, hand outstretched and intending to catch him should he lose his balance, her instinct the same now as it had been when they were children.

She slammed to a stop just out of reach.

What was she doing?

Varen caught himself on his own, shaking off the power that had gripped him as quickly as it had come, and he stared at her outstretched hand.

She composed herself and backed away. Averted her eyes, and tried to make her voice calm and detached as she said, "You are ultimately in the Dark God's control. I suppose that's all I really need to understand."

He didn't deny this. "I was able to come to you only *because* I agreed to summon those revenants. Not my ideal choice, as I said. But the chaos and destruction they created should abate him and hide my true purpose this morning—I hope. I also thought this might give you an opportunity to win over the Sadiran Queen. She's being difficult, isn't she?"

Cas kept her eyes on the nearby patch of blood-soaked snow and didn't reply.

"But now she's had another chance to see how helpful you can be."

Another chill crept up Cas's spine as she again wondered, *How closely has he been watching?*

The gods of the Dark Court could still come and go as they pleased, and they had no shortage of minions who could do the same. There was no limit to what he might know or what strings he could pull, for better or worse.

And yet...

She was grateful for the crystal in her hand, even if she couldn't fully trust the one who had given it to her. She cleared her throat. "Well. Thank you, I suppose," she said. "Hopefully this helps."

Varen acknowledged her words with a stiff nod. "And I should give you a warning, too... he'll keep using me. The Death magic has a counter in yours, and you're right—he wants to force you to use more and more of that magic. It's..." Another abrupt silence as something powerful but unseeable overcame him. Varen repeatedly tried and failed to roll the tension from his neck and shoulders and keep his head lifted. He eventually gave up and tucked his chin to his chest, his eyes closed and his breathing shallow.

Against her better judgment, Cas again reached out a hand to steady him. "Maybe I could slow your ascension down, somehow," she said quietly. "If my magic can—"

He cut her off with a bitter laugh, eyes flashing open and narrowing on her. "Don't be a fool."

She stubbornly kept her hand outstretched.

He only swiped it away and moved to brace himself against the nearest tree.

She followed, fists clenching from a combination of anger and stubbornness. "I could *help,* you idiot."

"You shouldn't be worried about saving me."

"I'm not." She *was,* but instead of telling him this, she matched his bitter tone and said, "I was merely being strategic. If you fall fully into his clutches, then it will compromise me and my plans. You know too much."

He tilted his head toward her, smiling as though he was

proud of her for finally finding the ruthless words he'd been hoping she'd say. "I will find a way to end things before that compromise comes. Don't you worry about that."

Cas's mouth ran dry as the images of Caden's death threatened again. She focused on the tree Varen leaned against instead of her brother's strange eyes, noting the broken and peeled places among the bark, counting the severed branches scattering the ground.

Her attention was soon drawn toward the city, pulled by a sudden breeze—and a howl that she was not convinced was entirely caused by that breeze.

"How many of those revenants are haunting this city?" she demanded.

"As many as the dead you left at the river. The spell to create them is not a selective one. They all rose."

Too many to count, in other words.

"I can't leave Ironedge to deal with these monsters."

Varen's expression turned almost regretful again, and she was struck once more by the thought that he was impossible. *They* were impossible. Why did she still want to try and make sense of him?

Stupid, stupid, stupid.

"I can draw them toward us," said Varen. "And I will drain the spell around some and send them back to the grave—but you will finish the rest."

Not a question, but a command, and Cas inwardly scoffed at the thought of obeying it. Of obeying *anything* he told her to do. But she again could not deny that she needed help, so she didn't argue with him.

"It will need to look like we were truly battling it out," said Varen. "A battle that I will ultimately lose."

Cas shifted her weight from one foot to the other. "If he finds out you helped me..."

"Then I will deal with the consequences."

"He'll be angry if you lose, too."

Varen's tone crept toward exasperation. "Can you do this or not?"

"I..." She forced herself to be still. "Yes. Of course I can."

"Good." He gave his hands a shake, causing little flourishes of shadow to appear and snake up his arms. His eyes glowed to an unsettling shade of red as he looked to the city. "Now try to keep up, sister."

He gave no more instruction than this before he was moving, sweeping into the streets with his shadows following like obedient dogs at his heels.

They moved together through the city. He paused every so often and did as he'd said he would—summoning bands of dark magic that drew hordes of the revenants toward them. Once the spirits had swallowed the two of them up, gathering like bees swarming a hive, his magic would change from dark shadows to pale threads of white that would violently choke the energy from the creatures.

Cas stayed close, using her own magic to clean up whatever lingering spirits remained after this initial choking.

They soon fell into a rhythm, repeating this same pattern over and over. Cas followed closely in her brother's steps, but she couldn't let her gaze linger on Varen—it threw off her concentration too much, seeing him so close and working in tandem with her.

What a strange morning this is turning out to be.

The city bristled with their combined powers, the air thick and rumbling with it. They were working together, but the energies still resisted the idea of this, adamantly sparking and pushing apart every time they touched. From afar, it *would* have seemed like the two of them were battling.

She lost count of how many revenants they put to rest. She could feel the weight of them all, each holding on, dragging her down, exhausting her powers a little more.

She pushed on, refusing to not keep up with her brother.

The largest group of revenants yet descended, and Varen made quick work of them. They fell like flowers shaken loose from a tree, floating down, curling and dying as they hit the ground, burying Cas in a sea of unsettling energy that made her cold down to the very depths of her soul.

So much energy, so many released ghosts, and yet more continued to swarm around them.

She could feel Varen watching her expectantly, waiting for her magic to finish off the rest of the horde. She tried. But the draining cold of his magic and the limits of her own were pressing in. Frustration made it increasingly difficult to concentrate. Over and over she tried, only to hit a wall, only to turn her irritated gaze toward her brother to find him still watching her.

Still waiting.

He cleared his throat. And she expected more exasperation in his tone, for him to taunt her, mock her, lash out at her with so many biting words as he'd done in the past.

But all he said, very quietly, was, "One more time. This is the last of them coming toward us, I think. One more time now, and finish them off."

She let her gaze linger for too long on his expectant face, and she was reminded of one of his memories—a vision she'd seen in one of the many crystals he'd given her—of him standing in a tower, eyes watching the palace gates as he thought the same two words, muttering them over and over to himself.

Come back.

She hadn't come back to him then, but she did now, somehow finding the strength to emerge from the cold and draw her magic along with her.

Light enveloped them and roared outward, overtaking the city as far as she could see. And then she *couldn't* see—not her brother, nor the things that haunted them, not even her own hands. The screech of revenants being ousted rang painfully in her ears, but they were eventually overcome by the hum of her power rising.

Then came silence.

She floated briefly in that silence, and she still felt unusually light even after she dropped back to the mortal plane, opened her eyes, and found herself kneeling on the cold ground.

Nothing moved, ghostly or otherwise. Time itself seemed to have stopped. She and her brother stood alone, apart from one another, neither daring to move toward the other, as if separated by a chasm that had suddenly split along the road.

She swallowed hard and started to speak, though she wasn't sure what to say. It didn't matter; they were interrupted by the sound of several people running toward them —Elander, followed quickly by Nessa and Laurent. Silverfoot bounded ahead of all three of them and leapt for Cas, a silver arrow shooting through the air into her arms. She held him tightly to her chest as she watched her brother take a step away from them all.

"Hurry up," said Varen, quietly, his eyes fixed on no one and nothing aside from her, "and save the ones you can."

He was gone an instant later.

Cas didn't move. Any sense of light was gone, leaving her so heavy that she *couldn't* move for a long moment.

Elander looked her over as he reached her side, gaze lingering on her leg—which was stained with blood from Zev's attack—and then on her thin shirt that was doing little to block the cold. He shrugged out of his coat and draped it over her shoulders before glancing toward the spot where Varen had disappeared. "Are you all right?"

She showed him the crystal Varen had given her, briefly recounting the things that had happened since they'd separated.

"He helped you?" Despite the evidence of it all around them, Elander's tone was still filled with doubt. The same skepticism clouded Cas's thoughts, and Varen's last words echoed through her mind, causing one question to rise above the rest, chilling her even more than the wind whipping the snow around them.

How many would she truly be able to save in the end?

CHAPTER 15

Cas clenched and unclenched her hands, over and over. It had started as an attempt to work the cold numbness from them. But now it had turned into a compulsion—the only thing that could keep her safe according to her anxious mind.

She couldn't stop. It was too dangerous to stop. Too risky to—

Her horse snorted and stomped impatiently beside her, waiting for her to finish adjusting its tack.

She placed her hands against its flank. Pressed into the muscle and tried to focus on the wall of strength rather than on her desire to move her hands.

Another impatient stamp of hooves.

"I'm getting there," she muttered, reaching underneath to adjust the girth strap.

Soryn had gifted their traveling party with several fresh horses, along with supplies to help hold them over until they reached Mistwilde. But she had otherwise remained distant, unwilling to help or commit to any plans beyond this.

We will see what becomes of you and your mission after you've spoken to the Mistwilde king, the Sadiran queen had told her. *If our paths are meant to cross again, they will.*

Not an outright dismissal any longer, but still not the renewed, powerful partnership she'd been hoping for, either.

Cas sighed and plunked her forehead against the horse, prompting the creature to whip its head around and empathetically nibble her hair.

Warmth flooded the space, easing some of the tension from her body. Cas knew where it was coming from even before she peered around the horse and saw the person approaching them. "Hello, Nessa."

Nessa smiled at her, but it was distracted and quickly on the verge of wilting, not at all her usual smile—not the one that lit up her whole face and the faces of everyone around her.

"What's wrong?"

Nessa fiddled with a small rip in her coat sleeve. "Something's changed."

Cas gave her a curious look.

"I don't know if it's the terrible weather, or the lingering Death magic, or something else...but it's much harder to summon my magic all of a sudden. I believe the Healing Goddess gave me an extra blessing when we were in Ciridan—even though she wouldn't outright *admit* to doing so, I left that city feeling more full of magic than I ever had. And it's persisted during our travels...until *now,* for some reason."

Cas stepped closer, reaching for her hand and stopping her from making the hole in her coat bigger.

"I've been praying to her and the Feather spirit ever since the day they visited my bedside, but I haven't felt them or encountered them in any other way since. And now I wonder if something's happened. I can't shake the fear of it.

Do you think...do you think the Dark God and his court might have gone after them?"

Cas couldn't bring herself to lie. "It's possible."

"If your magic drove him temporarily from this mortal plane, I worry he might be trying to attack our allies in other places—divine places. The Healing Goddess and her servant took a great risk, coming to us, helping me survive, and now..." She trailed off with a shuddering breath.

Cas waited for her to continue.

But Nessa stayed silent, occupying herself by brushing out the horse's mane with her fingers. It was obvious she wanted to say more.

Cas finished the last adjustments on the saddle before clearing her throat and asking, "Is that all that's bothering you?"

Nessa's gaze stayed fixed on the horse as she replied. "Seeing the dead come back to life like that," she whispered, "it just...it made me think. About what you did. About what I was. What I am now. So many have been lost and *haven't* come back, and I..."

"You're *you*. Nothing else," Cas said. "The revenants were not truly people brought back to life. They were ghosts, only shadows of living things—different from you."

It was a flimsy explanation, but Cas didn't know what else to say. She didn't truly understand all the things they'd been through, either. All the things she'd done. She just wanted to make everything better, to heal her friends and keep them safe. It was all she'd *ever* wanted—more than magic or crowns or anything else.

"I feel like I'm losing myself, magically and otherwise," said Nessa. "And it's not just me."

"Who else?"

She rubbed the mare's nose, smiling a bit and planting a kiss on it as the creature attempted to eat her sleeve. "Rhea doesn't want to say anything to you, but she's worried about the magical link between her and Silver...what might become of it now, after what happened to the spirit that magic derives from."

It took Cas only a moment to understand what Nessa meant. "Santi's corrupted..." she thought aloud, "and the Air spirit that served her..." Her chest felt tight as she remembered the frantic escape she and Elander had made from Kantrum. The sound of that spirit's cries of pain still haunted her.

Had the Sand Goddess killed her off completely?

"I hadn't thought about what might happen with Silver," Cas quietly admitted.

"It was all going to fade eventually, wasn't it?" said Nessa. "With what's happened to the Stone God and his disloyal followers, and what our ultimate goal is. But if the Air spirit is gone, and her goddess's magic is being corrupted by her new alliance with the Dark God...I just fear it might have sped up this problem."

Cas's eyes glazed over as she ran her fingers in repetitive circles over the horse's side, trying to think of something reassuring to say. "Maybe it won't, since Silver's magic is technically a corrupted version of the Air spirit's powers, anyway."

"Maybe." Nessa took a deep breath. "But I know Rhea's afraid. And I know *I'm* afraid."

Cas's hands stilled against the horse. She could manage no more reassuring words—they all felt too hollow, collapsing before she got them out—so she simply said, "Me too."

Nessa hesitated. "It just feels like pieces of us are slipping away. Like we're leaving a trail of them everywhere we go." She paused, using the heel of her hand to wipe away the tears collecting in her eyes. "Too many to pick up whenever it's all said and done."

Cas stood in silence with her for a long moment, until she managed to settle the anxiety still crawling through her skin and trying to twitch her fingers. Then she reached again for Nessa's hands, squeezing them tightly, and said, "We'll just have to pick up what we can. And then make new things to fill in the empty spaces."

Nessa didn't speak, and her eyes still shimmered in the dreary afternoon light. But the answer seemed to satisfy her for the moment—she eventually nodded and flashed a hint of a smile.

They worked together to finish readying Cas's horse and saddlebags before moving on to prepare others, and then Nessa left to gather the last of her things from the house she'd slept in.

The air felt heavier to Cas as she watched her leave, settling like a damp cloak over her shoulders, just as it had done after she watched Varen disappear.

How do you save everyone and everything at once?

Her horse snorted, almost as if in answer.

You don't.

As she took the reins and started to lead her horse toward the rest of their traveling party, she sensed a powerful energy approaching. She glanced over her shoulder and saw the Sundolian High Queen walking toward her, a trio of soldiers on either side of her.

"Queen Casia." She inclined her head in greeting. "Could we speak for a moment?"

Exhaustion and uncertainty made Cas's voice bitter. "Does Soryn know you're here?"

"She gave her blessing for this meeting."

"And what are we meeting about?"

The Sundolian Queen regarded her with a raised brow, but she didn't match Cas's clipped tone. "I traveled to this kingdom by way of the same Air-kind we used to send you to Soryn's aid some months ago," she said, calmly, each word precise and clear despite her accent. "Their magic is now fading, along with all magic that derives from the Stone God, but they should still have enough to more swiftly take you where you need to go—your goal is Mistwilde, I believe?"

Cas nearly dropped the reins.

"Not your entire army, I'm afraid," Alaya continued. "But enough of them to serve your purpose."

Cas still couldn't believe she'd heard her correctly. "You would help us? Give us so much, despite Soryn's wishes?"

"She is feeling..." The queen hesitated, perhaps searching for the proper Kethran word to use. "*Cold,*" she decided on. "But she understands what must be done, even if she does not welcome it."

Cas opened her mouth several times only to close it, hesitant to speak for fear that it might give this powerful woman reason to change her mind. When it came to matters of divine magic, the empire she ruled over had as much to lose as Soryn's kingdom did—if not more.

As if she could hear Cas's unspoken thoughts, the queen signaled for her soldiers to stand down while she walked toward a more private stretch of road, beckoning Cas to follow.

Once they were out of everyone's hearing range, she turned her golden eyes on Cas and said, "My empire stands on an...*edge* as well. Change will not be easy for any of us. There are no good choices. No certainty. No true clarity."

Cas pulled her coat more tightly around herself—or rather, Elander's coat, as he'd insisted she keep it on. The scent of him that clung to it was comforting, and she inhaled several deep lungfuls of it before she found her voice again. "I had no desire to be the one making these choices, for what it's worth," she told Alaya.

"I know." The queen's gaze drifted toward her guard. "So does Soryn, for what *that* is worth. And I will stay a little longer in Sadira and do what I can to continue to appeal to her on your behalf. I hope that you find the things you are seeking among the elves, in the meantime."

SORYN DID NOT COME to see them off.

The last time Cas had traveled via the Air-kind soldiers and the portals they created, she had been in awe of their magical abilities—the most powerful abilities she'd seen outside of the Air spirit and the Goddess of Time herself. But now, any sense of wonder was lost in the waves of uncertainty and fear surrounding them, and traveling was a bleak, solemn affair. Cas enlisted Elander and Laurent's help determining the soldiers that would go with them, and then this narrowed group of them stepped up to the portal, passed into it, and that was that.

But some of that awe returned as she stepped through to the other side.

The sight that greeted them took her breath away, and she briefly forgot about everything else.

A river flowed below them, its waters wild, tumbling, and glowing with a pale purplish light. There was a road across from it, lined with trees bearing leaves that glistened like they were made of colored glass—all manner of purples and blues and reds, each shade she noticed bolder and more beautiful than the last. Cliffs rose steeply on either side of the road, broken up by countless waterfalls cascading down, filling the air with a fine mist and a soothing rumbling that sank into her bones and gave her the courage of wild things.

She took a few bold steps forward. "That river is Mirdor, yes?"

Laurent nodded. "It stretches around the entire border they share with the human empire."

"I don't see a bridge," Zev said. "But I see a road that I assume we need to take?"

"We're going to take it," Laurent confirmed.

"Not really in the mood to swim."

"There *is* a bridge. But it only appears and carries the ones deemed worthy to enter Mistwilde. I swear I already explained this to you once...you truly don't listen when *anybody* talks, do you?"

Zev had already stopped listening, and was busy picking his way down the slope toward the river.

As he approached it, the already wild waters grew wilder, swelling and foaming and nearly spilling over onto the grass. A few of their party had cautiously followed his lead, and the waters grew rougher for every person that dared to approach the river's edge.

Cas ordered them all to retreat to the safety of the hillside she still stood upon, and then she turned to Elander and Laurent.

"What now?" she asked.

Elander hesitated. "It didn't do that when Laurent and I came here in the past. I'm not sure what's happening."

She held in a sigh.

Everything has to challenge us, doesn't it?

No matter—she would overcome this challenge, same as she had all the others before it. "The water you took from Lake Ulondar," she said, looking to Laurent, "you said it can help soothe this river's protective magic."

"Allegedly."

"Let's find out, shall we?"

He slipped the bag from his back and retrieved a canteen full of softly glowing water.

Cas took it from him and studied it, comparing it to the restless waves blocking their path. She didn't know how to use the lake's water, but she had not come this far to hesitate now, so she strode toward the river in search of more clues.

Silverfoot bounded after her, sniffing the gritty ground and pawing at loose patches of dirt and leaves. She crouched on the river's edge and Silverfoot followed, dipping his snout into the water, his fur bristling and ears twitching.

"You sense it too, don't you?" she whispered. "There's something very powerful sleeping in these waves."

He squirmed his way into her lap and nudged the hand she had wrapped around the canteen, spilling a few drops of its contents. She panicked briefly at the thought of losing the precious lake water—until she looked more closely at the places those drops had fallen.

She could have sworn the river water had turned clearer in these places.

She could think of nothing else to try, so she poured a handful of Ulondar's water into her palm, took a deep breath, and then tossed it across the river's surface.

She hadn't imagined it before.

The drops cleared Mirdor's waters as they hit it, revealing a river bottom that appeared to be only inches deep.

Cas stepped into the clear water before anyone could argue against it.

It happened instantly—a feeling of falling, as though she had stepped into a bottomless pit rather than shallow water. She was falling, falling, *falling* in a perfectly straight line, her hair and clothing whipping up around her, her stomach flipping wildly.

Her boots slammed onto spongy ground, jarring her to a stop.

Her hair and clothing sank back down, and though it all still floated a bit strangely around her, she could now see through it well enough to know that she had been transported to someplace entirely different.

Silverfoot was gone, along with the rest of her traveling party. The cliffs and the road they fenced in were no longer. Only the water remained, and it now stretched wider, farther into the distance than she could see.

A figure stood before her, knee deep in this water and wrapped in the same purplish glow that the river had been giving off before she stepped into it—an elf.

He watched her closely through indigo eyes that were clever but unsettling, too much color and not enough white, and his lips parted several times but he never spoke.

Somewhere in the place between her confusion and uncertainty, she found her own voice. "Are you the keeper of the River Mirdor?"

He took a step back through the water, eyes never leaving hers. The waves parted as he moved through them, peeling aside and revealing solid ground snaked through with veins of crystal.

He nodded to the revealed ground.

Daring her to follow?

There was a sinister expression on his face whenever she glimpsed it out of the corner of her eye—she would have sworn it. But it disappeared when she looked directly at him. The waters seemed rougher, too, when she was staring in any direction other than straight ahead.

Nowhere but forward, then.

After a few steps, the water began to collapse in her wake, so that she couldn't have turned around even if she'd *wanted* to. It soon lapped at her heels and slid over her boots. Then her ankles. Her calves. Deeper and deeper the farther she walked, until it had nearly reached her waist.

She felt like she was walking into her own grave.

When she looked back, she found an even higher wall of water behind her. *Impossible,* the way it rose straight up like that—an illusion? She wasn't going to test it. She kept moving forward, even though her legs had started to feel wobbly, and despite that same unsteadiness rising through the rest of her, causing an uncomfortable fluttering in her stomach and a trembling that she couldn't rid herself of, no matter how hard she tried.

The elf seemed to notice her shaking; he wasn't hiding the sinister look any longer. He wore it boldly and maliciously as his gaze bored into hers.

She only rebalanced herself and kept walking. "You don't frighten me," she said as she waded toward him. "I have faced far deeper waters than this."

He seemed to take this as a challenge. His hands motioned for her to stop. She did—an automatic reaction—and the water rose up and around her.

She kept perfectly still. Her time in Kantrum had

prepared her for this, in a way. And she had been drowning all her life before that, it sometimes felt like—sinking into waves of anxiety and fear where her surroundings grew murky and her breaths came heavy and slow—if they came at all.

So she didn't flinch as the water roared louder.

But then the river keeper briefly reappeared within the waves, his hands twisting to create another spell, and it was no longer simply water threatening to drown her.

It was *everything.*

Everything she had faced in her lifetime was suddenly swimming around her, dark visions of her past projected onto the waves, swirling and wrapping like a too tight embrace around her.

The cold orphanage she'd been hidden away in. The whipping that had left the scar on her jaw. The shadowy wolf that had once haunted her nightmares. The sword stabbing into Asra's frail body. The wolf saving her, betraying her, finding her again...

On the other side of this swirling, chaotic mess, the elven man continued to watch her—and her memories. He followed each new image with his eyes, looking rather pleased with himself. So she wasn't imagining what she'd seen. And all at once she realized...

He was reading her story.

Reading it and trying to determine what had brought her here, and for what purpose, and what she might do next. Testing her.

She stood taller and kept her balance, resisting the urge to curl into a tight ball as the waves and memories continued to rush.

The In-Between and the wild things they'd faced. Laurent lost beneath the sands in the Cobos Desert. A bridge made of lightning.

Zev dying on the shores of the Belaric Sea. The dark mark the Rook God had clawed into her skin. The blood Sarith had beaten from her. Elander's body falling beneath her brother's sword...

She had to close her eyes against this last image. When she opened them again, everything started to spin faster and faster—so fast she could only make out a few clear images.

Shadowslayer cutting through Caden.

Nessa going lifeless and cold in her arms.

Another life, another river trying to claim her, and Elander carrying her broken body away from the water...

And now came this moment—the next part of her story. She stared directly into the elf's eyes, no longer distracted by the scenes rotating viciously around her, by all these things that should have stopped her, broken her, knocked her down, dragged her under...

She stayed on her feet and kept her eyes lifted, and soon enough those things fell away.

A path opened before her.

The water receded, and the elf gave a slight bow before he dissolved into the retreating waves, leaving nothing but foam and a faint purple glow behind.

Cas returned to the mortal realm as abruptly as she'd left it, and she found herself standing in the center of the river. The water came up to her ankles. So shallow—and yet she couldn't see the bottom. But she didn't need to. She knew, with a certainty that she couldn't explain, that she would not sink. And her friends and soldiers would not sink, either, as long as she kept leading them forward.

"Come on," she said, beckoning.

She turned and started to walk, and soon she heard the sound of everyone following her. They made their way toward the road on the other side. As they stepped onto dry ground, the cliffs shimmered and shifted, revealing a second road carved through the rock.

They followed this road—Cas again had a feeling she couldn't explain, pulling her along—even as it led them beneath several waterfalls that tumbled violently downward. The waters never touched them, somehow, and the road went on and on until finally it curved and brought them fully out of sight of the mortal realm, and, finally, underneath an arch made of what looked like petrified wood. They slowed to a stop on the other side of this arch, their quiet gasps filling the air.

A city stretched out before them—*Irithyl*, Laurent told them. The Royal City.

The beauty that had first greeted them when they stepped through the Air portal had only been a taste compared to this—the vision their eyes feasted on now was nearly impossible to comprehend.

Water flowed everywhere Cas looked, falling over countless surfaces, gathering in turquoise pools, winding between buildings. There were no roads, only these winding rivers that calmly carried slender, white-sailed boats to and fro. The air glittered with mist that had caught the setting sunlight and turned to gold, and it smelled sweet and floral—likely from the pale blue flowers that covered many of the yards. The houses those yards belonged to were arranged in neat rows stacked precisely on top of one another, each one boasting countless windows of colorful glass. It somehow looked both perfectly planned and yet entirely natural—a wild city tamed by precise and thoughtful hands.

A palace stood in the center of it all, its spires twisting up into the orange-splashed sky, its emerald-colored banners flapping in the soft breeze. It almost appeared to float, lifting above most of the other structures in the city while the waterways that led to it were angled up and suspended like flooded bridges above the ground.

Cas was so busy staring at it all that she didn't notice the elven woman approaching them until she was almost directly before them.

She sat upon a horse with a shimmering golden coat, and her appearance was as breathtaking as the background she'd emerged from. She was not nearly as lithe as most of the elves Cas had encountered in Moreth and otherwise, but full-bodied and powerful-looking, with thick curls that reached nearly to her waist and shined like raven's wings. She tucked that hair behind her tapered ears before slipping gracefully from her horse's back, emerald coat fluttering around her as she dropped, and she stepped closer to Cas.

She had kind eyes—a welcome sight—that eagerly drank Cas in. They seemed to shift between different shades of blue and green.

She gave a slight bow, and then lifted both her fists out beside her before unclenching them and stretching them toward Cas and her party—a common greeting among those in her realm.

"Welcome, mortal queen," she said in a voice as smooth as the water that flowed all around them, "to the Realm of Mistwilde."

CHAPTER 16

The elven woman—who introduced herself as Anwyn—led Cas and her party deeper into Mistwilde, taking a winding path down a rock scattered hillside and eventually reaching a large dock at the edge of the palace grounds. From here they divided up into several of the slender boats Cas had seen from above. There was no wind, and yet *something* filled the white sails of these boats, carrying them onwards and upwards along the watery bridge that stretched to the front doors of the palace.

They left the boats behind at these imposing silver doors, but the waterways continued even once they were inside. There were proper hallways to walk along, but little streams flowed beside most of them, filled with small vessels swiftly carrying everything from messages, to supplies, to the occasional person. As with the boats outside, nothing seemed to be directing these vessels. They zipped smoothly about, crisscrossing the route Cas and her company were being guided along.

The halls felt almost like a series of rivers themselves,

narrowing and opening up in wild, unpredictable ways as they carved out a path through the palace. Anwyn moved without ceasing down these halls, past countless waterfalls and fountains that filled the air with the constant hum and trickle of water.

"Terrible place to be if you have to take a piss," Zev muttered, eying a small cascade flowing into a basin with elaborately carved beasts guarding its edges.

"Spare us the commentary, please," Rhea said, and Silverfoot agreed with a snort.

Cas's gaze shifted to Silver and lingered, remembering her conversation with Nessa. The elven realms suppressed divine magic—which would make the fading link between Rhea and Silverfoot even more pronounced.

She frowned, directing her focus back to Anwyn as the elven woman brought them through another set of doors. They were back outside, breathing in the heavy, damp air, climbing stairs circling a stone tower up to a dizzying height. Though it made her stomach flip to do it, Cas couldn't help peering down at the sparkling pools of water that dotted the grounds below, each one a different shade of blue burning in the early evening light.

They ended up in a circular room near the very top of the tower, massive in size and lined by still more waterfalls that tumbled into a circle of water edging the space. There was a throne at the top of this circle that looked to have been carved from driftwood, sealed and polished until it gleamed beneath the skylights running the length of the room.

Despite the water nearly overrunning the space, the air felt much lighter and less damp compared to outside. It was quieter here, as well, the roar of falling water subdued somehow—by a spell of some sort?

There were four bridges leading across the circle of water, each one stretching toward a small alcove attached to the main room. Someone was moving within one of these smaller areas.

Anwyn motioned for them to wait in the center of the throne room, and then she crossed the bridge, paused on the other side of it, and called out to this someone.

After a brief discussion in Mistwildian—followed by much rumbling and mumbling and the sound of shuffling books and papers coming from the alcove—an elven man finally emerged. He spoke swiftly to Anwyn in their language, directing her into the room in his place. As she disappeared inside, the man turned to face them.

Cas had seen his portrait in one of the books she'd studied back in Ciridan, so she knew who he was.

King Talos.

He looked considerably more *kingly* than the last elven king she had encountered. Clearly much older than Alder, his long brown hair was streaked with grey—a feature she had never seen in any elf before him, king or otherwise. *How old did an elf have to be to earn silvered hair?*

The creases around his eyes suggested his advanced age too, though they were more subtle. His face was still bright and alert, however old he might have been, his eyes twinkling behind round frames. Cas suspected they were not glasses meant to help with his vision, but *vesper* glasses, which were common creations among the elves, and which allowed a wearer to see things hidden in some texts—secrets that could usually only be revealed by certain periods of sun or moonlight. Alder had shown her a pair in Moreth as well. She covertly glanced at the books tucked under Talos's arm.

What secrets had he been trying to uncover within them?

He wore a flowing robe dyed the same shade of emerald as Anwyn's coat, carried a staff that extended as he tapped it against his thigh, and he walked toward them with a dignified limp, his right foot clearly struggling to keep up but his head lifted high and his shoulders pulled back.

Laurent was the first to speak as he approached, greeting him with a bow. "King Talos. As we discussed in our prior meetings, the Melechian Queen has joined us—I believe it's past time for the two of you to meet."

The elven king's gaze slid over Cas as Laurent introduced her.

She was used to this by now—the searching stare, the silent judgment. But there was something especially penetrating about the king's gaze. She wondered how many queens he'd hosted in his lifetime. How she measured up, and how she might set herself apart from them.

He limped over and settled onto his throne. "And to what..." he began, tapping his staff against the armrest and shrinking it once more, "do I owe this meeting? More attempts to sway me and my army into going to battle against your gods?"

His eyes were on Laurent as he spoke, but it was Cas who stepped forward and answered.

"That's only part of it." Her mind raced, trying to recall all she had planned to say, and all that had happened between the last visit Laurent and Elander had paid him and this moment. "It isn't just soldiers we seek, so much as your wisdom and the great, collective truths of this realm."

He snorted, though he didn't seem truly annoyed by her compliment.

Not even elves are immune to flattery.

"The stories I've heard of your realm, and your rule in

particular, are legendary," Cas pressed. "I know you hold great power here. Power to rival the gods themselves, to help navigate these frightening times we're living in—"

"Frightening times?" He chuckled, casually swiping the glasses from his nose and wiping them on the billowing sleeve of his shirt. "The gods don't frighten me."

Cas recalled her brother saying this exact thing months ago, and she shivered at the memory.

"I tried to explain this to your emissaries," continued Talos, "and they never gave a compelling enough argument to change my mind, but perhaps *you* can, since you're here..." He studied her with another of those long, penetrating stares. "What incentive do I have to help you, mortal queen?"

Cas started to reply, but Talos cut her off, clearly intent on listening to his own answer and no one else's.

"The divine cannot enter this realm," he said. "The mortal world could perish and we would sleep through it. It could burn for a hundred years and we still would not feel the heat from the fires—we have made certain of that. *You* are only in here because our River Keeper deemed you worthy, and then *I* decided to let that worthiness carry you through. But I was under no obligation to do so. The way into this realm can be shut at any time."

Cas fixed him with a hard stare. "Why would you let me in if you had no intentions of helping me?"

He hesitated.

"Because he was intrigued by what the River Keeper saw," came another voice—Anwyn's. She emerged from the alcove she'd disappeared into as she spoke, as if she'd been lingering at the doorway and simply waiting for an opportunity to shove her way into the conversation.

She stepped back into the room, the kindness in her eyes

replaced by a fierce stubbornness that immediately made Cas like her more than the king.

Talos summoned the elven woman to his side, muttering something to her in the Mistwildian language before lifting his eyes once more to Cas. "I wanted to speak with you, mortal queen. Nothing more." His gaze darted to Laurent and Elander. "They have told me much about your adventures, but to see them unfolding in the waters of Mirdor was indeed *intriguing*. You've been through much. Anyone who considers themselves a scholar and a lover of our world's intricate history would be interested in you and the history you are making."

"They *have* been through much," Anwyn agreed. "So why would you turn her away now? She isn't a book to be studied and mused over—this isn't *history,* Uncle, it is the present, and it is happening *now*. Wouldn't you prefer to make your mark upon it all before it becomes the tragic past?"

Another hiss of the Mistwildian language under his breath, and then he cleared his throat and spoke in the common tongue—though his gaze stayed mostly on Anwyn. "We were forsaken by the divine long ago, and we've managed to find our way over these centuries. Mortals can do the same."

"You don't understand," Cas argued, "the gods don't seek to simply *forsake* us. They seek to *destroy* us. And I'm not convinced they won't find a way to destroy you as well. All realms have weaknesses—including yours."

"Ah, but I don't have to convince you of anything, do I?"

Laurent placed a hand on Cas's shoulder, as if he could sense her growing frustration and how close she was coming to saying something regrettable. "You have other threats that could breach the defenses of Mistwilde," he said to Talos. "Neither mortal nor divine, but threats of your own blood."

The king's expression twisted in disgust. "You speak of the Morethian queen. She is—"

"She is not a queen," Nessa interrupted, so fiercely that both Cas and Laurent shifted toward her, preparing to hold her back if necessary.

Talos did not argue Nessa's point. He only studied the Feather-kind curiously for a moment before clearing his throat and sweeping his gaze back over the entire group before him. "Sarith is a problem that doesn't concern you."

"As we've told you before," Elander said, voice low and bordering on threatening, "you are mistaken about that. And we now know what she seeks in this realm," he added. "And *why* she seeks it. Information we thought you might be interested in."

In truth, they didn't *know*; they only guessed that it was the same as their own goal. *The Antaeum Point*. But Elander sounded convincing enough that for a moment it seemed the Mistwilde king was going to inquire further—they were balanced on the cusp of an understanding, a chance at an actual, fruitful discussion.

But several moments passed, and then he only fixed his eyes on Cas and said, "You can rest from your wars here, Mortal Queen. I swear that much to you. Horrors such as the ones that befell you in Moreth will not come to pass within the walls of my realm. But beyond these walls, I'm afraid our paths diverge considerably. We each have our own battles to focus on."

Zev and Nessa both cursed under their breath. Silverfoot growled in agreement, and Rhea started to reach for Cas's arm, while Laurent and Elander exchanged an uncertain look.

Cas moved free of them all and stepped to within a few feet of the king. She ignored the startled looks both Talos and Anwyn gave her—it was improper to come so close to the king's throne, no doubt—and before that king could speak, she shrugged out of her coat and rolled up her sleeves, revealing the scars Sarith had left upon her arms and shoulder.

"Our wars are the same," she said, "and there is no resting from them."

Talos kept his focus on her face, only allowing his gaze to flicker briefly to those scars she'd revealed. He still didn't speak.

Anwyn found her voice before her uncle did, staring unabashedly at the marks upon Cas's skin. "Those were made by a *scourge-blade,* weren't they?" she asked quietly. "A traditional weapon of this realm."

"Yes. As I'm sure the king already knows, with all of his infinite wisdom of the many battles I'm fighting."

She and Talos continued to stare one another down until the king got to his feet. He crossed back toward the room he'd been in when they arrived, not bothering with his staff this time, pausing at the bridge and studying his reflection in the water before he looked back and finally spoke.

"Sarith carries my old weapon—a gift I gave her mother—my sister—years ago. *Aluthol*—the Crownkeeper, it was called in those days, before it became as corrupted and stained with blood as she is. She's been seen with it along the outskirts of this realm, wielding it against my soldiers." He braced a hand against the bridge's ornate railing. "Bring it to me, and once *that* matter is dealt with, perhaps we can focus on our next war together." His eyes gleamed with mirth—as if he was telling a joke. As if he thought, *There is no chance she will agree to this.*

Cas was not in the mood for jokes.

So she bowed her head to the elven king, and made her voice as cold and clear as ice. "Consider it done."

HOURS LATER, while most of their group rested, Cas wandered the halls alone. It was not merely anxiety keeping her awake for once; it was just as much curiosity, her fascination with the Irithyl Palace and all its workings and splendor. There was something new, something beautiful, to look at around every corner she turned.

Sculptures lined many of the hallways, carved with such lifelike precision that Cas nearly greeted a few of them before realizing her mistake. That inner system of rivers—which she now noticed were distinguishable from one another by different gemstones embedded along their bottoms—proved even more intricate than she first thought. And there were the palace dwellers themselves, of course; the elves of this realm were each more stunning than the last, and all of them were seemingly trying to outdo the others with their extravagant cloaks and colorful jewelry.

But as beautiful as these things were, they eventually started to blur together, and Cas's mind turned regrettably back to the challenges looming before her. She started toward the floor where her friends were, intending to seek out Rhea and have a difficult conversation about her fading connection to Silver, when she saw Anwyn in the distance.

She was curious to know more about this niece of the

king, so Cas called out her name and then jogged to catch up with her.

They walked together for some time, Anwyn rattling off facts about the realm and excitedly introducing her to everyone they passed, until they came to a hall that dead-ended at yet another fountain. This one had several sculpted sparrows perched around its rim—a symbol associated with the king and his house, and Anwyn frowned as she stared at one of the stone birds.

"My uncle is a good king," she said. "But he is stubborn."

Cas could think of a few other words to describe him, but she kept these to herself.

"He wants to believe that elven problems are elven problems, mortal problems are mortal problems, and so on."

"It's a prevalent attitude among elves, I've noticed," said Cas.

Anwyn gave a wistful little smile.

"Not you, I take it?"

She shrugged. "I've always been fascinated by the divine myself." She held out her hand, and Cas was surprised to see smoke curling from the lines of her palm, and then a flash of fire—though it was gone as quickly as it came.

"Magic?"

Anwyn laughed. "If you could call it that. It's never more than a few embers." She glanced over her shoulder, and in a lower voice said, "But I wonder about what it might have been in the beginning."

"In the beginning?"

"For my ancestors, I mean." Anwyn settled down on the edge of the fountain, fingertips trailing through the water, a dreamy look on her face. "There are stories that say my great-great-grandmother on my mother's side fell in love with the

God of Fire. Unheard of, given the bitter war our kind were waging against the Marr at that point. And I am a small part of what became of that forbidden romance between an elf and a middle-god, all these generations later." She scooped up a handful of water and let it trickle down between her fingers. "I don't know if it's true, of course. The hatred for the divine still runs so deeply in my realm today that it's hard to imagine any sort of love existing between one of my kind and any divine being—much less one of the Marr, who essentially stole our place at the right hand of the Moraki."

Cas sat down beside her, letting her gaze drift to the reflection of sparrows in the water, trying to imagine such things for herself.

"But I do believe our fates are all intertwined, regardless of what race or family we were born into," said Anwyn. "And I admire you for trying to bring the broken kingdoms back together, and for extending a hand toward the elven realms as well, trying to unite us all." Her gaze drifted in the direction of Cas's scarred arms, now covered again by coat sleeves, and her voice grew distant as she added, "And I'm sorry for what happened in Moreth."

Cas shuffled where she sat, not wanting to linger on those things that had happened. "Speaking of family...the king is your uncle, and he is also Sarith's uncle. So that means..."

"Yes; she is my cousin. We grew up together—close in age, and my dearest friend and confidante."

"But that closeness is strained now, I assume?"

Anwyn pulled her hands from the water and clenched the gauzy folds of her dress tightly in her fists. "I hardly recognized her the last time she visited these halls. War has a way of remolding people. As do crowns. And she got too close to both of these things and let them change her. It's...unfortunate."

Cas looked away, thinking of herself, her brother, their relationship, the way it all seemed to constantly be twisting and turning into something new. She swallowed hard to clear the uncomfortable lump forming in her throat. "Yes. It is."

"I don't know what will become of her before the end." Anwyn hesitated. "But if there is any way I can help you...*stop* her, then please. Tell me. And I will do it."

Cas nodded in thanks, but then let the conversation drop. It was clearly making Anwyn uncomfortable. She might prove a helpful ally in the future; there was no sense in driving her into a deeper, more tense silence now.

The elven woman went back to swirling circles in the water with her fingers. She appeared lost in thought for several minutes before she excused herself and left Cas alone to resume her wandering. So Cas continued to her friends' rooms alone—but Rhea was nowhere to be found.

She kept moving, eventually stumbling upon Elander, who stood by himself on a balcony that, unsurprisingly, overlooked another pool of water. Cascading falls fed the pool, tumbling down from towering rock walls that surrounded the small body of water. The rock face was embedded with crystals, glittering and bright, and the sight of Elander standing among it all seemed yet another beautiful work of art in this palace that was full of them.

She crept up behind him and slid her arms around his waist, sinking her face into the strong lines of his back, breathing in his earth and winter scent. Despite how quietly she moved, she didn't startle him. He kept his eyes on the water but wrapped his arm around her own, squeezing her more tightly against him.

They stood like this for several moments, until Cas managed to pull herself from his warmth, and she stepped around to face him instead. "Alone for the first time in what feels like forever."

He intertwined his fingers with hers and pulled her closer, planting a kiss on her forehead. "So we are."

Her heart fluttered in her chest, fully prepared to soar—but something in his expression clipped its wings. "You seem distracted."

She expected him to deny it, to not admit anything was wrong; it had been the usual cadence of so many of their conversations.

But now he shook his head and said, "Sorry."

"What is it?"

He met her gaze—the same stubborn, unyielding one she'd given the elven king earlier. He sighed. It seemed he'd finally learned there was no avoiding her question when she gave him that look, and his lips quirked into a defeated smile. "It's just..." He gestured to the pool below them. "Water, of all things."

"Water?"

"It's everywhere in this place, which is unfortunate, as I've begun to...Hate it. Fear it."

She let go of his hand and moved to the balcony railing, leaning over and studying the rippling reflections of rock and gemstone. "Why is that?"

"Let's count the reasons." She glanced back as he lifted his gaze to the moon, a bright orange disc in a mostly cloudless sky, and his eyes appeared darker than usual—haunted—in spite of the light now falling into them. "Do you remember the night you fled the Ciridan Palace? You were shot by one of Varen's soldiers, and you fell into the Lotheran River and nearly drowned."

"And you pulled my body from it and carried me away," she reminded him.

"Then came the River Serine, when I watched the ice spreading, trapping you in the water underneath."

"You pulled me from that, too."

He shook his head. "And then Kantrum. The grey, the silence, the moment I thought I'd lost you for good, it was—"

"Need I remind you?" She stepped close again, reaching up and pressing a hand to his cheek, pulling his gaze back down to hers. "You carried me out of those waters, too. It seems to be a recurring theme with us."

"It...yes, it does." He appeared to be trying to think of an argument, but then he gave in with a laugh—though it was quiet and somber. "It does, doesn't it? But it also feels like it's come too close, too many times. And one of these times I'm going to be too slow and... I have nightmares. Nightmares of you slipping away in the waves, your hand just out of reach of mine. And when I watched you walking into the Mirdor earlier, it was like living out one of those nightmares. I can't seem to shake the image of it, even now."

She considered everything he'd said for a long moment. Then, in a voice made soft and certain by all they'd been through, she repeated the words he'd said to her countless times over the past months when she'd woken from nightmares of her own. "I haven't slipped away to anywhere. I'm right here."

He stared without speaking, his chest rising and falling with slow, deliberate breaths, his hand tracing the edges of her face as if recommitting it to memory.

She stretched taller, looping her arms around his neck so she could pull him down to meet her in a kiss. He was hesitant at first, muscles still tense and guarded against all the vulnerable things they'd been discussing.

But then he kissed her back, pushing a hand through her hair to grip her head and pull her more completely against his mouth. He leaned toward the balcony railing and she went with him, her lips crashing into his, her weight settling against his body. She pressed as tightly as she could to hold him in place; he'd been her anchor so many times in the past. She wanted to be the same for him.

She pulled away a minute later—only because she needed to take a deep breath. He didn't move to continue the kiss, but his eyes never left hers. His arms circled her waist, keeping her close, as if he was afraid she might sink out of his reach in that very moment. "I've never felt fear like this before," he said. "I never used to be afraid of anything."

She again hesitated before answering. There were so many things she wanted to say to him in that moment; it took time to sort through them all. "When we rebuild our palace—our forever home, after the war—we can move it away from the Lotheran River. Just to be safe. I've always felt most at home in the mountains, anyhow. So, somewhere far away from the water, far away from the memories of it and that original palace it ran alongside."

He didn't reply right away, aside from wrapping her up and kissing her again, holding her body flush against his until his heart thundered so closely to her own that she couldn't tell whose beat was whose.

"After the war," he repeated softly.

She could hear the uncertainty still clinging to the edge of the words—not quite fear now, but still not his normal confident tone.

"There is always an after," she whispered. "The stormy waters can't last forever."

He took a deep breath.

She mirrored his next deep breath, inhaling the same heavy air as she gazed up at him. "So here's to everything after."

He smiled at this echo of his own words and the promise they'd made before leaving Ciridan.

They stood silently, her head against his chest, for several minutes before he spoke again, in a voice that had regained most of its usual confidence. "Tomorrow morning, Laurent and I are leading a team to search the places where Sarith and her soldiers have been spotted. That weapon the king mentioned...we are going to retrieve it, one way or another."

She lifted her head. "I'm going with you."

His brow furrowed, but he didn't object. This battle belonged to both of them, and she would not be left behind.

They were quiet for another long moment before Cas pulled away and began pacing the balcony, turning their conversation over and around in her mind. She couldn't remember him ever admitting to being afraid before. Rhea rarely admitted to such things either, but Cas was certain that was what had made her impossible to find this evening.

Fear.

All of her friends were in danger of succumbing to it, and she wished she knew how to stop it from needling its way deeper into their ranks.

"You look like you're plotting something," Elander commented.

She managed a slight grin. "As I believe I told you when we first met—I usually am."

"One of the many things I love about you." He reached for her hand once more, drawing her back toward him. "Are you going to share this plot with me?"

She averted her eyes. "I'm simply thinking of the moment we find her. Not *if* we will find her—but *when,* and how satisfying it will be to make her pay for the things she's done. I don't dream of death and bloodshed often. But for her, my heart seems to have made an exception. And I will be glad to introduce my sword to her neck."

Elander was silent for so long that she wondered if she'd actually managed to startle him this time. But when she looked back, he only smiled at her before lifting his gaze back to the sky.

"My vicious queen." His eyes were distant, gazing into the moon that turned their usual pale blue to a haunting shade of red. "You will have to beat me to it."

CHAPTER 17

There were three dead elves upon the northernmost bend of the Mirdor River, their violet-tinted blood shining in the late afternoon sun.

The unusual color of this blood was unique to Mistwilde elves, Laurent had told them, so there was little doubt about where these three had originated from. And they looked to have been guards or soldiers of some sort, judging by the armor they wore and the weapons they carried.

Morbid as it was, Cas couldn't help the surge of excitement that rippled through her as she inspected them.

Finally, a sign left by our enemy.

Nearly a week had passed since their arrival to Mistwilde. And she was finding it similar to Moreth in at least one regard; the strange, backwards magic that teemed in the air made the realm feel even more removed from the mortal one than it actually was. It felt like they'd been there for nearly a year, as if the days were slipping away too easily, and with too little done during them.

They had continued to meet with the king and his

council on a regular basis, trying to appeal to that king. He remained amicable and accommodating, but entirely unmoved when they spoke of their divine wars; he only kept insisting on having his sword recovered from Sarith and returned to his possession.

A promise to him that they intended to keep—but not the only matter they had to deal with.

It was maddening, knowing the Antaeum Point they were after could be so close to them, and yet they didn't have the ability to *reach* it. Cas felt she could almost sense it at times. Could hear it calling to her, could taste it on the tip of her tongue. She felt like she was starving and the elves were dangling food just out of her reach.

She'd survived her hunger spasms by focusing most of her energy on the matter of Moreth's false queen. Five days had brought five separate missions, different approaches that had led them along the various borders of Mistwilde—but each mission they'd set out on had proven as fruitless as the last.

Until now.

Thus the excitement she felt as she looked over the dead ones before them.

It lasted until Elander knelt beside one of the fallen elves and touched a hand to its arm. He drew back instantly, and Cas felt a stirring in the air, a shiver of unexpected power across her skin.

"Divine magic?"

Elander nodded. "Subdued by the elven realm's spells, even on this distant border, but still unmistakable. It feels like magic tainted by the Dark God. Though I can't tell what we're dealing with, exactly. It's very...*muddled,* with the way magic is shifting and being tainted and twisted by that god."

Cas knelt as well, but avoided touching the stiff bodies. Silverfoot was perched upon her shoulder, fervently sniffing at the blood-tinted air as he relayed all they were seeing back to Rhea, who had gone a separate way with another group of their allies.

"Not Sarith, then?"

Elander shook his head at her question, concern etched across his face, and Cas quickly grasped his meaning.

"...But perhaps servants of the Dark God who are *aiding* Sarith."

"That's what I fear."

Laurent nodded in agreement as he came up beside them, glaring in disgust at the two slash marks that crisscrossed each of the elves' throats. "The way they're marked there," he added, "that was done by Moreth soldiers, most likely. It's an old, barbaric tradition that started in wars long past. And it seems it was done after these three were already dead—otherwise there would be far more blood."

They moved silently around the scene, studying it for additional clues.

Cas eventually broke the quiet, her fingers anxiously scratching Silverfoot's ears as she spoke. "So elves marked these kills, but their blades weren't responsible for causing the deaths. They simply wanted to make sure someone knew they had been here, too, I guess?"

"A warning?" suggested one of the Mistwilde soldiers who had accompanied them, and everyone present agreed this was likely the case.

There were eight of them in total looking over the murder scene. Sufficient, Cas had thought, and the small number had allowed them to move quickly and quietly to this point. But it seemed *too* small of a number now, as she wondered about what might have been responsible for the bodies.

The Fire God? Ice? Death? Or something else entirely?

What sort of monster had been sent?

And where was it now?

Everything felt like a threat. Every odd flicker of warmth seemed like it could be heralding a monster wielding Fire magic. Every chill breeze was a potential sign of the Ice Goddess. Every shadow meant Death was coming—and the shadows were numerous, dancing ominously over the bleak landscape. Too many shadows for this time of day, it seemed like.

Silverfoot had wandered away from their group. He paced the edges of their search area, his ears flicking and his tail stiff. His eyes were glowing, but not as brightly as they usually did from his magic. He occasionally stopped to shake his head, as though trying to clear it and allow the magic to flow better.

Struggling to send and receive images with Rhea?

Threads of unease twisted through Cas.

She walked over and scooped him up. The fox shook his head again and pawed at his face and ears, clearly agitated, while she tried in vain to soothe him.

They had parted ways with Rhea and the others at a diverging point a few miles back. There had been two roads that formed a circle, each side curving around a small mountain to the same eventual point, according to their Mistwildian guide. They had gone one way, while Rhea, Zev, and Nessa led a team along the other. Silver was to be the linking point between them, keeping them aware of the other team's movements. Rhea had insisted she and Silver could do this, even if that vision she and the fox shared had grown tenuous as of late.

It isn't gone, she'd sworn, *and it will be as useful to us as it's always been.*

But now it seemed impossible to deny that Silver was struggling, his magic fading after the Air spirit's demise. And Rhea...

What would become of them?

Elander made his way toward Cas, studying Silverfoot as he came. He was no doubt worrying about the logistical side of this development—what it would mean to lose what had once been a reliable communication method between them all—but he didn't mention it.

Cas hugged Silverfoot and pressed her cheek against his fur. "We should hurry to the meeting point," she said, without lifting her face from the fox's fur. "I think he's anxious to get back to Rhea."

Elander hesitated, glancing back at the dead elves, but ultimately he didn't argue. They collected a bag twisted around one of the elf's arms, along with Morethian emblems they cut from the clothing of all three of them—proof for the Mistwilde King that they were still chasing their goals—and they mounted their horses and set off at a quick trot.

There was no one waiting for them at the agreed-upon point.

They paused, exchanging uncertain glances. Several moments passed in silence before Elander cleared his throat, looked toward the road Rhea and the others should have been making their way along, and calmly said, "Hopefully they were slowed down because they stumbled upon more useful evidence for us."

"Hopefully." Cas's voice sounded considerably less calm. She nudged her horse into movement, riding a short distance down the road before circling back, gaze searching the trees and hills that surrounded them—but there was nothing to find.

A chill breeze swept over them, and strange shadows swept after it, making Cas's horse restless.

She led the beast in a winding path from one side of the road to the other, trying to calm it, before pulling it to a stop, taking Silverfoot from his place over her shoulder, and situating him on the saddle in front of her. She pressed her forehead to his and ruffled the fur of his face, attempting to soothe him once more before she asked him to try and connect to Rhea.

The fox gazed at her through eyes that still did not glow as they should have, no matter how hard he seemed to be concentrating. Occasionally he blinked, and they were brighter for an instant afterward, but that was all.

Then suddenly he jerked as if he'd been shocked by something, the twitch so violent that the horse he balanced on leapt nearly straight up in the air, kicking wildly. Cas settled them both while Elander drew his horse directly beside hers, taking a hold of its headgear so she could focus on Silverfoot.

"What's wrong?" she asked, as though the fox could answer her—because he had proven, countless times, to be capable of understanding and answering in his own way. But this time, he only curled up, miserable and shaking, in her lap. What this meant—whether he couldn't connect to Rhea at all, or that something terrible had happened to her—Cas couldn't tell.

Something caught her eye before she could further question things: Movement in the sandy hills directly in front of them, and the sound of boots scraping over uneven ground. A shadow. No...

A person?

She looked closer, and they were gone.

A ghost?

She shivered, thinking of the revenants they'd encountered in Ironedge, and she squinted in hopes of seeing something more solid.

Nothing there.

There was no road in that direction; the only road beyond this point was one that curved sharply east, back toward Kethra. The others wouldn't have taken it without waiting for everybody. But they *might* have decided to explore these sandy hills while they waited. Cas could almost picture Nessa and Zev daring each other to climb higher and faster over the dunes.

A vast lake lay on the other side of these dunes, according to the Mistwilde soldiers accompanying them. Cas rode closer, until the ground became too shifty for her horse to find purchase, then she leapt from its back. She took a bag attached to the saddle and fixed it across her body, emptying its contents before tucking Silverfoot's shaking body inside. She readjusted Shadowslayer and the sheath at her hip, and then she turned and scrambled up the sandy ridge.

Elander and Laurent both dismounted and followed her. It was a tricky climb, the sand extremely loose and the slopes nearly vertical in places, but they made it to a relatively flat ledge where prickly trees grew and provided limbs to grab. They paused here to catch their breath. They were high enough now that Cas could see for a long way down every road in the area, but she still saw no sign of Rhea and the others.

She followed Elander and Laurent's lead as they sank into quiet concentration, listening for unusual sounds, feeling for any more magic that might be in the area.

"I think I smell blood," Laurent commented after a minute.

Cas's eyes flashed open in alarm. She didn't doubt Laurent's inhuman senses—though she *wanted* to. Her gaze shot toward the remainder of the hill they had to climb. She started to claw her way toward the peak, but Elander reached for her arm, holding her still while more of their riders caught up to them.

Three stayed with the horses at the roadside, but the other two followed Cas's lead to the height of the dunes and found themselves overlooking the lake.

Selakiir. Or the Vanishing Lake, as the Mistwilde soldiers said it was often called, owing to the number of people who had never been recovered after the waters claimed them. It was so vast she could not see the other side of it. She scanned its shores until, on a particularly wide stretch of gleaming sand, she spotted something that made her breath catch.

Bodies.

Rhea and the rest of that other group *had* beaten them to the meeting point.

And now two of that group were lying motionless on the ground below, their coats—once the brilliant green of the Mistwilde banner—darkened by what appeared to be blood. More blood had oozed into the white sand beside them.

Cas nearly lost her balance. Loose pebbles and sand skittered wildly out from under her as she leaned closer to the carnage, and it took both Laurent and Elander grabbing hold of her this time to keep her from rushing forward into what would likely have been a dangerous—if not deadly—race down the hillside.

She clenched Elander's arm so tightly she lost the feeling in her fingers. "Where are the rest of them? *Where are the rest?*"

They found their balance and then picked their way down as quickly and carefully as they could. They were halfway to the bottom when a strange rumbling began from deep within the hillside.

Cas quickly sidestepped to the nearest sturdy looking perch, balancing herself atop a smooth bit of rock, crouching down and clenching its edges while she searched for the source of the rumbling.

Her gaze eventually fell upon several sparkling blue stones embedded in the nearby ground. She stared at them for a moment, and they seemed to stare back—a ridiculous idea.

But then they *blinked*.

She would have sworn those were eyes, not jewels. A terrifying thought occurred to her. "This is some servant of the Mountain God at work, isn't it?" she called to Elander, who had taken refuge against a slab of stone similar to the one she clung to.

He nodded. The gods themselves would not set foot on elven lands, but they had all manner of created beasts who roamed more freely—weakened by elven air, as were all divine things, but apparently still powerful enough to cause trouble.

Elander started to explain further, but the rumble within the hillside became a roar, and suddenly the entire slope was collapsing around them.

A large rock struck Cas's shoulder, sending her tumbling

from her sturdy spot. Her face met the ground. Her entire head felt too heavy to lift, her eyes too heavy to hold open, and as sand and stone cascaded down upon her, darkness overtook her vision and carried her away.

When Cas woke, it was nighttime, and she was buried up to her waist in sandy earth and rocks. She carefully twisted and turned, trying break free, trying to better see and understand what had happened.

Bodies were partially buried all around her, none of them moving.

Black dots swam in her vision. She nearly passed out once more from shock, but somehow, she managed a breath before the darkness could take her back. Then another. She clenched fistfuls of sandy dirt and let it fall between her fingers, focusing on the soothing, shushing sound of it, on the feel of it sliding over her palm. She could still feel. She was still *alive*.

She forced her eyes to stay open and keep looking around.

So much dirt.

So many bodies.

She finally wiggled free of her almost-grave and rolled for a few feet, coughing and sputtering, before pushing to her hands and knees and inspecting herself. Shadowslayer was still hanging haphazardly from her hip, and the bag she had slung across herself was intact—but it was empty.

Silverfoot was nowhere to be found.

Panic threatened again. Her eyes stung from a mixture of clinging sand and threatening tears. Her lungs burned and her heart felt like a heavy stone in her chest, but she kept moving, crawling back to the wrecked hillside.

She found Elander, and then Laurent, and then their soldiers—all were accounted for, all of them unconscious but still breathing.

One by one, she tried unsuccessfully to rouse them.

The sand continued to shift in places, little landslides sliding down, minor in scale but still loud in the eerily quiet night. She scanned the area for signs of the Mountain God's minions. She saw none, but she was still afraid of another massive collapse, so she mustered all of her strength and dragged each body from the clutches of the earth, pulling them as far as she could toward the lake.

They still didn't wake, even after she splashed frigid water onto their faces. She wandered back to the base of the dunes and tried shouting for the three soldiers they'd left on the other side.

No one answered.

The sky was clear, no cover of clouds to protect her from the moon and starlight that suddenly seemed penetrating. She felt cold and lost, completely and utterly alone.

Her gaze fell upon what she *thought* was the spot where she'd seen the bodies on the beach. They were gone. But upon closer inspection...their blood remained. A trail of it led away from the beach, between dunes that glowed pale blue in the moonlight, and into a forest of brambles and small, spiny trees.

Would it lead her to Rhea and the others?

Cas stared at the trail for a moment, squeezing Shadowslayer's pommel, trying to decide what to do.

She got to her feet and started to walk.

She couldn't go far—she wouldn't leave Elander and the

others in such a vulnerable state—but something dark and unnatural was at work, and she would not figure out what was happening by standing still.

She trudged her way across the sand and cut through the dense thicket of trees, wincing as branches snagged at her hair and clothing. Soon enough, Shadowslayer's edge sliced away the last of the branches holding her back, and Cas broke into a clear path that sloped down toward a dried-up creek bed.

There, stretched out among the dust and water-smoothed stones, was a third, bent and bloodied body.

Rhea.

Cas froze. Her feet felt disconnected from the rest of her, preventing her from sprinting forward like she wanted to, from racing to Rhea's side to check for breathing and a beating heart. The paralysis was like armor three sizes too big, draping heavily across her shoulders and chest, holding her back. Protecting her.

Because in her heart she already knew the answer.

There was no pulse to check for.

When she focused, Cas could sense life-forces, a side-effect of carrying so much of the Life Goddess herself. Not an exact art, but she knew the energy of all of her friends by now. And she sensed nothing in this clearing—no life aside from her own.

This couldn't be.

She finally shook free of the paralysis and staggered forward, her lips quivering, repeating a single line over and over—

"This isn't real."

Not real, not real, NOT REAL.

But no matter how loudly she shouted it in her mind and

otherwise, the scene before her did not change. As she drew closer, she saw the realness of it with startling, heart-wrenching clarity—the bruises upon Rhea's face, the blood trickling from her mouth, the dagger that had fallen, clattered to the ground several feet away. There was blood covering that fallen blade.

She had fought until the very end.

Cas's legs gave out in a rush of weakness. She caught herself just before slamming face-first into the ground, her knees jarring against stone and palms pressing into sharp pebbles.

Her vision swam, and in the corners of it she thought she saw more strange shadows like the ones she'd witnessed at the last murder scene, and the ones that had led her to climb the dunes…

What were they?

She closed her eyes tightly, willing them away. She could make this go away. She was light, her sword the enemy of darkness, and no shadow—of Death or otherwise—could overcome her. She had brought Nessa back from the abyss.

She could do it again.

She opened her eyes and reached a hand out, brushed it over Rhea's skin, arm shaking as she tried to find her power.

But all she found was cold. It was all she could dredge up —any warmth she summoned was frozen by the time it reached the surface, any light that sparked was swallowed up by still more shadows. And the air…that damnable elven air suffocated her attempts from the start. She stared at her hands, furious with herself. With *everything.*

I should be able to manage more than this.

She sensed movement behind her. A moment later, Silverfoot padded around her, weaving his way cautiously, hesitantly, to his master's side. He sniffed at her fallen form and his body went rigid. A soft whine vibrated in his throat.

He looked back and forth between Cas and Rhea. Grabbed Cas's sleeve in his mouth and tugged, pulling her hand back to Rhea's cold skin.

Cas tried again for warmth, for magic that might somehow fix everything.

Nothing happened.

Silverfoot's nose lifted her hand back up every time she let it fall, willing her to keep trying, until finally she drew her hands away and wrapped her arms tightly around herself. She couldn't try anymore. She couldn't *fail* anymore. Silverfoot squirmed his way into her lap and wiggled underneath her arms, pawing and pushing desperately against her chest, trying to unwrap her arms.

Finally, he gave up and collapsed, his little body impossibly heavy against her.

"I'm so sorry, Silver," she whispered, while that awful, familiar thought roared between her ears—

You can't save everybody.

Cas was not sure how long she sat there. Long enough to lose the feeling in the legs tucked beneath her. Long enough that her eyes grew dry and raw and itchy, and Silverfoot's side was soaked through with her tears, and even then, she still did not move. Neither did the fox—he barely breathed, as though this ability had been intertwined as tightly as his vision with Rhea's, and now it was too much, too awful, to carry on breathing without her.

Cas heard footsteps. She wanted to ignore them. But they were growing louder. Closer.

Somehow, she made herself stand to face whoever was approaching. Silverfoot rolled from her embrace and stayed on the ground, curled against Rhea's side, his snout nudging her hand up and trying to drape it between his ears, desperate for her to scratch there as she so often had.

Cas looked away from the sight and steeled herself against whatever was coming. Strange shadows had gathered around the clearing without her realizing it, closing the space into a tight circle. She cautiously moved around the edges of it, trying to find the path she'd taken from the beach.

A voice split the quiet, cold and crawling like frost over Cas's skin. "A word of warning."

Cas spun around and found herself looking upon a familiar face. An elven woman with golden hair and eyes dark as the cold sky above.

Not Sarith, but nearly as terrifying. *Nalia*—the elven queen's second in command. The one who had so gleefully followed the orders to carve scars into Cas's skin.

She stepped closer, circling Cas, who followed only with her eyes. Nalia had no weapon in her hands now, but she still seemed to be searching for places to strike.

Cas's reply came out in a snarl, sharpened by grief and growing rage. "What *warning* do you have for me?"

Nalia smiled. "That if you keep searching, you are only going to stumble upon more things you don't want to find."

Shadowslayer shook in Cas's hand as she turned to square herself up with the elf. She jabbed the blade in Rhea's direction without taking her eyes off the enemy. "Did you do this?"

"Of course not." Nalia shook her head, that familiar sadistic glee dancing in her eyes. "It was *you*."

Cas was so confused—and horrified—by the idea that she couldn't reply right away.

"You know the magnitude of the things you seek. What you will change in the process...and *destroy*. Yet you cut violently onward, and you haven't thought once of how vulnerable it's made your friends and allies."

"That's a lie."

"*Is* it?"

I've thought about it plenty.

Nalia's laughter was quiet and menacing as she tucked a hand under her chin and let her gaze drift lazily back to Rhea. "Well, hopefully she knew you cared. Otherwise, her untimely death is even more of a tragedy, isn't it?"

Cas couldn't help the way her gaze followed Nalia's, or the way it froze upon Rhea's still body. Silverfoot had wedged himself under her arm, nuzzling up to her the way he often did when they slept. She looked as though she was sleeping now.

But she wasn't.

Never would be again.

And something inside of Cas *snapped* at this thought.

She cleared the space between her and Nalia in the blink of an eye. Shadowslayer was withdrawn in the next instant, and the sparks that exploded around her overtook the shadows swirling through the air. For a fraction of a moment, Cas saw nothing except her target illuminated, and her power unfurled with such force that she feared nothing and no one—elven or god or otherwise.

Nalia leapt back and then sideways, the speed and grace of her race on full display. She came to rest lightly upon a fallen tree and flung her long coat aside, revealing the weapon at her hip. It appeared to be a sword until she withdrew it, and then the whip-like attachment became visible, as did the shining barb at the very end of that steel whip.

That weapon.

A scourge-blade.

Cas stumbled at the sight and the memories it awakened. She recovered quickly—

But not quickly enough.

As she twisted aside and tried to lift her sword into a guard position, the whip of the scourge-blade flew out and wrapped around her throat.

She dropped Shadowslayer, both hands flying to her neck, trying to wedge fingers between the whip and her skin. She managed a single finger—enough to allow her a quick, choked breath—but pulling the whip farther away proved impossible, while trying to twist free only made it tighten, only pulled the barb deeper into her flesh. She felt blood on her fingertips and went still. Her vision blurred.

Nalia's face swam in that blurriness before her, her devil smile the only thing Cas could clearly make out. She watched it stretch wider as Nalia yanked her weapon toward her, cutting off what little breath Cas was still managing.

All sense of feeling left her, and Cas slipped once more into darkness, the sound of laughter following her down.

CHAPTER 18

Elander opened his eyes to a sky dotted with bright stars.

He breathed in deeply. Coughed. Rolled from his back to his side and pushed himself upright. There were bodies all around him—Laurent, and the two soldiers who had accompanied them—but he immediately noticed the one body that was missing.

"Casia?" Her name came out in a cough. He got unsteadily to his feet and searched through the darkness, finding nothing. He walked all the way to the far edge of the beach…

Only to come back to his starting point and find her waiting there.

Had she been here this entire time?

She stood waist deep in the lake. He had missed her at first because of the way her hair reflected the moonlight, shining as bright as the reflection of that heavenly body upon the dark waves—and because she wasn't moving, wasn't making a sound.

He stepped uncertainly toward the water, hesitating just

out of its reach as he called out to her. "Casia? What are you doing?"

She didn't reply.

Something is wrong.

The thought struck him like a knife to the chest, and he was torn between a desire to draw his sword and dive in after her. He called out to her again. This time she moved, lifting her head and appearing to study the moon for a long moment before she finally replied.

"I saw her in the water."

"What? Saw who?"

She tilted her face to the shore. "Rhea."

Her head twisted farther toward him, but her eyes never quite managed to meet his. There was something trailing down her chin, a stain branching over her throat.

Blood?

He scanned the water, searching for the source of it. For whatever new enemy he needed to fight. But all was silent, all was calm, and he had nothing to fight aside from his own racing pulse.

He reached out his hand, beckoning. "Come back to the shore."

"I can't."

"You can't?"

"She's still down there. She's…she's going to *drown*!" Her voice was growing frantic, and it drew him toward her despite his fear, despite his uncertainty, just as it always did.

It seems to be a recurring theme with us.

He was almost close enough to reach for her when she disappeared beneath the surface.

It happened so quickly, so smoothly, that it looked as though she'd stepped purposefully from a drop-off in the lakebed. The water was barely disturbed, still and clear enough that he could see several feet down.

Yet he couldn't see *her*.

He waited for some sign of movement.

None came.

Something in the back of his mind still whispered that this was not right, that there was something strange at work. Something much louder argued that it didn't matter—he couldn't let her sink any deeper.

The louder voice won.

He dove, twisting and spinning downward until he had moved beyond the wobbly beams of moonlight and had nothing to guide him aside from the pulse of his own magic calling out to Casia's.

That pulse was weaker than normal, suffocated by the realm's air and the increasing amount of water above him. But he kept swimming downward, and soon she floated just ahead of him, her body limp, edges faintly glowing in a way that made her appear ghost-like. It was Kantrum all over again.

Only with a different ending this time.

Because though he managed to reach her and gather her to his chest, same as he had in the River Drow, something had taken hold of her—something that ripped her violently from his grasp when he tried to push back toward the surface.

He caught her and tried again.

Useless, again.

No matter how many times he tried to pull her toward the surface, something always wrapped around her, always caught her, always pulled her away from him. The water churned more violently with every failed attempt, and within the murky clouds he saw tendrils of red—that *was* blood on her throat, and every time she was jerked away from him, it agitated her wound.

I'm hurting more than I'm helping.

He treaded water for an instant, that terrible thought pounding in his head until he felt something grab him—a hand circling his arm and yanking, trying to drag him away from Casia.

He fought it as hard as he could until a particularly violent bloom of blood filled the water all around him. Horror held him still for an instant—long enough for the hold on his arm to tighten just before *something* yanked him back into the cool night air.

He sank again almost immediately, but not before the chill brought a moment of clarity. As it settled over him, he realized he could see the bottom of the lake. It wasn't as deep as it had seemed. Casia was not in danger of sinking, she was simply floating, waiting, calmly calling him back down.

What was going on?

Had she been this calm the whole time?

No. She'd changed.

He realized it because the scene was *still* rearranging as he watched, the bottom of the lake moving up and down seemingly at will, the water clearing and darkening over and over, Casia shifting and fading from his sight—all of it changing in ways that made no natural sense. It *wasn't* natural. It was shifting to match his racing thoughts. To take advantage of his fears.

And on the edges of it all, tendrils of black bloomed and floated about like the blood in the water.

Shadow magic.

He only had to think it—to name it in his mind—and the

spell was broken in the next beat of his heart. A beat that was too fast, too frantic, and that made him suddenly aware of the immense pain in his chest. The burning in his lungs. Aware that Casia was not in the water beneath him—never had been—but that *he* had dove deeper into that water.

Too deep.

Every part of him felt spent, weary beyond reason. He wanted to sink back into the embrace of shadows and float peacefully downward, even though he knew the things they created were not real.

His head broke through the surface instead. He'd made no effort to swim upward—it was clear now that someone was dragging him from the bottom of the lake. He vaguely felt the arms wrapped around him, could hear the person's heaves for breath interspersed with increasingly agitated cursing.

He struggled against their hold, though he wasn't sure *why*. He didn't truly want to go back to the dark depths, yet he still felt partially under their spell, and wrong to think he could simply leave them behind.

Perhaps if he could just get back to them, he could make sense of everything...

He broke free of his captor and dove, only to be yanked back, forced again to the surface.

He freed himself again and was pulled back even more violently. Over and over it followed this pattern, until he broke through the surface one final time and found a fist closing in on his face before he could dive back down.

It struck hard enough to make his thoughts of depths and darkness rapidly disperse. He was aware of everything—painfully aware. And also bleeding from his nose, he realized, after gingerly touching a hand to his face.

"Are you awake now?"

Elander blinked and saw Zev standing beside him, clutching his coat and keeping him from diving with one hand while his other hand drew back into a fist.

"Are you? Or do I need to hit your stupid face again?"

Elander couldn't catch his breath enough to answer. He started to jerk free, and Zev swung again—but this time Elander caught his fist and shoved him away.

"I'm awake," he snarled.

"Sorry," Zev said, slowly lowering his fist. "I was just making sure." And he *did* look somewhat sorry—and confused. There were two more soldiers halfway between them and the shore, also looking thoroughly confused.

Elander took a step away from Zev. They stood for a moment, chest deep in the frigid lake, finding their balance.

"Shadow magic," Elander offered in explanation, washing away the blood on his face with a handful of water. "It...I nearly fell for it."

"No kidding. You nearly drowned—your face was an unsettling shade of blue when I first pulled you up."

Elander swallowed hard. His throbbing nose didn't seem too high a price, suddenly. "Thank you," he muttered.

"Never mind it—you can make up for it by helping her." He pointed to the shore, where Laurent was crouched beside a body that was surrounded by what appeared to be birds made of smoke. The smoky creatures swooped and dove over and over, dissipating and then reappearing just as quickly. Laurent held Shadowslayer outstretched above the still form, and it seemed to be keeping most of the creatures at bay. Rhea and Nessa watched from a cautious distance, while Silverfoot snapped and swatted at any twists of smoke that came too close to them.

Elander couldn't clearly see the body on the ground, but the pull on his heart and magic told him it was Casia, and he was wading toward the shore in the next breath, his dizziness and the pain in his nose forgotten.

Zev and the two soldiers caught up with him. "Nothing we've tried wakes her," said Zev. "No one but Laurent can get close to those shadowy...*things* around her without being overtaken by them."

"Those things are known as faral." He winced at the grim reminder of his old life and the company he once kept. "They used to answer to Tara. But now..."

"They answer to the Dark God instead?"

"If I had to guess."

He'd had more experience than most with Shadow magic and the creatures that wielded it—but breaking free of the spell for himself was one thing. Driving it away from others was different. Shadow magic was not a typical offensive attack; it wove its way into a target's very mind, and expelling it was often complicated and dangerous.

Laurent stepped aside and passed Shadowslayer over as he backed away. Sweat beaded his forehead and his breathing was slightly ragged from the effort of trying to resist the faral attacks.

Elander knelt beside Casia. He felt a surge of strength as he touched her shoulder—their magic meeting. It sparked enough power that he managed to create a shield around the two of them, driving back several of the farals. Some remained birds, perching on nearby trees and glaring through glowing white eyes, while others shifted into lanky beasts that crouched to watch them, their shadows bristling like fur standing on end.

Once they had room to breathe, he rolled Casia onto

her back. She was so limp that he braced himself for a terrible, corpse-like version of her, but her cheeks were flushed with life and still warm, as though she was only sleeping. But somehow this was worse—so alive, yet trapped, the only outward sign of the attack she was enduring the occasional darkness that surged over her skin like a short-lived bruise.

No matter how he shook her or called out to her, it was as Zev had told him: She couldn't seem to hear him or feel him. Her pulse raced wildly from the fear and anxiety the faral visions caused...

He wasn't going to be able to reach her through that relentless, pounding rhythm.

"Nessa," he called, his eyes on the faral looming over them. "We could use whatever magic you can come up with."

The Feather-kind didn't hesitate to rush to his side, swatting furiously at a swooping faral as she came. The creature only grew in size, larger wings of smoke unfurling with a sound like a crackling fire, before it dove at her once more.

She stood her ground. The air warmed for a burst from her magic—enough that the creature was dissuaded, and then it promptly decided she wasn't worth the effort. She had a tenaciousness about her, Elander had to admit, and he was starting to admire it.

She dropped to her knees on the other side of Casia, eyes lifting to Elander for direction.

"Focus it toward her. I need you to calm her down enough that she can feel my magic reaching for hers."

Nessa nodded and immediately went to work, clasping one of Casia's hands between both of hers and leaning closer.

It took longer than it should have, and came only in weak bursts at first—Casia had told him that Nessa feared her magic had started weakening in the past week, and he felt the proof of it now.

Nevertheless, Nessa persisted, and the secondhand energy of her magic eventually settled over him and made him feel more relaxed. He fought it off, trying to stay focused on Casia. But it proved too much after a moment. His eyes blinked shut. And when they reopened, it was to a beautiful sight.

Casia was awake.

He started to breathe a sigh of relief, to gather her up in his arms, but—

No.

This wasn't real. He saw them just before he fell entirely under their spell: the dark shadows creeping along the edges of his vision, trying to overtake the scene and shift it as they'd done in the lake.

Rather than pulling her out of the spell, he was being drawn into it alongside her.

He bowed his head and closed his eyes. His hand gripped Casia's arm, his focus entirely on the solid feel of her. On her *real* body, not whatever nightmare version of her this magic was trying to conjure up.

"Wake up, Casia."

"I can't."

She finally responded. He wasn't certain if it was her real voice or not, but he chanced another attempt to communicate. "Yes, you can."

"I can't. It's...something is holding me down. Something is wrong."

Don't open your eyes, he commanded himself, over and over. *None of it is real. Don't look at it. Don't think about it. Don't give it a foothold.*

Silence. Stillness. It stretched on for what felt like another lifetime between them. Then came her voice, barely a whisper—

"It's dark here, isn't it?"

He didn't answer. He fought to ignore the fear in her voice, to resist the urge he felt to sink closer and meet her in the darkness. He had sworn to always meet her there, to sit with her in the waves of fear and anxiety. But he couldn't do it this time. It would only lead to both of them drowning. So he did the most painful thing he could have done in that moment.

He *waited.*

He didn't move closer to her, even when her breathing started coming in gasps. Even when her body twisted and turned, writhing about in the clutches of the faral's magic. Even when she went still as a corpse once more, and her voice became pained and thin as she whispered, "It's getting darker."

Even then, he kept perfectly still with a hand on her shoulder, nothing more.

"Don't leave me here alone," she pleaded.

You aren't alone.

He wanted to shout it. But he stayed silent until a sound like a gurgling breath—the last desperate inhale before drowning—echoed in the quiet. He still didn't speak in response to it, but he did inhale deeper, as if he could breathe in enough for her, too, and his exhale was accompanied by power that rose without any conscious thought. The raw, unbridled power that had been granted to him by Solatis, that marked him as a guardian of her most precious creations. A guardian of *Casia.*

Somehow, he had to protect her.

A weary but full breath—mirroring his own—preceded her next words. "It's so dark."

Her voice had changed. Maybe he was imagining it. He almost *certainly* was imagining it. But there seemed to be a weight to it that hadn't been there before…

He blinked his eyes open.

She was right. It *was* dark. All around them were shadows and smoke, not just in the shape of crows and other beasts now, but of people and countless other things—gods and monsters that felt familiar, oppressive, and that pressed ever closer, no matter how hard he tried to make them go away. Their cold persisted, driving away the last of the soothing warmth Nessa had summoned.

It frightened him even more than his nightmares of watching Casia drown—this familiar, cold darkness that seemed to always be lingering on the edges of his life, waiting to call him back. Waiting for a moment of weakness. To remind him of all the times he'd hurt her, all the mistakes he'd made, all the moments he couldn't take back.

Casia's eyes were still closed. The dark waves no longer moved over her skin—this was not a shadow vision, he decided. He was looking at the real her, at her true mouth moving, trying to speak. He couldn't hear any words, but he could read her lips easily enough.

Dark.

It's so dark.

He didn't let his gaze linger on the shadows around them. He kept it on her.

"It *is* dark," he agreed quietly. "But the dawn is coming soon, I think." He brushed the sweat-soaked hair from her forehead, let his hand linger there as he closed his eyes once more. His body tingled with a different sort of warmth—not

Nessa's, but something much hotter. Violent, almost. The heat of a sun exploding into existence. And in the burning stillness that followed he finally felt it—answering magic.

Light met light, wave after wave of it building, spreading out and creating a barrier around them. It forced the faral to retreat farther, and soon he heard Casia coughing, struggling to sit up in the brightness before falling into his waiting arms.

Another surge of power shivered through him as he wrapped her more tightly to him. His eyes were still closed, and yet he could see it clearly in his mind—the barrier they had created expanding so that it surrounded more than just the two of them. He held her until it reached all the way to the lake and far beyond.

Then he opened his eyes.

He was aware of all of the people staring at them, of the slight glow that had overtaken those people and everything else, but he could only stare at her.

Casia stared back, and she had to swallow several times before she got words out. "You're bleeding."

A corner of his mouth inched upward. *Of all the things for her to worry about right now...*

Zev was there before Elander could speak, shoving his way between them. "It was for his own good."

"You hit him?"

"His own good," Zev repeated.

Casia gave him a withering look.

He grinned. "Though I did enjoy it, I won't lie."

"It was for the best," Elander admitted, the lingering feeling of gratitude making his voice slightly less hostile than usual toward the Fire-kind. "And hopefully someday I can repay the favor."

Casia arched a brow. "Of punching him, I assume you mean."

"Whatever's best for him," Elander said with a shrug.

She fixed him with a stern look at first, but then came a break in the gloom that had settled over them—she smiled back at him.

The sight of it chased away the last bits of darkness in his mind.

He pulled her to her feet. She briefly steadied herself against him before hurrying to her friends and embracing each of them in turn. She held on longest to Rhea, drawing back only after one of the faral struck the barrier they'd created.

It didn't break through, but it caused a strange sensation to ripple through Elander as the power of it was tested—and through Casia too, judging by how she jumped.

She walked the edges of that barrier, studying it. He joined her, as did Laurent. The shield was already fading under the realm's spell. But as weak as it was, it still seemed to be doing its job; most of the shadow creatures on the other side cowered at a distance, and the few who gathered enough courage to strike it were quickly driven back by flashes of light.

"What are those things?"

"Faral," Elander told her. "Creatures born of Shadow magic. They use that magic to dig into your mind and root out your deepest fears, which they then use against you."

Casia's gaze drifted back to Rhea as he spoke. Her body seemed to seize up for a moment, as though she'd forgotten how to breathe.

What had she seen while under the faral's spell?

He waited, but she didn't seem to want to talk about

those visions. He didn't make her. He didn't particularly want to discuss what he'd seen, either.

"It's over now," he said quietly. "And it was nothing except trickery."

She nodded, but her eyes never left Rhea. Her fingers dug into her palms, and her voice was tight, quiet, and full of anger when she spoke again. "Every time I think our enemies can't sink any lower, they manage to surprise me."

"Fear has long been a tool of evil," Laurent said. "Usually when they get desperate—so at least we know we're making them feel more desperate."

"They're mistaken if they think it's a tool that will work against me," she said, as much to herself as them. "I've been carrying on in spite of my fear for my entire life, and I don't plan to stop now."

OVER THE NEXT HOUR, Casia withdrew into her thoughts, moving along the created barrier and reinforcing it with a haunted but determined look on her face.

Elander let her be, joining Zev and the others as they worked to make sure everyone and everything they'd left Mistwilde with was accounted for. There was another route around the steep dunes he'd climbed over, it turned out, and they were able to lead the riders they'd left on the other side back to them.

Once they were all together, they went about setting up camp at the lake's edge, having decided not to risk anymore travel for the night. They soon had tents pitched and a campfire roaring, and all of them gathered around the warm blaze —aside from Casia, who remained on the edge of their campsite, speaking with Laurent and one of the Mistwilde soldiers.

No one around the fire felt much like talking. Not even Zev. He lasted no more than half an hour before he got to his feet and stretched.

"Well, I don't know about all of you," he said, "but *I'm* thoroughly traumatized enough for one evening, so I think I'm going to call it a night." He didn't wait for anyone to reply before he retired to the nearest tent.

He was quickly followed by the majority of the others, aside from the ones assigned to the first watch.

Elander had put up the tent he and Casia had shared countless times in the past, but he opted for carrying his bedroll close to the fire and sleeping under nothing but the sky instead. He had never liked the confines of tents when he was on edge like this. No tent was going to protect them from anything they faced; it would only slow down his counter attack. Casia felt the same, he knew, and so he gathered a second roll of blankets, preparing it for whenever she managed to settle her thoughts and find her way back to him.

Though he doubted either of them would get much sleep.

MORNING CAME, but Elander didn't realize it when he first opened his eyes—eyes that he had only closed an hour ago. The sky was still unusually dark, a foreboding, steely shade of grey, even after his sight fully adjusted. It always had a dark tint to it lately, it seemed like.

And it was getting darker by the day.

When he sat up fully, he spotted Casia nearly in the same place she'd been before he fell asleep, standing at the lake's edge with her arms folded around herself. She appeared to be studying the sky's reflection in the water.

He walked over to her.

"Do you think it's the unstable state of divine magic that's making the sky look so strange?" She didn't take her gaze from the reflection of it as she spoke. "All the shifting energies that Malaphar and everything else has caused? The constant cloudiness feels almost like a symptom of the greater sickness. And it keeps getting worse. Darker. Like he's determined to black out even the sun itself before our final battle."

Elander stood beside her for a moment, studying the same stretch of sky, feeling for those unstable energies and attempting to understand it all as much as she was.

He soon gave up on this and lowered his gaze, studying her instead. His faint-hearted yet fearless queen. His clarity, no matter how dark the skies became.

"I don't doubt he's trying," he told her. "But I don't think he can extinguish the sun."

She inhaled deeply, steeling herself before glancing his way. Her eyes held his for a moment, shimmering with unshed tears. She rapidly blinked them away and looked back to the water just as quickly.

"Did you sleep last night?" he asked.

She gave a barely noticeable shake of her head.

He hesitated. "We could go back to the palace if you need to. Regroup and refresh."

She only shook her head again. "I sent riders out at dawn to scout the trails on both the eastern and western sides of the lake. I go back with Crownkeeper or not at all. I'm..." Her fingers had started to tap against her side. She paused to focus on stilling them, clenching them into a fist that she tucked under her arm. "Tired," she finished. "But there will be no rest for me in that palace. Not while the sky looks like this and the shadows keep pressing in."

Elander nodded. He was worried about her, but he felt the same. They couldn't go back yet.

This feeling was reinforced—and the fate of the day sealed—only moments later, when the two riders Casia had sent came racing up the beach toward them.

The rider in front leapt from his saddle before his horse had come to a full stop. His face was bright red and his voice winded from the hard ride as he finally said the three words Elander had been waiting to hear for what felt like an eternity—

"She's close by."

CHAPTER 19

Several waterways ran away from the eastern side of the lake, each one they encountered more twisted than the last.

They followed the fourth branching river they came upon, trusting the scout's reported sighting of multiple riders traveling along the northern side of this river. The scout believed they had been members of Sarith's personal guard, judging by their armor and the dress of their horses.

It quickly proved the most promising trail they'd followed yet. Elander noted countless hoof prints and broken foliage that suggested many horses had recently passed this way. No birds sang. No creatures rooted among the leaves, nor scurried between the branches above. Even the wind had grown calmer, the breezes almost hesitant, as though frightened into silence.

"Sarith will be very familiar with this part of the realm," said one of the Mistwilde soldiers as they rode cautiously along. "There was once a sprawling residence on this side of the river—Mistedge. It was her family's home for a time, given to her father by King Talos. Unfortunately, that gift caused another crack in the already strained relationship between them, as Rumil—Sarith's father—believed his brother was trying to push him out of the family and away from the crown by building him such an elaborate home so far away from the central palace and the royal city." He lowered his voice before adding, "He wasn't entirely wrong."

Elander peered through the trees on either side of him, searching for signs of movement but still finding none. The path they trotted along grew increasingly overgrown. His skin crawled with warning, heart speeding up with every strange sound and shadow he noticed.

"Anwyn mentioned this place to me," Casia said. "When the disagreements between the brothers came to a head decades ago, Sarith's father apparently set fire to the main residence of Mistedge. There are no buildings still entirely intact, she told me."

"Correct," said the soldier. "But some of the magic that protected the grounds remains. So we should tread carefully."

"What kind of magic are we talking about?" asked Zev.

"It's hard to—"

Silverfoot cut the explanation off with a sharp bark. An instant later, the horse at the front of their party reared, nearly throwing its rider to the ground.

Elander jerked his horse to a stop alongside the others, watching as the ground before that rearing horse crumbled swiftly away, leaving a deep ravine.

Seconds later, the earth moved again, closing the wound and smoothing it over as though the gash had never been there at all.

They all stared.

Nobody moved.

Nobody spoke, until finally Rhea cleared her throat and said, "Silver sensed that coming—he was growling well before it happened."

"The horse obviously knew enough to stop in time as well," added Nessa.

"These woods are silent because the animals know better than to tread here," muttered Laurent. "So we'll follow their lead."

They did precisely this as they slowly continued along, following the growls of Silverfoot and the uneasy steps of their horses, pausing to throw stones at suspicious areas where those horses refused to trod. The stones triggered the spells as well as any movement did, and they managed to reveal several would-be death pits in this manner.

But there was more than shifting ground to contend with. The deeper they rode, the quieter and darker their surroundings became—a quiet darkness that seemed unnatural. Even the air itself was untrustworthy; they would walk through what appeared to be clear patches of forest only to feel the air shifting, sliding like gritty sand over their skin. It felt almost as if they had passed through Air-kind portals. Those portals never took them outside of the forest...

But Elander swore the trees and bushes around them shifted every time they passed through one of these unnatural air pockets.

After a few minutes of silently trotting along, the soldier continued, in a voice much quieter than before. "Rumil's father was one of the elves who first experimented with creating the unnatural crystals of magic that so many still use in the Kethran Empire. And Rumil himself was allegedly involved with even more of this questionable, fringe magic. Some say the fires that burned the Mistedge manor were, in truth, accidentally set—an experimental spell gone wrong."

They walked on, Casia moving to the front of the group as the first glimpses of something grand came into view—grey towers peeking through the evergreen trees. Her attention was so captivated by one of these towers, by a tattered banner still flying from its top, that she ignored her horse's frightened signals, urging him onward until it was almost too late.

Silverfoot's bark brought her back to her senses. She veered sharply aside and, with some effort, brought her spooked mount to a controlled stop.

Elander felt her heartbeat—her magic—speeding up right alongside his own, followed by her desperate attempts to settle it. She signaled to Nessa, who fired an arrow directly into the space her horse had nearly stepped into, revealing the trap awaiting them.

Unlike the ones they'd encountered thus far, this trap did not collapse the ground. It heaved it upward instead, launching earth and stones into a chaotic cloud that swirled menacingly for several moments, uprooting several trees before it settled. Their party scrambled backwards, narrowly avoiding the shower of rocks and limbs and dirt.

When the dust cleared, they finally saw it through the cleared trees: The main dwelling of Mistedge.

Much of it blended with the rocky hillside rising at its back, its towers made of the same stone and jutting about in a way that mimicked the wild landscape, which made it difficult to judge the true size of it.

"The ruins of Mistedge," their most-informative soldier announced, cautiously leading them closer.

Ruins was an appropriate enough description, though it still had an unmistakable grandness about it. The main section was wrapped in moss and littered with fallen branches and leaves, and parts of it had collapsed, while others still bore what looked like fire damage around their broken edges. But as they carefully made their way around the front of the building, the damage was less noticeable. The front of the building was faced in white rock, which stood out among the grey and the green, making the sheer size of it apparent—it stretched too wide for Elander to see the actual end of it.

They dismounted, secured the horses, and moved to search the interior for signs that someone had recently been through, or even camped within, what remained of the rooms.

"Stay together," Casia ordered—which wasn't difficult, as most of the rooms inside were expansive, and several were missing walls. They swept from edge to edge of the residence as a large group, avoiding more pockets of strange, unpredictable magic—wayward spells that split the ground, that breathed life into the overgrown plants and turned them hostile, that seared the air and made it difficult to breathe at times.

After a close call with a stone pillar that cracked and collapsed as they passed by—nearly bringing part of the roof down on top of them—Elander and Casia risked trying a bit of magic themselves; they worked together to wrap their party in a shield. His own power came eagerly, as if it knew precisely what was at stake in this desolate place—that this was not the time to ration his magic.

She's close by.

He couldn't explain how he knew this, he simply *did.*

Casia drew closer to him, as if she felt the same truth coursing through her as well. The closer she drew to him, the more powerful his magic became, surging with no more effort than breathing required. His senses seemed to heighten with her nearness too—so much so that he felt the next trap coming even before Silverfoot gave his customary warning bark.

He heard a tiny crack from above, spreading through a wooden beam supporting what was left of the ceiling. His gaze swept along that ceiling and he noticed a strange waviness to the air, like a sign of sweltering heat on a summer day. It engulfed the beam, splitting it in two, and he had a vision of it all falling, wood breaking and burying them—

He didn't think. He only reacted. He grabbed a fistful of Casia's coat and slung her out of harm's way just as the beam snapped and brought part of the roof clattering down. A second beam snapped to his left, and he narrowly avoided the deluge it triggered by half-jumping, half-stumbling backward.

He escaped the brunt of the falling wood and stones, but in the process he blindly passed through yet another strange pocket of air. He felt the same uncomfortable grittiness on his skin as before, and there was no mistaking the unnatural shifting that accompanied it this time. He blinked, and the lighting had changed. The walls had closed in. The roof was suddenly gone, there was a strange humming in his ears, a chill biting at the back of his neck...

He had been transported to somewhere else.

And he was alone.

His magic surged, reaching for Casia. No response. He felt nothing—not of her or anyone else. His magic still felt more powerful than usual, yet centered directly around him, unable to stretch far beyond where he stood. Something was pressing back at the edges, trapping it around him.

He gripped Caden's sword and started to walk, coming upon a room that was missing a significant portion of its ceiling. A second story was visible through the largest of the gaps, and it appeared to be mostly intact—he could even make out a few broken pieces of furniture. Beyond that, he saw the jagged silhouettes of distant trees through a fallen wall, as well as a dark grey sky peeking through a hole in the roof.

He still didn't see—or sense—Casia or the rest of their group.

He had started to turn back when a voice trailed down from somewhere above, icy and smooth, freezing him in place.

"I've finally caught something useful in my snares, it seems."

That voice.

Months' worth of smoldering, restless violence burned through Elander's blood at the sound of it. His hand went again to the grip of Caden's sword, and he lifted his gaze and spotted Sarith in the room above, lazily unfolding from one of the broken chairs and coming to sit upon a break in the floor, her legs dangling freely down toward him.

He kept his voice as chillingly calm as hers, refusing to take the bait of the mocking smile she greeted him with. "And what *usefulness* do you believe I'm going to provide you with?"

She studied her nails for a moment before replying. "That remains to be seen, I suppose. Why don't you start us off by telling me what brings you here, of all places?"

He considered not dignifying her with a response, but the

words slipped out of him in a growl, heavy and dark and cold as a grave. "We have unfinished business, you and I."

"We certainly do." She stood and stretched. "Though rest assured—I have been *trying* to finish our business since the moment you all left my side in Moreth. So I'm only too happy to see you here now. Though I can't imagine why you've come to this realm. Mistwilde is a bit out of the way, isn't it? Given all the other things you should be focusing on. The mortal realm is a bit of a *mess,* isn't it? Tragic, really."

"You know why we're here."

She smiled brighter, clearly not caring to deny the accusation.

"And we don't intend to stay long."

"*Really*? Because my sources tell me you've already been in this realm for a week—and time flies when the end of the world is at stake, you know."

He hesitated, unable to immediately shake the unease that rippled through him at her mention of *sources*. How many traitors were sneaking around within the palace of Mistwilde?

"Never mind how long it's been," he said darkly. "We'll deal with all our messes in due time."

"You think so?"

When he didn't reply to this, she laughed softly and then dropped, smooth and silent as a cat, to the floor he stood on.

"You follow her regardless of the hopelessness that surrounds her and her ambitions, don't you?" she asked, stalking closer. "Like some lovesick pet." Her laughter was louder this time, echoing in the suffocating space. "It's very endearing. In a *pathetic* sort of way."

He ignored the insult, instead focusing on discreetly

studying their surroundings, searching for signs of magic, noting the places where the floors and walls seemed weakest, along with the gleaming hilt of the weapon at Sarith's hip.

Crownkeeper?

"Pathetic..." Sarith continued, "because I think you know as well as I do that she is not ruthless enough for the role that's been thrust upon her. The Mistwilde king will not give her what she seeks, regardless of what you want to believe. He is an old, stubborn fool. And the things he possesses... such things must be *taken.* And I daresay your little queen does not possess the power to *take.* She thinks too much of what she could give, and she's blind to the true nature of this broken world and what it takes to survive it."

"Pathetic, you say..." Elander again refused to take her bait, responding in a perfectly calm tone. "And yet you were too afraid to face her."

"I was aiming for her," Sarith said, flatly. "You got in my way. So I'll deal with you first—but don't worry, she's next. And I have others keeping her company in the meantime."

Others?

His nerves sparked further to life, but he again kept calm, hiding his true concern. "Separating us because you realized, of course, that you would never win if you tried to face all of us at once. Coward."

She smiled.

"One-by-one, you think you can manage us, or mind-by-mind—because I assume the faral beasts were your idea as well."

"I do love the intimacy of Shadow magic," she said, shrugging. "And of one-on-one conversations such as this."

"Let's *talk,* then," he said, no longer able to keep his hand from reaching and pulling Caden's sword free of its sheath. "Just the two of us."

"I would love nothing more," she agreed, tossing the long braid of her dark hair behind her shoulder and lifting a hand. There was something pinched between the fingers of that hand, something that sparkled as it caught a weak beam of sunlight—the only beam of light filtering in through the broken skeleton of the manor and finding its way to them.

A magic crystal?

He could feel the power emanating from it. Could feel more unnatural power pressing all around, but it no longer felt suffocating. He was expanding beyond it, his senses still heightening, his own power swelling, lifting him into that most sacred form—the one fueled by the same oath that had carried him through lifetimes and led him back to Casia over and over again.

Protect her.

He had failed before.

He would not fail this time.

Without another word he swept forward, sword slicing toward the false elven queen.

Sarith moved as quickly as any elf, and then some—but she still only narrowly avoided being sliced across the middle.

A slight gasp escaped her at the closeness of the attack, but she recovered quickly, her sharp laughter filling the air as she danced away from him and tossed the crystal into the air. Its glittering became a burst of energy that screamed through the air and rattled the bits of broken manor all around them.

Suddenly Sarith was not alone.

One, two, three—Elander lost count of the number of soldiers pouring into the space, emerging seemingly from the air. Elven soldiers who moved with speed and grace far beyond that of humans, who wielded their blades with deadly precision and were relentless in their attacks.

It didn't matter. He maneuvered around their first strikes, parried their next, and then knocked them aside as if they were made of straw, his heightened speed greater than theirs, his strength enough to send them careening into far-off walls, one by one, as he cut a path back to Sarith.

She stood her ground even as he drew to within inches of her.

"So much for *intimacy*, I suppose," he said, glancing at the trail of dead soldiers behind him.

She only sneered at him and leapt back as he attacked, avoiding the swing of his sword by mere inches once again. She landed in a pile of debris. Knelt as if to catch her balance, but shot upright just as quickly and flung a broken slab of stone at him.

As he knocked it aside, she reached into her coat and withdrew another crystal, using it to shift their surroundings and summon more soldiers to her aid.

And again Elander cut them down and found his way back to her.

She stood her ground once more, though her legs faltered slightly this time, nearly collapsing beneath her as he pressed nearer.

"I'm here for you, not them," Elander said, backing her toward the nearest wall. "Drag this out as long as you like. It still ends the same way, I promise you."

Sarith stopped sneering at him. Her hand wrapped around the hilt at her hip and she swiftly withdrew the scourge-blade—that ancient weapon of Mistwilde.

Elander hesitated just long enough to study it.

There was a large emerald secured in its pommel, with wing-like symbols etched into the handle branching out from that centered gem. Both these things were symbols of the king—he'd seen them countless times now, in countless different forms, after so many visits to that stubborn old king.

So this was *Aluthol.* The so-called Crownkeeper.

He hadn't witnessed this weapon cutting into Casia's skin, but he knew it was the same whip. He swore he could sense the drops of her blood, of the magic in that blood, that still stained it. It sent more power roaring through him—so much power that he lost himself for a moment. He was moving, but he wasn't entirely sure *where* or *how.*

He only knew he wanted to kill the one responsible for spilling that blood.

When his awareness returned, he had her by the throat, her body lifted and pinned to the wall.

Her eyes were wide with panic.

Good.

It wasn't enough to simply end her. He wanted her to panic. He wanted her to feel fear, and despair, and sheer *agony* along with the pain up until her very last breath—every single damn feeling that she had inflicted upon Casia. He would repay it all tenfold.

A cold wind blew before he could lift his sword, followed swiftly by voices and footsteps; he had a feeling that whatever spell Sarith had used to separate him from the others was fading, leaving their battle open for anyone to intervene.

As soon as he suspected this, it happened as if on cue—movement behind him—and he couldn't be certain if they were his soldiers or Sarith's.

He sensed an arrow flying toward his back, forcing him to release Sarith and spin aside to avoid it.

Sarith dropped to her knees, coughing.

He shifted his attention to a new flood of soldiers. He no longer needed the sword he held. He was bristling with power, overflowing with it, the furious light breaking from his body in waves that turned nearly solid as they raced around the space, molding into the familiar shape of wolves that swallowed up every soldier that dared to approach him.

When he spun back to face Sarith, the pack spun as well, diving together and rising up into the form of a single beast that momentarily eclipsed his own body.

He *was* the beast, the beast was him, and there was no separating them as they stalked toward their prey.

Sarith's eyes were the only thing Elander saw among the waves of magic and light that had built between them, and only because they seemed to glow, turning brighter and brighter with her growing desperation and madness.

She swung her weapon over and over.

He avoided it again and again, stalking closer until she stumbled, and then he moved to strike—

Somehow, she managed another swing of her weapon as she fell, and this time she hit his side, wrapping the barbed whip around and dragging it across, digging in deeply enough that he felt it through the armor of magic that surrounded him.

It stayed lodged in him, even as his magic overtook it and sank in, making the weapon shake. Even then, Sarith held tightly, and the blade and its whip did not break apart as other weapons might have—it was elven-made, and made well enough that it withstood even the divine essence wrapped around Elander.

He finally grabbed the whip and ripped its barb free of his skin himself, ripping Sarith off her feet in the same motion. She tried to catch herself against the wall but failed, rolling down and crumpling into a heap on the floor.

He took a step toward her, but sharp pain shot through his side, bringing him to an abrupt stop and causing him to drop his sword. Blood pooled at his feet. *So much of it.* The wound was much deeper than he'd realized at first.

The light beast he'd summoned began to lose its shape.

More of Sarith's soldiers were closing in, while Sarith herself remained half-collapsed against the wall, arms braced behind her, chest heaving for breath. Her smile slowly returned as she watched the wolf around Elander breaking, the light scattering and shifting around them.

She staggered to her feet, laughing as she rose. "Did you *really* think such a beast could finish me off? I don't know what you truly are, what full powers you may possess—nor do I care. I have cut down kings, and I will cut down gods soon enough, and you are nothing more than an annoying insect that I simply need to crush. You end *here*."

She swung the scourge-blade with a renewed, mad strength.

Elander veered aside and caught the extending whip, avoiding the strike she'd aimed for his throat, but causing the barbed tip to wrap around and bite into the skin of his forearm instead. That barb sank deeply into him, sending more blood cascading down to join the rivers already winding around him.

He held tighter and jerked her toward him, ripping her off her feet.

She held just as tightly to the weapon and fell back, pulling the whip taut as she did, forcing it to dig deeper.

His teeth clenched and his breath left him in an automatic gasp—but he hardly noticed the pain that followed. Because in that moment he felt something far more powerful than any pain he'd ever experienced.

His eyes darted briefly upward.

And he smiled.

Sarith bared her teeth in a feral expression. "Why are you grinning, fool? Your god-like arrogance persists even now, doesn't it? You are outnumbered, your beast is *vanquished*—as you will soon be." She laughed again, breathier this time, as her mad stare focused once more on the scattered pieces of his light floating around him. "And yet you're *smiling*."

"Yes."

"*Yes?*"

"Because your eyes are on the wrong beast."

He lifted his gaze to the ceiling, and this time he let it linger there.

The false queen and all of her soldiers followed his lead, their eyes widening as they saw the figure standing in the room above them with a towering, tiger-like beast of light crouched and waiting at her side.

Elander released his hold on the whip. Sarith clumsily unraveled it and stumbled back, her hand fumbling to adjust her grip on the weapon's hilt as she turned and tried to take on a more ready stance.

It was already too late.

And Elander's only regret was that he was not in a position to see Sarith's face as Casia's tiger descended, bringing with it a furious storm of lightning, slashing its way through Sarith's remaining guards before leaping and wrapping its teeth and claws around her.

When Casia finally called the beast off, the soldiers were

all dead. The elven queen was on her back, her weapon lying uselessly on the ground, several feet away from her.

Casia dropped down to their level.

Sarith scrambled to sit upright as she came closer, words tripping from her mouth as the lightning beast prowled near to her once more. "How did you get here? How did you pass through our spells? And Nalia—where is Nalia?"

"She's dead," said Casia as she wiped a smudge of blood—presumably Nalia's—from her cheek. She withdrew her sword. Her tiger stalked back to her side, curling around her and opening its jaws wide as Casia added, "And you're next."

The declaration stirred the floundering bits of Elander's power back to life, swirling them together, pressing them again into a distinguishable shape. He picked up his fallen sword. The wolf finished reforming, only to break apart into a pack of light beasts once more—enough to partially surround Sarith's broken body.

Casia's beast followed a similar transformation, peeling apart until they numbered enough to form a circle with Elander's, enclosing their target in a blinding ring of light.

They stood on opposite sides of this ring, Sarith between them.

Casia's eyes found his, and he remembered their conversation from the Irithyl Palace.

You will have to beat me to it, he'd told her.

She was thinking the same thing—he could tell by the smirk flirting with her lips. And he could read the unspoken suggestion that flashed in her eyes a moment later.

Together, then?

He nodded.

Together.

His sword plunged into Sarith's back. Shadowslayer followed in the next breath, plunging into her chest. And as they withdrew their blades, the circle of beasts converged upon Sarith's form, devouring it, filling the space with light and drowning out the sound of her screams.

CHAPTER 20

It was nearly midnight when they returned to the palace in Irithyl.

Cas led the way up the winding staircase to the throne room, Crownkeeper in her hands, Elander and the others following closely behind her. She gave only a tired, pointed look to the guards by the door, and they hastily bowed and let her inside.

She didn't wait for them to announce her.

She announced herself as she stormed into the room, interrupting the conversation Talos was having with one of his attendants and causing him to nearly jump out of his throne.

She strode directly up to him and threw Crownkeeper at his feet, waiting until the clattering echo of steel upon marble had faded before she said, "Tomorrow morning, you will take me to the Antaeum Point that we *both* know exists deep inside this palace, and you will tell me everything you know about it. No more games between us. I will give you a few hours to prepare, to summon whatever servants and scholars you need to bring along for this. I'm going to take a bath in the meantime and wash the filth and memory of your niece from my skin."

He stared at her, eyes wide, lips parted but not speaking.

"Any objections?" Elander asked—though it was not so much a question as a challenge.

A challenge that Talos opted not to meet. He merely gave a single, solemn bow of his head before ordering the attendant he'd been speaking with to lead them away, to arrange for whatever they might need before morning.

Cas didn't wait for this attendant either; she was already halfway to the stairs before he caught up to them and started to bombard them with questions about food and clothing and other such comforts.

Once they reached the foyer at the bottom of the steps, Cas finally paused her march long enough to answer him, and then to turn to each of her friends in turn, taking in their faces.

They'd made it back.

They were all still here.

She breathed in deep, trying to settle the rush of anxious energy that had been driving her all day long. They had traveled at a rapid pace, driven by her eagerness, by her almost obsessive need to drop Crownkeeper at Talos's feet. Her fixation had blinded her to any exhaustion or pain that she or anyone else might have felt.

Now that it was done, she felt all her other fears and obsessions catching up and pressing in all at once, threatening to unbalance her.

"Tomorrow will be a long day," she told her friends, "we should rest."

They all agreed, but they still lingered around her until

Silverfoot gave a mighty yawn that triggered several more within their circle. They admitted exhaustion one after the other, and one by one they left, until only Cas and Elander remained.

Her eyes swept over his chest, his arm—the places she knew had been ripped apart by the blade she'd dropped in the throne room.

His coat covered most of the bloody evidence. But she could still see it in her mind as clearly as she could see the moments before it had happened, when she'd found herself separated from him and everyone else.

She'd been cornered by Nalia when she'd felt it—his power reaching out to her, pulling hers out. The same power that had kept her from drowning in the River Drow. It had lifted her sword and swung it with the power of a goddess, putting an end to those elven women who had haunted her nightmares for so long.

Her skin still tingled with the remnants of that power, a humming that grew more intense every time she looked at Elander.

All these hours later, it still hadn't settled.

"Come on," she told him, "we need to take care of your wounds before we go to sleep."

"They've more or less healed already, as I told you earlier." He gave her a small smile, shaking his head. "You really weren't listening to me, were you?"

She recalled it vaguely now—her asking to see his wounds, insisting they stop to tend to them, and him refusing to take the time to do it. Her obsession with returning to Irithyl had prevented her from arguing the matter too thoroughly.

But she insisted on it now. They ducked into a secluded

corner that afforded them more privacy, where he shrugged out of his coat and peeled aside the tattered cloth of his shirt, fully revealing the damage done to his side and forearm.

Cas braced herself for the worst as she drew closer to him. But he was right—the bleeding had clearly stopped long ago, and scars had started to form over even the deepest-looking gashes.

"Whatever power flows through me whenever I reach that guardian state…it seems to make my healing abilities similar to what they were as a god," he said. "Otherwise, I likely would have bled to death before we made it back to the city."

"It still needs to be properly cleaned and bandaged," she pointed out. Her fingers traced the edges of the largest mark. It looked painful—the scar bright red and angry—even if it was no longer open and bleeding.

He caught her wrist and stopped her wandering touch. His grip made her stomach flutter, turning that humming in her skin into more powerful vibrations.

So much power.

She settled it as best she could, somehow keeping her voice level as she said, "I know where we can go to take care of it."

He regarded her with a curious look.

"I told the king I intended to wash this mission from my body. And I had somewhere in mind."

She took his hand and pulled him along before he could protest, leading him through the palace, toward a spot that Anwyn had shown her days ago.

They came to a narrow hall lined with flickering wall sconces. At the end of it, the space flared dramatically outward into a room which housed dozens of natural pools rimmed in smooth stone, fed by underground springs that kept the turquoise waters warm enough to fill the air with steam.

She turned back to Elander, hesitating. "Water, I know. Too much of it, maybe?"

His face was impossible to read.

"We don't have to stay here long," she said. "But Anwyn told me that these pools have healing and rejuvenating powers. So I thought it might be wise to use their waters while we had a moment."

He didn't object, so Cas found a servant who led them down another hallway, through a set of wooden doors, and into a private chamber that featured several different pools of varying sizes, shapes, and depths. A staircase of stone led to even more pools above, and some of these higher pools cascaded down into the lower level, creating cascading walls, while the outermost basins were open to the outside, no ceiling between them and the heavens above.

The skies over Irithyl were not as clouded as they were on the edges of Mistwilde and in the mortal empire beyond; she could still see the stars here.

It felt like it had been ages since she'd last looked upon them.

She kept her eyes on their distant twinkling while they waited for the servant to return with towels and clean clothing. Even then, she only glanced back for a quick word of thanks before he left.

Her gaze immediately found the sky again as she partially undressed, kicking off her boots and leggings, stepping into the nearest pool and testing its warmth and alleged healing properties. She longed to wade deeper, to go to the pools on the very edge and float among the reflection of stars, to sink into them and forget about everything for a bit.

But she returned to Elander's side first, to where he'd taken a seat at the edge of a pool and put his feet in the water. She tugged insistently on his coat until he slipped it off, and pressed him further until he'd done the same with his tattered shirt. Then her focus shifted to the pile of towels the servant had left for them.

Elander didn't protest as she cleaned away the bit of dried blood he hadn't managed to wipe away himself. He stayed on the edge of the pool while she stood in the nearly waist-deep water before him, her hands working gently over his side, and then over his forearm.

And to her surprise, the beginnings of a smile soon twitched his lips.

"What is that look for?"

"You don't like blood. I don't like water. Yet here we are."

She absently smiled back, her focus mostly on examining the marred skin of his arm, fingers carefully avoiding the places that still looked tender. There weren't many of those places, thankfully; it looked like these scars had formed weeks ago rather than hours ago. But it was still difficult to *believe* this, even as she stared at it with her own eyes.

"We have to do what we have to do, don't we?" she said.

He didn't reply.

She kept working, and when she drew back minutes later, she found his eyes had closed. He looked peaceful, lost in thought, until her hand brushed his skin once more, which made him suck in a deep breath and shake his head.

"Are you okay?" she asked.

He nodded. "It's not pain. It's just...it's been a long day of trying to quiet this power you stir in me, that's all. The danger's passed for now, but my body is still very... *aware* of you. All of you."

She swallowed hard as another shiver of *awareness* tingled through her as well. "You too, hm?"

His eyes flashed open, and her heart skipped several beats at the powerful...*untamed* look he gave her. "Since the moment you returned to me in Mistedge," he told her.

She averted her gaze so she could stay focused on her task of squeezing out the cloth in her hands. "I thought this power we shared might settle, the more we used it."

"Nothing between us feels settled at the moment."

She agreed. She felt lightheaded, and it had nothing to do with the pleasant, disarming warmth of the water she stood in, and everything to do with the rough edge his voice had taken on.

Elander took the cloth from her hand, finished rinsing and wringing it out, and then gently brushed away something on her throat.

"I'm not sure what it says about me," he mused as he worked the cloth across the side of her face, "that I found it incredibly arousing, watching you wipe the blood of our enemies from your cheek earlier."

She gave him a teasing grin. "Probably that you're a twisted, questionable soul."

"Maybe so."

"But I'm not complaining, so long as you're *my* twisted, questionable soul."

His smile quirked, and then he mirrored her actions from moments ago, slipping off her clothing as she'd done with his, until his hands could roam freely over her skin. "Forever and always," he assured her.

Her eyes darted briefly toward the door, making sure the servant had closed it securely.

His fingers came to rest beneath her chin, shifting her gaze to his. His smile fell away as his eyes fixed on hers, their pale blue appearing darker against the bright pools all around them—dark and wild with a smoldering heat that built in the space between them, making the steaming water almost unbearably hot.

"Let me finish cleaning up," she whispered, "and then we can go somewhere else if you want. We could..."

He shook his head, fingers dragging toward her mouth as she spoke, tracing her bottom lip and causing a fluttering in her chest that made her words trail off.

"We can stay right where we are," he said.

She started to reply, but he slid down from the edge to meet her before she could, his arms wrapping her up and steadying her against him as he tilted his face toward hers.

"I can't wait another moment for this," he said, letting his lips brush over hers with the faintest bit of teasing pressure, "water be damned."

She forgot whatever she'd started to say.

They cast off what little remained of their clothing and then waded deeper together.

The water in their pool was a particularly milky shade of blue, and in the darkness, it hid everything under the surface. Perhaps because she couldn't see, Cas was overcome with the desire to touch, to draw closer to Elander and find the lines of his body among the warm waves of concealing water.

She traced all of him, scars and smoothness and corded muscle alike.

He was still at first, watching her with a slightly mesmerized smile on his lips. Then he caught her hand and guided it toward his stomach, then lower, and she took him in her grasp and stroked until his head tipped back and a soft curse slipped through his lips.

After a moment he composed himself and brought his gaze back to hers, leaning down to steal a few quick kisses while his fingertips glided once more over her skin. He had memorized her body, she was certain, yet he explored it as though it was the first time—with reverent hands that moved slowly, savoring every dip and curve before finally settling against her hips, his fingers digging in and curving her body toward his.

He pulled her closer. Nothing but water separated them now—and in places, not even that.

His hard length met the softness at her center, and a rush of power wrapped in need bloomed in her, making her feel slightly dizzy.

He steadied her again and then lifted her up, guiding her legs around his waist and supporting her thighs with his hands so she could reach his mouth more easily. Her arms hooked around his neck and locked tightly as she pressed her mouth to his. His hands moved along her thighs, taking a more secure grip and using it to press her harder to his body. All the most sensitive parts of her were crushed against the firm ridges of his muscles, held there by his inhuman strength.

She wrapped her legs more tightly around him. His kiss became hungrier, his grip tighter, and her dizziness was back —but she welcomed it. She floated blissfully in the waves of it, knowing he held her, knowing he wouldn't let her fall.

As they drew away from the kiss to catch their breath, she realized that he had lifted her completely out of the pool. Chills had erupted across her skin, and she shivered with sudden awareness. He noticed, and carried her toward a neighboring pool—one that rose slightly higher than the one they currently stood in—and placed her on the smooth edge of it.

Warm water cascaded down from this pool into the one below, washing over her and spiking heat that spread all the way to the tips of her fingers and toes. Her new position evened out their heights as well, allowing him to kiss her while he slipped one hand around the small of her back and the other pressed against her inner thigh.

She sighed with pleasure and gripped the stone around her more securely as he pushed her leg wider, pulling her center more fully into the flowing current of water. Another soft sound escaped her as he did, and it occurred to her that he hadn't brought her to this warm waterfall simply to drive away the chill on her skin. That water shifting between the pools, cascading around her, underneath her, between her thighs...

It was torment.

Delicious, wonderful torment.

An involuntary shudder went through her, and as his mouth was pressed against the curve of her shoulder, she felt the wicked smile he gave in response to it.

"You're enjoying that too much, I think," he teased.

She couldn't deny it. She was enjoying it so much she couldn't have spoken *to* deny it, even if she'd wanted to. And then he made it worse, or *better*—gods, she didn't know—as he worked his fingers alongside the water, touching and tapping, opening her to the warm current as it slipped and slid against her.

She drew one leg toward herself, curling away from him.

It felt too good to allow him to keep going—but not as good as it would feel to have *him*.

She wouldn't be sated by mere water and touch. This need that had been building all day, this magic shared between them...it had transcended even the oppressive magic of this realm and the weight of all their wars, and it would not be settled until she had him *completely*, until he was inside of her, one with her in flesh and spirit and every other possible way.

"We need a more shallow pool," she breathed.

Another hint of something wild flashed in his eyes at the suggestion. He offered his hand and helped her down from the ledge, then carried her to a neighboring pool. It was as deep as the last one they'd swam in, but rather than being surrounded by carved stone, it sloped gently toward a natural edge—a beach of fine sand. Elander left her in the water and went to gather their towels, spreading them along the sand, creating further cushioning before wading back to her.

She let him pull her out of the water and then down to her knees, but she resisted when he tried to lay her on her back, putting a hand upon his chest and pressing him down onto his back instead.

He arched a brow, resisting halfheartedly—it seemed they would never make it through a day without challenging each other at least once—but it took little more than the sight of her crawling over his body to win him over. He laid back and simply admired her as she straddled him, his hands stroking her sides before rising to her face, pushing her hair back and holding it out of her way as she brought her lips to his. Her kisses soon traveled lower, down over his throat and chest and stomach. He inhaled sharply as her mouth pressed just below his navel, and she smiled, fully prepared to pay him back for the wonderful agony he'd caused her a few moments ago.

She took him into her mouth, moving as slowly as the water at first, rising and falling as the pool lapped at their feet, pushed by a slight breeze.

As she began to move more quickly, more confidently, he curled partway up so his hands could press into her hair and hold it back for her once more—but he didn't last long in this position before a shiver overtook him and he dropped back to the sand, his hand pulling away from her hair and raking through his own.

"You're enjoying this too much, I think," Cas teased, drawing a cross between a laugh and a deep moan from his throat. He sat up again and his hand cradled her head, guiding it back down, sinking himself deeper into her throat.

"It's because you're entirely too damn good at it," he informed her when she came up for air a moment later.

He was fixated on her lips as he spoke, on the drops of himself that clung to them.

She felt heat building between them again, preparing to combust.

They both moved at once, crashing back together with a force that took her breath away. He was faster, and there was no resisting him this time—he was too strong, and the way he lifted her, spun her around, pinned her underneath him… she didn't *want* to resist him. She wanted him on top of her. She wanted the weight of him pressing her down, the length of him pushing into her, wanted to greedily take her fill of him until she could no longer think straight.

His fingers came first, quick and hard, testing her wetness and massaging, coaxing more of it out of her before he guided himself in with a powerful thrust that made her cry out—a cry that had been building for what felt like an eternity.

He drove deeper, lowering himself closer to her, his mouth paying tribute to her breasts and sucking their tips into hardened peaks. Another deep thrust forced a second cry from her lips, and he kissed a path up toward her ear, pausing to whisper, "That sound. That beautiful *sound.* I've been waiting to hear it all day."

His warm breath sent a trembling through her skin, making her voice hitch as she replied. "Make it worth the wait, then."

He rose enthusiastically to this challenge, wrapping his arms around her legs and pulling her harder against him while he pushed, penetrating so deeply that when her mouth fell open this time, no actual sound came out—she could scarcely breathe, much less cry out.

Her back arched. Her hands went to the sand on either side of her as Elander guided her legs farther apart, and her fingers dug into the grittiness as he moved more furiously against her.

Her eyes had closed at some point. She saw pinpricks of light in the dark—like the stars she'd been coveting earlier, only much closer. They lingered even as her eyes blinked open, and she was no longer thinking of that night sky, but only of the sky she'd imagined when she had first caught Elander's gaze in this lifetime...of all the times she had lost herself in that particular expanse of blue.

She would never tire of losing herself in it.

And she was slipping once more into it now, oblivious to everything except the way he was watching her, the way he moved against her, giving more and more of himself until he reached the very edge of his restraint.

She met him at that edge, her hands abandoning the sand as he came. Reaching for him, clutching his back, holding tightly to feel the release rippling through his muscles. It shivered through her as well—the final push she needed to let go and join him, letting the last of her control fall away.

Several moments later, they sank back toward reality together. He collapsed against her, rolling slightly to one side so his full weight didn't crush her. They didn't speak, only stayed in this position, wrapped up in the calm and clarity of after, perfectly satisfied for a few blissful minutes.

He moved before she did, rising with a content sigh and wading back into the pool. She followed, her head still spinning, toes still tingling.

She wandered toward the ledge of the pool, a shimmering catching her eye. Piled along that ledge were smooth stones of various colors and shapes. She picked one up and absently ran her fingers over it. There were four distinct splashes of white upon its face, which made her think of the jewels in the sacred stone—the Heart of the Sun—embedded in her sword.

She clutched it against her chest, not willing to fully go back to thoughts of swords just yet. Her gaze circled the space around them instead, watching the steam rising, and she moved nearer to a waterfall spilling from a pool above, cupping her hand underneath it and letting the water collect and trail through her fingers.

"It's so peaceful here," she said after a moment.

"It is," Elander agreed, reaching for the stone. He studied it as she had, and she wondered if he was thinking about all it resembled, too.

Then he lifted it into the falling water beside her, angling it so it made that water shoot directly into her face.

Cas let out a squeal and retaliated by swiping her arm through the pool, hurling a wave back at him. He ducked to avoid it, disappearing under the surface.

She tried to snatch him and drag him back, but he was too quick; he was already behind her somehow, and he grabbed her around the middle as he popped back up, dragging her backwards—directly under that falling water.

She slipped loose and swept under the surface, sending a massive wall of water rushing at him when she came back up for air.

He returned the fire, and they were oblivious to the rest of the world for several minutes afterward, lost in their attempts to out-splash the other one until he caught her and wrapped her in a crushing hug, pinning her arms to her sides.

She couldn't put up a proper fight any longer—she was too busy laughing.

Laughing.

Gods, when was the last time she'd truly laughed like this? So hard that her sides hurt and her lungs burned?

She couldn't remember.

He hugged her more tightly. "Do you surrender?"

"Are you going to try and drown me under that waterfall again if I say no?"

"Maybe."

"Then I suppose I do," she laughed. Struggling against his strength was useless anyway. "For now."

He loosened his hold but kept his arms draped around her. She settled back against his chest, eyes closing as she focused on the feel of his heart beating against her.

When he finally let her go, she found herself drawn back to the waterfall. She stood beneath it on purpose this time, head tilted back, letting the warm water fall upon her forehead and down through her hair, washing the last traces of the week's horrors from it.

She was intimately aware of Elander watching her, and a slight smile curved her lips. "Are you thinking of trying to drown me again?"

He chuckled. "No."

"What is it, then?"

"I was just thinking of what the elves claim about these pools."

She gave him a curious look and moved out of the falling water, squeezing it from her hair as she stepped closer to him.

"This does feel like healing water," he said.

Her smile brightened. "Yes," she agreed, "it does."

CHAPTER 21

Early the next morning, Cas and her friends gathered in a small room tucked away in a dark corner of the palace, its features bland and unremarkable save for the black door centered in its back wall, which had all manner of different symbols carved into it. At a glance, they resembled many of the divine marks she was familiar with, but upon closer inspection Cas could see that most of them had been altered in small—but significant—ways.

Through this door, the Antaeum Point awaited.

Two Mistwilde elves joined them—Anwyn, as well as an older male who introduced himself as Kylian, a Master Keeper of Records and Laws of the Realm.

Kylian looked considerably less enthusiastic than Anwyn about what lay ahead of them.

The king himself would not accompany them for this task; it would be a dark journey into the very depths of the palace, the path narrow, tight, and potentially full of wayward pockets of magic—not unlike the unpredictable magic they'd contended with in Mistedge. This was not an oft-traveled path, aside from a few well-trained scholars, and dangerous things festered in unused spaces. Kylian was one of those well-trained travelers, but he made no guarantees regarding their safety or return.

Cas herself was prepared for anything at this point, her blood still racing from the events of the day before. But she was worried about others in their group—a concern that only heightened when she felt Silverfoot brush against her leg. She took Rhea's arm and pulled her aside, but she only managed to voice a few syllables of concern before she was cut off.

"We'll manage," Rhea insisted.

"Are you sure?"

"I once promised you I would follow you to the end of the world, didn't I? And now we're off to the center of it, it seems. Makes no difference to me and Silver."

"I just—"

"Leave it at that, love," Rhea said, gently but firmly. She reminded Cas of Asra whenever she took on that tone, and her heart clenched, squeezing away the words of protest she'd started to say. They were the only two people who had ever managed to quiet her arguments so completely.

"You criticize my stubbornness," mused Cas, "but I'm growing convinced that at least some of it was inherited directly from you."

Rhea smiled. "You're welcome."

So they all went together, as promised, with Kylian leading the way and Anwyn bringing up the rear.

After descending at least ten levels of winding staircases, they came upon a second black door. Kylian pressed his palm to a strange symbol of interconnected circles in the center, and it slowly swung open.

"Only an elf from Mistwilde can open this," he informed them, "and only certain bloodlines, at that. If anybody else tried it, they would meet a very painful end." His gaze lifted to the ceiling, where Cas thought she saw...*something* moving. She felt an uncomfortable pulling on her skin—a pull that she had learned to associate with backwards elven magic.

Anwyn huffed at the dramatic tone of Kylian's voice, waving their attention away from the questionable thing above and urging them through the doorway that led below.

Cas and the others pressed closer to her as she guided them into a narrow passage that sloped steeply downward, following a trickling stream filled with stones glowing with a soft blue light.

The air grew colder as they walked. The water flowed more and more sluggishly, frost appearing along its edges, creeping farther toward the center and growing thicker until it was solid ice they were descending alongside. The stones—only just visible through the increasingly deep ice—provided no more light at this point. There were torches spaced periodically along their walk, however, and Kylian removed one and carried it along with them. But its light seemed small and overwhelmed by the growing dark, its flame flickering precariously as though it was one ill breath away from going out and leaving them in total blackness.

Cas tried to think of brighter things.

She ended up picturing the last Antaeum Point's location —the island off the northern shores of Kethra. Even though the memories of that island were haunting and confusing, Cas still would have preferred visiting it as opposed to treading deeper into this darkness. And the goddess she had met there...the memory of her voice and her light filled Cas with the warmth she needed to keep moving.

She held tightly to those memories as she walked on, drawing courage from them and whispering that same encouragement to her friends. Both Zev and Nessa summoned what magic they could manage after her rallying efforts, providing more comfort and warmth—though not much.

Hopelessness threatened, but before it could overwhelm them, they reached a more expansive space, and the air felt somehow less oppressive. Cas spotted what looked like lights of some kind; crystals affixed to the stone wall and wrapped in iron cages. Kylian put his torch beneath the one closest to them, whispering a word in the ancient Mistwilde language as he did.

Instantly, the crystal ignited, as did more lights along the length of the wall, stretching farther than they could see.

They followed the trail of blazing light into a vast underground cavern.

Ice coated most surfaces here, spikes of it hanging down from the ceiling, patches of it glistening on the grey walls, bits of frost crunching beneath their boots. In the middle of it all, a frozen lake awaited them.

And hovering above this lake of ice was a spinning cloud of darkness.

It spun so tightly, so quickly, that at times it appeared to be a solid thing, an actual orb they might have been able to pluck from the air if it had been smaller. But it was far from small; it was the size of a modest house, and its energy extended even beyond that, swaths of dark blue and purple waving like ribbons toward the outer perimeters of the lake.

The very center of it was much paler in comparison to its edges—a light shade of lavender, save for a spot of black in the very center, which made Cas think of an eye.

"I've never gotten this close to it," Anwyn said, voice hushed with awe.

"And we would be wise to not get any closer," Kylian said, pointedly.

But Cas's feet were already moving, bringing her toward the lake. The energy whipping around the point felt like it was pulling her, subtly sloping the very ground she stood upon and trying to tip her toward it.

"You can't tell her not to do things," she heard Zev muttering to their guides. "Because it will only make her want to do it, nine out of ten times."

She hesitated long enough to glance back and say, "I didn't come all this way just to *look* at it. I need to examine it more closely at least."

Zev took a deep, bracing breath and shook his head, but he followed her as she crept closer, as did the rest of her friends.

Anwyn soon followed them, too. Even Kylian gave in after a moment, jogging after them—though only so he could cut swiftly into their path and order them to a stop before they got within reach of the point's waving arms of energy.

Cas didn't argue against these orders; Shadowslayer had started to tremble against her hip, distracting her. She withdrew it and found the symbols upon its blade pulsing, flashing like a warning.

Trying to protect her?

She pressed her palm against the glowing symbols on the blade. Her mind focused on one symbol in particular—the symbol of Sky—until a few lines of turquoise energy peeled free and circled around her. They were barely noticeable with all the competing energies they had to contend with, and she doubted they would shield her from much. But Shadowslayer had stopped shaking for the time being.

Kylian was staring at that blade with a curious expression in his amber colored eyes, fingers thoughtfully rubbing his sharp chin.

Cas kept the conversation on the Antaeum Point, rolling the unease from her neck and shoulders and then taking another step toward the swirling mass as she asked, "How was this made?"

Kylian studied Shadowslayer for a moment longer before lifting his gaze back to the Point. "Through many sacrifices of divine-blessed mortals, to start with."

Nessa recoiled. "How wonderfully barbaric."

"They were *willing* sacrifices," Kylian continued, a bit testily. "From mortals who had been blessed with the Dark God's power, but who came to realize the sort of devastation that such power could wield—and thus sought a way to create a safeguard against it."

"Or were convinced by our ancestors that this was what they needed to do," Anwyn put in.

"Either way," Kylian continued, not bothering to warm the iciness in his voice now, "it was created using their divine-blessed blood as a base of the spell. The ones who created it were able to extract the Dark One's power from this blood and use it to finish tying this Point to him. Ties that were reinforced by all manner of complicated rituals performed by the ancient ones of our kind..."

"Ancient ones who detested the gods to the point of insanity," Anwyn added.

Kylian's voice turned solemn. "Yes. They poured all of

that malice and insanity—everything they could muster—into creating this Point they hoped might continue to fester, becoming a vulnerability great enough to one day cause the downfall of the ones who had caused *their* downfall."

"Lucky for us," Zev said.

"Yes…but *unluckily* for you, the ones who created it did not leave proper instructions for how to finish the job. It has swirled on and on for centuries now, presumably tightening its bond with that Dark God, but doing nothing to temper him. Our past leaders have tried outright destroying it, even, as some scholars believe this would create a counterflow of power that would destabilize, if not outright obliterate, the Chaosbringer."

Cas's skin shivered with possibility.

"But obviously that destruction hasn't been successful," muttered Zev.

Kylian shook his head. "I personally don't believe a fool-proof method of destroying the Point—or otherwise undoing or sealing off that god's power—exists. Our king doesn't believe in it either." His gaze slid over Cas, and he stopped just short of a disdainful sniff. "But you were insistent, I'm told. And so here we are, because you were unwilling to trust the wisdom of a king many decades your senior…"

Cas glared back at him. "Forgive me, but I've come to realize that the wisdom of elves is rarely firsthand. They're very good at hiding behind their thrones and books and pretending to understand the world, but if one wants something actually done, they're better off *insisting* on doing it themselves."

Kylian looked too flustered to speak for a moment—Cas

suspected people rarely spoke back to this pompous creature.

Anwyn fidgeted with the emerald beads around her neck and avoided looking at either of them.

Laurent cleared his throat. "We have a Blood crystal with more information on the matter of dealing with this Point, don't we?" he reminded them.

"Yes," Cas said, frowning, "but the usual spell to activate it didn't work when I tried—because of the wards against divine magic in this realm, I suspect."

"Or because the one who created that crystal is now gone," Elander added quietly, "and the spell is waning as a result." He avoided Cas's gaze, obviously not willing to speculate further about the matter of Caden and those special crystals he'd created for them. They weren't the same as crystals she'd used in the past; she'd yet to fully make sense of them and their magic, and maybe never would.

"We're already here now," Zev pointed out, "so Cas is right, as much as it pains me to say that. We should at least try to examine it closer. Maybe run an experiment of our own."

Kylian looked unsettled by the idea, but he still had not recovered enough to argue against it.

Anwyn shifted her weight nervously from foot to foot, excitement brightening her features.

Rhea's eyes were closed. She kept very still as Silverfoot cautiously darted around the outskirts of the Point and its power, her focus obviously on the thoughts and images the fox was sending her way. "Using an opposite power seems like a possibility," she ventured after a moment. "Something born of the Sun Goddess should be able to negate this, shouldn't it?"

"Others have tried that in the past, of course," said Kylian.

Cas tapped her fingers anxiously against the handle of her sword. "But how *much* of that divine power did they try?"

Kylian didn't have an answer for this.

"Not as much as Casia and Elander possess, I'm sure," said Laurent.

Kylian still did not reply, and Cas did not hesitate long enough for him to find an argument.

"We have to start somewhere," she said, sheathing her sword but keeping her hand clenched around its pommel as she stepped closer to the spinning blackness. Elander followed cautiously behind her, his hand pressing against her back every time she lost her nerve and started to hesitate.

Stepping onto the iced-over lake was like walking headlong into a blizzard. The cold grew increasingly more biting, the energy whipped at their bodies like blistering wind, and the howl of power was shrill and haunting, making Cas want to press her hands to her ears.

They were nearly close enough to reach out and touch the outermost bits of swirling energy when Kylian found his voice, shouting to be heard over the raging, wailing power. "The king would not approve of this!"

He started toward them, but Anwyn caught his arm and held him back. The elven woman's gaze locked on Cas, that combination of fear and exhilaration still shining in them. She urged Cas on with a nod of her head.

Cas nodded back, and her attention shifted to Elander. They communicated without the need for words, their magic rising in unison, fighting against the whips of the Point's energy that struck out and tried to push them back. The ropes of Sky-kind power Cas had summoned earlier thickened, expanding into a true shield that was further bolstered by Elander's power.

How many times had they used this power to chase away the darkness?

This is just another chance to do the same thing.

They kept moving, attempting to create a shield that would fully cover not themselves, but the mass of energy before them. Contain it—that was their first objective, and then they might crush it into something smaller, something they could stand a chance of controlling or even eradicating completely.

But every time they came close to covering it, a bolt of dark energy would sneak free, starting a chain reaction that rose into a storm that quickly overwhelmed them and their magic.

A particularly violent tempest of resistance sent Cas stumbling backward.

Elander only just managed to catch her before she crash landed painfully against the ice. She watched in terror as dark energy kept coming toward her, branching around them and viciously striking the ice beneath her. She expected the dark power to cut straight through and drop them into frigid water underneath.

But this frozen water seemed to be a continuation of the strange power that filled the space—it didn't chip or flake the way normal ice would have.

Cautiously, scarcely daring to breathe, they retreated to the edge of the lake. Cas clenched and unclenched her hands, focusing on breathing in time with the movements, staving off the panic trying to rise in her. Elander's eyes were still on the Point, and his expression was grim—a rare look of defeat on his normally confident face.

"You will have to come up with a better plan," Kylian said, a touch of smugness in his tone. He clearly did not expect them to try again. Just as his king had not expected Cas to truly go after that sword he'd asked for.

Time to prove a second elf wrong.

Shadowslayer was shining again, so powerfully it couldn't be contained within its sheath. The light seeped out and was drawn to her, setting her entire body aglow. It made her feel warm. Powerful. *Invincible.*

She unsheathed the sword, and the dark tendrils of the Point visibly pulled back. Curious, she swung a test swipe toward the center of the lake.

The tendrils curled even more drastically away from her.

Flinching already...and she had not even attempted to draw any of her true power out yet.

Elander read the plan forming in her mind, again without her saying a word. Concern knitted his brows together, but he didn't move to stop her. "Be careful," he whispered.

She agreed, taking a deep breath.

She lifted Shadowslayer and marched forward once more, focusing on the light that wrapped around the blade, intertwining it with her own and guiding the power into a tapered end—a spectral extension of the blade itself. Once it felt solid and steady, she held tightly to the physical sword but stabbed the energy forward, piercing the Point with the sharp extension of light.

The initial impact knocked her to her knees, but she managed to stay upright, to hold steady despite the waves of darkness shedding from the Point and rolling around her.

Elander continued to summon as well, sending waves of protective magic that wrapped around her, shielding her from the worst of the breaking darkness.

As more and more of the Point's layers peeled away, she could see what she thought was the center of it—an orb of purple that shifted between all the colors of a bruise as it spun, suspended in the air. She could *feel* it, pulling her—and all magic—toward it. And she heard…*voices.* Quiet voices that she didn't understand, though she thought she recognized the languages they were speaking in. Fire, Death, Ice, Serpent-kind… The languages of the Dark Court.

She thought of Kylian's story of the blood sacrificed at the altar of this Point, and she wondered if the whispers she heard were echoes of the ones who'd given that blood.

The possibility was unsettling, but she drove it away with the same mantra as before: *The dark yields to the light. We've driven away the darkness countless times in the past. We can do it again.*

She squeezed her sword tighter, willing more of its power and her own to the surface. Each squeeze brought another wave surging forward, until finally…

The darkness swirling around her stopped.

Everything seemed to stop, and then to dissipate, until only she and the orb in the Point's center remained, and the orb no longer spun—it had become a solid shade of crimson.

She swung her sword toward it, sending forth a spear of light that struck the orb and broke into a net of electricity, encircling it. The orb absorbed more and more of this lightning until it began to reflect this power instead of darkness, its surface taking on the streaked blues and glowing greys of a sky after a storm. Everything somehow grew more silent, more still…

Then came a sound like an axe splitting a log.

There was no warning beyond this—it went from peaceful to chaotic in a blink as a new, terrible energy exploded outward, striking Cas's sword and throwing her onto her back. She crashed against the ground and Shadowslayer flew from her grasp, hitting the ice and spinning to a stop several dozen feet away.

She scrambled to pick it up, but an enormous amount of dark energy overwhelmed her as soon as she reached for it, knocking her backward with even more violence than the first explosion.

She lay motionless on the ground for several moments before the feeling came back to her arms and legs.

She crawled once more to her sword, but she didn't touch it this time.

She simply stared.

Its blade swirled with dark clouds. The Heart of the Sun —which usually glowed so brilliantly within its pommel— pulsed with the same darkness.

And all the jewels upon the Heart's face had cracked.

CHAPTER 22

Cas couldn't breathe.

This isn't happening.

Desperation overtook her, sending her crawling once more for her blade. It was moving now, wrapped in shadows that were shaking it, clanging it against the ice.

Elander grabbed her and pulled her away before she could touch it. She struggled against his hold, but he was relentless, dragging her until they were well out of reach of the weapon and any of the tendrils of darkness it released into the air.

She fell back against him, stomach twisting, nearly doubling over from the painful urge she felt to vomit. Her friends rushed to her side, gathering between her and the cursed blade, trying to make sense of what had happened. They blocked her view of Shadowslayer, but she could still *feel* it.

And it felt as though she herself lay upon the ice, shivering and fighting for control among the dark energies engulfing it.

When the sound of cracking metal rang sharp in the air, she felt that too—as if something inside of herself had cracked.

A terrible, heavy silence followed this cracking sound. So, so *heavy*, like she was suffocating under a deep pile of snow.

She squirmed out of Elander's grasp. But this was as far as she made it. Her arm stayed braced against him as she rose unsteadily to her feet, and her gaze was blurry, focused only in the direction of the blade—and not truly focusing even on that—so she didn't realize what was happening in the room around her.

Not until she heard Nessa say, "The Point is...*gone*."

They all turned and faced the center of the lake once more.

The air still looked wavy and unsettled above the ice, but that distortion had no definite shape. The floating orb was gone, as were all the ribbons of power that had swirled in and around it.

Meanwhile, a new energy continued to rage within Shadowslayer's blade. As dark as it had been above the lake—twisting currents of deep blue and purple, with a black dot in the very center of it, opening and closing like an eye...

"It isn't gone," Cas breathed in realization. "It's *moved*."

There was no other explanation—not that anyone could come up with just then.

The Point had somehow been transferred into her weapon.

And that dark point had swallowed up all of the light the sword usually carried, which had to be the reason for the awful sickness churning through Cas—the reason she couldn't breathe. Because her power, intertwined so tightly with that sword, was being choked. Suffocated.

But at least the darkness was contained.

For now.

Kylian stared at her without speaking for a long moment. His voice was tight with fear and disbelief when he finally demanded, "What kind of sword is this?"

Laurent answered when Cas didn't manage to—the calm among the chaos, as usual. "One created by the Goddess of Life herself," he said. "The goddess with the original gift of foresight…I wonder if she ultimately intended for it to be used this way?"

"Who knows," said Zev, slowly approaching the fallen blade and crouching beside it.

It was settling as the seconds passed. It no longer shivered, and the darkness it had absorbed seemed to be fully contained within the blade, with no stray bits of it dancing in the air around it anymore.

Zev cautiously withdrew the knife at his boot and stretched it toward Shadowslayer's hilt, as if to flip it over and better inspect it.

Silverfoot barked, making Zev jump and snatch his weapon back. His sister was upon him a moment later, grabbing the collar of his shirt and pulling him farther away.

"I feel like this should go without saying," Rhea hissed, "but let's *not* poke the potentially deadly, cursed thing with a knife."

"Your idiotic curiosity will be the death of all of us before the end," Laurent grumbled.

"In my defense," said Zev, "Cas poked it first."

Cas finally got her legs to move. She circled the blade, keeping it at an arm's length. She didn't reach for it as Zev had, though she couldn't deny that she *wanted* to. "We can't just leave it here."

No one—not even Elander, who was nearly as connected to the sword as she was—seemed to have an answer for *what next*?

It was Kylian who eventually broke the uneasy silence once more. "We'll need more help to deal with this," he muttered, ushering the group of them off the ice and back toward the tunnel they'd taken down to the Point.

Cas remained too stunned to argue or come up with a better plan, so she numbly followed the others as they funneled back toward the palace.

The glow of the torch Kylian carried this time seemed even weaker than before. Likely only her imagination, but knowing that still didn't stop her fears from growing in the dark. So much of her magic had been guided and formed with the help of her sword...

How much magic could she manage without it?

AFTER HOURS OF DELIBERATION, Shadowslayer remained below, while Cas and her friends moved nervously among the palace above.

The king and his council would not give her sword back. It was the new Antaeum Point, that council argued, and they were the keepers of the Point—not her. She would not be allowed to retrieve it until they had come up with a plan, or at least a better understanding of what had happened.

Cas disagreed with their decision.

Vehemently.

But she was also outnumbered—a fact that she was well

aware of, but that the elves repeatedly reminded her about. After the third meeting on the matter, she grew tired of talking in circles and stomped from the king's study without looking back.

She stormed without any real direction through the halls, eventually making her way up to a rooftop terrace that overlooked a marshy stretch of land on the palace's southern side. She stood in the chill air, watching the sun slipping lower, wishing she'd grabbed a coat while wondering what was happening beyond the horizon.

The skies remained clear here, but she knew they were much darker in the places she couldn't see.

What had become of Soryn? Of Ciridan? Of her brother, her followers, and all the divine beings who had sworn to help her? They were overdue for a meeting with those divine allies.

Their business here was taking too long, and now it seemed destined to take *longer*, and the thought made her almost as sick as losing her sword.

Elander found her a few minutes later. He didn't speak right away, merely leaned against the railing and watched a white bird swooping in and out of the sun-splashed swampiness below them.

Her magic stirred as it always did with his arrival, which normally brought *good* feelings along with it. But now it made her want to try reaching out to her sword, too—even though she knew its magic wouldn't reach back—and she was left with nothing but a hollow sensation in the pit of her stomach.

She exhaled a long, shuddering breath. "I feel as if I've lost a limb."

Elander stepped closer, reaching and trailing his hands up

and down her arms, letting his eyes travel the length of her body. "They all seem intact to me."

"You're too calm about this."

He chuckled. "I'm not calm. But the *elves* are calm—even when they shouldn't be. So I am simply mirroring their culture for the sake of blending in and keeping their favor."

She inhaled deeply, preparing another argument. But she couldn't come up with one, so she gave him a wry smile instead. "It's so annoying when you remain rational despite my best attempts to panic."

He returned the smile, wrapping her in a loose, one-armed embrace and kissing the top of her head. She leaned into him, closing her eyes for a moment, searching for balance.

"Well," she sighed after a few moments, "I can be a queen without a sword, I suppose."

He glanced down at her, tightening his hold around her waist. "You? Yes. I don't think there even needs to be a crown in your case; it's implied at this point."

She gave him a more earnest smile, which lasted until she glanced once more toward the distant horizon.

"Something tells me you've already started plotting how to save the world without a sword, anyway," Elander added. "So I'm not overly concerned."

Her cheeks warmed a bit at the look he gave her—admiring and expectant. And he was right, of course.

He knew her entirely too well.

"I was planning to go back to the mortal realm this evening," she admitted, slipping out of his hold and moving to the edge of the roof. "At least to the borderlands. We'll see if the Blood crystal Varen gave me works more clearly there, and gather what news we can of the outside world. Let the elves debate the sword and the Point until they're mad with indecision—I won't stand around here while they do it. We have too many other things to do."

He nodded in agreement, and a solemn quiet overtook them.

Silverfoot bounded up the steps to the roof shortly thereafter. He was followed promptly by Rhea and Laurent. Cas relayed her plan to them while Silver rummaged and dug through one of the raised gardens that were evenly spaced along the rooftop.

"You need to go," Rhea agreed, "but some of us should stay and keep council with Talos, I believe. If we all leave, I fear he isn't going to let us back in. We need to keep a foot in the door and try to mitigate things after this latest…*complication* we've brought to his realm."

Cas didn't like the idea of dividing up, but she agreed it was necessary. Rhea volunteered herself and her brother to stay behind, and Cas started to suggest Elander stay as well—he was the most persuasive of their group, and could likely win back at least some of the king's favor. But she couldn't bring herself to say this. She selfishly wanted him close. She felt vulnerable and off-balance without her sword, and he settled her nerves better than anything else—perhaps even better than Nessa's magic.

He likely wouldn't have agreed to stay, anyhow; as calm as he appeared on the surface, she knew better despite her teasing. He simply hid his nerves better than she did. And she doubted he would be letting her out of his sight any time soon, with her sword compromised and her powers shifting uncertainly because of it.

"We should bring Nessa outside, too," she thought aloud. "She helped steady me through the experiments with the

Blood crystals in the past. And we can gage the state of the Stone Court and its magic by how well she manages to use her power."

"Good thinking," Rhea agreed.

Laurent had been busying himself with fixing the patches of garden that Silverfoot had disturbed, but he paused at the mention of Nessa, his hand stopping just short of snatching Silver as he trotted past with a flower hanging from his jaws.

"And Laurent should probably stay here," Rhea added. "Since the king and his advisors seem least offended by his presence."

"Of course," he agreed quickly—but Cas didn't miss the way he'd averted his eyes at the suggestion, or the subtle crease of worry that had formed on his forehead.

She said nothing for the moment, but once Elander and Rhea left to prepare for their various tasks, she couldn't help but sidle closer to Laurent, crouching down to help right more of the flowers Silverfoot had upturned.

"You could go with us too, you know," she said, casually. "If it would make you feel better."

He shook his head. "Someone has to keep Zev from making the situation with the elven king and his council worse. I think Rhea is at her limit with him."

She couldn't argue this point.

"You'll be fine without me. Nessa will be more useful than I would be. She's very..." He trailed off, shaking his head.

They continued sorting through the gardens in silence for a few moments, until Cas's fingers brushed a drooping flower with pale yellow petals. "These look like the same blossoms Nessa planted along the paths behind the palace back in Ciridan." She braced a hand against the ground, steadying herself and trying not to think of what had likely become of those flowers since they'd left.

"They are," Laurent informed her. "I mean...I believe they are."

Cas watched him carefully tending to the blooms, plucking the dead petals away and shifting the dirt this way and that, until she couldn't keep her thoughts to herself any longer. "I think you should tell her how you feel."

He stood and brushed a bit of soil from his pant leg. "I have no idea what you're talking about."

Cas sank back on her heels, sighing as she watched him head for the stairs.

But he paused at the top of those stairs, tapping his fingers against the railing, and he tilted his head back toward her just long enough to say, "Just promise you'll keep her safe, please."

She couldn't truly promise any such thing, and they both knew it.

Cas still nodded.

"I will," she said.

CHAPTER 23

Early that evening, Cas, Elander, and Nessa followed a duo of elven guides out of the city and into the wilds beyond it. A guard made up of a dozen of their own soldiers accompanied them as well. They took a proper bridge over the Mirdor River this time, then followed a twisting road through the thick forest on the other side, curving back and forth for no less than an hour before the elven riders stopped at the edge of a field and bowed, indicating they had traveled as far as they intended to travel.

Cas led the way from this point, through the field and its swaying grass streaked through with some kind of pungent, purple flowers that reached to her horse's chest.

As they came to the other side of the field, the world changed.

The instant they stepped free of it, passing from Mistwilde into the mortal realm, it was as though someone had blown out a lantern.

Dark streaks covered a tea-colored sky, giving it the appearance of water spilled over ink and old parchment. The air felt damp, moisture settling on her skin and making her clothes heavy, yet no rain nor snow fell, and the ground and vegetation looked as though they hadn't seen rain in months—even though Cas knew this wasn't true.

An eye-watering scent assaulted them as they rode deeper into the mortal lands, a combination of dust and acrid smoke and fumes. Elander and Nessa drew closer to her, squeezing in from either side, warming away some of the fear threatening to slow her down. Their soldiers drew closer as well, creating a more formidable line behind them.

But even their presence could not keep the terror from gripping Cas's heart as she stared at the sky, searching for a sun she couldn't readily find.

"It's only been a little over a *week*."

She didn't realize she'd said this horrified thought aloud until Nessa replied, in a voice barely above a whisper, "A week too long, it seems. I expected things to look bad, but not *this* bad."

Elander was staring at the sky with an equally horrified look on his face.

He can't extinguish the sun, he'd told her.

It was true—the glow of it was still there. But it was weak, diffused, and the glow's exact origin was impossible to pinpoint among the murkiness.

How much longer until it's eclipsed completely?

Cas nudged her horse into motion, afraid they would all lose their nerve if they didn't keep moving. "We're going to visit Feyedge and speak to the people there about what they've seen over this past week. Let's hurry while we still have some daylight left."

Feyedge was the mortal town closest to the Mistwilde border. Many of the people who lived there made their living peddling elvish wares—both real and fake—to curious travelers who came to glimpse the edges of Mistwilde, even if they couldn't enter it. They were no strangers to odd happenings, and they were a superstitious lot; they would have been watching carefully and taking notes on any changes in the air.

Elander trailed some distance behind Cas, a torn expression on his face—thinking of the Blood crystal she had tucked in her saddlebag, most likely. It was their priority, they'd decided before leaving.

But it didn't seem safe to use it out in the open, directly under these angry skies. So Cas kept moving. And despite his obvious misgivings, Elander eventually kicked his horse into a faster gait and caught up with her.

Feyedge was only a ten minute ride. The day seemed to be fading away at an unnatural pace, and their horses grew sluggish and clumsy as though hours of hard riding had passed rather than minutes, but they reached their destination in one piece and darted toward the arch of twisting wood and the fluttering purple banners that marked the city's gates.

They expected resistance here. Cas recited her story for the guards in her head over and over as they approached, preparing to do whatever it took to win them over. But when they arrived, those guards—four of them in total—could not listen to any of her plans and pleas.

Because they were all dead.

Cas leapt from her horse's saddle and crouched down beside the closest guard, using his own fallen sword to carefully roll him onto his back and inspect him. She saw no wounds. No blood. No obvious sign of injury—only ashen skin, bloodless lips, slightly sunken cheeks. The life and soul had been leached from his body. The others around him looked similar. The same grey hair, colorless eyes, pale skin…

"Fading Sickness," Nessa whispered, standing and stumbling away from the body she'd been inspecting.

Cas fought the urge to glance at her own Fade-marked appearance in the reflective surface of one of the fallen guard's helmets.

She strode from the gatehouse into the city, securing her horse on a nearby hitching post, and ordered their soldiers to split into three groups and scout the area, to get a better idea of what they faced and seek out any way they might be able to help. She raced along the nearly deserted streets, seeking the same things herself.

It proved a pointless endeavor; she heard people shouting, crying out to one another, caught glimpses of them scurrying about in a panic—but no one was willing to talk to her or any of her soldiers for very long. Most houses were barricaded shut, curtains drawn over the windows. Some of those windows had black cloths upon them as well—a common marker of death throughout the empire.

The deeper she ventured, the faster it all seemed to spin around her: the fearful cries and hushed voices; the black cloths; the pale faces; the sky and its dark, foreboding streaks that she swore were growing heavier, sinking closer…

She rejoined her companions near the gate a short time later, all of them having come to the same grim conclusion.

"This town is beyond our help," Elander said. "We shouldn't linger. Whatever beasts Malaphar sent to infect these people could still be nearby."

"The Sickness…are surges of it happening in other towns, too?" Cas turned toward Elander, eyes wide in search of an explanation, even though she knew he had no way of answering the question any better than she did. Desperation had made her ask it, and that same despair made her want to get on her horse and race along all the villages on the eastern coast, to see what was happening firsthand.

Counting their dead wouldn't do anything to slow their enemy down. She knew this. And yet it didn't make the weight of those dead any easier to bear.

"We've taken too long in Mistwilde," she whispered, numbly.

"Things are escalating even more quickly than we feared…" Elander's brow furrowed as he watched a group of townspeople huddled together and hurrying down the street, terror written all over their faces as they kept stealing glances at the sky. "But it was always going to get uglier toward the end, as Malaphar draws closer to his ultimate goals, regardless of what we focused on. We couldn't have been everywhere at once to prevent it. You know that."

Cas closed her eyes against the thought. But she nodded —an automatic reflex at this point, acknowledging these inevitable failures.

"The crystal," Nessa urged, "we need to focus on it, now. On the bigger picture."

Cas agreed, and she kept going despite her dizziness, searching for a relatively safe place where they could manage that focus.

They found an empty building on the outskirts of town and locked themselves inside of it. Their soldiers spread out around the perimeter, keeping the building within sight while staying far enough away to not draw attention to it.

Elander checked the rest of the house for any potential

trouble while Cas shrugged the bag from her back, took the Blood crystal from it, and summoned Nessa to her side.

"The house is clear, but let's be quick," Elander said, returning to them.

Cas nodded and knelt down, bracing a hand against a table covered in cobwebs and dust. Nessa crouched beside her, reaching to wrap a hand around her arm. The feather-shaped mark on her skin flickered as she focused on summoning her magic. Cas eagerly awaited that warm magic —she was desperate for it after what they'd seen outside—but even after minutes had passed, the air around them remained cold.

"I'm sorry." Frustration filled Nessa's voice. "It's coming so slowly these days. I just can't seem to—"

"It's fine," Cas assured her, even as her stomach twisted into knots. "Just do the best you can. I'll manage the rest."

Determination hardened Nessa's expression as she gripped Cas's arm more tightly.

Cas took a deep breath and focused on reciting the words to bring the crystal in her palm to life, prepared to slip into the dark memories it contained with or without Nessa's supporting magic.

It took much longer than it should have. Whether from her own fear, or because the elven airs had tainted it, or because its power had grown less potent in the wake of Caden's death, she couldn't be sure—but *something* was clearly tempering this crystal's power, just as something was weakening Nessa's.

But after several minutes, Cas felt it: the telltale pressure on her chest that told her the spell was beginning to work.

"I'm right here," Nessa encouraged. "We can do this."

Cas felt a flicker of warm magic. Still faint, but she held to it like a rope as the Blood crystal's memory continued to unfold around her.

It finally happened: She blinked, Nessa and Elander were gone, and grey fog rolled along the edges of the new scene she found herself within. Familiar sensations...but it still felt unlike the countless memory-filled crystals she'd used before.

She sank fully into this memory with a violent jolt, and it was as if she had slammed her head into the floor of it, causing a dizziness that turned everything she saw into unstable shadows edged in soft red light.

She heard voices. As fuzzy as the things she saw, yet she was certain she recognized at least one of them as her father's.

Once she heard his voice—and named it in her mind—one of the silhouettes took on a more definite shape, making it clear that this was indeed another memory featuring Anric de Solasen.

He was in a study of some kind—a blurry desk and shelves upon shelves of books behind him—and he was speaking to a man who had laid out piles of notes and diagrams across a desk. Cas stood at the door, keeping watch. Or rather, *Lord Orbryn* stood at the door; this was another one of his memories, divined from the blood of his murdered body, she was fairly certain.

The lord had only partially paid attention to whatever meeting was taking place within this room; the memory kept shifting to the hallway, watching and listening for any potential intruders, which left whatever was being said within the study frustratingly unclear.

But Anric's raised voice soon snapped Orbryn's full attention toward the room.

"Your conclusion," Anric growled at the figure beside him, "get to it."

The other's reply was feeble but clear. "Certain monsters can only be felled by other monsters. Some darknesses resist even the brightest of lights. This Point was made by darkness and sacrifice, and therefore only darkness and sacrifice can *unmake* it, which means—"

A loud *pop,* followed by the distant sound of shattering glass, wrenched Cas from the memory.

Panic bloomed fast and hot in her chest, but she had been so *close* to hearing something useful, if she could just keep listening...

She closed her eyes and tried to refocus.

The scene in the King-Emperor's study flickered partially back into view. Cas was aware of the memory while simultaneously being aware of the present, of her racing heart and Nessa's uncertain fidgeting.

Her father's voice was rising again, almost clear once more...

Another loud *pop* jerked her all the way back to the present.

This time, after closing her eyes and concentrating, Cas opened them to find only Nessa before her. She blinked several more times, trying to bring Anric and his study back without success.

The crystal in her hand had cracked, and its center no longer pulsed red with any magic.

It was over.

She flung the dead crystal aside as she held in a curse.

"I'm sorry," Nessa stammered, "I tried to help you stay focused, but it..."

"It's not your fault," Cas said, massaging the space

between her eyes, trying to ward off the headache starting to build. "What is going on?"

It was Elander who replied, in a grave tone, "We need to get back to Mistwilde." He stood by the window, cautiously peering through the cracked, dust-caked panes.

Cas rose unsteadily to her feet.

Nessa offered her a shoulder for balance, and together they made their way through the dark room to the window and looked outside to see...

Fire.

There were three houses standing apart from the rest of the city, rising on a hill just beyond its protective walls. All three of them burned bright against the tea-colored sky, their windows shattered and full of quickly swelling flames.

Far in the distance, Cas saw what appeared to be the source of it all—a bird, larger than any she'd ever seen, wrapped in flame, with wings that sent embers and smoke hurtling toward the city with every flap.

"A servant of the Fire God?" Cas asked.

Elander shook his head. "That isn't his servant."

Cas reached habitually for the comfort of a sword that wasn't at her hip. She had only an average elven blade there, resistant to divine magic, yes, but incapable of creating any of its own. She still squeezed its handle tightly as Elander took a deep breath and said:

"That's the God of Fire himself."

CHAPTER 24

"If I had to guess," Elander said, "I'd say they knew we were in Mistwilde, and they concentrated on attacking Feyedge for this very reason."

"They were hoping we would notice it..." Nessa said, understanding, "so they could draw us out."

"So the smartest thing for us to do is pretend we haven't noticed anything at all," Elander said, "and hope we haven't actually been spotted by the Fire God or anyone who's accompanied him."

Cas inwardly recoiled at the thought of leaving the town to burn, but when Elander fixed his expectant gaze on her, she still gave a stiff nod. "Yes," she agreed, quietly. "We need to live to fight another day. Let's gather everyone and slip away while we can."

They moved stealthily out of the house and into the city, quietly calling out to the soldiers who had been standing guard. Once they were all accounted for, they raced through the city, heading away from the field the Fire God continued to soar above, keeping to side roads and using the cover of shadows as well as they could. Night was falling fast, the dark streaks of foul energy in the sky growing even darker and obscuring the moonlight—which at least made it easier to go unnoticed.

Once they were clear of the city and its buildings, they had a distant but unobstructed view of the flying god. His flaming body burned so brightly against the sky that it was impossible to ignore it.

Cas's skin felt hot, as though she was much closer to the fires he was setting. And if she didn't move faster, she *would* be close—several more houses on the edge of the city looked to have caught fire, and a terrible wind had arisen, fanning those flames farther, higher, hotter…

She tore her eyes away and forced herself to keep moving, knowing it would be foolish to try and stop this rampage, no matter how badly she wanted to.

But when one of her soldiers cried out in alarm, her gaze snapped automatically back in the direction of the city, and she saw something that made her heart simultaneously clench and soar.

A second shape-shifted being was streaking toward the God of Fire—another bird wrapped in magic, only in lightning instead of flames.

Nephele?

Cas slowed to a stop, awestruck as the two divine beings collided. The resulting explosion sent shockwaves of power exploding outward, reaching Cas and her company even as far away as they stood. The ground shook, several of the horses reared, and Cas struggled to settle her own mount before drawing it up between Elander and Nessa's.

"The Goddess of Storms..." Cas began, uncertainly. "Should we..."

Elander averted his gaze. "We'll catch up with her soon."

Cas knew he was thinking the same thing she was.

We'll catch up, assuming she survives this.

"Is there no way we could help?" Nessa asked.

Elander had already turned his anxious horse and started to trot quickly away as he said, "This is a battlefield for gods. And we have no clear way of slaying gods at the moment."

Nessa still hesitated, terror shining in her wide eyes, but Cas urged her into motion and quickly followed her—though she had to fight the urge to look back herself.

Looking back would do them no good. Not when all she had was a broken, confiscated sword, a broken crystal, and far too many questions without answers. She was not useless without her sword, but escape made more sense at the moment. And Nephele was capable of winning this fight without their help.

Wasn't she?

Cas made herself focus only on escaping—not just for herself, but her soldiers. "What is the safest route back to Mistwilde?"

"The closest land the elves claim lies due east of here," answered one of those soldiers. "It isn't where our guides were planning to meet us, but there should be enough elven magic teeming in the air that it will deter the gods from following us once we reach it. And once the area around it is clear, we can sneak our way back to our planned entrance into the realm."

Cas agreed to this plan, sending the soldier to the front to lead the way alongside Nessa while she and Elander brought up the rear.

They had nearly made it to the shelter of a sparse forest when Cas felt power closing in on them—such an enormous wave of it that it nearly flattened her against her horse's back even as she raced on toward the trees.

The gods were drawing closer.

They weren't chasing Cas and her company; they were merely locked in a fierce battle, twisting and diving this way and that, completely oblivious to anything outside of each other. Again and again they crashed together, wings of fire and lightning tangling, clawed feet and sharp beaks slashing, wayward sparks and embers showering down over the landscape below them.

Cas thought she could feel the ebb and flow of Nephele's magic, along with every hit that magic sustained from their enemy—perhaps from the connection she had to the goddesses of the Sun Court. She saw Elander veer uncertainly from their path more than once, distracted by the same connection. But he kept pressing on, not looking back…

Until the Goddess of Storms hit the ground nearby, her massive form rolling violently across the earth, flailing wings taking out trees and burning a deep rut through the grass and dirt as she slid.

Elander jerked his horse to a stop, as did Cas. Their eyes met for a brief, horrified second, but before they could decide what to do, the God of Fire was upon them, hurtling flames with every rapid, reckless beat of his wings.

A particularly large ball of fire struck the grass directly in front of one of their soldiers. His horse bolted with such force that the rider ended up sideways, hanging out of the saddle and bouncing like a lifeless doll against the horse's sweat-slicked, panting sides.

Cas kicked her own horse into a gallop without thinking, racing to cut off the path of the straying rider. She charged in front of the panicked horse and summoned a weak line of Sky magic—just enough to create a barrier that forced it to stop, to turn around and gallop toward relative safety.

Cas turned and followed swiftly after them.

The god above was faster.

A line of fire shot in front of her, cutting her off from the rest of her group. She twisted around, and more fire followed, encircling her with clear, calculated precision.

The god was targeting her now.

Her horse reared. She jumped from the saddle to avoid being catapulted from it, rolling as she hit the ground and then springing up to her feet and trying to take on a formidable stance. She backed her way around the circle, searching the flames with eyes already watering from the heat and the smoke.

She saw him approaching seconds later. No longer a bird but a man, a demon with eyes like glowing rubies and a flame-wrapped spear clutched in his massive hand.

But the God of Fire never reached her.

A rush of breathtaking cold overtook the space before he could, dropping them both to their knees.

Cas instinctively crouched lower, covering her face. Peering out from under her arm, she saw the fire around her changing, writhing about as though doused by a sudden downpour. But it wasn't *rain* smothering its power—it was the cold, the rush of magic weaving into the flames, eventually turning them pale and sluggish. Draining them.

Death magic.

The heat from the flames soon disappeared entirely.

Cas lifted her head and found herself surrounded by

oddly white and heatless flames...and then by shadows. A figure materialized among these shadows, rising up and branching out into a solid form, like ink spilling into the shape of a man.

Her brother.

He stood in front of her, facing the last spot she'd seen the God of Fire. Ribbons of pale blue floated and snapped in the air around his body, protecting him.

Protecting her.

She glanced to her right and saw a section of the fire ring drained completely away, just wide enough for a person to slip through.

Varen pointed her toward it. "Get on your horse and hurry back to the elven realm. Now."

Despite all the things she wanted to say to him, she recognized the danger of the situation she'd found herself in. So she started to obey, stumbling to her feet and frantically searching for her horse.

A sphere of fire dropped down from above, slamming into the ground, igniting the grass and creating a *whoosh* of heat and power that sent them both flying through the air.

Cas landed hard on her side, arm jamming into her ribs in an awkward, painful way that she was certain would leave a nasty bruise. Wincing, she pushed upright. Her vision was still watery, blurry, burning—but she was no longer surrounded by fire; she had been flung clear of the circle of it. In the distance she saw her soldiers on the move, some of them gathered around the fallen Storm Goddess while others were spreading out and searching, calling out words she couldn't hear over the howl of wind and the crackling of burning grass.

Looking for her?

She could have run to them.

She almost did.

Then she glanced in the opposite direction and saw Varen lying on the ground, unmoving.

He's fine. He's a god. The God of Fire won't kill one of his own court.

She got to her feet, holding her side and backing away, staggering several steps in the direction of her soldiers...

Her eyes stayed on Varen.

They were *still* on Varen as the God of Fire made himself known with a roar that brought embers floating up from the ground all around them.

A sudden wind swirled those embers toward the Fire God, engulfing his body in a bright glow that swelled into a brilliant blaze, and in the next breath he was emerging from the flames as a beast more dragon-like than bird-like. His arms extended toward the sky and kept going, reaching into wings that dripped molten red liquid and threw off flickers of fire with every flap that propelled him upwards.

Another explosive ball of flame pummeled the ground before Cas's feet, creating a violent updraft of heat and wind. She was knocked back once more, but caught herself this time—just barely—landing delicately on the tips of her toes and fingers. Her gaze immediately went to the sky, seeking the Fire God, bracing for his next attack.

The swirling embers around him had stretched into a burning net, and it was falling toward Varen.

Cas launched into a sprint, reaching her brother just before the wall of fire fell upon him.

She wrapped him tightly in her arms, rolling several feet

and then scrambling several more, dragging him with her and trying to stay ahead of the fire. As she pulled him closer, her magic pressed outward, building slowly at first before finally bursting into a shield that pushed back the flames trying to swallow them up.

The shield continued to grow around them until they were fully cocooned, cut off from everything outside.

Even without her sword, she had managed it, just as she'd managed it when she was a child. Despite the risks, despite the fear, despite the disaster it might lead to...Despite it all, she remained steady, her arms wrapped tightly around Varen, her magic protecting them both.

Nearly a minute passed. Cas didn't move, afraid one wrong motion might make her magic collapse under the Fire God's incredible power.

Varen finally twitched. Coughed. "I told you to run."

"Have you really learned *nothing* about me since the beginning of this mess?" she mumbled. "You should know by now that I'm terrible at following orders."

His lips twisted in a pained, humorless smile. He kept forcing his eyes open whenever they tried to droop shut, watching the barrier surrounding them with an unsettling stare, as though he expected it to flicker away if he dared to blink.

When a long moment passed and it still held, he closed his eyes and sank more fully against Cas.

Cas remained still. She could feel the fires pressing against her shield. The sound and scenery outside of them remained muffled by her magic, but she was intensely aware of it all the same.

She looked down at her brother. He'd hit the ground

hard; hard enough that pebbles had embedded into his face. Blood trickled from a scrape on his forehead. She brushed the dirt and rocks and blood from his skin, then instantly drew her hand back, clenching it into a fist as she shook her head. Her heart felt like it had lodged in her throat despite her best efforts to keep it down.

They couldn't stay like this.

She knew they needed to move, but something strange overtook her when she started to, and it held her in place for another moment—a feeling of familiarity. A flicker of memory followed...one that she was almost certain had not come from any crystal Varen had given her.

This memory was *hers*.

It simply fell into her head, sudden and soft around the edges, but clear: The two of them together in a garden, collecting fallen flower petals. Then she was running, him chasing until he tripped, and she turned and found him sprawled out on the ground behind her. Blood wound a bright path against his face in the memory, just as it did now. And she shook his shoulder now as she had then, her voice coming out small and afraid, as if she were that child once more.

"Ren?"

It took several more tries before he slowly opened his eyes and said, "You used to call me that when we were little."

She nodded.

"Mother hated it."

"Did she?"

He lifted his eyes to the sky—to what they could see of it through the haze of Cas's magic. The tint of that magic made it look closer to blue than it had in a long time.

"So many of my earliest memories are of her," Varen said, "and they're only about the things she hated."

Cas didn't reply, fighting the ache in her heart to know more. She simply sat with that ache, with the fear of fire pushing in and reaching them, and she wondered if her brother had committed these things to memory because knowing what the queen hated made it easier to not do those things—which made it easier to survive.

Surviving. That was all they'd both been doing for so long.

They'd grown so talented at it.

But surviving was not the same thing as living, and it was devastating to think about how hard they had worked to survive...just to end up here, bleeding and surrounded by flames, on opposite sides of a war she couldn't imagine them both making it through.

"She always told you to pronounce my full name, because otherwise you sounded like an ignorant child who could hardly speak." Varen sat up, pushing away her attempts to help steady him. "But we *were* children who could hardly speak, weren't we?"

Cas again said nothing; her throat felt too raw. *Everything* felt too raw. She stood and went to the barrier she'd created, reinforcing a few places where it had started to crack while still watching her brother out of the corner of her eye.

"I wonder what might have been, sometimes, if Father had not gotten mixed up in deals and duels with gods," said Varen. "If we'd had a chance to speak as something other than children, before everything became so...*complicated*." He got to his feet, his balance swaying slightly.

Cas tried again to offer her hand, and again, he ignored it.

"I'm fine," he muttered, rolling a bit of tension from his shoulders—a very human-like gesture, even as the air around him began to shift, his cold magic rising to the surface and his eyes taking on an unsettling glow. "I simply forgot how powerfully *violent* the gods can be." His gaze drifted toward a smudge of orange—a fire—growing brighter on the other side of their shield. "Particularly this one."

Cas's hands clenched and unclenched as she tried to stave off the anxious tingling in them. "You saved me from that violent god. It was very obvious to anyone watching. And the God of Fire will tell the one he serves—the one *you* are supposed to be serving. He will be *furious* with you."

"You forget how vain and ambitious the gods of the Dark Court are." He gave her a grim smile. "They all want to be the one to sit at Malaphar's right hand, and it is a constant battle to prove that they belong there... I'll just tell him I warded the Fire God off so that I could take care of you myself and earn more favor."

Cas took a deep, steadying breath.

"Not the most important matter, either way." He kept his eyes on the growing firelight beyond the barrier. "Have you managed to use that crystal I gave you?"

She begrudgingly accepted the change of subject. "Yes."

"Good. So you have what you need to finish things."

"But I didn't really *finish* anything," she admitted. "We were interrupted before I could hear and see everything contained in the Blood-divined memory. *This Point was made by darkness and sacrifice, and therefore only darkness and sacrifice can unmake it*—those words were clear, but I don't know what they mean."

He frowned, eyebrows pinching together in thought.

"I didn't hear the rest, and now I don't think the crystal can be salvaged or—"

A sound like ice cracking whipped their attention toward

the shield. Another weak point was forming. Cas could clearly see fire now—not just a hazy spot of it, but the outline of individual flames reaching toward them.

"You'll have to piece it together as best you can," said Varen, calmly. "I managed it for Dawnskeep. Father managed to do so for the prior Point."

Cas knew this, but she couldn't help feeling as though she had too many pieces to put together. She was gathering them as best she could, but they were all falling, more of them tumbling from her arms every time she tried to readjust her hold. "The Antaeum Point has moved from where it was in Mistwilde," she told Varen. "I transferred it to my sword, somehow, and Shadowslayer is containing the power of it, but now I can't use that sword."

His face was difficult to read. Intrigued? Afraid? Confused? His expression seemed a combination of all these things. Then a flash of what might have been understanding crossed it. But before he could share whatever revelation he might have had, another crack split their shield—the largest crack so far.

Cas briefly felt the heat from the Fire God's spells singeing her skin before Varen's magic overtook it, draining it and leaving chills on her skin instead. It was better than being burned...but Cas still hated this cold, the way it sank in and disoriented her, making her forget all the warmth she'd ever known.

"When the time comes," Varen said, "I have a feeling you'll figure out what to do." His voice had taken on a hollow, resigned tone, and there was no more time to discuss it; the fires outside roared brighter, and Cas could sense both Elander and the Storm Goddess drawing closer, everyone and everything funneling toward a chaotic end.

"Now, just as before," Varen continued, quickly, "we'll fight for the sake of appearances. Drive me away from you and your followers. Make it look convincing."

The world afforded them a few more seconds of silence. Her shield held longer than they thought it would as she stood there, scarcely breathing, studying her brother's face. The blood she hadn't managed to wipe away, the eyes that no longer looked human.

She didn't *want* to drive him away.

Every parting felt like it might be their last, and she was not ready for this to end. Not like this.

"Varen, I—"

The silence shattered.

Her magic collapsed, sending a wave of heat and her own failing power rushing over them. Varen drained it before it could flatten them, filling the air with more of that unbearable cold. As soon as it all settled—as soon as they risked being seen by the world outside—Varen turned on her without warning.

His hands rose at his sides, swirling shadow beasts into existence to do his bidding, sending them lunging toward Cas's chest.

She stumbled back, managing just enough magic to create a shield between them, warding them off. They continued to prowl around her, circling in search of an opening.

The Goddess of Storms had recovered enough to dive back into battle with the God of Fire. Their bright forms tumbled and tore at one another just beyond where Cas and her brother stood.

So Varen was able to focus fully on her. Through the smoke and magic-filled air, their eyes briefly met, and he shook his head at her as his lips formed an obvious command. *Fight back.*

The shadow creatures became more solid, their muscles clear and defined as they crouched and prepared to spring.

Cas wanted to lunge past them and tackle her brother to the ground as she had before. To wrap him up. To *fight*, but only as they had as children—scuffling and rolling in the dirt until one of them surrendered and they bickered but eventually made up. To fight as *children*, not as gods or kings or queens or whatever they were now.

This is wrong.

The beasts leapt, claws leaving dark streaks in the air as they came.

Tears stung Cas's eyes as lightning sprang to her fingertips, not as solid as what she usually managed with her sword, but solid enough. She shoved her sparking hands forward, making the creatures recoil in mid-air. As she swung closer to them, they crouched and began to fade, seeping into the dark ground.

They disappeared, and she twisted around to face her brother, the lightning at her hands building into more violent storms as she moved. She drew a hand back, but stopped just short of releasing the power circling around it. She couldn't make herself cast that magic directly at him.

Varen shook his head at her hesitation, the familiar disapproving, slightly smug look on his face. He slowly lifted his hands out beside him, summoning again. Not creatures this time, but pure blades of shadowy energy that he aimed at her. He didn't stab them immediately forward, pausing just long enough to give her a chance to summon a defense.

Cas's hands still refused to move.

It didn't matter.

Elander darted in front of her, and he shared none of her hesitation. He was pure action and anger, his light blinding as it swept forward and engulfed the shadow blades, crushing them into pieces, into wisps of black energy that scattered wildly in every direction.

Behind him came not one, but two goddesses—not Nephele, but the goddesses of the Moon and Sky, both surrounded by furious and brilliant waves of magic. The goddesses guided part of that magic toward Cas, combining it to create a powerful shield for her.

Elander focused on Varen, brandishing Caden's sword, which crackled with lightning he'd summoned and twisted around the blade.

Cas ducked the building shield and dove for Elander's arm, wrapping herself against it and trying to drag him to a stop. "This is wrong," she said, voice breaking. "*This is wrong*!"

Elander couldn't hear her over the roar of all the various magics—or maybe he chose to ignore her. He pulled free and kept his focus on Varen.

But Cas had slowed him down enough that Varen had put a considerable distance between them, and Varen was still backing away. Only when she caught his eyes once more did he draw to a stop. He blinked slowly, almost painfully, as if he was trying and failing to drag his gaze away from her. He finally managed it—one last glance her way before a resolute bow of his head. A goodbye.

For the last time?

Cas's breath hitched at the thought. She forced herself to keep moving as Varen disappeared in a flash of shadow and smoke, and she turned to the last place she'd seen Nephele and the Fire God battling.

They had both abandoned their bird forms and stood

instead as humanoid beings squaring off with one another, weapons of magic drawn and bristling with power.

The Fire God's attention shifted briefly, watching Elander approaching with the other two goddesses—and eventually Cas as well—following in his wake.

Seeing the odds shifting so dramatically, the fiery god hesitated only a moment before he followed Varen's lead and disappeared in a swirl of dark smoke.

Cas and her allies waited, tense and prepared for any tricks he might attempt...

He didn't return.

The Sky and Moon Goddesses had wrapped the city of Feyedge in shields of magic, keeping the fires from spreading beyond the places that had already burned, and now Nephele stepped toward the destruction to put the lingering fires completely out.

Cas watched, numbly, as the Storm Goddess conjured up dark clouds that poured water onto the twisting flames. The scene was soon eerily dark, filled with steam and smoke, and Cas shivered as she stared at the burned hellscape, trying to recognize shapes, to get her bearings and make sense of all that had just happened.

Elander drew closer to her—a shape she quickly recognized even in the ashes and smoke. He took her hand, stroking his thumb against the palm of her shaking hand.

"Nessa led our soldiers onward toward Mistwilde," he told her. "They should be safe." He looked her over, eyes filled with concern. He didn't ask if she was okay—he clearly already knew the answer was *no,* and that she would lie and say *yes,* and so he simply skipped the words and wrapped his arms around her instead.

She pressed tightly to him, safe but still aching,

surrounded by warm power and yet still shivering from the memory of her brother's magic. Of his voice. She couldn't get the image of his face from her mind. She couldn't stop looking at the blood on her hands—his blood.

And she couldn't stop thinking about all the wounds between them that she could not heal.

CHAPTER 25

"Whatever you've heard or imagined about the state of this mortal realm," said Nephele as she returned to them, "I assure you, it's worse."

Elander shot her a withering look, but Nephele, true to form, did not hold back with her commentary.

"This scene mirrors one that has become common all over this empire and beyond," she continued, pointing at the destruction around them. "Scenes that suggest we're careening ever more swiftly toward the end of this realm."

Casia had inhaled sharply at the word *end,* and Elander sensed her balance swaying. He subtly reached a hand toward the small of her back, preparing to steady her if necessary.

"So I hope you all have made some sort of significant progress toward *stopping* that end," Nephele said.

"We're still working on it," Elander said bluntly.

Nephele opened her mouth, clearly prepared to berate

them for not working hard or fast enough, but the Moon Goddess cut her off.

"We're here because earlier today we felt a strange, unsettling surge of your magic," said Inya, her shimmering eyes shifting between Elander and Casia.

"You felt it?" Elander couldn't keep the uneasy chill from creeping down his spine. "Even through the backwards spells that hover over Mistwilde?"

Inya frowned. "Yes. We thought you might be in trouble—more trouble than usual—so we came to find you. But we were distracted by the Fire God along the way. We found him committing similar atrocities in Silverbank, some thirty miles south of here. We drove him away from that seaside village, and then followed him to this one."

"And you said he's created similar scenes elsewhere..." Casia said. "But how many? It's scarcely been more than a week—how much damage could he possibly have caused in that time?"

"The divine move with impressive speed when they want to," the Sky Goddess muttered.

Indre's voice surprised Elander—that she had bothered to speak, and that she'd accompanied the other two goddesses into this battlefield to begin with. Despite the brief help she'd given them in the past, she'd been quick to return to her indifferent existence, and he'd expected her to stay there until the end; it didn't bode well for their cause if things had escalated to the point that even *she* had decided to step back into the fray.

Was this truly the end?

"As for how many," Nephele added, "we've lost count. And it's not just him. The Ice Goddess has created her share of destruction as well—as have all the other Marr who have switched their allegiance to *Him*. It isn't just the divine, either. There are pockets of mortals and elves who are *also* clamoring to be seen as supporters of the Dark God. The armies of Ethswen and Moreth, led by Sarith, for example, have made no secret of their desire to serve him in exchange for being spared and given favor in whatever new world he's trying to create."

"We already knew that last part," Casia said miserably.

"Though no one is being led by Sarith any longer," Elander added, unable to keep the dark hint of smugness from his tone.

Indre's thin brows rose high above her indigo eyes. "So the rumors of that are true?"

"Even without that elven usurper queen," Nephele pressed, "there are no shortage of others to lead the corrupted masses. Chaos still threatens every corner of this world."

The group of them stood without speaking for a long moment, studying the evidence of that chaos surrounding them.

The Moon Goddess nudged an ash-covered pile of dirt with her foot. She took a deep breath, as though steadying herself and drawing in courage. "Though for what it's worth," she said, "there are also mortal armies rebelling against the idea of his reign."

Casia lifted her gaze, and Elander saw a flash of hope in her eyes. He wished he could cling as stubbornly to that hope as she did, that he could shake off the uneasy chill still gripping him.

"A rebellious army continues to grow in Sadira," said the Moon Goddess. "And the ones you left behind in Ciridan are still organizing too, drawing more and more to their cause.

They saw the true state of things after the battle that occurred at your palace, and they're rallying accordingly."

"As we trusted they would." Casia closed her eyes for a moment, as though basking in this rare beam of positive news. "Good."

Inya gave her a small, encouraging smile.

Nephele and her sister exchanged a less encouraged look, but kept their concerns to themselves for once. They fell silent again, the Sky Goddess's gaze narrowing on Casia and studying her for a long, uncomfortable moment.

"That strange surge of magic..." she prompted. "What *was* that?"

"I...I think I know what you're talking about." Casia looked toward the elven realm they'd left behind, visibly steeling herself before she told them of the incident in the depths of the Irithyl Palace—the reason she did not currently carry the weapon Solatis had given her.

The goddesses were momentarily speechless once she'd finished, and Nephele's voice was soft, less assured than usual, when she finally spoke again.

"The jewels on the Heart actually *shattered*?"

"And when they did, it felt as if a part of me shattered with them," Casia replied. "I still feel off-balance, as though more of my power was tied into that sword than I realized, and now it's...*gone*. Or being suffocated."

"So the Point is still intact, only moved."

Casia nodded, and then told them, too, of the Blood crystal and of her hopes to use the information contained within it to finish dealing with the Point.

Elander listened as intently as the goddesses. After she'd been interrupted while using the crystal back at the city, the look on her face had been easy enough to read—she felt like this part of their mission had failed. Still, he'd hoped she would be able to put more of the memory together; that they would all be able to make better sense of it once they'd made it to the other side of their latest battle.

But nothing Casia said made that unease in him settle—every word only made it *worse*.

"A Point created in darkness and sacrifice..." Inya repeated.

"And it must be unmade by the same methods," said Casia. "But what sort of darkness? What sort of sacrifice?"

Nephele shook her head. "Any guess we could make would be mere conjecture. But it doesn't sound *good* for us, does it?"

Elander turned away from the group for a moment, fixing his gaze on the distant city—or what he could see of it through the thick haze of steam and smoke still hanging around. He didn't want Casia to see the concern in his expression.

The Moon Goddess was again the one to offer a more hopeful explanation. "The mortal scholar you saw within that memory could be wrong. Light *can* overcome even the darkest powers—we've seen it before." Elander turned back to them as the goddess looked to Casia, eyes fixing on her cheek and glazing over in thought. "You sacrificed yourself and took on Malaphar's mark, stepping into the darkness of his power and control to save others...and you withstood that power and eventually made it back to the light. Your sword has now done the same thing, hasn't it? Its light is sacrificed, but the darkness was contained by it, put into a more manageable form. Maybe it's only a matter of holding back the dark until the light resurfaces and crushes the Point out of existence—or seals it, or what have you."

The Storm Goddess shook her head. "But it was Solatis—the Light herself—who ultimately dispelled such darkness before. Now Solatis is gone. And she's gone partly *because* of all she sacrificed to bring Casia and Elander back to the light."

Casia held her hand out before her, summoning a tiny spark and thoughtfully twisting it around as she considered Nephele's words.

"So even if I was able to help my sword destroy the darkness that makes up the Point, it might mean..." Her words trailed off, lost in a sudden howl of wind. She didn't try to find those words again, or to raise her voice above the harsh breeze. She didn't need to.

It was clear that everyone present was already thinking the same thing.

No one said it—not even Nephele—for which Elander was grateful. He could barely stand to *think* it. There had to be another way, another solution that didn't involve Casia sacrificing any more than she already had. He refused to believe anything else.

The wind howled on, the sparks around Casia's hand extinguished, and the five of them stood in the hazy darkness, contemplating.

Finally, Nephele breathed a sigh and, in a tired but determined voice, she said, "Assuming we can find a way to deal with this Point—eventually—what should our next move be, in the meantime? We can't stand still. Our enemies are growing more organized, their attacks more efficient. Our forces, in comparison, are scattered and struggling to know where to go."

Inya nodded in agreement and added, "Also, if the Dark

God was not aware you were in Mistwilde, he is aware of it now."

"You can't hide in that elven realm forever," said the Sky Goddess.

"We didn't go there to *hide*," Elander reminded her savagely, fighting off the reflexive urge he had to reach for his sword.

The goddess turned toward him, eyes darkening and strands of hair lifting as her power bristled to life. Nephele moved to stand between them, playing peacemaker for perhaps the first time in her existence.

Casia managed a much calmer tone than Elander had as she glared at the Sky Goddess and said, "I went there to see the Antaeum Point dealt with. And I will figure out how to deal with it before we leave—I just need a little more time." She shifted her focus to Nephele. "You all can still travel more quickly than any other messenger I could send, right?"

"Quickly enough," Nephele said, arching an intrigued brow.

"We need messengers far and wide, to gather these scattered allies and direct them, prepare them for what's coming. Soryn, the ones keeping Ciridan for us—all of them. Tell them I am close to a solution, and once I have it, I will be marching out from the realm of Mistwilde to face whatever wrath the Dark God brings. Maybe marching toward an ending, as you said. Or maybe not." Her gaze swept over the ruined fields and the city smoldering in the distance, and Elander saw the way her brow creased, and the subtle movement of her lips as she was calculating—trying to determine how many days the world might manage to survive, how long they could stand to keep trying to unravel the mysteries of the last Sealing Point.

Despair flashed in her eyes before she averted her gaze from all of them.

Not long enough.

She shook off that despair and calmly decided on a number. "One more week," she told Nephele. "One more week, and we should all be prepared to face the end, whatever it may be."

The Storm Goddess studied her without speaking for several beats. Nephele was usually difficult to read, but Elander thought he understood his old friend this time, as he was thinking the same thing she was—how far Casia had come since the first meeting they'd had in Stormhaven. It simultaneously filled him with awe and made him sick to his stomach, thinking of all she'd been through to get to the point of being able to command everything from elven kings to ancient goddesses without flinching.

"Very well, then," said Nephele. "We'll move quickly." She gave Casia a slight bow, and then she was off, stretching her hands toward the sky as though beginning an elegant dance. As she swept those hands down, they became wings that lifted her up, and her body turned to lightning that took on the familiar shape of a massive bird.

Her sister followed without another word, twisting into a similar shape that disappeared even more swiftly into the distant sky.

The Moon Goddess remained, her soft gaze fixed on Casia. Her hand reached to brush a stray strand of Casia's hair from her face, and then it fell to her shoulder, holding there as if steadying her.

It felt like an intimate touch meant for a private conversation, so Elander stepped away to give them some space.

The goddesses had corralled their horses with a

makeshift fence of magic; he went to collect them, and to check and secure their bags, while Casia and Inya finished their conversation.

He returned to her side just as Inya planted a kiss on Casia's forehead. She then dismissed herself with a slight bow like Nephele had, her body shifting to ribbons the color of moonlight as she bent. Those ribbons took swiftly to the sky as if whipped upward by a sudden, violent wind, and they formed a serpentine shape that weaved swiftly between the clouds and streaks of darkness.

Casia watched the sky for a long time after the goddesses had disappeared from sight, her brow furrowed, arms hugged around her middle, fingers tapping against her side. Some of those fingers were covered in what looked like blood.

Her brother's?

"We need to hurry and catch up to the others," he said, "before they get worried and send a search party after us."

She nodded and swung onto her horse's back without another word.

They galloped through the drifting mists, not slowing their pace until they were well out of sight of the battlefield and winding deep into the forests beyond it.

As the scent of smoke gave way to the heavy aroma of pine, Elander took the map from one of his saddlebags and looked it over. This was not the same way they had traveled out of Mistwilde, but he was fairly certain it was the same path Nessa and the others had taken.

They moved slower, searching for signs that the others had traveled along this route. Elander had just paused to study a cluster of trampled ground and broken branches when Casia abruptly broke the silence.

"Do you think it's true? That this will be the end?"

He hesitated, unsure how to answer, and Casia continued before he could find the words.

"I suppose that's a stupid question, isn't it? Given the evidence all around us."

"It isn't stupid," he said quietly. "We've made it this far by questioning our supposed endings and rebelling against them, haven't we?"

She managed a slight nod and an agreeable, if short-lived, smile. They rode in silence, side-by-side, for several more minutes, until the air started to tingle with the familiar feel of elven magic. The sky seemed to lighten as well, more moonlight reaching them in spite of the trees that were thicker than ever.

Casia inhaled sharply and slowed her horse to a stop.

"What's wrong?"

She was staring at something just ahead, fists clenched tight on the reins and eyes wide and unblinking, as if watching a nightmare unfolding—but Elander saw nothing nightmarish. Nothing moved aside from scattered leaves drifting down, knocked loose by a gentle breeze.

"Casia?"

She gave her head a little shake. Turning her face away, she said, "I just need a moment to let everything the goddesses told us...settle. Before we go back to Mistwilde. Before I face the others."

He didn't like the idea of stopping, but he dismounted as she did, taking the reins of her horse along with his own, leading them both to a nearby stream to drink.

He kept watch while Casia walked along the stream, studying her moonlit reflection for a few minutes before kneeling down and washing her hands in the cold water, rinsing away the blood.

He wondered what had taken place between her and her brother earlier, while they were confined within the shield of her magic. But he didn't ask. He only kept a watchful eye on her while also scouting their surroundings and planning their next steps, occasionally summoning small sparks of magic to investigate dark shadows more thoroughly.

Casia soon moved away from the stream and leaned against a large tree, sliding down it and settling among the dead leaves and limbs at the base of the trunk. She drew her legs toward her, resting her elbows upon them and pressing her hands to her forehead.

Concern eating a pit in his chest, Elander secured their horses and stepped closer to her. He still didn't speak; he wasn't sure what to say. Nothing he could have said felt like enough in the aftermath of the day's events.

Casia kept her head lowered, but she was the one to eventually break the silence as she quietly but clearly said, "I am not afraid of death."

He leaned against the tree, folding his arms across his chest. "I think you've more than proven that over these past months."

She laughed a quiet, humorless laugh. "I just meant…that if the world can keep going after we're gone…then it would be enough. I've thought that for some time now, and I've been preparing myself for whatever sacrifice it might take to keep it going." She picked at a dead leaf crushed under her boot. "If there was a way we might all survive, then of course it would be better, but it…" She trailed off, shaking her head. "And you and I, anyway…we were given *two* lifetimes. So how could we selfishly ask for any more than that?"

He frowned, but otherwise didn't reply; the question didn't seem to have an answer.

She was silent for several minutes, eyes glazing over in thought, before she spoke again. "I don't need any of it. Not the crowns or vows or forever homes on mountaintops—they were a hope, a trick to get us to this point. And so what if they never happen? Plenty of queens have suffered worse things throughout the bloody history of this empire, haven't they? At least...at least, there was a *possibility* in my case. And a love powerful enough to break a world. *Nothing can break things so completely*, as the Healing Goddess said."

"And nothing can heal them so fully," he reminded her.

She smiled sadly. "Right. Of course." She closed her eyes. "But it all just feels...*broken* now, doesn't it?"

He wished he could disagree. He simply couldn't bring himself to do it.

"I can still picture it, although it's much blurrier now," she said, softly. "The wedding, the heirs, the growing old together. And you... you would have stood by my side through all of it. I believe that."

The idea of hope felt false and unfair at the moment, so he didn't offer any. He simply reached for her hand, and as she took it and let him pull her to her feet, he said, "Yes. I would have."

She stared into his eyes, unblinking even as her bottom lip quivered. She was afraid—so was he—and it felt as though they were attending a private funeral, grieving all the things that might have been, committing them to memory while they still could.

But she never cowered or looked away, no matter how the darkness seemed to gather and press around them, and soon his faint-hearted queen became fearless once more, reaching up and pressing her hands through his hair, pulling his lips down to meet hers.

She kissed him as fiercely as she wielded a sword. He returned it just as fiercely, wrapping her tightly in his arms and crushing her to him, taking her in until he knew nothing beyond her smoke-tinted taste, her soft skin, the way she trembled when he whispered those three simple words against her lips.

I love you, I love you, I love you.

When they pulled away minutes later, she took hold of his hands and still looked only to him—not at the path ahead or behind them, or at any of the dark places looming all around, as she said, "The Moon Goddess might have been right. There might still be a chance of the light coming back. A chance we don't end in darkness."

He could tell she was struggling to picture such an ending even as she said it. He was, too…and yet he found the strength to agree with her.

"I don't think we end in darkness." It was strange, how he found it easier to believe in things for her sake rather than his own. "And even if it comes, it won't last forever," he added, squeezing her hands. "*There is always an after,* as someone told me not very long ago."

CHAPTER 26

A short time later, they came upon Nessa and the others waiting for them at a sharp bend of the Mirdor River.

They didn't linger here, pausing only long enough for Cas to wrap Nessa in a swift hug and check her over. Then they were off again, filling Nessa in on all she'd missed as they rode along, racing through the trees and making their way toward the hazy, distant glow of the city of Irithyl.

Before Cas had a chance to finish recapping all that had taken place in the fields outside of Feyedge, another group of riders met them, hailing from the palace and led by a frantic Anwyn—who had apparently spent the last several hours scouring the edges of the realm, hoping to find them and bring them in.

She raced quickly up to Cas, pulling up just short of their horses colliding. "Thank goodness you're back," the elven woman gasped out. "There's trouble in the palace. Your sword is...it's...*just hurry,* please!" She turned and galloped toward the city with no more explanation than this.

Thoroughly confused, her heart clenching with dread, Cas followed along with the others. The rest of her friends met them as they passed through the gates to the palace grounds, accompanied by servants who took hold of their horses as soon as they dismounted.

Cas's focus was on getting to her sword, but her gaze automatically followed Nessa as she leapt from her horse and went straight to Laurent, burying her face against his chest. Or the way Laurent took her in without hesitation, his eyes closing and his arms tightening in a way that seemed protective and soft and completely out of character for the elf she'd come to know. When his eyes opened, they found Cas, his gaze slowing her down for half a step. He gave a subtle nod that seemed to say several things at once—a welcome, a concerned curiosity, a thank you.

Just promise you'll keep her safe.

This latest mission felt like it had been a failure in so many ways, but she'd managed this much at least.

Cas briefly greeted the rest of her friends before she followed Anwyn at a near sprint into the palace, winding through the halls with such reckless speed that she was soon hopelessly lost, completely at the mercy of whatever direction Anwyn chose to take her. They slowed only when Elander caught up to them and grabbed Anwyn's arm, forcing her to a stop.

"What is going on?" he demanded. "I'm not a fan of sprinting blindly into whatever dangers await us."

Anwyn wrenched free of his hold and kept moving, though she slowed to a more reasonable pace. "The instant Casia left this realm, the sword...*turned* on the ones keeping it," she explained in between attempts to catch her breath. "And some of the dark that the blade was holding in escaped, and the power of it overwhelmed the ones standing guard. One of those guards is dead. The others escaped—barely. They've locked the blade alone in a room, and no one has entered that room since. But I fear the walls are not going to hold much longer. They're already cracking. The door has started to cave even though it's made of materials that usually withstand divine magic. The doors of the rooms all around it are caving in as well, and no one can even walk the hallway that leads up to the blade's room without risking injury or madness. We've tried *everything* we could think of to temper the darkness. Nothing works. It hasn't yielded to any charms or spells we've used—they hardly seem to faze it."

Minutes later, they reached the head of the hallway in question and paused there, staring at the distant, damaged door. Anwyn had not exaggerated the woeful energy of this setting; the air was so thick with foulness that it was difficult to move or even breathe within it.

But even through the noxious waves rolling toward them, Cas could sense what lay beyond that door. When she closed her eyes and concentrated, she thought she could *see* it—an ocean of blackness and the shadow of her sword, even blacker, in the center of it all.

And when she focused harder, she could *feel* something deep within the shadowed blade—a glimmer of light. Drowning. It was *drowning*, and she had to get to it. *Now*.

Her friends caught up and folded in around her, breaking her concentration, all of them wearing the same concerned expression.

"It might not yield to you either," Laurent warned, starting to reach for her. He ended up closing his hand into a fist instead, and he didn't try to hold her back when she took a few steps down the hall, though she could tell from his expression that he *wanted* to—they all wanted to.

"Have you forgotten what it did to you when you approached it before?" Zev asked. "It's only grown more chaotic, more violent..."

She paused and tilted her face toward him. "If it keeps raging further and further out of control, then this entire realm will be at risk. What else should we do?"

She waited, giving all of her companions a chance to answer.

No one said anything.

So she turned back to the task before her. She bowed her head and thought of the fires blazing around Feyedge, of the bodies drained of life, of blood spilling and skies growing dark. Of the days they'd already lost, the time they didn't have to waste...

She braced herself and walked on, drawing what magic she could to the surface in spite of her exhaustion, pushing back against the dark waves of energy that crawled like spiders over her skin. She felt Elander behind her, his magic connected to hers. It was like a lifeline stretching after her, his presence an anchor that made her feel like she could always find her way back to the light, no matter how far down this dark hallway she went.

I don't think we end in darkness.

He'd said it so easily. And she'd believed it just as easily—so when she came to the end of the hallway, she didn't hesitate to throw herself into the darkness.

She pushed the door open.

Power flooded over her, threatening to buckle her knees. She gripped the splintered door frame and stayed on her feet, managing one step after another all the way to the other side of the room.

Against the far wall, her sword waited, suspended in the air, trapped in the midst of twisting black and purple clouds. It was not the same smooth, tightly coiled cloudiness they'd first encountered below the palace—it was chaos, a churning mass of energies all fighting for dominance.

It reminded her of the chaos that the Sun Goddess had originally pulled Shadowslayer from. She vividly recalled watching Solatis reach into that turbulent mass of darkness and power and withdraw the gleaming blade—a weapon so beautiful it had taken her breath away.

She pictured that beautiful sight now—the Goddess and the unblemished sword—and she held the image tightly in her mind as she reached into the dark clouds.

Cold bit at her skin, eating its way to the bone. She swiftly lost all feeling in her arm from the elbow downward, and yet she kept moving, trusting that her connection to Shadowslayer would put it back in its rightful owner's hand once more.

The moment her fingers brushed the hilt, she could feel again. She gripped it and squeezed until the numbness left her fingers and warm strength coursed from the sword up her arm. It was short-lived, swiftly overtaken by the power of the Antaeum Point, but it was enough to give Cas what she needed to heave the sword free and fully into her hold.

As she withdrew it from the cloudiness, that mass collapsed swiftly, creating a powerful suction that nearly sent her toppling forward. The pressure was so immense she feared it was going to leave her permanently embedded in the rattling floorboards beneath her.

She crouched down and tried to find her center once

more, but it was like kneeling in the middle of a cyclone. A deafening roar rose all around her, followed by wind that ripped at her hair and clothing, leaving nothing for her to do except curl into herself and hold tightly to the blade that shook and tried to fly from her grasp over and over again.

She held on, breathing her way through, until the sword and her surroundings finally calmed. The blade remained dark, cursed, *broken* compared to what it had been—but the Point was contained within it once more, and all was quiet.

Cas had hardly moved, yet she felt more drained now than she had after battling actual gods outside of Feyedge.

She heard footsteps behind her. People cautiously drawing closer to the room. Staring at her. But she couldn't speak, couldn't turn to face them—she was too exhausted to even lift her head. And relief did not come quickly, even now that she had the sword firmly back in her possession; it still required her constant awareness. If she let her guard down, the energy within its blade swiftly turned darker and more restless, threatening to rage out of control again.

She felt someone moving past her, surveying her and the newly-settled room. Then came a voice she vaguely recognized —the king, she thought, and confirmed it a moment later when she finally found the strength and balance to lift her head.

He was staring at the sword in her hands.

She held it more tightly, determined not to allow him to take it from her again.

His eyes didn't leave it even as he addressed her. "You picked it up."

"Someone had to."

He considered this for a long moment, slowly shifting all of his focus to her. "Doesn't it hurt to hold it?"

She swallowed hard, trying to soothe her suddenly dry throat, unsure of how to reply.

Hurt was not the right word.

Or perhaps it was—perhaps, if she hadn't been so used to the feel of impossible magic and pressure, she might have felt pain from it. But all she felt was…

"Heavy," she told the king. "It's heavy. I suppose it would be painful if I focused on that, but I don't anymore. I can't. I'm too focused on keeping it all under control."

"So despite the weight of this burden, you don't hesitate to carry it," he said, "even if it pains you."

It wasn't really a question, but she answered him anyway. "The Goddess of Life chose me to carry this burden. And I swore I would do it. The light cannot always overcome the dark, but it must rise to meet it. That was the task I was given, and I haven't turned away from it yet. I don't plan to start now."

The king didn't answer—perhaps because the room was growing more crowded by the minute, more and more people intruding on their conversation.

Cas was grateful for those people, for the way her friends gathered like guards around her, and for the feel of Elander's hand closing around her arm, steadying her as she rose back to her feet. She kept her eyes on the elven king, expectant, until finally it happened—

He bowed his head slightly, and something like reverence flashed in his eyes as he looked up at her and quietly said, "I think that I better understand your plight now, Mortal Queen."

She stilled, not daring so much as a breath over this new, potentially fragile understanding between them.

"And it seems *you* are to be the keeper of the Point, after all," he added, "for better or worse."

He ordered the palace dwellers who had intruded to disperse, to leave her and the sword alone, and Cas's nerves finally began to settle.

She returned the bow the king had given her and then focused on that sword, double-checking the sheath encasing it for damage.

It felt heavier than usual in her arms, but its weight seemed to lessen as her friends gathered around her once more. Suppressing the dark point in the blade became almost second-nature as she passed the hour in their presence, walking the halls while she, Elander, and Nessa filled the others in on all that had taken place in the borderlands.

As the conversation wound down and the palace grew quieter, Cas found herself, as she so often did, drawn toward Elander, ready to slip away and spend the night wrapped in his arms.

Once the rest of their group headed toward their own rooms, he drifted to her side, looking her over as he came.

"I'm okay," she said, before he could ask.

He nodded, taking one of her hands and squeezing it. Suddenly he was staring at her the way he had just before she'd kissed him in the forest earlier that day—with the weight of lifetimes in his eyes, and his lips parted as though on the cusp of a thousand things he wanted to say.

"Are *you* okay?" she asked, smiling a bit uncertainly.

"Yes." He returned her smile, though his eyes remained distant with thought.

She studied him a moment more before giving up on this particular guessing game and starting to walk, tugging him along with her. "I'm okay," she repeated. "But I'm exhausted."

He followed without speaking. Neither of them spoke until he drew to a stop outside the door to her room, hesitating to follow her inside.

She gave him a confused look. "Aren't you coming to bed?"

"Soon," he told her. "I need to speak with the king about something first. I won't be long. Go rest."

Curiosity burned inside her, but she was too tired to indulge it. He planted a swift kiss on her lips, and then he was gone, disappearing around the corner before she could find the words to ask him to stay.

Another wave of exhaustion pushed her through the door. She wandered into her room, leaned Shadowslayer against the wall, stripped off her outer clothes and weapons, and then collapsed onto the bed, focusing on the lingering taste of Elander's kiss instead of the pressure and fear she felt whenever she glanced toward her sword.

She was asleep within minutes.

THE NEXT MORNING, Cas woke up alone.

It was only her and her sword, which remained relatively calm and quiet in its place against the wall, right where she'd left it.

She remembered Elander joining her in the middle of the night, she was almost certain of it. His earth and winter scent clung to the pillow beside her, and the sheets still held his shape; he hadn't been gone long.

She thought of the last conversation they'd had, how quickly he'd slipped away to go speak with the king, not inviting any questions on the matter. The same curiosity that had gripped her then pulled her from the bed now, making her move quickly despite the exhaustion still weighing her down.

She washed and dressed, and she was twisting her hair into a braid when she heard a soft knock—Elander announcing his return.

"Good morning," he said, pushing his way inside, arms laden with a tray full of food and drink—breakfast. He'd brought breakfast, and he was smiling as though there was somehow nothing on his mind other than eating it with her.

She breathed a soft sigh. It was silly, maybe, but the sight of him standing in the doorway, sunlight streaming over his handsome face, preparing to do something so normal as having breakfast with her....she could have melted into a puddle right then and there. She wanted to sink into the peace of the moment and stay in it forever.

"You're catering directly to my room now?" she mused as she finished tying off her braid. "What's the occasion?"

"The occasion," he said, setting the tray on the dresser before her, "is that you went to bed without eating last night."

She frowned in thought, trying to recall the blur of events that had preceded her collapsing into bed. "I did, didn't I?"

"You were sound asleep when I returned." He poured a steaming cup of *yamash*, the elvish take on coffee, and handed it to her after adding her usual splash of cream and dusting of cinnamon—luxuries they hadn't often had time for during these past months. She was surprised he remembered them, and that he thought they had time to enjoy these luxuries this morning, given all that awaited them.

What was he up to?

"Sound asleep...and snoring so loudly I thought I'd stumbled upon some otherworldly beast rather than the queen I was looking for," he added, teasingly.

"If you'd fallen asleep along with me, you probably wouldn't have noticed—but I distinctly remember waiting *forever* for you last night," she countered, sipping at her drink, which he'd made precisely right. "You were gone much longer than you said you'd be."

He acquiesced with a wave of his hand, busying himself with preparing his own drink.

She studied him as she continued to sip, her suspicion growing. "What did you ask the king about yesterday?"

He didn't look up from the mug he was stirring, but she could see the trace of a smile on his lips.

"Elander?"

He shook his head, his smile brightening. "Eat," he insisted.

She ate, taking her drink and a pastry filled with some sort of cream and moving to the cushioned window seat, sitting cross-legged upon it while soaking up the warmth of the sunrise filtering through the colorful glass panes. Elander joined her a minute later, leaning his shoulder against the wall and staring at the world outside as he absently sipped his drink.

He remained unusually quiet, even after several minutes passed. In the silence she could hear the energy humming around Shadowslayer, and her eyes were soon drawn to it in spite of her efforts not to let it disrupt the peace she was enjoying.

"Shadowslayer is calmer this morning," she commented. "The darkness seems to have lightened a bit."

"It spent the entire night at your side," he replied, not

taking his eyes off the sunrise. "And you have that effect on the darkness."

Her cheeks warmed despite the casual, offhanded way he'd said it. She went back to nibbling on her breakfast, gaze following his and watching the sun as it continued to rise over the distant forest, spilling light into the nearby city and defining all its points and edges. All of the colorful glass windows were particularly breathtaking in this lighting.

Her chest felt tight as she stared at them and thought of where she'd been such a short time ago—of the darkness and devastation waiting just over the horizon. She tried to guard her mind against the memory of the Sky Goddess's words, but they infiltrated her thoughts all the same.

You can't hide in that elven realm forever.

She started to turn and move away from the beauty that suddenly felt wrong—unearned—but Elander caught her arm and held her still. His hand swept to her chin, tilting her gaze up to his, and she had the feeling—as she often did when he looked at her this way—that he could read her thoughts, her fears, her *everything*.

He said, "Walk with me for a minute?"

A simple request, but her heart leapt into her throat for some reason, leaving her unable to answer with anything but a nod. He placed his cup back on the tray and left the room without another word, and she only watched him go at first. Something in his tone had made her stomach and legs as unsteady as her voice.

She came to her senses soon enough and jogged to catch up. "You're up to something. And I wish you'd tell me what."

Another half-smile curved his lips, but he only kept walking, taking her by the hand and leading her alongside him. They walked for the better part of an hour, it felt like, until she became convinced that he didn't actually have a destination in mind. She started to tease him about the matter, when suddenly they were interrupted by someone walking toward them.

"Anwyn?"

The elven woman approached without hesitation, and Elander greeted her as though he'd expected to run into her. She had something in her hands—a short sword wrapped in a silk cloth. She unwrapped it and offered it to Cas, telling her it was a gift from the king, and then she dismissed herself, smiling as she went.

Unable to stifle her curiosity, Cas withdrew it partially from its emerald-studded sheath and looked it over.

It was more stunning even than Shadowslayer, the gold and white symbols upon its iron more intricate and more numerous. They appeared to be imprinted on the blade itself, not etched or painted, but somehow a part of that iron—as though the metal had already bore these markings when it was harvested from the earth. She knew of no mortal technique that could have caused such an illusion, and she wondered at the magic that had gone into creating such a beautiful object—and at what other magic might be slumbering within those markings.

They walked on, leaving the palace and strolling into the gardens, Elander still lost in thought, Cas still studying the blade. She was so entranced with it—so busy trying to unravel the various symbols from each other—that at one point she nearly walked straight into a rose bush, making Elander chuckle as he caught her sleeve and prevented the thorny collision.

She finally pulled her attention away from her gift and took in their surroundings. They had put quite a ways between themselves and the palace at this point. The yard around them was clearly kept, yet wild, trimmed and cleared for walking, but without any obvious pattern to the various bushes and flowers growing all around them. She'd never seen such bright flowers, such bold shades of pink and orange and yellow. But as beautiful as they were, she still found her eyes drawn back to the blade after a moment.

"You like the sword, I take it?" Elander asked.

"It's beautiful." The word seemed inadequate. "I've never seen markings like these before. I would be hesitant to use it in an actual battle, afraid I might stain it."

"It's a Savnas blade. A ceremonial blade," he told her, "used for over a century by the elves of this realm—but not for battles."

"...Ceremonial?"

"Yes."

"What kind of a ceremony?" She suspected she already knew the answer, and her heart fluttered wildly as she asked the question. Her gaze was still fixed on the blade. When she gathered the courage to lift her eyes, she found him staring at her as though no blade separated them. As though *nothing* separated them, or ever had, or ever could.

"Elander." His name left her as a whisper, a hopeful sigh, and then she asked him one final time, "What did you speak to the king about?"

He smiled as he had before, but he finally gave her an answer. "This isn't the way it was meant to happen, I know. And it doesn't have to happen if you don't want it to."

A wave of dizziness nearly overcame her, and she realized that she had been holding her breath. She willed herself to release it, and then slowly inhale another. *Exhale. Inhale. Exhale...*

"But it would be official," he continued, "an elven king is as good as any mortal one, in this case. The elves have different traditions, different words and vows than we might have otherwise had...but none of that makes a difference to me, really, as long as you're my wife at the end of the day."

Wife.

Her breath caught again at the word, but she managed to keep her head lifted and her gaze fixed on his. She could keep breathing as long as she kept her eyes on him. She had told him as much when he'd first asked her to marry him—that she needed him to remind her how to breathe as she navigated crowns and wars and whatever else, and it was more true now than ever. He was her guardian, her king, her anchor.

And now she would be his wife.

There was no question, no hesitation left in her.

But before she could tell him this, there came a sudden rustling in a nearby bush. She tensed, drawing closer to Elander. Another rustle—and this time an excited, anxious whimper followed it. She recognized that sound.

"Silver?"

At the mention of his name, the fox gave up any attempt at hiding and bounded happily toward her, leaping into her arms so excitedly she nearly stumbled and fell as she tried to catch and secure him.

Cas struggled to keep her arms wrapped around his lanky body as he wiggled and barked at a line of bushes in the distance. Cas's eyes narrowed in the same direction, and after a moment, she understood. "You were eavesdropping, weren't you?"

His ears twitched as he gave the loudest bark yet.

Cas took a few steps in the direction he was looking in,

and she heard a muffled voice—Nessa's, she was fairly certain—say, "*Ugh*, he's given us away."

Her friends still remained hidden until Cas called out, "I know you're there." A bit of shifting, and a boot was suddenly sticking out from underneath one of those bushes. "And I'm less than impressed by your stealth abilities, for the record," she added, drily.

They tumbled out of the bushes one by one—all four of them—Zev and Nessa poking and shoving at each other, while Rhea and Laurent managed a bit more dignity, strolling casually toward her while picking stray leaves from their clothing.

Cas looked them over, unable to keep the grin from spreading across her face. "How are you all the same group I used to trust with my life when it came to jobs that required secrecy?"

"We hardly needed to apply much *stealth* to this particular mission." Zev countered. "It's not as if we didn't all already know what was happening."

Cas cut her eyes toward Elander, who lifted his palms in a declaration of innocence.

"I didn't tell him anything, I swear."

"He didn't have to," Zev said. "Did you honestly think I wouldn't *guess*?"

"We all guessed," Rhea added, smiling. "I hardly needed Silver's vision to see what was destined to happen between you two."

Laurent rolled his eyes in a good-natured manner. "It's almost like we know you well enough to read you by this point."

Cas gave him a skeptical look. "Even you?"

"Even me."

"And he has the emotional awareness of a pile of sticks," Zev pointed out.

Laurent didn't disagree with this assessment.

Cas's smile widened as she looked at each of her friend's faces in turn. "I didn't want to keep it from you," she told them, smile fading slightly. "I wanted you all to know as soon as we'd decided, I just wasn't sure what would become of us, and I didn't know how…how to…"

Rhea came to stand beside her, linking their arms together. "You don't have to explain yourself."

Nessa nodded in agreement, and not even Zev had a snarky word to offer. He seemed genuinely happy—they all did. More happy than Cas remembered them being in a very long time, which made *her* happy. Ridiculously, deliriously happy.

She looked back to Elander, who offered her a shrug. "It was destined to happen, one way or another, as Rhea said."

She felt as though she was truly noticing the warmth of the sun for the very first time as she hugged Rhea's arm tighter and said, "Then I suppose there's only one thing left for us to do."

CHAPTER 27

In the light of a setting sun, beneath a pink and orange splashed sky, Cas stood with Rhea and Nessa at the top of a staircase overlooking a vast garden.

The Palace of Irithyl rose behind them, reflections from its colorful windows casting rainbows against the cobblestone paths. The ground was littered with white flowers, most of them freshly freed from the trees by the warm breeze that carried a hint of honey beneath its thick floral scent.

Farther down one of the cobblestone paths, against a backdrop of more flowering trees, Elander stood with Laurent and the King of Mistwilde, waiting.

Cas wore an ivory dress with a plunging neckline, made up of layers of sheer fabric, its top layer embellished with golden designs that subtly resembled suns with shimmering, outward stretching rays. It draped straight and elegantly to the floor until she moved, at which point the delicate train lifted and flowed out behind her, billowing in such an ethereal manner that Cas thought it might have been magic at work—though Anwyn had insisted it wasn't.

Her hair fell around her in long, loose waves, and upon it sat a golden circlet with sides resembling feathers twisted together—a borrowed crown once worn by an ancient elven queen, lent to her as a sign of the newly-established trust and respect between her rule and that of the Mistwilde elves.

Nessa, looking stunning in skirts of pale blue and silver, bounced happily about, adjusting the many layers of Cas's dress, while Rhea, in a sage-colored dress with shimmering pearls woven delicately through her curls, recited the steps of the upcoming ceremony that Cas had already forgotten.

Zev joined them a few moments later, a gold-rimmed glass in each hand. His formal tunic matched his sister's, its rich color making his eyes seem a brighter green than usual. Silverfoot trotted after him, wearing a similar-colored collar studded with pearlescent stones.

"This is your last chance to back out, you know," Zev informed Cas with a grin, earning him a swat from both his sister and Nessa. He managed to dodge both—practiced as he was at it—while keeping the cups in his hands upright, not spilling a single drop from them.

"What's in the cups?" Nessa asked.

"A sampling of a special elvish spirit—*mythwater,* they call it. For Cas's nerves."

Rhea muttered something indistinguishable, while Nessa's eyes narrowed suspiciously.

"Is this going to leave me… *indisposed* for my own wedding?" asked Cas.

"Of course not." He chuckled. "When have I ever steered you wrong when it comes to alcohol?"

"Is that a serious question?"

"No—and on second thought, don't answer it. Here, just drink."

She took the glass from him and gave it a dubious sniff; the smell was a mixture of sweet and tart, like perfectly ripened raspberries. Tempting, she had to admit. Her fingers tapped against the glass, considering. "If I drink this, you have to walk me into this affair and make sure I don't get dizzy from it or anything foolish like that."

He met her gaze. His eyes turned serious for half an instant, and Cas felt a blush creeping across her cheeks.

"I can do that, I suppose," he said. "Though I'm not sure I can keep you from looking like a fool."

"No doubt having you hanging off her arm won't help with *that*," Rhea said, giving them a wry look that soon gave way to a more tender smile.

Nessa still looked mildly suspicious as she watched Cas and Zev toss the contents of the cups back after the count of three, but she simply gave a happy sigh and went back to smoothing the layers of Cas's dress.

Silverfoot had made his way down toward Elander and the others, but he returned to them now, plopping down at Rhea's feet and looking up at her expectantly.

"They're waiting on us," Rhea informed them.

Nessa straightened the circlet on Cas's head one last time before taking Rhea's arm and leading her on to that small crowd waiting in the distance.

Cas and Zev followed a few moments later.

The air seemed to grow thicker and more perfumed as they descended the stairs. Her heart raced, and soon she was feeling a bit lightheaded. The mythwater actually *had* calmed her somewhat, but her pulse still sped up with every step they took, her anxiety unable to tell the difference between true battles and bold but welcome, wonderful things.

Zev knew this, of course. Knew that it likely would have been worse if not for the way he kept teasing her—offering to change directions and escort her to the nearest tavern instead, or else made her laugh by gathering up handfuls of fallen flowers and showering her with them to help 'enhance' her appearance.

He finally straightened up and walked properly once they were within view of other people, but he still kept up his teasing, leaning closer and whispering, "Don't assume I won't beat him up just because he's going to be your husband now. I'm still going to be close by to take care of you if necessary."

She shook her head, smiling. "I'll keep that in mind."

They walked on together, finding their way to a path that narrowed and stretched through rows of rose bushes, eventually leading to a small pavilion hedged in by rock walls and cascading water.

It was a small, intimate affair, with only a handful of noble elves gathered alongside Cas's friends to bear witness, but it was all she needed. It was all she *wanted*—the gently falling water, the warm sunlight filtering over them, the lilting notes of a harp-like instrument being played nearby.

And then, *finally,* the smile spreading slowly across Elander's face as he caught sight of her walking toward him.

In that moment, she wanted nothing more than to look upon him and that smile for all the rest of her days, however many or few they were.

He was the perfect complement to her in an elegant ivory tunic and a doublet embroidered with golden thread, his hair loosely tied back. Rings of emerald and gold decorated his fingers, shining as brilliantly as the circlet on Cas's head—gifts from the king himself. That king stood to his right, and Laurent waited next to him with the Savnas blade resting on a cushion in his hands.

Cas nearly slowed to a stop without meaning to, but Zev kept her moving, guiding her toward the raised platform Elander and the others stood on and kissing her cheek before moving to take a seat.

She walked the rest of the way to Elander on her own, taking his hand and stepping up to him. Time seemed to freeze as their eyes met, as they both tried and failed to find words. Only one word was playing over and over in her thoughts—

Finally, finally, finally.

Elander's gaze darted briefly to Zev. "I assume he was trying to talk you out of this while escorting you down here," he whispered.

Cas smiled. "For the entire walk."

He shook with quiet laughter.

"But I'm stubborn. So I still made it back to you."

He reached to free one of the flowers Zev had tossed into her hair, tucking it behind her ear instead. "And thank the gods for that."

The king stepped toward them and began to read from an ancient-looking book, and Cas tried to listen to each and every word, but found this difficult between her racing heart and the distracting weight and warmth of Elander's hands against hers.

She blinked, and the first part of the ceremony was over. Laurent was beside her a moment later, offering the sword to them.

They took it, each gripping the hilt with one hand and holding it upright between them. Cas pressed a hand to one flat side of the blade, while Elander pressed his to the opposite side, and the elven king stepped forward as Laurent bowed his head and stepped away.

The king said something in the Mistwilde language, making the blade glow with soft amethyst light. Warmth filled the steel and flooded into Cas's skin, a burning that stopped just short of being painful.

It lasted only seconds, but the marks it left behind—as the king declared—would last forever.

They pulled their hands away. Laurent took the sword once more, returning it to its cushioned resting place, while Cas and Elander lifted their hands with their palms facing outward.

The blade's branding had left two identical symbols upon their skin, in the center of each palm. They resembled trees with curved trunks, intricate roots, and branches curling to one side and catching what looked like a small sun.

The sword and its magic chose the mark and the meaning, she'd been told, and no two were created exactly the same. There were elves well-studied in the symbolism of such things, and they would be able to reveal the full meaning behind these particular marks, but all she truly cared about was the fact that they matched—an outward sign of the inward connection she'd felt to Elander for so long.

They pressed those marks together as a chorus of voices rose from the ones gathered all around them. The voices were speaking in the same ancient language the king had used to recite the blade's spell, but there was a common tongue version of this same verse that Anwyn had shared with Cas earlier that day:

May sun and solace rise to meet you
Blade and courage always keep you
Through wealth of light
or depths of night
Until time takes your final breaths
and both your souls find rest

The words were beautiful, as were the voices speaking them in a rhythmic, undulating fashion. Almost like music. But as they rose and fell over them, Elander's palm moved, fingers finding the spaces between hers and squeezing tightly, and a separate vow began floating through Cas's mind—the words he had spoken to her on the hillside back in Ciridan.

She had repeated them in her head countless times since that day.

And as the voices of the others began to trail away, she found herself reciting these familiar words out loud, soft enough for only Elander to hear. "Across lifetimes, through endings and beginnings, with all that I have, all that I've ever had..."

Recognition warmed his expression, and he repeated more of that conversation in the same soft but certain tone, "I never stopped loving you. And I never will. I've made that vow before—nearly every time I've looked at you in this lifetime and every other—and I make it again now."

She nodded. *As do I.* "Always. Every beat of my heart and breath from my lungs is yours now."

There was more she wanted to say. More feelings that she suspected she would never be able to properly put into words. But as the last of the voices faded around them and the music in the distance stopped, the words no longer mattered.

He kissed her and everything else fell away—the world, the wars, all her worries about the right words and everything else. Only the two of them, now *one*, existed, and it took the loud cheers of the crowd surrounding them to wake her and pull her from what felt like the most beautiful dream she'd ever had.

They were swept away, along with that crowd, toward a larger pavilion nearby. A delicate, decorative fence of gold encased it, but the top remained open to embrace the twilight sky. Strings of ivy and twinkling lights wove through the fence, and the stone beneath their feet was embedded with sparkling stones that resembled the stars winking into existence above them. Mouth-watering aromas soon filled the air—spiced meats, sweet fruits, vanilla and honey from the *vedas* cakes that were famous in this realm. Wine was poured without restraint, and music played, growing increasingly loud and jovial as the evening went on.

Neither of them had ever cared much for dancing. But Cas felt like dancing now, and Elander was more than willing to oblige, and perfectly capable of leading her along even to the complicated notes of elvish music; they glided effortlessly over the shimmering stone, a vision of gold and elegance in the glittering lights.

She danced her way through the evening, occasionally taking turns with Zev and Laurent, as well—and even with the Mistwilde king himself at one point—but always finding her way back to Elander before too long. As the music grew softer and their guests began to politely disperse, she took two glasses of wine and found her way to his side once more.

He took a glass in one hand and her hand in the other, spinning her slowly out in time with the music, then drawing her back to him. They stared into each other's eyes for a long moment, lost once more to the world around them. He started to raise his glass, nodding to the one she still held. "To everything after?"

She smiled but shook her head at the familiar-by-now line.

"No?"

"Not tonight. Tonight, I think it's just…to *this*." She clutched her wine glass to her chest, toward her heart that felt close to bursting. "To everything now, to everyone present."

He considered the words as he studied her, eyes filled with adoration, and then he lifted his glass in a full, proper toast. "To tonight, then."

Cas lifted hers as well, her smile brightening as she looked at the people around them. At Zev, who was busy trying to teach several skeptical-looking elves a classic drinking game from the mortal realm, at Rhea talking and laughing with the king as though they were old friends, at Laurent and Nessa dancing slowly off to one side, oblivious to anyone who might have been watching them.

This.

This was why she kept fighting. It was not for the light on the distant horizon, or the one waiting on the other side of the storm, but the lights right here in the storm with her, laughing and dancing and *living* in spite of the darkness raging around them.

Everything after was important.

Hope was important.

But more than this, it came down to surviving—no, *living* —and feeling each of these waves, these moments as they broke over her.

There is always an after, she had told Elander. *On to the other side,* as her friends had grown so fond of saying. But another thought had occurred to her tonight—that even if they never made it to after, they had made it to *now,* and this was worth celebrating even without the promise of anything else.

So they celebrated until the moon was high and the night air cold and crisp, and when their hearts were full, their feet sore from dancing and their stomachs aching from laughter, they finally said good night to all who remained at their celebration, and she and Elander slipped away with the sound of music fading behind them.

They headed toward their shared room, slightly drunk off not only wine but each other's presence. They ended up taking several detours along the way, stopping to sneak kisses and caresses every time they found themselves in a relatively private stretch of the palace. But eventually they made it to their destination, where they found a servant waiting alongside a pile of gifts, who offered to bring them anything else they might wish for before retiring for the night.

As Cas was thanking them, the magnitude of the day hit her all at once. It was overwhelming—even if it was for good reasons. She excused herself, removing her borrowed crown and placing it safely on the dresser, then stepped out onto the balcony, craving the quiet and the cool air.

She was staring at the stars when Elander finished talking to the servant, dismissed them, and joined her outside.

He said nothing, only pressed close and smoothed a hand against the small of her back, then up along her spine, tracing a path through the thin fabric of her dress. The sheer layers of that dress did nothing to dull the sensation of his fingertips against her. She closed her eyes and focused on those fingers as they traveled up to her shoulders, sliding the strap down on one side, revealing more skin.

He kissed a trail across her bare shoulder and along the curve of her neck, making her shiver, while his hands roamed up and down her body. One of those hands reached around and came to rest against her stomach, pulling her firmly back against him. He held her in place while he continued to kiss her neck, to caress and nibble at the sensitive spots around her ear. Her body reacted as it always did when he teased this spot, twisting and pressing hungrily back against him, urging him to keep going.

His hold moved from her stomach to take her by the hand, and he used the grip to twirl her around and push her back just far enough to allow him to admire the full sight of her.

She stood in the bright moonlight, heat pooling in her lower stomach as he stared unabashedly at her. She was still mostly clothed, but it didn't feel like it.

Nearly a minute passed. He made no move to finish removing those clothes, which brought a teasing smile to her face. "Is something wrong? It's not like you to hesitate to undress me."

He returned the smile, still holding onto her, his hand a powerful, steadying weight between them. "Have you ever had a gift that was almost too beautiful to unwrap?"

The heat in her center began to spread, tingling throughout her entire body.

"*Almost* being the key word in that sentence." He closed the distance between them again, his hands resuming their exploration, this time finding their way to the clasp at the dress's back. He unhooked it. He slipped the other strap from her shoulder as well, but continued to take his time, even then, dragging his fingers with excruciatingly delicate motions along the edges of her dress, unraveling it bit by bit and taking the time to kiss, to taste and savor each inch of her skin as he uncovered it.

As he slipped the fabric down to her waist, he backed her toward the balcony railing, holding her steady and in place against it. He cupped one of her breasts, his mouth dipping toward its peak, taking it between his lips. Her head tipped back as lips gave way to gently biting teeth. A gasp escaped her, and he rolled the dress down to her hips in response, exposing her stomach so he could traverse the lines of it with both his tongue and his fingertips.

Heat continued to build around and within her, making her heart pound and her thoughts turn wild. She took his hands and guided them into rolling the dress even lower—along with everything underneath it—and he offered no resistance, his nails digging into her skin as he dragged the fabric away from it. He didn't slip the dress fully from her body, but left it gathered around her knees, effectively binding her legs.

He knelt before her. His hands moved along her thighs, up to the needy throbbing at their center, his fingertips mapping out a route for his mouth to follow. And he followed without hesitation, lips pressing and tongue tracing, slipping in and claiming her until her knees felt weak, her balance threatening to give way even as her hands held more tightly to the railing behind her.

Her legs started to buckle completely. He caught her and straightened, lifting her onto her tiptoes, securing her against him with one strong hand while using the other to strip the dress completely off.

She regained her balance and sought to even out their clothing, deftly unbuttoning his jacket and pulling at the tunic underneath. She got these fully removed and his belt undone before she gave into the urge to crash back into him.

They tangled together, her hands roving over his newly-bared skin, one leg wrapping around him while his hand sank into her upper thigh, lifting her higher, more fully into every kiss.

After a minute he slipped free and backed slowly away from her, a smirk flirting with his lips as he pulled his belt fully off and finished undressing.

She followed.

He took her hand as he sank down onto the edge of the bed, pulling her into his lap. Her knees pressed against his thighs as she leaned forward and crushed her lips to his. She rocked against him, hips rising and falling without slowing, challenging his balance and control until he was flat on his back, fighting off a groan, and it was her turn to smirk.

He laughed at the sight of that smirk and sat up again, taking her face in both hands and drawing her in for a slow, lingering kiss.

"I love you," he breathed as he pulled away. The words—and the way he looked at her as he said them—made her heart skip into an even faster rhythm. She stopped teasing him and simply wrapped her arms around his neck, drawing him in for another slow kiss.

His hand slid across her lower back, then lower, taking a

commanding hold on her legs and pulling them out beside him, making it easier for her to sink more fully into his lap.

"Now arch your back and lift your hips," he ordered, one of his hands slipping between her legs and pushing up, persuading her to comply. "I want to be inside my wife."

The words sent a quiver of need rattling through her, so intense that it nearly made her collapse against him, but she did as he told her to.

He kept his hand between her legs as she moved, massaging and teasing before he guided himself into her. His hands then went to her hips, pulling her down gently at first, easing her onto him. Her mouth fell open as he jerked her more viciously toward him, and his expression mirrored hers before he leaned forward and buried his face in the waves of her hair.

She caved toward him, overcome by the sensation of him filling her so completely. He held her in this position for a moment, then nudged her hair aside as he trailed his lips along her jaw, up to her ear, and whispered, "Why don't you move those hips like you were doing before?"

Her chest heaved as she tried to catch her breath. Every inch of her skin felt alive as she leaned back, baring herself more fully before him. She kept her arms around his neck as she moved back against him, rising and falling in time with the pounding of their hearts, the rhythm soon turning faster and more furious. He slid one hand against her lower back, helping her balance, while the other came to rest on one of her hips, clenching a little more tightly with each rolling movement she made.

His eyes were closed at first, concentrated on the feel of their joining. When they finally flashed open again and his gaze took hers—full of desire and burning need—it sent a shock of pure pleasure straight to her core, nearly doubling her over.

One side of his mouth lifted at this—that all he had to do was *look* at her and it nearly sent her over the edge. She was close, and he knew it, and he responded by putting both hands on her hips and bringing her slowly to a stop. He held her in place as he leaned back against the bed, giving the pleasure still throbbing through her time to build and travel through every inch of her body.

Then his hips were moving instead of hers, his strength taking over, hands gripping and positioning her to fully meet each of his thrusts. His touch traveled from her lower back down over her curves, digging into the backs of her thighs and spreading her legs wider to take him in more fully.

It felt so good that she nearly lost her balance despite his strong hold. She curled downward, pressing closer to his body, molding herself to his hot skin and planting kisses along his chest in-between trying to catch her breath.

He slid them closer to the edge of the bed and braced his legs against the ground, allowing him to push more deeply into her, wrapping his arms tightly around her body and pulling her closer as he did. Her lips parted and she nearly cried out, but he leaned up and took her face in his hands as before, and his mouth was against hers before any sound escaped.

Stars filled her vision as he kissed her, an entire sky that she fully, willingly lost herself within. The stars spun faster as he kissed her more deeply and she hungrily kissed him back, no longer concerned with things like *breathing*.

He wrapped her legs around his waist, lifted her, and had her pressed up against the nearest wall a moment later.

The cool wall shocked her senses briefly back into focus, just long enough to make her aware of every place he was touching her, of the hum of his magical energy tangling with hers, and of how powerfully, effortlessly he held her against that wall.

Her hand reached forward, pushed through his hair and cupped his jaw. She caught a glimpse of the new symbol gracing her palm. The ceremony and all that had followed it flashed through her mind, bringing with it waves of ecstasy that carried her toward a release unlike any she'd ever experienced.

He kissed her over and over as she rode the surges and ebbs of it, his fingers trailing over her hyper-sensitive skin, pulling every last ounce of pleasure free.

Once her body had gone nearly limp against him, he carried her back to the bed. He pinned her hands to the mattress and rode her to his own finish, and the sensation of him emptying into her triggered a second climax of her own. He kissed her through this one as well, staying inside of her, the heat from his body wrapping around her and making her feel safe and removed from everything outside of the two of them.

She stayed curled in the same position even as he rolled away, reveling in the pleasant little aftershocks that continued to shoot through her. When she finally opened her eyes and sought Elander's face minutes later, she found him already looking at her, gaze full of wonder, as though he had just woken up beside her for the very first time.

Her heart clenched, trying to guard against the flood of confusing emotions waking inside of her. There were tears in her eyes before she could fight them off.

Concern flashed across Elander's face as he sat up.

"I'm fine," she said quickly, sitting up as well. "I'm not sad. I'm *not*, it's just..."

She didn't know how to explain it; what she felt in that moment could not be described by words like *sad* or *happy*. She wasn't entirely sure if there *was* a word that could explain the mess of feelings unfolding in her.

Human, maybe.

"I don't need all those future plans, as I told you," Cas said, quietly, "but now that I've tasted them, I don't know how to let them go, that's all. My head knows what's likely to become of us, but my heart doesn't want to listen."

That's the problem with loving deeply, she'd once said to him. *It means you have to hurt deeply too.*

She'd lived that lesson over and over these past months, and yet she had continued to love and set herself up for hurt over and over again. And even now, sitting in the dark, knowing the hurt and horrors that awaited them in the coming days, she lifted her gaze to her husband and found the courage to say, "But just so you know, I wouldn't have changed a thing that happened tonight. Whatever comes next, I'm still happy. And thankful."

Elander took her hand, tracing the new mark gracing her palm, his fingers light against her skin and his expression thoughtful. It was several moments before he replied.

"The elves have their meaning behind all these marks," he said, fingers still tracing the lines of hers. "But I already know what it means. It's a promise. And whatever is coming...if this is to be our ending, then believe me when I say I will be waiting for you in whatever comes next—whether in this lifetime or another. I will find you again. I swear it."

She took a deep breath, finally managing to stop the tears from building in her eyes. To smile, even. "Nowhere I could go," she whispered.

He wiped away the last tears clinging to her lashes. "Nowhere you could go," he agreed.

CHAPTER 28

Elander woke before dawn the next morning, but he kept perfectly still for several minutes, wishing he could extend the night indefinitely. It felt as if it had passed unnaturally quickly, as though some cruel spell was at work.

Eventually, he sat up, and the world seemed to spin even faster. He looked to his right, seeking and finding the one thing that usually slowed his racing fears and brought him balance—*her.*

His soulmate. His queen. His wife.

His wife.

Everything he had ever wanted, and everything he was so terrified to lose. They were official now, and that somehow made everything both more beautiful and more terrible, as though the world had finally revealed its true colors and been fully illuminated, for better or worse.

As quietly as possible, he slipped from their bed and dressed. He expected her to stir regardless of how silent he was, but she didn't, so he pulled the blankets more securely around her and then went out into the palace alone.

There were countless people he needed to meet with, endless strategies to discuss, and now they were a day behind with their planning.

Casia would be upset with him for not waking her and including her in these discussions, but he would fill her in later; she was sleeping soundly for once, and he didn't want to disturb her.

Not when it could be the last chance for her to truly rest for some time.

He shook the uneasy thoughts from his head and walked faster, tracking down servants who eventually led him to Laurent and Rhea. The two of them were gathered around a table in a small meeting room, poring over correspondence from their allies, both near and far, and from various informants they had stationed throughout the empire. Untouched platters of food and drink sat between them. Neither of them looked as though they had slept much—if at all.

"Any news from Moreth?" Elander asked. The other elven realm within the Kethran Empire was the ally he was most eager to hear good news about; it had been under Sarith's thumb ever since her husband's murder—and arguably, even before that—but with her death, they hoped a wave of change would come swiftly enough to help them with their looming battles.

"General Kolvar believes the tide is shifting quickly," Laurent told him, accepting a drink of some sort from one of the servants flitting in and out of the room.

This general had helped them in the past, when their prior business in Moreth had taken a turn for the worst. He had been in that realm for the past several weeks, working in secret to try and maintain some sort of hold over those who were allies to Casia and her tenuous crown.

"The ones who were already aware of him and his undercover operations are rallying around him, of course," Laurent continued. "But there are former minions of Sarith claiming loyalty to him now as well, and their numbers are greater than we'd expected."

"But it's risky, trusting numbers without being able to properly vet them," Rhea added. "We don't truly know who is loyal to our causes and who isn't after the mess with Sarith. It will take time to sort through the ranks and organize them."

Elander frowned. "Time we don't have."

"Exactly," Laurent agreed.

"But here's something more positive," Rhea offered, reaching for a letter that Silverfoot had clamped between his jaws and carried to her. "The goddess's birds dropped it off with our watchers near the border this morning."

The *magari,* she meant—messenger birds that Nephele had long used to carry information throughout this realm and others. They could move as quick as a flash of lightning, but still posed a risk—they would be hard not to spot against the empire's increasingly dark skies, for starters. But they had much bigger risks to worry about now, he supposed.

"The armies centered near Ciridan have gained more bodies from the north. There are rumors that Alnor's former rulers are sending the help themselves—which is a victory in and of itself."

The king and queen of that fallen kingdom had not been heard from in years; their exile, and the mysteries surrounding it, had become something of a legend throughout the realms.

These fires they faced were truly drawing all manner of beings toward them, weren't they?

"And those bolstered armies have started to move," Rhea continued. "Some units have already crossed into Sadira."

"And the Sadiran Queen?"

"Permitting them passage without incident, as far as we know. But we haven't been able to pinpoint her location over the last few days. Hopefully, she's just sheltered somewhere to regroup."

They spent the next hour discussing these matters further. Nessa and Zev eventually joined them. Casia was the last to arrive, having gotten sidetracked by a separate meeting with the king.

As she came inside, she laid Shadowslayer against the wall, where it kept mostly still, save for an occasional twitch that scraped its sheath against the ivory plaster. The darkness in it swirled on, obvious even through the sheath, drawing Elander's eyes to it unless he consciously fought against the pull. Even when he wasn't looking at it, he still felt it pulling, the sensation like shards of glass dragging over his skin. Unpleasant, but the risk of leaving it unattended—separate from Casia—was worse.

Casia accepted the cup of tea Nessa gave her as she sat down, her face a steel wall while she took in the sight of all the letters and notes spread upon the table, and the map with markings of all the confirmed locations that had been attacked, burned, or otherwise decimated by their enemies. It was a grim map with far too many markings, but if she was overwhelmed by what she'd walked in on, she didn't show it.

She simply took a deep breath and got to work.

Another hour of discussion had passed when her attention briefly darted away, first to her sword, then to the door.

She excused herself from the table they had all gathered around, hesitating after she stood, her right hand clenching and unclenching.

"Time to see about the matter of the sword and the Point?" Laurent guessed.

"Yes." Her gaze tracked toward Elander, but she seemed to stare right through him, lost in whatever images she held in her mind even as she said, "I thought we could try neutralizing it together, this time."

He agreed, rising to follow her as she carefully picked up the sword and left the room, leading him to a large room at the edge of the palace.

Three of this room's walls were made of glass, as was a large part of its ceiling, affording them plenty of sunlight. Casia stood in a bright patch of this light for a moment, catching her breath—along with her courage—and then she decided against the enclosed room and moved outside instead.

She unsheathed the sword and placed it on a set of stairs that led up to a raised platform overlooking the outdoor space, positioning the weapon at eye-level against one of the risers.

The blade was darker than Elander remembered—or perhaps it only seemed so because of how bright everything else was.

"Do you remember when I healed the girl in Belwind? During our first mission together?" Casia asked.

It felt like an age ago, but he nodded. "Vividly."

"I thought we could try something similar."

He considered the plan for a moment. "Reflecting and redirecting the dark energy? As the Moon Goddess does."

She nodded. "We can expel and scatter it, and perhaps

then we could neutralize the scattered pieces in some way. Bit by bit, if necessary."

It was as good as any place to start the day's experiments, so they both took their place on either side of the stairs. He lifted a hand toward the resting sword, and waited until Casia did the same, until he felt her magic rising, slipping into the space between them.

The magic began to bleed from him a moment later, drawn out more easily and swiftly in response to hers. He directed it toward the sword and kept his eyes on the crescent-shaped symbol at the base of the blade, willing it to ignite the way it usually did whenever Casia accessed this kind of magic. That symbol—along with the others—was lost among the black energy.

Even as their light magic overtook it, briefly causing the metal to glow with a sickly pale shade, the symbol still remained lost.

They continued to summon power all the same. Shadowslayer seemed to be absorbing it. Not an outright failure maybe, if they could feed enough power into it to displace the other power that had overtaken it. But...

Could they really push the darkness out?

As soon as he started to question their methods, he felt a twisting in his gut, as though something had taken hold of his magic and attempted to wrench it from his control.

And the blade *did* expel and scatter magic—but not the dark magic that had taken up residence within it.

Instead it was their *own* magic that came flying back at them, with a force that sent them both stumbling backward. The ball of hot, unstable Sun energy hit the windows beside them and dispersed rapidly, bouncing brightly off the glass and leaving them momentarily blinded.

Elander kept his eyes tightly shut until the heat had faded. When he blinked them open again, nothing had changed. The symbols on the blade remained dark, the energy within it still hummed, low and ominous, and the sun itself seemed to have dimmed.

Casia cursed.

Elander swallowed his own curse. "We'll try again later," he told her, trying to mask the concern in his voice. "Let's focus on other things while we recuperate."

OVER THE NEXT TWO DAYS, they tried again. And again, and again—so many times that Elander eventually lost count. Each attempt, they approached with renewed hope. Each one turned into another failure that ended the same way—with one or both of them on the ground, cursing.

Their fifth attempt—*or was it the sixth?*—of the second day ended with an explosion of rebounding light so violent that it knocked the breath from Elander's lungs as he hit the ground. Casia landed several feet away from him, and she was alarmingly still for far too long before she managed to push to her hands and knees and give her head a little shake.

Even after she came back to her senses, she stayed on the ground, resting against the palace wall with her knees drawn toward her and her head bowed low.

Elander stood and leaned against the wall beside her, tilting his head back, staring at a wisp of cloud in the distant sky to try and keep the world from spinning around him. "We need a new plan."

Casia didn't disagree. She was quiet for several minutes before she answered. "I want to believe what the Moon Goddess said…about us having enough power between us to overcome the Point's darkness. But I'm afraid that's wishful thinking. And we're running out of time. We've made plans, we've sent word to too many people to delay things much longer. I may just have to carry the sword with me, darkness and all, as we march out into the mortal realm. Or maybe..." She trailed off, rapping her knuckles together in frustration.

Darkness and all...

The words had sent a powerful shiver through him, threatening his balance even as the palace wall held him up. "The ancient magic in the air of Mistwilde is likely helping to subdue its dark energy. Taking it outside while it's still in this state seems...risky."

"What else can we do?"

He didn't have an immediate answer for this.

"I'm afraid of what will happen if we take the blade outside, obviously. But my magic won't be suppressed at that point, either. Nor will yours. So that's...something to consider, at least."

She didn't sound particularly confident about this plan, nor was she in a hurry to move, clearly waiting and willing to listen to any other idea he might have had.

Elander didn't answer at first. But a few minutes later, he *was* struck by a sudden possibility. Not one he particularly liked—but several more minutes passed, and he could think of nothing else. So he said, "Rest here for a moment. There's something I want to try."

She gave him a curious look, but she seemed too tired to inquire further.

He disappeared back into the palace and moved swiftly through it, searching for Zev. Unsurprisingly, he found him near one of the kitchens, sampling various dishes leftover from the wedding feast.

Was he ever not eating?

Elander wasted no time with pleasantries. "I need you for a moment."

Zev grinned that foolish grin of his. "You're finally admitting you need me. I'm so touched."

Elander scowled. "Just hurry up, please. Casia is waiting."

At the mention of her name, Zev proceeded to stuff the entire rest of a small cake into his mouth in one bite, indicating for Elander to lead the way as he did.

Casia was back on her feet when they returned to her, refocused and pacing back and forth before her sword, studying it.

She glanced up as they approached, giving Elander a curious frown when she noticed he wasn't alone.

"We haven't tried any power that's derived from the Dark God yet," Elander offered in explanation.

Zev stepped to Casia's side, fire dancing at his fingertips, his eyes narrowed on Shadowslayer. He had, to his credit, shifted quickly from gorging himself into a ready and helpful, focused form.

Casia still hesitated, reluctant—even now—to get anyone else involved in these dark and dangerous things. But she eventually pointed him toward the sword and said, "Fine. Let's see what happens when you use your magic against it."

He complied, igniting the flickers around his fingers into a more proper plume of flame that he sent spinning, wrapping around the blade.

That blade went silent as the flames hit it, flashing briefly to a bright shade of orange. Then it grew as dark as before, its humming returning with deeper, more disturbing notes. Elander braced himself, preparing to parry whatever tainted ball of magic the sword threw back at them...

But no magic came.

They were all silent until Elander cleared his throat and stated the obvious, "It didn't repel it, the way it's been doing with Sun magic."

Casia cautiously stepped closer. "But it doesn't seem to have altered it in any permanent way, either."

A few more similar experiments yielded similar results, prompting Elander to reluctantly share the rest of the plan that had started to form in his head.

"I don't think we've been approaching this from the right angle," he said. "Or that we're truly considering what it *originally* required to create this Point."

Casia was quick to guess at his meaning, though it was clear from the troubled look on her face that she didn't want to understand what he was suggesting. She quietly said, "It wasn't purely magic that was sacrificed to create the original Point. There was blood involved as well."

Zev seemed to fight off the urge to recoil, but he nodded, his focus undeterred. With no more hesitation than this, he took the knife from the sheath at his ankle and cut a clean, shallow line across his palm. After squeezing his hand together to draw more blood to the surface, he held it above Shadowslayer and let a few crimson drops fall upon the blade.

The sword shivered as the drops hit it.

They stared at it, waiting. In vain, at first. But then came a strange shift in the power around the sword—a disorienting moment in which Elander felt...*nothing*. No power, ill or otherwise. It happened so quickly that he thought he'd imagined it until he noticed the way Casia was staring at him.

"Did you feel that?"

He nodded.

"It disrupted the energy, though it was only for an instant. It seems to have bounced back just as quickly."

The three of them were quiet, contemplative.

"A Point created in darkness and sacrifice," Elander thought aloud, "and only in darkness and sacrifice can it be unraveled..."

"So we need a sacrifice that's large enough and dark enough to shatter it," Cas said.

"Anwyn said it took the sacrifices of multiple Dark Court minions to create it," Zev pointed out. "We can't just round up a few dozen magic users and approach it the same way?"

Elander shook his head. "If the magic and blood sacrificed is too little, I fear it might merely keep absorbing it, which will only make it more powerful."

Zev turned the words over in silence, taking the time for a rare bit of careful consideration before he spoke again. "We have to overload it to the level of breaking, essentially. Push it beyond the limits it was originally intended to hold."

"Exactly."

He and Zev both moved closer to the sword, nervous but excited by this potential breakthrough. Casia, in comparison, had gone very quiet and still, her arms wrapping tightly around herself as she stared at her sword.

"Are you all right?" Elander asked, glancing over his shoulder.

"I'm not planning to sacrifice myself, so don't worry," Zev added, offering her a smile that she didn't return. "We're obviously going to have to turn this blade on the upper-god himself, somehow." He mimed swinging a sword through the air, stabbing it into the god in question. "Bathe it in his blood and watch it crumple and suck his power away along with it... that will be satisfying, won't it?"

Elander kept his tone and expectations more tempered. "It gives us a possibility, at least, even if it will be a dangerous plan to carry out."

Casia nodded quickly in agreement. "I agree. And I'm fine. Just the sight of blood in general—you know how I am."

They did, and yet this didn't seem like her usual distress surrounding her memories of blood. But Elander couldn't pinpoint precisely what seemed off about her reaction, and she moved to collect the sword and put it securely back in its sheath before he could find the words to question her.

"I'm okay," she reassured him, kissing him on the cheek. "I think I just need a break."

She hurried off alone, leaving Zev and Elander staring after her, both of them wearing concerned frowns.

"It's not like her to admit she needs a break," Zev commented.

"No. It's not."

Elander wanted to follow her and inquire further. But the cruelty of time reared its ugly head once more, in the form of a palace servant arriving, reminding him that he was due for a meeting with Laurent and several of the ranked officers of the Mistwilde army.

Too much to do, too little time.

This meeting couldn't wait, so he forced his concerns about Casia down and kept moving.

One meeting turned into several more, into discussions not only with soldiers but with council members and then the king himself—several of which grew heated and exhaustingly long.

Once he was finally finished, he sought Casia once more, but by this point she was nowhere to be found. Nessa assured him she was safe—she'd gone to *Elleras,* the quiet hilltop gardens the elves used as a place of retreat and meditation, and she didn't want to be disturbed. He fought the urge to go check on her—just to make certain she *was* safe—and instead he busied himself with more meetings and preparations. There was certainly no shortage of things to do.

He eventually found her in their room when he retired to it much later that evening, but by this point his wife was already asleep, her fists clenched tightly as if preparing to fight off the coming nightmares.

THE NEXT DAYS passed in a blur of planning and preparation, the Palace of Irithyl now fully immersed in and moving to the rhythms of war.

The king had ended up pledging even more than they'd hoped to their cause—over three hundred of his finest soldiers. They would join the ones left behind with Soryn in Ironedge nearly two weeks ago, who had started marching toward Mistwilde and their queen even before Casia had officially sent word for them to do so. And plenty of others were following their lead. Those others would all be converging from different corners of the empire soon, and together they would be enough.

Enough.

They had to keep believing that, to keep pressing on in spite of the bleak odds.

What else could they do?

Each day brought fresh problems and bad news that chipped away at their morale, yet they carried on.

On the sixth day after their trip to the mortal realm and

their meeting with the goddesses, the messengers bringing ill news from the outside world numbered almost too many to count. But still Elander kept moving, inspecting weapons and armor, mapping routes, answering questions, sorting out disputes between soldiers.

He had only just finished dealing with one problem when Zev intercepted him, beckoning him to follow as he headed to face *another* problem. "Cas is looking for both of us," he said. "There's finally been news from the northern borders. And apparently, it's not good."

Casia didn't speak when they reached her, only handed over a piece of parchment that looked as though it had been read and worked between her hands countless times.

Elander held it at arm's length so Zev could read it as well.

From its hastily scratched contents, they learned that Edolin and Droskin—two of the largest towns along the Ethswen and Sadiran border—were destroyed, one of them encased in ice, the other still smoldering from flames that had devoured the entirety of its expansive network of roads and bridges in a single night.

Meanwhile, a series of earthquakes had been felt along the northern edges of those cities, driving out the survivors still clinging to their homes and trying to save them—the God of the Mountain at work.

The surviving inhabitants of the border cities had fled south, only to run directly into a waiting mortal army, who had butchered their numbers further before moving into Edolin and Droskin to establish their own order within the ruins.

The Dark Court and its new allies were cooperating better than ever, it seemed.

Laurent and Nessa joined them a few minutes later, Rhea and Silverfoot not far behind them. They each took in the latest bad news with the practiced, stoic expressions they had nearly perfected by this point. Uneasy silence followed, lasting for several minutes before Laurent finally interrupted it, staring out of the window and rapping his knuckles against the sill as he spoke.

"It's only a matter of time before Malaphar himself makes an appearance," he said. "His followers grow bolder every hour, laying out a carpet of blood and destruction to welcome him back into this realm."

Casia picked up Shadowslayer, which had been resting against the wall. It rattled in its sheath, and Elander fought off the urge to wince as he felt waves of dark energy siphoning off it.

The energy settled as Casia gripped the sword's handle more tightly. She drew it to her side and concentrated on keeping the tip pointed at the ground, her arm oddly stiff, as if fighting off the urge to lift it and start swinging.

After a minute, she did swing it—calmly and fluidly, twisting and stabbing it with practiced movements around the room as she spoke, almost more to herself than anyone present. "We need to weaken Malaphar to give ourselves a chance to get close and draw blood. But to weaken him, we have to get close enough to draw blood. I keep playing through the different scenarios of this upcoming battle in my head, and it just goes around in circles."

Elander didn't want to admit to it, but his thoughts had been circling in similar ways.

"We have a lot of help on our side," Nessa said stubbornly. "Enough to create diversions and give us a chance, and goddesses who will be able to shield you while you take that chance—we'll find some way of taking care of what we need to do."

Rhea nodded in agreement, placing her hand on Casia's arm and stopping her aimless slicing and stabbing. "The leaders here are more or less in agreement with this plan, right? You shared your beliefs about what will happen if—or *when*—you're able to strike the Dark God with Shadowslayer, and nobody has come up with any objections."

"The fact that you got them all to agree on something—even Kylian—gives me hope, personally," said Laurent.

Casia sheathed her sword, her moment of doubt seeming to pass nearly as quickly as it had overtaken her. "You're right, of course," she said decisively. "And this remains the plan… We'll hope for the best but expect the worst, as we always have."

"We'll need a plan for *after*, too," Rhea pointed out. "If the Point breaks, there's a chance Shadowslayer breaks as well, and that will leave Casia vulnerable."

"She won't be vulnerable," Elander said. "I'll be right behind her."

"We'll *all* be right behind her," Zev said, and the others agreed.

"You may be carrying that sword on your own," said Nessa, before Casia could protest, "but we're going to make it to the other side of this together."

"So now the only question is whether or not we're ready to make our way toward that other side," said Laurent.

"The week's time we mentioned to our divine allies is nearly up," Elander said.

Casia's eyes met his, full of emotion that she quickly blinked away. The last conversation from their wedding night whispered through his mind, making his chest feel tight.

If this is to be our ending...

She tilted her head away from him—away from everyone—as she replied. "Every day we wait, we risk another mortal city falling. I don't think we'll ever truly be ready for what comes next, even if we had months to prepare for it. We have to move."

Uncomfortable silence overtook them, but no one disagreed.

Laurent moved first. "I'll go inform the king and help him spread the word."

LATER THAT EVENING, Elander made his way to Elleras, those hills of sanctuary that rose to the north side of the palace.

He found Casia here as he'd expected he might, standing alone beside one of the many small shrines strewn across the ridges. This particular shrine featured a statue of an elven woman tucked between two sturdy trees, her scarred face lifted toward the sky. A banner of ribbons and brown and golden-red feathers hung between the trees.

The elves had established a sanctum here partly because it was the highest point in the city. From its loftiest hills, one could see and consider the big picture, the world past Irithyl and above the forest that wrapped around it, and farther even than that—far enough to see the sky beginning to change, the ill air of the mortal realms overtaking the protective magic of Mistwilde and darkening its edges.

Casia kept her gaze on that distant rim of darkness as

Elander approached, though her face did angle toward him a moment later. "It's almost time, isn't it?"

Time.

He was so...*tired* of that word. He wanted to throw it—and all the questions surrounding it—away.

Time? We have all the time we could ever need. Don't worry about it. Don't even think of it.

Instead, he leaned against a nearby tree, grateful for the support it provided to his weary body and soul, and he said, "The soldiers Mistwilde has promised to our cause are making final preparations. They're expecting to ride out at dawn, based on the whispers I've heard. But they're awaiting your orders to confirm this plan, of course."

She took a long time replying.

"*Dawn,*" she said, quietly.

A corner of his mouth edged up. "The timing seems appropriate, given that the Queen of the Dawn will be leading the way."

"And the King."

He stepped to her side and took her hand. It shook slightly against his, whether from the chill air, or nerves, or some combination of both. He found the mark they shared and traced it with his thumb, following the lines of the tree, from its roots up to the curled branches and the sun tucked within them.

"It's appropriate for another reason," she informed him.

"And what is that?"

She faced him more fully, the soft smile on her lips not quite driving away the solemn look in her eyes. "Because we don't end in darkness, right?"

He smiled back. "No. We don't."

"If this is the end, then we will go out with the sun rising around us; it will be the brightest light this world has ever known."

She looked back to the city, but his gaze lingered on her for a moment, struck by the way the setting sun's light made all the edges of her seem to glow.

The brightest light this world has ever known.

"I have no doubt," he told her.

CHAPTER 29

Dawn came, and Elander and Casia led the way out of Mistwilde with the sun rising against their backs, its warmth urging them and the rest of their riders onward, its light filling them with something like hope.

Only half of their Mistwilde army followed them now; the rest remained on the edges of the elven realm, waiting, preparing to emerge once they received the agreed-upon signal. The plan—the hope—was that they would be able to use surprise and misdirection to their advantage.

All together they were almost certainly outnumbered, even if all the ones they'd called to meet them actually answered that call.

But their enemies didn't need to know *how* outnumbered.

The destination he and Casia were leading their current troops toward was Hallowforge, a fortress already secured by their allies, which they planned to use as a stronghold and base for their upcoming battles. This was the point all their soldiers would ultimately be converging toward, and after nearly an hour of swift riding, Elander spotted a welcome sight: the gold and white banners of Hallowforge, and the shimmer of a shield of magic surrounding it.

That shield sent another shot of hope straight to his veins—it meant the Moon Goddess had already been here, providing even more fortification to the stone towers and the elaborate walls fencing the fortress in, just as they'd asked her to do.

This place was ancient, built by the elves in the early days following their divine exile. It had long been considered a sacred site by them—the location of countless major battles and final stands—and so they had worked to maintain it for centuries. Only more recently, as those elves withdrew more and more from mortal societies, had it started to show signs of decay.

But it remained sturdy enough now, particularly with the help of magic, and it looked calm and ready to serve their purposes well.

So far so good.

As they approached it, Elander spurred his mount faster to catch up with Casia's, his gaze on the sword bouncing against her horse's side.

His breath caught as he stared at it, whether from his own nerves, or in reaction to the Point contained within it, he wasn't certain.

"How does the sword feel?" he asked, drawing closer.

Casia kept her eyes on their destination even as her hand went to Shadowslayer's sheath, tapping anxiously against it. "Unsettled." She shifted in the saddle, sitting up a little straighter. "But I have it under control for now."

He nodded. *So far so good.* He kept repeating that line to himself over and over as they rode into the fortress, trying to make himself believe in it. He didn't look at the sky as they rode, as it had grown increasingly dark with every mile they put between themselves and Mistwilde.

At Hallowforge's main gate, they were met by a group of heavily armed soldiers, who were wary until Cas showed them her sword and Elander showed them the rings given to him by King Talos—proof that they weren't vipers cloaked by Mimic-kind magic or otherwise.

Most of their welcoming party hailed from the Gulf Region to the southwest. The Mistwilde king had vouched for their trustworthiness, though his dealings with them—as his dealings with most mortals—had been brief.

As the soldiers took their horses and moved ahead to tend to them, Zev was—unsurprisingly—the first to quietly voice his doubts about the situation. "How do we know we can trust the ones gathered here?"

"We don't," said Laurent flatly.

"I'm certain there are at least a few traitors lurking within these walls, just waiting for a chance to betray us," Elander added. "So keep your eyes open."

Zev started to reply, but they were interrupted as one of the greeting soldiers rejoined them. He brought Casia and her inner circle to the man who had overseen most of the readying of this fortress—Farak was his name, a hulking brute of a battle-scarred captain who had fought in the service of the former Sadiran king and queen.

Farak led them toward a private room in one of the towers before briefing them on the current situation. Two other soldiers joined them along the way, carrying small torches to provide them with more light.

"The Goddess Inya was here in the early days of our tasks, guiding us," Farak informed them. His voice was gruff and businesslike, as though visits from goddesses were a routine occurrence for him.

Elander got the impression that this man had seen enough to not be rattled by much—including divine creatures.

"But she left some time ago," he continued, "off to help more of the soldiers marching toward our cause. There were skirmishes reported near Olan, specifically. Thought her protection would be more useful there, especially since she knew you'd be arriving at this fortress soon, and she believed you were capable of providing just as much protection."

He moved to the room's only window, a small rectangle that likely would have afforded them little sunlight even on a bright day. With the darkness currently engulfing the sky, it was more or less useless.

"Barriers have been maintained by the handful of Moon and Sky-kind humans we've managed to recruit to our cause," Farak said, pointing to the distant glistening in the air that signified that barrier.

The walls around Hallowforge were elaborate as well, a spiraling labyrinth full of secret passages and pathways, making it difficult to overtake even without the added protection of magic.

"And now that you're here," Farak added, "hopefully you two can help reinforce the places that have weakened."

Elander felt the man's gaze on him, but he couldn't look away from the window. From up high, the world looked even darker somehow, and the number of people moving about the fortress and fortifying its defenses seemed scattered and insufficient.

"Of course," Casia answered for them.

Elander nodded, still watching the world outside as a bird

struck the barrier. It was momentarily stunned and dropped like a rock...only to catch itself partway to the ground and shove its way through one of the weakened places, squawking loudly as it came.

And though he didn't typically believe in signs or superstitions, he couldn't help feeling as though it was a bad omen.

TWO DAYS PASSED in relative peace while they continued to prepare.

More soldiers arrived every few hours, folding into their ranks and swelling them to the point that they spilled out of the fortress and into encampments established in the woods and on hilltops nearby.

It was encouraging to see their numbers grow, and yet Elander knew that greater numbers also meant a greater possibility of traitors among them. He had spent much of the past days in interrogation mode, watching for any spies trying to slip past their defenses.

He tried not to think of past lives and lost things, but Caden would have been helpful to have now. Not only for his mind-reading magic, but for that confident, arrogant attitude of his that had been contagious.

Elander never thought he would miss that attitude, but the hole its absence had left behind felt most apparent in moments like these, while staring down an upcoming battle without his old companions by his side.

But every time images of what might have been snuck into his head, he quickly shook them off and got back to work.

The goddesses of the Sun Court had not accompanied

any of the arriving soldiers—they were still busy elsewhere with other problems, according to the messenger birds Nephele sent. But a group of the incoming soldiers *had* been escorted by one of the Moon Goddess's most trusted servants—the Mist spirit, Kiri.

The spirit lingered even after the ones it had accompanied had settled in. This spirit had been no friend of Elander's in the past—he didn't care for the creature's prank-loving nature—but he was glad for its presence now; it served as a tangible sign to the doubters among them that divine help was here, and more was coming.

The spirit quickly developed a habit of following Casia wherever she went throughout the fortress, trailing her like a faithful hound ready to obey any command.

When she wasn't around, he settled for Elander—which was why Elander wasn't startled any time Kiri suddenly appeared, usually heralded by a swirl of mist.

He was sitting beside a stone table in a rugged, overgrown yard in the fortress's center when he spotted that telltale mist, and watched it clear to reveal the spirit clinging to the underside of the table. Another prank and attempt to catch him off-guard. Even though it hadn't worked, a ripple of the spirit's chime-like laughter still rang through the air.

"No time for that nonsense," Elander said quietly.

The spirit swung onto the bench beside him and tilted its narrow, deer-like head, questioning. Elander subtly nodded toward the two men who were deep in conversation on the far side of the yard.

He hadn't come to this run-down, tucked-away space to spy on these men. He'd come here in hopes of a moment of peace to clear his head.

But his gaze kept drifting toward the men, to the taller

one in particular; he couldn't help but notice the way this soldier kept reaching for the handle of his sword, the way his stance never seemed to settle, the way his gaze never truly met the eyes of the person he was talking to.

Why was he so nervous?

It was an old habit from his time as the God of Death, noticing these things—he'd once been able to sense a frightened heart from a mile away. To smell a person's fear, even, or taste their apprehension on the air. And though he couldn't do it any longer, he still had a bad feeling about this man and the nervous way he shifted about.

All of them had reason to be afraid, given what awaited them in the coming days.

But in his experience, traitors tended to smell and taste the most like fear.

He'd stared too long; the man sensed it and turned to stare back.

He recognized Elander quickly and gave a hasty bow, a nervous smile, and then turned and promptly hurried away. The other man followed after only a cursory glance in Elander's direction.

Elander dragged his gaze away and fixed it on the Mist spirit, thinking; the goddess this spirit served could reveal not only paths, but also the true forms of things.

The spirit was staring at the space where the men had been talking, its head tilting this way and that, curious.

"You sensed something off about that too, didn't you?" Elander muttered.

The spirit's glowing white eyes blinked slowly, making Elander think of the moon shifting in and out of wind-swept clouds. Its long face lifted in the direction the men had disappeared into, and after a few sniffs at the air, he shifted into clouds of mist that reformed into a body at the last spot the nervous man had been standing. He explored the area for a moment before returning to Elander in the same manner he'd left, peering up at him, expectant.

"Follow him," Elander ordered. "And see what you can uncover."

Casia entered the yard just as the conversation finished, and she watched the spirit bounding away, amusement brightening her eyes as she looked back to Elander.

"You two are friends now, hm?"

He leaned back on the bench, stretching his legs out and trying to shake off the tension that had settled in his muscles. "As much as I'm *friends* with any of our allies in this strange place we've found ourselves in."

She hugged her arms around herself, looking thoughtful as she circled the space and came to a stop beside the path that led into a larger yard beyond. Groups of soldiers were currently gathering in that yard, sorting through weapons and armor. She watched them for a moment before she said, "Do you remember the first time I encountered that spirit? You weren't pleased."

He arched a brow. "Because you encountered him after charging recklessly into a cursed forest, as I recall."

"*If the lesser-spirits really are trying to communicate with you, nothing good will come from it,* you said. Right after you shouted at me in front of your soldiers, as *I* recall."

He cringed a bit at the memory. Their beginning in this lifetime had certainly been...rocky. "Times have changed a bit, haven't they?"

She settled down on the bench beside him, wrapping her arm around his and leaning against him with a sigh. "Just a bit."

Another two days passed. The number of soldiers joining the fortress slowed to a trickle, the sightings of enemies grew closer and more numerous, and snatches of anxious whispers throughout the fortress soon became full, loud conversations filled with doubt and criticism.

"More are coming," Casia assured them all, regardless of how harshly they spoke about her and her plans. "It takes time to cross the empire, and some of our allies had a greater distance to travel than others. Keep preparing as though they will arrive at any moment—because they very well might."

Elander was quick to agree with her and silence the ones who didn't, as were the rest of her friends; they couldn't afford infighting on top of everything else.

But in private, they all worried as much as anyone about the lack of incoming bodies.

The skies were growing darker. The correspondence from Nephele and their other divine allies had stopped—whether because the enemies pressing in made it too risky, or because of some other, more ominous reason.

As the end of the fourth day drew to a close, Elander found Casia sitting alone with Nessa on top of one of the lower towers, leaning her back against the parapet with Shadowslayer resting in its sheath at her feet.

He felt dark energy emanating from the sword—more than he had ever felt before. But there was a distinct warmth in the air too, burying some of that unstable energy.

Warmth from weak remnants of Feather-kind magic?

Casia hadn't asked Nessa to use magic since the day in Feyedge; if she'd requested help now, the situation must have been dire.

"What's going on?" he asked.

Casia kept her eyes on the sword as she replied. "It's been acting strangely over the past hour or so. Reacting to what's approaching, I'm afraid."

"To what's approaching…" A chilling realization overtook him. "The scouts we sent across the river have returned?" It had been over a day since they'd sent them, and some had started to suspect they wouldn't be coming back.

She nodded. "Just a short time ago. I was coming to find you, to share their report, when Shadowslayer demanded my attention. It felt like the Point had started to shift again, as though it was trying to pull me and all of my magic into it. I had to stop and focus to try and calm that energy…which is why I'm sitting on the ground." She leaned her head back against the stone, clearly fighting off the urge to close her eyes.

She looked exhausted, but Elander swallowed down his concerns about her for the moment and tried to remain focused on the bigger picture. "What news did those scouts bring?"

"The bad kind," said Nessa.

"Is there any other kind here lately?" Elander mused.

"Armies are marching from both Riverhill and Eriton," Nessa explained. "Together, they're two thousand strong. At *least*."

The number made him dizzy.

"We're on the cusp of the end," Casia said. "And Shadowslayer knows it. I don't think I can keep it balanced and under control for much longer."

Elander crouched down before the sword, stopping just short of picking it up. He wanted to carry it for her, but worried he might throw off her concentrated effort to keep its power under control if he tried anything.

She said nothing as his hand traveled along the sheath, but her body seemed to involuntarily tense whenever that sheath was touched. It seemed as if more and more of her was getting twisted up with this weapon.

But how much more?

And what was going to happen to her if—or *when*—the sword and the Point it carried shattered?

He straightened back to his full height, turning his attention to what he could see of their own army beyond the low walls of the tower. He braced a hand against that wall, still feeling dizzy from the possibility of *two-thousand* marching toward them. Their numbers were less than half that. And the ones below were moving frantically about—unusually so, as if they'd forgotten all their efforts to organize and prepare themselves.

Do they already know what's approaching?

He didn't doubt it; bad news had a way of spreading like wildfires in the wind.

They were trying to decide what to do next when the Mist spirit suddenly appeared.

There was no sneaking about, nor any laughter this time; a cloud of mist simply descended between Elander and the others, shifting quickly into the more solid, familiar shape of the spirit. He looked eager and pleased with himself, Elander thought—a dog intent on getting a treat after doing a trick.

That nervous soldier, Elander remembered after a moment of thought.

It had only been a day, but so much had happened between that moment and now that Elander had nearly forgotten about ordering the spirit to track that man—and he was now more concerned about the news the scouts had brought, anyway.

But the spirit was insistent, his big eyes shifting pointedly between Elander and the bridge leading back into the fortress.

"There's something he wants to show us, I think," Nessa said, taking a few cautious steps toward the bridge.

Casia and Elander exchanged a concerned look. She gave in first, rising to her feet, cautiously securing Shadowslayer at her hip, and urging the Mist spirit to lead her on as he had several times in the past.

Elander followed at a distance, focusing on the spirit while also listening for any trouble that might be brewing in the distance.

The spirit took them to one of the small barracks set apart from the main fortress. After several twisting hallways, they came to a door that was locked. This didn't stop him; he simply melted into mist that slipped under the door, opening it from the other side after a bit of fumbling with the handle.

Once inside, he darted for one of several beds lining the wall. His antlers stabbed into a bag underneath it, lifting it and shaking it, spilling its contents.

A small knife, encased in a painted leather sheath, hit the floor—among other trinkets—and the spirit nudged it toward Elander's boot.

Elander picked it up, pulling it free of its sheath and studying the strangely polished, colorful stone it had been carved from.

"This is a *shole* knife." He lifted it carefully between them. "They're common in Ethswen, particularly the markets of the capital city. Carved from the petrified wood that's found along the edges of the Moreth Desert—more for decorative or sentimental use rather than actual battle."

Casia frowned. "The knife looks worn but its sheath looks new—or freshly painted."

"Were they painting over something?" Nessa wondered.

"Seems like it," Casia said, picking away a scrap of the top layer with her nail. "What was on it before?" She turned to the Mist spirit as she asked the question, extending the object toward him.

The spirit darted cautiously around her outstretched hand, sniffing at the sheath and drawing back several times before he seemed to decide what to do.

Then he lifted his long face toward the object and breathed out a shimmering fog that wrapped around the sheath, briefly lifting it a few inches above Casia's palm.

Within seconds of it dropping back against her skin, a symbol bled through the top layer of paint—a golden tree against a red backdrop.

"The royal crest of Ethswen?"

Elander nodded as he took the sheath from Casia's hand, skin crawling with unease as he turned it over, considering the implications.

"Not all people from Ethswen are bad," Nessa began, uncertainly. "It isn't really proof of—"

"Digging through the personal belongings of a soldier who's sworn his life to you and your cause? How very *noble* of you, Queen."

Casia's gaze snapped toward the sudden voice, eyes narrowing on the man who stood in the doorway—the same man Elander had ordered the spirit to track.

She turned to face him more fully. "Have you truly sworn to it, I wonder?"

The man started toward her, but Elander stepped into his path, holding the knife and its sheath up for him to see. "This dagger and sheath once bore the symbols of the Ethswen royal family. But I've asked around about you. And I know you told Farak and several others that you come from Herrath, and that you've never even *been* to that kingdom where so many of our enemies hail from."

"Is it a crime to receive gifts from this kingdom?"

"No," said Nessa. "Which makes it suspicious that you would lie about it. Almost as if you were afraid of anyone digging more deeply into your connections to that place."

His eyes went to the spirit. He seemed to be calculating, realizing who this creature was, that there was no lie that he could tell that would be more convincing than Kiri's magic.

His knees bent, preparing to sprint.

Elander moved faster, blocking the door. Casia closed in on him from the other side, lightning dancing around her hand, while Nessa pulled the bow from her back and started to nock an arrow.

Shadowslayer gave a sudden violent tremble, and Casia's gaze darted toward the window—toward their distant, bigger problems on the horizon—for a fraction of a second before she looked back to Elander. Her thoughts were easy enough to read.

We need to deal with this quickly.

Elander darted forward, slamming a hand into the man's chest and pinning him to the wall. "You have thirty seconds to give me an explanation that will convince me to spare your life."

No explanation came.

But as Elander tightened his hold and pressed closer, the man finally spoke, his words laced with laughter—the half-mad tone of a man who clearly thought himself a martyr. "Do you think I am the only one who hasn't truly devoted himself to this futile attempt at a final stand?"

Elander pushed him harder against the wall. "How many more?"

The man smiled. "Enough that some of us have managed to slip away. To send messages and let your enemies know to hurry and strike before your full strength is gathered...and your time is nearly up, by my calculations."

"How *many* slipped away? And where did they go? *Who did they plan to speak to?*"

The man only sneered in response.

"If you won't help us, then we have no room for you here," said Casia. "No space to spare for traitors in this crowded fortress."

"I have been as *helpful* as I intend to be," said the man.

Elander glanced at Casia, who nodded, voice a combination of ice and exhaustion as she said, "Kill him."

Nessa made a little noise of protest, but took only a half-step toward them before drawing to a stop, resigning herself and simply looking away.

Elander drew Caden's sword. He considered trying one last time to wrench information from this cretin—but then came the alarming sound of shouts and horns blaring warnings in the distance, making the man's smile grow wider.

"So it begins," the traitor mused. "What a shame I won't get to see the start of the new world our most powerful God is building."

Casia's nose wrinkled in disgust before she turned and started for the door.

As she turned away, Elander struck, plunging his sword into the man's chest and twisting, keeping him speared against the wall until the last of the life had faded from his eyes.

He yanked the blade free, stepping back to allow the body to tumble to the floor. After cleaning his sword on the back of the man's shirt, he caught up to Casia and Nessa in the hallway, and together the three of them headed for the nearest watchtower, intending to see for themselves what all the noise was about.

"That man could have been bluffing," Nessa said, breathless as they raced along. "He sounded out of his mind to me. Like he wanted us to think he knew more than he actually did."

"Maybe," Casia said, picking up her pace and rounding the next corner so quickly she nearly crashed into Laurent, who looked flustered at the sight of her—at least by his standards.

"Hurry," he said, beckoning them on toward the spiraling steps of the watchtower.

This particular tower had five separate levels, and Laurent flew gracefully up toward the highest of them, finally reaching a small room with a rusted old ladder in its center. The ladder led to a wooden door in the ceiling. He scaled it without hesitation, and the door landed with a heavy *thud* as he flung it open and pulled himself up out of sight.

Casia followed. She reached the top and let out a gasp just as Elander started up the ladder. He climbed faster, heaving himself through the floor and into the sickly-colored daylight.

Casia stood near the edge, arms braced against the wall, head bowed against the horror taking shape below them.

The sky was a putrid yellow streaked with purple and

black. Beneath it, from every direction they could see, armies carrying enemy banners marched toward them.

Everyone atop the watchtower was silent. Still. Horns continued to sound all around the fortress, each of their warning blares drawing rallying, bloodthirsty cries from the approaching hordes.

A merciless pounding started in Elander's head and would not stop, while the smiling face of the man he had just killed flashed in his mind, the traitor's words ringing hollow and haunting in his ears.

So it begins.

CHAPTER 30

Nessa was the last to climb onto the roof. As she took in the sight of their approaching enemies she stumbled, barely catching herself against the protective wall. "There are…*so many.*"

"We were expecting to be outnumbered," Laurent said quietly, coming to stand at her side.

"Yes, but not this outnumbered, this early in the battle." She looked toward the corner of the barracks they'd just come from. "And there are traitors among us who have been giving away our numbers and positions—which means there are even *more* enemies rushing toward us as we speak."

"And these are only our mortal enemies," Elander added, grimly. "The gods are watching too. Letting mortals lead the charge while they stand back and wait for the easiest moment to finish things."

"Making those mortals prove their loyalty to the Dark Court before they intervene?" Laurent wondered.

Elander nodded—he'd had the same dismal thought.

Nessa's voice was nearly lost among the sounds of the rising chaos below as she asked, "What do we do?"

Casia turned away from that chaos, reaching for Shadowslayer's handle and giving it a tight squeeze. "The numbers are obviously not in our favor," she said. "Meeting them all outright will lead to nothing but a quick massacre. We'll have to hold a defensive position until more of our allies come."

Laurent started to shake his head. "And if more *don't*—"

Casia's gaze snapped toward him, cutting him off. "They'll come."

His jaw tightened, but he bowed out of the argument with a sigh and turned his attention back to the approaching enemies. "I suppose there's nothing to do but hope they will."

"Until then, the barriers of magic must hold." Casia turned toward Elander, desperation briefly flickering in her eyes.

"They will hold," he vowed. "We'll gather everyone capable of reinforcing them, prepare them to act, and use any other method we can to bolster the fortress's actual walls."

"What about the traitors in our midst?" asked Nessa.

"Never mind them," Casia muttered. "They've already collected enough of our plans to do their damage, anyway. We don't have the resources to defend from every angle, so we'll focus on the most pressing attack—which at the moment is coming from outside."

Their plan decided, they dispersed, each heading in a different direction to spread the orders out as swiftly as possible.

Elander raced for the north-facing field, where he encountered Zev. Together, they worked to command all of the soldiers in the area, sending most of them toward the inner walls of the fortress while any useful magic users were sent to meet Casia at the barrier of magic.

They raced from one edge of the field to the other, finishing the task swiftly. Elander had started to make his way back toward the fortress when he heard Zev say, "They've...stopped. They're turning around."

Elander paused, glancing in the direction Zev was pointing and seeing it for himself—the lines of approaching soldiers were moving farther and farther away, retreating until they were merely strips of dark silhouettes in the distance.

"Why doesn't this feel like a good thing?" Zev asked.

Thinking the same, Elander scanned the area all around the retreating army, looking for whatever had chased it away.

He saw nothing. It was perfectly calm, the evening suddenly so quiet he could hear Casia and Laurent shouting orders in the distance, even though he couldn't see them. Their voices seemed to echo, making their surroundings feel eerily empty. *Exposed*.

Then the shouting stopped, cutting off abruptly as if they too had just noticed the odd retreat of their enemies. The wind stilled. Birds and beasts had long fled the area, and nothing else—not even Zev—made noise, making Elander very aware of every beat of his own heart.

A strange sound began moments later, drowning out that beat. Like dirt falling, pattering against stone. It grew louder as something began to take shape in the distance—clouds of dust rising up, collecting into a billowing mass that nearly stretched up to the sick-colored sky.

A sandstorm?

It fanned out between the fortress and their enemies who had been marching toward it, and then it started its own deadly advance, heading straight for the fortress.

Elander's stomach dropped as he watched the shifting of this storm, realizing immediately that there was nothing natural about its gritty clouds. Seconds later, he caught sight of its source—a beast stalking through the center mass of swirling sand, twisting into the shape of a lioness with a lean, white body and deep black eyes shining like pits of tar among the dust.

He and Laurent had been wrong.

Apparently, not *all* of the gods were willing to let mortals draw the first blood.

Zev took several steps backward. "Is that..."

"The Goddess of Time? Yes."

"Just when I thought it couldn't get any worse."

"Did you *really* think that?"

"It's just a saying."

"A foolish one, given our history. And it's about to get *much* worse." Elander was still moving, still motioning the last few soldiers toward the fortress. He gave Zev a shove, prompting him back into motion as well. "Keep ordering everyone to fall back—we need to draw in closer than planned. We're still spread too thin to defend against whatever gods have decided that now is the time to make their appearance."

After another shove, Zev snapped back to awareness and did as Elander said.

Elander was preparing to turn and run for the walls himself when he spotted a figure far in the distance—Casia, racing across the field on horseback, silver hair streaking out behind her, hand lifted toward the oncoming storm.

Light flew from her fingertips, weaving into a shield for the sand to hit and dissipate against. She wasn't stopping the storm, only slowing it down, giving their soldiers a chance to retreat into the relative safety of Hallowforge's walls, and their other, lesser magic users time to reposition the barrier of magic.

She successfully protected all but a few stragglers. But once most of the soldiers were safe, hundreds of feet separated her from them. The barrier around the fortress was still shifting into its new position while the wall of churning sand pressed closer and closer to Casia, threatening to engulf her every time she started to turn and focus on riding to safety.

A soldier passed by Elander, leading his horse away from the danger. Elander took the reins from him and jumped onto the horse's back, breaking into a gallop toward Casia.

He was nearly within shouting distance when a whirlwind of twisting sand broke free of the descending wall and overtook him without warning.

It was not simply *sand*. There was magic in it—Time magic that disoriented him, making him lose track of how long he'd been trapped within it. He felt like he had been pushing through the storm for hours already. Like he was hopelessly lost, and there was no point in continuing to search—it was over, he had taken too long and Casia was surely gone by now…

No.

He closed his eyes tightly, willing himself to focus on his breathing and the beat of his heart rather than on the sand sifting over him.

It's only been seconds.

In the next second—before he could lose himself again—

he was summoning his own magic, creating a shield around his body to keep the sand and the ill wind from touching his skin. Once the shield was in place, he gave himself over more fully to the magic, letting it pull him, guide him through the haze and lead him toward Casia.

Her expression was eerily vacant when he found her—the Time magic was taking hold of her as well.

He shouted her name once, twice, three times, and on the third try she finally snapped back to the present and realized the danger she was in.

She swayed in the saddle, hands fumbling to catch herself. The reins slipped from her grasp. Her horse panicked and began to buck wildly. She leapt from the beast, somehow landing gracefully and snatching the reins back. She tried to settle the horse, but let it go after a violent toss of its head nearly slung her across the field.

Elander rode closer, grabbing her and hoisting her into the saddle in front of him. He handed her the reins while he focused on drawing out more magic to protect them, and together they galloped toward clearer air.

The weight of two riders was nearly too much for his tired horse. They moved more and more slowly while the storm continued to chase, growing more violent, battering against his shield. Sand cascaded down and rose up simultaneously, like a sentient creature trying to catch them in its jaws.

It was moments away from succeeding when threads of turquoise energy streaked past and wove into the barrier Elander had created. Within seconds it had overtaken his barrier completely, stretching it both outward and upward, creating a wall nearly as solid as the stone ones surrounding the fortress.

His heart unclenched a bit as he caught a glimpse of the new magic's source—dozens of soldiers running toward the storm rather than away from it, led by the queen of Sadira.

A roar rose from deep within the cloud of sand, sending it billowing out in one last desperate attempt to swallow them.

Soryn and her most powerful magic users pushed forward, cutting it off. The Sky Goddess herself appeared beside the Sadiran queen, her body surrounded in a bluish-green glow and her hands outstretched, shaping and reinforcing the magic shield with small, precise movements of her hands.

Elander spurred his exhausted horse faster. He wasn't sure how many soldiers Soryn had with her, or how long they could hold up against the Time Goddess's storm, but the faster they could all return to the fortress and regroup, the better.

They made it to the original barrier erected around the fortress's grounds. Casia lifted a hand and controlled a small section of the magic, peeling it away, allowing them to pass through without breaking their stride.

Once they were well within the guarded zone, Elander hopped from the saddle, helped Casia down, and handed the horse over to one of the soldiers who had rushed out to meet them.

He scarcely had time to ask Casia if she was okay before she was already moving again, striding in the direction they'd just raced away from.

He caught her arm and held her back.

She didn't fight against his hold, but she refused to head deeper into safety, too busy searching the chaotic scene of dust and magic for signs of what was happening with their allies.

Another deafening roar rattled the ground and sent explosions of sand into the air, fully swallowing up any and all flashes of Sky magic.

CHAPTER 31

Casia's hand flew to her mouth. She took a few steps forward before a sudden crack of thunder boomed through the air, cutting her off. The Goddess of Storms appeared with a flash of bright sparks that stung as they showered over Elander's skin.

"Catch your breath, Queen," Nephele said, "and let us help." She raced for the sandstorm without waiting for a reply.

The Moon Goddess emerged seemingly from nowhere seconds later. She paused only long enough to give Casia a reassuring squeeze on the shoulder, then she sprinted after Nephele, her magic building, shimmering specks of it trailing out behind her.

Casia's idea of *catching her breath* was racing back and forth along the perimeters of their stronghold, making sure all of their soldiers were safe and preparing for their next move. Her gaze continuously darted toward the roaring sand and the last place they'd seen Soryn.

Several minutes passed.

Soryn did not reappear.

The sandstorm continued to roar and shift. Sparks of lightning occasionally lit the sky around it, only to be doused by sand over and over.

Finally, there came a sound like sails snapping in the wind, followed by an explosive shield of white and turquoise energy taking shape, curving against the wall of sand and pushing it back—Moon and Sky-magic. Elander briefly saw what looked like the Goddess of Time stalking along the edges of the encroaching shield before her sandstorm scattered and collapsed, devouring her form.

Casia slowed to a stop, watching and waiting, her expression mirroring the anxious feeling twisting Elander's stomach into knots. She still looked as if she might bolt toward the battle at any moment. He stepped closer, preparing to stop her again if necessary.

They waited, hardly moving, scarcely breathing.

Nephele finally passed through the shield with the Sadiran Queen in her arms.

The young queen looked half-dazed, bleeding profusely from a wound on her shoulder, yet she still looked furious at having been pulled away from the battle. Her stubbornness reminded him of Casia.

No wonder they got along so well at the start.

Soryn was placated only by the sudden appearance of the Healing Goddess, who took her from Nephele and swept her away, carrying her deeper inside the fortress's walls without so much as a word to anyone. The Feather spirit appeared as well, following dutifully at her goddess's heels.

Elander and Casia followed the divine creatures into an atrium with patchy grass and an open ceiling, watching silently as she laid Soryn on the ground and inspected her wound. The goddess's magic felt weaker than it had when they'd last encountered her; Elander was surprised to see her still on this mortal plane at all. He thought the Feather spirit looked odd too, the edges of her faint and ghostlike, as if she was only seconds away from disappearing and heading for other realms.

Luckily, even the goddess's weakened magic made quick work of stopping the blood flowing from Soryn's shoulder.

The Sky Goddess soon strode into the space as well. Her face seemed less severe than normal as she looked over the Sadiran queen, Elander thought, as if she'd developed an unusual fondness toward this human who bore her mark.

As the Healing Goddess finished her work and stepped away, Casia knelt at Soryn's side. "You came."

"Well…" Soryn trailed off, eyes shifting between the Healing Goddess and the Sky Goddess before looking back to Casia. "You all seem to keep much better company than some of the other rulers of this empire. And they were very insistent that I come to your aid."

"What of the company *you* usually keep?" Elander asked. "The Dragon Queen and her followers?"

Soryn winced, either from pain or from her concerns about that company. "There are more battles taking place elsewhere," she said. "Which is why we were late. I stayed with our Sundolian allies for as long as I could before it became apparent that the more consequential battle would be here."

An explosion of sound in the distance rattled them, as if to remind them of all the potential *consequences* they faced.

Soryn's head snapped toward the noise. Elander and Casia helped her stand, and together they hurried up a set of nearby steps that led to a small landing where they could glimpse what was taking place in the distance.

The barrier created by the goddesses to push the sandstorm back still held, but it was weakening, its energy a jumbled mess of fading light.

It wasn't only sand battering against it, breaking it up. Now there were flames as well—an inferno building, searing the shield away section by section, threatening to engulf it completely.

The God of Fire?

Shadowslayer had started to shake, the Point it harbored stirred by the apparent arrival of a more powerful servant of the Dark God. Casia gripped it tightly with both hands as her eyes met the Sky Goddess's.

Without a word exchanged between them, the goddess understood and was off, lifting into the form of a bird that swooped back down to the battlefield and met the Goddess of the Moon where she stood alone, facing the shattering shields.

The goddesses worked together once more, both using their magic to create more layers of protection—an outer shield of pearlescent energy reflecting the dust and fire, and a second line of Sky magic blocking any threats that managed to slip through the first line.

The Goddess of Storms soared above them, the edges of her bird form wild and sparking, difficult to make out among the rising residue of competing magical energies. Her attacks made her position easier to follow—bolts that shot from the dark sky, picking off any soldiers that snuck their way through before the shields were fully placed and secured.

She continued to patrol even after the other two

goddesses returned to Elander and the others. Soryn left to see to her own soldiers, but as she walked away, they were joined by the rest of their innermost circle.

The conversation swiftly turned tense while their enemies continued to gather and pound at their doorstep.

"We can't just keep rebuilding shields," Zev said. "We don't have the resources to survive an indefinite siege."

"Farak believes we can put together a formidable offensive maneuver," Laurent said. "Our numbers are more even now that Soryn's army has arrived. Some had arrived from Moreth just before the Time Goddess's attack as well. We just need to organize and get into position before we drop our shields."

"An offensive maneuver right into the flames of the waiting Fire God and whatever else is hiding behind him?" Rhea's worried tone was accompanied by a soft, uncertain whine from Silverfoot.

Nessa gave the fox a reassuring pat, even as despair overtook her own expression. "We're still outnumbered, even with the new arrivals. And the gods we're facing..."

"Are not invincible," insisted the Moon Goddess. "Once Malaphar is drawn out and destroyed, dealing with his servants will be easier."

"It will weaken them," said the Sky Goddess, shaking her head, "but it won't make them immediately disappear."

The Moon Goddess frowned. "Not immediately, no. But it will be a significant victory."

"And whatever corrupted energy he's given to the Mountain and Time deities won't have truly taken root in them," added the Healing Goddess, "so when Malaphar goes, the magic he gave them will go, too—and more quickly than it will fade from his true servants, I'd expect."

"So only the God of Fire, and possibly the Ice Goddess, will still need to be dealt with," Casia said. "And the mortal armies, of course. Though without the gods backing them up, hopefully they'll fold quickly."

"The Ice Goddess hasn't been spotted in the mortal world since her assault on Edolin," Inya informed them. "Growing tired of her master's games, we can only hope...or perhaps remembering she once had a conscious where mortals were concerned."

"Whatever the reason, it seems she's joined the Serpent Goddess in turning her attention away from this mortal realm. And we already know the new God of Death is not a reliable follower of his master. So if nothing else, at least Malaphar's true court is more or less in shambles."

"And the Mountain God?" Nessa asked.

"He was rumored to be working closely with Sarith and her followers in Moreth," said Inya. "Since that self-proclaimed queen's demise, there haven't been any sightings of him that we're aware of."

Hope fluttered through Elander—only to be swiftly deflated moments later, as Shadowslayer gave another wild tremble. Casia's hand had reached for the sword even before he felt it tremble; it was already becoming second nature to her.

Nephele glided over to them a few minutes later, shrinking and shifting back into her human form before landing lightly at the top of the steps.

The sight of all the goddesses together gave Elander another brief flash of hope—along with an idea. He quickly explained their failed attempts at sealing the Antaeum Point to the goddesses, as well as the plan they had to use Malaphar's own power against it—a plan he still wanted to find an alternative to.

"Most of the Sun Court is here now," he said. "Maybe we should try one last time to combine our magic and overpower the Dark energy in the Point?"

Casia looked doubtful, but she still nodded. "It's worth a try," she said, pulling the sword from its sheath and staring into the energies swirling restlessly within its blade. "But let's hurry."

They moved to a more secluded corner of the fortress grounds, one with more open space and fewer people. Once there, the five of them—Casia, Elander, and the three remaining goddesses of the Sun Court—gathered around the blade and repeated the exercises Casia and Elander had attempted in Mistwilde, sending currents of all their different but aligned powers into its cursed blade.

The sword shivered and spun, taking each new strand of power in...only to twist them up and violently spit them back out.

They tried several times, but each attempt proved fruitless—and increasingly dangerous.

Their final try caused a rebound of tainted Sun magic to strike one of the fortress walls, sending a section of stone crumbling alarmingly close to a pair of soldiers standing near it.

Nephele gave up on their experiments after this, walking away as she flatly declared, "This is a dangerous waste of time and resources we don't have."

Elander couldn't disagree. No matter how badly he wished otherwise, it seemed the Point would not be undone by light; it would have to be carried into the dark and dealt with, whatever the consequences.

Casia's head was bowed low, fists clenching and unclenching as she waited for the irritation in the sword to settle; for it to yield once more to her touch.

Nessa started to reach for her, the feather-shaped symbol on her skin glowing faintly. "Perhaps we could—"

"Enough," Casia said, eyes hardening to steel and voice devoid of emotion as she turned away from Nessa's offer of comforting magic. "The Storm Goddess is right. There is only one way this ends, and we all know it. Let's just be glad I can still carry this sword to that end."

No one said anything, but Elander doubted anyone present felt *glad*.

Casia picked the sword up all the same and returned it to its sheath, taking a few minutes to grip it tightly, settling its anxious energy before turning and starting to give out new orders.

Nessa, Rhea, and the Healing Goddess and her servant spirit were sent to help take care of any soldiers who had been injured or weakened, to make certain their forces were as close to full strength as possible. Laurent, Zev, and the Goddess of Storms went to find Farak and Soryn, to help plan their attack strategy for when their shields came down.

Once they'd dispersed, Casia paused only a moment to catch her breath, then turned and walked toward the same watchtower they'd followed Laurent to earlier. Elander and the Sky and Moon Goddesses went with her. They climbed only to the tower's middle level, high enough to see far into the distance without risking the vulnerability of the open roof.

There were no lights, just two evenly spaced windows. The sky was dark enough that Elander thought it might be late evening, though the exact time was impossible to tell.

The Moon Goddess conjured a few strands of magic, filling the room with a soft glow. The hours pressed on while they observed from their tower, Casia and Elander both occasionally leaving it to go check in with the preparations being made all around the fortress.

Casia returned from one of these checks and went immediately to the window, bracing her hands against the stone sill as if she expected the world to start rattling at any moment.

A few minutes later, it happened—a sudden and complete darkness overtook everything outside, followed by an immense pressure that made it feel as if the tower was closing in around them. Shadowslayer moved as though an invisible hand had taken ahold of it, slicing wildly through the air, forcing Casia to remove it from her belt and drop it to the ground.

The dim light of the veiled stars eventually returned, but their surroundings continued to shiver and suffer from that odd heaviness, as if everything was being crushed in the fist of a mad god.

Elander knelt, placing a hand on the floor for balance. Casia gripped the sill more tightly. Both of the goddesses lifted their faces toward the window almost in unison, eyes wide.

No one moved aside from this. Not right away. There was no need to look outside, no need to more closely inspect the cause of that awful, dark pressure. There was no doubt about who had caused it.

There was no need to speak of it, either—but Casia said it anyway, her voice like a stone dropping into the uneasy quiet. "He's out there. Close by."

Finally, the pressure subsided.

Casia picked up her sword, which still rattled in its sheath like a beast trying to shake free of its cage.

Elander took a deep breath, trying to settle his nerves so they didn't show in his voice. "Well, we've drawn him out. As planned."

"*Plans*," scoffed the Sky Goddess, her nervousness on full display. "Our barriers are about to come crashing down. He will break through and crush all the people gathered so tightly together in this fortress; we've only made it easier for him to kill more efficiently."

Several moments passed in near total silence. Elander could feel each of his heartbeats like enemy fists pounding on the doors to the room they stood in. The Fire God's inferno built more violently against the distant shields, still not quite breaking through, but burning boldly enough to cast ominous patterns of shadows and flames against the tower room's walls.

Casia took a step back from the window.

Elander knew what she was going to say before she said it. Knew that the time had come to face their ending, whatever it might be. He still wasn't ready—would likely *never* be ready—to let her rise to meet that ending.

But he kept perfectly still as she turned, fixed her eyes on the Sky Goddess, and said, "He won't break through the shields and crush anyone within this fortress. Because I am going to ride out and meet him."

CHAPTER 32

Casia did not ride out alone.

She might have if given the chance—but Elander refused, of course. Her friends all descended upon them as they walked out of the watchtower too, as though they had developed an ability to sense when she was trying to face her battles alone. She didn't argue against them going with her. They didn't argue with her plans to march toward their ending, whatever it might be. The time for debate had passed.

They readied their horses and started that final march with few words said between them, stopping once they were clear of the fortress's walls but still a fair distance from the shields the goddesses had created.

Those shields were still intact, but rumbling as if they could erupt and shatter at any moment. Cracks had formed in places, the fractures filled with fire that flowed like molten rock.

The sky crackled and flashed with unstable energy. The earth showed signs of despair as well, patches of grass scorched away and little fissures reaching all the way to where Elander's horse stood. The air smelled of metal and burning things, save for the occasional hint of jasmine from the far-off hills, carried to them by stronger gusts of wind.

The scent of the flowers made Elander think of Sulah's Hill, back in Ciridan—a memory that somehow both strengthened his resolve and made his heart feel as though it was caving inward, trying to escape what was coming.

Casia rode a few hundred feet away from the fortress before drawing to a halt and surveying the battlefield, both the horrors ahead and the army taking shape behind her.

Elander, Zev, Nessa, and Laurent drew their horses into an even line alongside hers. Silverfoot had wedged himself into the saddle next to Zev, prepared to provide sight to Rhea and the other soldiers waiting in the fortress with her, linking them to the heart of the battle.

The Healing Goddess and her servant had stayed at Rhea's side to help keep order and manage reinforcements and other things, while the Storm Goddess had shapeshifted and resumed her position above the battlefield, ready to take aim at the Fire God once the shields dropped—eager, she'd said, to finish what they had started outside of Feyedge.

The Sky and Moon Goddesses had their sights on the shields they'd created. On the signal, they would do away with them abruptly enough to catch their enemies off-guard.

Behind them, part of their mortal army had formed ranks. More were hiding in the fortress and in the hills behind it, spreading out to conceal their true numbers.

Soryn waited to lead a group of those hidden soldiers from the east.

Farak waited to lead another group from the west.

All was ready, quiet, and oddly still, every breath held and body braced for impact.

"It's settled," Laurent said, glancing toward Elander and Casia. "You two focus on finding your way toward Malaphar, and the rest of us will deal with distracting everyone and everything else."

They stared at the fractured shields, each silently grappling with the enormity of the task ahead.

Zev cut his eyes toward Casia. "Just a simple search and find mission," he said, breaking the tense silence threatening to settle. "No pressure or anything."

Nessa managed a nervous laugh while the corners of Casia's lips turned upward a bit.

Laurent's tone remained serious to the very end. "Everyone knows their assignments, so let's pretend it *is* just another mission, and we'll see you two on the other side." He looked to Casia first, then to Elander, gaze lingering only long enough for a quiet understanding to pass between them. Having said everything he apparently needed to say, he guided his horse out of their line, preparing to help draw attention away from them as planned.

Nessa pulled her horse directly next to Casia's and reached for her hand, giving it a squeeze and filling the air with a burst of her warm magic before leaving and following Laurent. Zev followed her, but not before presenting Casia and Elander with a teasing salute and reminding them not to mess up.

Casia stared after them as they went. Her throat bobbed. A dozen different emotions flashed upon her face before finally settling on one—determination. She looked back to the shields looming before them.

A shadow moved among those shields, lashing against

their magic and rattling them, expanding the glowing cracks. Dark energy seeped through the fissures. It felt as it had in the tower—like unmistakable evil; mad power and pressure that could only have come from the darkest of gods.

Their horses pranced nervously. Casia grabbed Shadowslayer and held tightly, trying to keep the darkness contained. As she did, Elander settled his mount and stepped it closer to hers, catching her eye one final time.

Another shadow rattled the shields, but they did not look away from one another.

The world reduced to the two of them and their thundering heartbeats. All they had been, all they had made it through, all they had vowed. All of it had somehow led to this final hour, to the very edge of the world's ruin or revival.

"The brightest light this world has ever known," he reminded her.

She nodded, letting go of the sword's hilt and taking a firm grip on the reins as she turned once more to face the waiting shadows.

Here it comes.

Elander breathed in slowly, willing the world to slow as well.

It didn't.

The Moon and Sky Goddesses swept past them before they could utter another word. Their shields gave way with a sound like shattering glass, collapsing and sending a warm, powerful wind rushing over everything.

There was a brief pause, a moment suspended among that wind.

Then everything seemed to spring into motion all at once —the two sides racing forward, colliding with the sounds of pounding hooves, of battle cries, of steel striking steel and shields and flesh.

Mortals and monsters alike clashed. Human soldiers made up the bulk of both sides, but there were beasts that answered to the Dark Court here as well; Elander saw no less than a dozen of the Fire God's hellhounds leading the charge to his left, and he kept catching glimpses of shadowy wisps that he was fairly certain were revenants just waiting for the first bits of wounded flesh to infect.

A massive shadow overtook them, sweltering heat accompanying it, and Elander didn't have to look up to know that the God of Fire himself had joined the fray.

The Storm Goddess intercepted him mid-dive, her form a blur of bright wings and wicked, lightning-wrapped talons. The crackle of electricity and the explosion of smoke and flame drowned out all other sounds for several moments.

But even as the battle overhead raged, Elander's attention stayed on the Sky and Moon Goddesses below. Laurent and the others followed closely behind these goddesses as they summoned lines of magic and guided them this way and that, using them like barricades to push the enemy aside and open up a path.

Elander and Casia rode deeper into the enemy's side by way of this path. Elander provided protection while Casia focused on Shadowslayer, withdrawing it and letting it guide her. It had clearly, violently reacted to Malaphar's pulses of power earlier, so their plan was to follow these stronger reactions, to use them to seek the god's magic and pinpoint his precise location.

Her balance was threatened every time one of those reactions occurred. Elander stayed close, protecting her not just from the soldiers or beasts that slipped through the goddesses' barricades, but from the sword itself whenever the more intense shivers of power overtook it.

His own magic felt stronger than ever, bolstered by the presence of the Sun Court and by the danger closing in around his queen.

Whatever power had been given to him as her guardian in whatever lifetime, he would lay it all down right here on this battlefield if it meant they lived to see another day. And the magic sleeping in him seemed to understand his resolve, waking more and more confidently with every spark he summoned.

Casia moved with the same confidence.

Every time an enemy tried to slow her down, Elander was there, cutting them off with a swing of his sword or with blasts of light or stormy magic.

They covered hundreds of feet in this manner, the area around them growing more and more empty as their enemies caught sight of the dead left in their wake and lost their nerve, accordingly.

Soon they had created enough of a clearing to pause and consider their next move. Elander started to suggest doing so, when Shadowslayer shook with a sudden tremor so powerful it forced Casia to lean back in her saddle, drawing her horse to a stop.

She pressed closer to the horse's back, centering her balance so she could use both hands to try and keep her sword under control.

The blade continued to move on its own, the tip of it twitching, almost bending to the left—like an arrow pointing their gazes toward the tree-dotted hills rising and rolling in that direction.

A shroud of smog drifted over the crests of the hills. The

trees it blanketed twitched with the same fervor as Casia's sword, bending in ways that seemed impossible. Pressure settled on Elander's chest, making his muscles shake with every attempt at a deep inhale. A foul, powerful wind stirred, wrapping around them and stealing the remainder of his breaths away.

He's nearby.

Or, at least he had been—and recently. Likely stalking his way along the ridge, watching the chaos he'd sowed as it bloomed, as it led to carnage and blood and so many broken things in the battlefield below him.

With little more than a glance to coordinate, they were moving again, charging toward the hill. Casia led with her sword outstretched, Elander right behind her.

Heat and shadows overtook them, followed by a line of fire falling from the sky and igniting directly in front of them.

Elander's horse veered wildly to the right.

Casia's darted in the opposite direction.

Before Elander could race back to her, another ball of fire struck the ground and exploded outward, forcing him even farther away.

It happened just as it had outside of Feyedge—he was on one side, Casia was on the other.

He wouldn't stay separated from her this time, even if it meant jumping through the fire.

He surrounded himself with a shield of magic and spurred his horse back into motion. It reared to a stop inches away from the ring of flames. Despite the protection around it, the creature refused to move. After several failed attempts to coax it forward, Elander leapt from the saddle and sprinted through the wall of fire on foot.

More fire greeted him on the other side, plumes of it rising in every direction he turned. His shield protected him from the worst of the heat, but he could still feel the fire pressing against that shield, suffocating his magic and making it feel heavier and harder to control as the moments passed.

Cursing, he continued to search, fighting his way toward any open, unburned space he saw. These spaces were igniting more and more rapidly, with towering flames and smoke making it impossible to see Casia or anything else clearly.

He saw what looked like an open path and darted for it.

A trio of the Fire God's bloodthirsty hounds waited at the end of it.

They spotted him, baring their teeth and crouching, creeping forward before lunging with such supernatural speed they appeared as nothing more than hurtling balls of flame. He briefly lost them against the walls of actual flames rising all around, and he only just managed to duck to avoid a set of fiery claws across his face.

A shadow overtook him, followed again by blinding magic and heat—not from fire this time but from bolts of lightning that caged the attacking hounds and swiftly turned their bodies to nothing more than charred husks.

Nephele.

She landed gracefully just ahead of him, shifting once more to her human form as she did. Her back remained to him as she fought off a dog who had escaped her initial assault.

Another fire-hound leapt at her through one of the walls of fire, but Elander sprinted between them and intercepted it, withdrawing Caden's sword and plunging it into the creature's chest in one smooth motion. He held the impaled creature until it stopped writhing and whimpering, then dislodged it with a powerful snap of his arm.

At the sound of its body thumping against the ground, Nephele spun around to face him, panting heavily. "Aren't you supposed to be with your queen?"

"Aren't you supposed to be taking care of the God of Fire?"

Nephele smirked and pointed toward a section of fading flames—to a figure on the other side of it that was rising slowly, pulling fire toward him and obscuring his form as they watched.

"I'm working on it," said the Storm Goddess, her dark skin suddenly bright and dancing with lightning.

Elander motioned to the destruction all around them. "Your methods are sloppy and reckless, as usual."

"I've got this under control."

He frowned, not entirely convinced she did, but when she jerked her head toward a parting in the flames and told him to find Casia, he didn't need telling twice.

He raced for the clearing, finally breaking free of the fire and smoke.

Several of the god's dog-like beasts gave chase, snapping at his heels. He cut them down one after the other, meeting lunging bodies with his blade and summoning shields to repel their flaming attacks, leaving a trail of blood and scorched earth behind him.

The hills he and Casia had been trying to reach finally rose directly in front of him. He dealt with the last of the beasts pursuing him, stabbing it into the ground only to turn and find a row of enemy soldiers awaiting him at the base of the hills.

They took one look at him—at his burned and bloody self, alone—and charged more confidently than they should have.

His patience officially used up, Elander rapidly summoned lines of electricity, snaking them around the soldiers, cutting down a dozen bodies with little more than a few furious movements of his hands.

He had his sights set on the ridge above, and nothing would slow him now. He readied his sword and spun and slashed over and over again, cutting his way through the enemies his magic hadn't already felled.

He could feel occasional flickers of Casia's magic. But they were faint, and all the Dark energy in the air threatened to drown them out completely.

He sheathed his sword, broke away from the main battle, and raced up the hill, hoping he'd find clearer air and better focus higher up. Halfway to the summit, the dark and sinister sky grew even darker—the few visible stars had been blotted out by a gathering cloud.

A cloud of *sand*.

It was similar to the ones they'd faced earlier, except each of the grains of sand within this storm shimmered more like glass—and they cut like it, too, tiny blades brushing over the few patches of his unprotected skin and sending blood bubbling to the surface.

He shielded his eyes and pulled his hood over his head, dropping to his knees as he summoned more protective magic. He wasn't afraid of fighting through pain or blood—only of losing more time, of the Sand Goddess's magic making him too disoriented and too blind to continue searching for Casia.

With a barrier wrapped around him, he resumed his

climb up the hillside, ignoring the blood on his face and the burning that started in his muscles as the slope grew increasingly steep.

The sand continued to fall around him as he climbed, but he pushed through, eventually reaching a flat ledge among the hills that provided a relatively safe vantage point.

He paced the area, searching the chaotic battle below, reaching out with his magic and willing it to find Casia. To let her know he was still there. If he could just catch a glimpse of her, a spark of her power—

A sudden burst of sand exploded over the ledge and scraped at his shield, forcing him to drop back and focus on securing that shield.

No sooner had he managed this when another wave of magic flashed down from somewhere above. It avoided him and instead overtook the sandstorm, swallowing it, shrinking it almost as abruptly as it had exploded toward him. The magic controlling the cloud faded—*drained*—and the grains of sand fell like natural sand should have, trickling harmlessly down the hillside.

Elander twisted around and saw a familiar figure standing on the ridge above—Varen.

One distraction for another.

The God of Death slid down the slope, stirring up dust that tangled with the shadows surrounding him as he made his way toward Elander. "Where is my sister?"

Elander lowered his shield but remained tense, still unable to fully trust or make sense of this man—this *god*—before him. "If I knew, I'd already be running in that direction." He went back to summoning magic to try and draw a response from hers. "The chaos is making it difficult to track her."

Too much darkness drowning her out.

He shook off the thought and kept trying.

Varen walked the ledge beside him, surveying the battle for himself. "It's difficult for me as well, for what it's worth. Though that's partly because you two feel very similar these days—I thought I was following her magic, not yours."

"Sorry to disappoint you."

"No matter."

A ripple of power went over them, and they both looked to the same spot in the distance, to where a streak of deep purple had slashed its way across the unstable sky. That energy, and the pressure that followed...

"The Dark God has her in his sights," said Varen, matter-of-factly.

Elander found the pommel of Caden's sword and clenched it tightly. "Or she has him in *hers*."

"She's trying to chase him down, is she?"

Elander didn't reply.

"She will reach him, I'm sure. But..."

Elander continued feeling for Casia, but he couldn't help the way his head tilted curiously toward Varen.

"Her plan to slay him will fail," Varen said.

"How do you know?"

"I glimpsed her at the beginning of this battle, from a distance, and her sword...it still pulses with the Antaeum Point's energy. I could feel it even from far off."

There seemed no point in hiding anything now, so Elander nodded. "...We tried but failed to overcome it with Sun magic," he admitted. "Only the blood of one with the Dark God's magic seemed to negate any of the Point's energy."

"She thinks she can use his own power against him,

doesn't she? Dark blood to overcome darkness; a monster to slay a monster..." He didn't pause for Elander to confirm one way or the other. "I should have seen this coming," he continued, voice calm and matter-of-fact as ever. "She never learned to come at a problem from an angle...always charging headfirst into the dark, that one."

His eyes glazed over, and for a long moment he seemed to have forgotten about their conversation entirely.

Finally, he blinked and lowered his unsettling stare to Elander once more. "Though I suppose I wouldn't be here if she hadn't done so all those years ago. And neither would you, for that matter."

Elander didn't want to talk about that now, but Varen continued to stare—his gaze had paused on Elander's hand, caught on the mark the Savnas blade had burned into it.

As he considered the mark, an emotion Elander couldn't readily name overtook Varen's features, something shifting between understanding and sorrow, and then, oddly enough...*peace*.

He finally looked away, moving on to something in the distance. "I'll go find her," he told Elander. "But you should be prepared to follow soon after, to help her finish things."

"...I was already prepared for that."

"Good." Varen started to turn around but hesitated, glancing back, not quite meeting Elander's eyes. "And one more thing."

Elander tilted his head to show he was listening even as he went back to scanning the battlefield below, searching for signs of Casia.

"If you both somehow survive this, do me a favor."

He stopped searching the wreckage and fully met Varen's gaze.

"Take care of her, won't you? And find a way to convince her not to blame herself, whatever that takes."

They stared at each other for another long moment, Elander feeling as if he was looking upon the man before him for the very first time. His throat closed to the point where he couldn't properly speak, so he merely nodded.

"Thank you," Varen said.

Then he was gone, disappearing in a swirl of pale magic and shadows.

CHAPTER 33

Cas opened her eyes to fire—a great ring of it closing around her, its bright glare obscuring everything beyond her immediate surroundings. Smoke and embers swirled, blinding her further. They made her cough, her chest ache, but they were nothing compared to the immense, crushing ripple of power that had woken her up.

She sat up, dazed, not remembering how she'd ended up on the charred ground. Her soreness made her certain she'd been thrown against it. Her horse was gone. Her sword was…

Where was it?

Panic brought her to her feet. After a moment of frantic searching she spotted it at the base of a burned tree. She stumbled for a few steps and then began to run, leaping over piles of smoldering grass, darting to avoid falling embers, finally dropping to her knees beside her weapon and carefully reaching toward it.

Once it was calm, she picked it up. Another ripple of

power rushed through the air. Shadowslayer felt it, too, and tried once more to respond with violent shaking.

While her battle with it raged on, she heard the larger battle doing the same in the distance. Her soldiers, her friends...all of them were still fighting. The veil of smoke and flame, along with the haze of magical residue, continued to thicken, making them seem a thousand miles away. She felt trapped and alone with her sword and its darkness—the same sort of loneliness that had always accompanied her frequent panic attacks.

But she would not panic now.

She held Shadowslayer tightly in her arms, reaching once more for the part of her that was still buried deeply within the blade. She would not be overwhelmed, and neither would the sword, so long as she held to the light inside of them both and kept going.

She rose once more to her feet and started to walk in the direction of the awful, dark power she'd felt. She remained braced for another wave of that power, but it didn't come. After several minutes, she instead felt *light*—a surge of it powerful enough to answer her own magic.

She walked faster, picturing Elander's face, imagining his magic twisting into hers and fortifying it. He was close by, she was certain of it. Looking for her, most likely.

But she didn't find Elander.

The light she'd felt had come from the Goddess of the Moon, who emerged from the smoke in her canine form, her silky white fur stained with ash and blood.

Inya trotted to her side and paused there, looking to the distance, toward a slash of purplish energy that had ripped through the starless sky.

As they stared at it together, another of those dark ripples of energy fell over them. Cas loosed a shuddering breath as it passed.

"He's close," she said—not really a question, but the goddess's bright eyes blinked slowly as if in answer before she bowed her slender head, and then her entire body, lowering herself so Cas could more easily climb onto her back.

Cas didn't hesitate. She fixed her sword to her belt and then hoisted herself up, grabbing fistfuls of fur to hold on—gently at first, but more tightly as the goddess launched without warning into a full sprint.

They raced across the dark battlefield, weaving and dodging attacks, leaping over fallen bodies and summoning occasional blasts of magic to push their way through crowds.

They passed through fire and hordes of battling soldiers, finally coming to a clearer section of field that allowed them to truly pick up speed.

The pulses of dark power continued to break over them, growing stronger and more numerous as they ran. It felt as if Malaphar *knew* he'd caught their attention, as if he was trying to lure them away from everything else, calling them to a private battle he was certain he would win.

He would regret that call very soon.

The goddess rarely spoke while in her shifted form, but Cas thought she could hear her soothing voice drifting through her head as they raced onward.

Hold on tightly, Shadowslayer.

Cas did, leaning forward and squeezing her legs more firmly against Inya's sides. They moved even faster, scaling hills without hesitation, bouncing from one steep slope to the next, the world around them becoming little more than blurs of color and sound until they were high above the rest of the battle.

Another shiver of power in the air—the strongest yet—nearly made Inya lose her footing on the steep hill they were climbing. They leapt to more even ground and continued to move, veering toward where the darkness seemed strongest.

They both spotted him at the same moment—a figure cutting a terrible, monstrous silhouette against an adjacent and partially burned hillside. Shadows rose and fell over the hills all around him, disrupted only by the glowing edges of burned bushes and tufts of grass lit by wayward embers. Wind howled around him, continuing to send dancing bits of fire over the area, igniting more patches as they drifted down.

Cas sat up straighter, while the goddess slowed to a stop before she seemed to realize what she was doing. Cas squeezed her legs against her sides again, urging her to move. The goddess shook back into awareness, and they swept into a wide arc around their target, making their way to a nearby plateau that would give them more room to maneuver.

The Dark God turned but didn't give chase. The shadows draped over the hillside came to life with even this subtle movement, lifting and wrapping around his body, doubling its size. Tripling it, maybe. It was impossible to tell what was shadow and what was flesh, and the answer seemed to be shifting as they watched, some of the shadows actually solidifying and *becoming* flesh.

Cas kept her focus on his eyes, on this one part of him that seemed constant. They locked onto hers with equal boldness. Her world narrowed to them, the pale orbs set in an even paler face, and even though a considerable stretch of uneven earth separated them, Cas felt as if she was mere feet away, staring directly into his gaze. It was like staring out over a sea, one so vast and deep it made her feel small and insignificant.

She was neither of those things.

"Get me closer to him," she ordered.

The shadows around him grew, swallowing up the drifting embers and everything else until the darkness surrounding them was absolute. Cas could see only the space directly around her, and only because of the constant, subtle glow of the goddess carrying her.

Then came the goddess's voice, clear and ringing in her head—

Ready your sword.

Cas withdrew it, still holding tightly to the goddess's fur with her other hand. Warm energy radiated between the goddess and her, chasing away the last of the empty chill caused by Malaphar's pale eyes.

Magic rose up from Inya's body, strands of silver-white wrapping around both Cas and her weapon until they were both as bright as the moon itself. The light stretched in all directions, illuminating the path ahead.

The goddess charged forward, her paws swift and soundless upon the ground.

They were within thirty feet of their target.

Twenty.

Ten.

Inya slammed to a stop at the same moment Cas rose up and leapt from her back, and the combined momentum allowed her to soar an impressive distance, her sword outstretched and ready as she descended on the Dark God.

She struck Malaphar's chest, Shadowslayer guided by the

pathfinding magic the goddess had wrapped around it; there was a small opening in the center of the black, scale-like armor he wore, and this was where her magicked blade sank deeply into. Deep enough that the weapon became a firmly-fixed object that Cas could brace herself against.

She gripped it tightly, throwing all of her weight into trying to shove it deeper.

Blackish-red blood oozed over the blade and onto her arms. The scent of metal and heat, mixed with something like dirt, was nearly overwhelming. She held her breath and held tighter to the sword, bracing herself for the swift disappearance of the energy trapped in its blade, for a strange emptiness like the one that had followed their experiments with Zev and his blood.

The emptiness never came.

A massive hand wrapped around the back of her neck, claws digging through the thick collar of her coat and reaching skin.

The Dark God pried her away from him as if she was little more than an insect crawling against his chest. She had only one thought as he did—that she could not let him get his hands on her sword. She again threw all of her weight into holding it, dragging it out with her as the god wrenched her away.

He ripped it completely out of his body, the scrape of its sharp edge upon armor and the sickening, slippery gushing of blood accompanying his deep laughter.

And then he flung her away, sword and all.

She slammed and slid her way down into a rocky crevice between two steep hills, Shadowslayer clattering after her. Its blade was so black she almost lost sight of it in the night. There was still blood on it—it was almost entirely covered—

but there had been no negation of the dark energy plaguing it. Not even for a moment.

Now what?

Every inch of her body ached, but she picked up the sword, sheathed it, and scrambled out of the narrow space. Fighting through the pain and the suffocating energy of her sword, she rose into a more formidable stance, expecting the Dark God to dive down at any moment.

But when she looked up, she didn't see his shadow descending.

She saw only light, far above—the brilliant silver-white light of the Moon Goddess and her magic.

As she watched, shadows swarmed around that light, eclipsing it.

Cas dropped to one knee, holding her breath.

A minute later she saw the silver-white dog falling down the steepest of the hills surrounding them, her light trailing out behind her, waning like a star shooting toward its death.

She finally came to rest with her body centered between two leafless trees, and the light surrounding her simply...*went out.*

Cas continued to stare. The falling light had been so bright that it lingered even after its source was extinguished, little white dots of it dancing before her eyes. Then her vision adjusted to the new darkness. The goddess was lost in the night, all was dark, and Cas was alone again.

She barely had time to comprehend this before a *whoosh* of wind and energy overtook her.

Malaphar landed a few feet from where she knelt, his arrival shaking the ground so violently she would have lost her balance if she'd still been standing.

She pulled her sword closer. Her power that slept within

it, buried underneath the layers of darkness...she couldn't feel it anymore, no matter how hard she tried to reach for it.

The Dark God drew his own blade from the shadows swarming around him. "This is disappointing," he said, voice sharp and echoing, like ice cracking on a cold, silent night.

Cas stood up, stubbornly clutching her sword, useless as she knew it would be.

"Solatis was so *convinced* you would be the champion queen of mortal-kind," the god continued, "I thought this last battle would at least be more entertaining."

He gave no more warning than this before sweeping his blade forward.

She danced out of reach of the weapon itself, but shadows exploded from the tip and gave chase, wrapping like a whip around her legs. She instinctively stabbed Shadowslayer toward the binding. It didn't drive the dark rope away, but the blade absorbed some of its magic, loosening its hold and allowing Cas to break free.

It was a short-lived victory, as the god simply summoned more darkness, forcing the blade to absorb it until it shook so wildly that Cas had no choice but to cast it aside.

As it thudded against the ground, more shadowy bindings snapped toward her. She rolled to the right, summoning lightning to her hands as she went, fending off the reaching shadows.

The distant sky was alive with lightning as well—the Storm Goddess still fighting. She could feel that goddess's power even from a distance. She could breathe it in, draw from it, rely on it. The magic of the Sky Goddess bristled in the air as well. And the Moon Goddess...even though she seemed to have fallen, there was light left behind. Even if Cas could not easily see it, she could *feel* it.

And sword or no sword, she could still carry their light.

Her lightning struck more of the reaching shadows, winding around them, stopping their pursuit of her. The tangled magic tumbled and fought, suspended in the air for several seconds before it ignited in an explosion of power that sent them both stumbling backward.

They circled one another, continuing to trade strikes of magic until Cas found herself backed dangerously close to a steep edge. Below her stretched a rocky slope. The ground shifted beneath her boots, little pebbles and clumps of dirt slipping free and threatening to take her with them.

As she tried to leap toward more solid footing, Malaphar rushed forward, sword at the ready.

She twisted out of his path, lost her balance, and landed on her back as she veered wildly away from the steep, rocky hill.

He followed an instant later, ripping the sword he held into two separate blades, into curves of shadow that hardened and shone like obsidian as he twisted them and stabbed them toward her chest.

She summoned a shield of light, stopping the swords mere inches away from her body. The shadowy weapons scattered as they met her light, leaving only the god himself looming over her.

She rolled from beneath him and staggered back upright.

The shadows she'd scattered simply returned to his body, building into his figure until he towered even higher above her. He didn't bother to reform his sword, or any weapon at all—he simply stalked closer to her, one hand lifting, its clawed fingers flexing.

She reinforced her shield as she tried and failed to catch her breath.

He clawed a hand into the shield. Squeezed. She thought he was attempting to break it apart with nothing more than the sheer strength of his grip. But no—there was more magic seeping out of his palm too, threads of black poison infusing into her magic and creating cracks in the barrier.

She held steady. Several moments passed. Her muscles shook, sweat beaded her skin, but the shield held, and held, and *held*—

Then it began to collapse inward. To push against her body, buckling her knees. To *crack,* allowing little bits of darkness to slip through and land against her skin. Those bits didn't hurt right away. But she could feel them sinking in and spreading, warmth in her veins that turned quickly to burning. Soon her entire body felt as though it was on fire. It was all she could focus on—the most painful thing she had experienced in her long, colorful history of painful things.

Her knees gave way, slamming her into the ground.

She needed to get up, to find some way to expel his poison from her. But she could scarcely breathe from the pain, much less move.

Light, she thought, desperately. *I need to summon more of it.*

She couldn't budge, not even to lift her hand and reinforce her breaking shield.

Someone else moved on her behalf—wolves of light surged over the edge of the steep hill and prowled around her, snapping at the god and his shadows, herding them away.

Elander.

She could feel him in between the miserable throbs of pain and flashes of fire, could see his face in her mind even as darkness tried to overtake her thoughts. She forced herself not to collapse further, bracing a hand against the ground and searching through the haze of wolves and light to find him.

He was nowhere to be seen.

She settled for beckoning one of the beasts closer to her, wrapping her arms around its neck and focusing on its magic to help bring her own power to the surface. Her body sank partially into it. It wasn't a fully solid creature, but it was enough to steady her.

The burning in her veins eased. With her next exhale, her body expelled light along with breath, reforming the barrier around her. Thin at first, but thickening rapidly, sealing her off from the Dark God.

The last thing she saw before it closed her off completely was that god disappearing under a horde of wolves as his angry roar filled the air—an awful, earth-shaking roar that rattled Cas's teeth and made chills erupt over her skin.

She held tighter to the wolf before her, her awareness slipping away as she buried herself in its light and warmth.

CHAPTER 34

When Cas's focus returned, the wolves remained. They were pacing the edges of a dome of reflective, protective magic—her barrier, only it had somehow expanded to cover the entire hilltop, even without a conscious effort from her.

Malaphar was nowhere to be seen.

But she was not alone. The battle had closed in all around her. Through her shield she could see fire and other types of magic flying in all directions, could hear the clang and clatter of weapons, the pounding of footsteps, the chorus of frantic, raised voices…

And her brother was standing just inside the very edge of her protective shield, watching it all unfold.

"Varen?"

He didn't turn around.

She pushed to her feet and went to his side. He glanced her way but still didn't speak. They stood together for a long moment, staring at the mayhem just beyond them until she could no longer stand the silence.

Her eyes darted to Shadowslayer, which lay on the ground at the dome's opposite edge, and her voice cracked as it came out. "I failed."

"Spectacularly so." Varen turned to face her more fully. A trace of a clever smile lit his face, reminiscent of the times she'd stumbled upon him in his library after he'd just discovered some new fact or imagined some new theory. "But you had the right idea," he told her. "You just missed an important detail, I believe."

She moved to pick up her sword, but stopped mid-reach as he continued.

"It isn't a sacrifice if you have to *take* it from him. It must be given willingly."

She left the sword on the ground, staring at the purple and black energy swirling bolder than ever in its blade, understanding dawning over her and making her muscles seize up.

Zev had been willing that day in the palace yard.

The ones who had originally created the Antaeum Point, according to the story the Mistwilde elves told, had been more than willing to sacrifice whatever it took—they had been *desperate*, even, to create a weakness for the gods they loathed.

As desperate as her brother.

"We were right," she said, quietly. "Weren't we? When blood infused with Dark magic hits the Point, it causes a disruption in its power. And enough drops of such blood will overwhelm it. Destroy it. Darkness to overcome darkness..."

"It will require more than *drops* I'm afraid."

She stared at him.

He didn't elaborate.

He didn't have to. Cas already knew what he meant. What

he had planned. Perhaps she'd known for some time, but she'd buried the knowledge without realizing it, some subconscious attempt at protecting herself.

She swallowed the dryness from her ash-filled throat. "Did you know all along that it would come to this?"

"I had ideas, even before I ascended. Caden was useful, as I'd hoped—able to steal more details. Enough that I started to piece the last of it together. And I would have told you more of my thoughts and plans before now, but it would have risked too much—if Malaphar suspected us of working together, then we wouldn't have made it to this night, to this...*opportunity* before us. You wouldn't have been able to move the Point so conveniently to me."

"And now it doesn't matter if he knows we're working together..."

"Right. Because now we've finally come to the end of things." Another slight smile, this one grim but victorious, curled his lips. "One last sacrifice, and the gods lose this round. So you haven't failed, really—in fact, I couldn't have done this without you."

The gods lose.

For so long, she had thought she was waging a war against her brother, against her past and the atrocities her bloodline had committed.

Now she understood the way Varen saw it—the way he had *always* seen it.

It had always been a battle between him and the gods.

Let the gods rage, he'd told her once. *They do not frighten me.*

He truly *hadn't* looked afraid back then. He didn't look afraid now, either. He looked almost...peaceful.

And Casia hated him in that moment—hated him for the way he seemed to have accepted this fate when she could not, for the way her heart felt heavy with grief, with a love that made no sense to her and likely never would now, because how, *how* would she make sense of it all if he was gone?

How could she?

He picked up her sword and offered it to her.

She didn't take it. "You don't want me to do this."

He kept the sword outstretched. "It never really mattered what I wanted."

Another stone piled onto her already too-heavy heart.

Cas took the sword from him, even as she shook her head and whispered, "There must be another way."

"Even if there *is,* surely you realize that we don't have time to find it?"

The shield around them trembled as a rush of magic struck it, as if the universe felt the need to remind them how very little time they truly had.

"Come on now, my dear sister. Are you a queen or not?"

She wiped the sweat from her palms, gripped her sword more tightly, took a step back. She couldn't do this. She *wouldn't* do this.

He followed her. "I know you didn't want this role. I didn't want to be king, either. But here we are. And if it helps, I think you'll be better suited to the crown than I was. Here's a chance to prove it to everyone who might still doubt you."

Her eyes watered and burned, but she refused to blink, refused to look away from her brother.

Another burst of magic struck their shield.

Varen studied the spot of impact for a moment before fixing his eyes back on her. "He's coming. Either he destroys me or you do, and only *one* of these options is going to give our world a chance to survive beyond tomorrow."

He moved closer. She fought the urge to take another step away from him. To run. *Where would she go?* Shadowslayer shook in her hands as she lifted it and pointed it at him; its weight seemed to have tripled.

"Strike hard and strike fast," he whispered, eyes on the sword. "I don't want to linger."

She took a deep breath.

Varen summoned a current of pale magic to his hand. With a flick of his wrist, it stretched into a spear-like shape.

Another hit rattled the shield around them.

Varen sprang toward her in the next instant, stabbing the spear of magic forward, sending a wave of cold power washing over her. Even as the chill gripped her, Cas side-stepped the attack, pulling her sword in close, refusing to strike back.

They darted through the confined space, twisting and turning, the space continuing to fill with Death energy that made her movements increasingly sluggish and clumsy.

She stumbled.

The javelin of magic struck toward her throat.

Reflex brought her sword up to knock it aside at the last moment.

With divine speed, Varen recovered and attacked once more in the span of a heartbeat, forcing her to use her sword to parry again, again, and again, until she had fallen into a rhythm and was no longer thinking about her movements. She didn't have to think.

She didn't *want* to think.

But her mind still raced, traveling to the past instead of the present, reliving the moment in the mountains weeks ago when Varen had pulled her from the ledge and she'd demanded answers from him.

Why did you agree to become a god?

And his reply, as smooth and certain as the attacks he made against her now—

Because the alternative would have been you becoming one.

He had found a way to protect her, just as she had protected him all those years ago. A circle. One that she did not want to see completed, and yet it was closing a little more with every breath she took, with every beat of her heart that she could not slow down, no matter how hard she tried to.

Thump.

Another stab knocked aside.

Thump. Thump.

Shadowslayer seemed to move on its own.

Thumpthumpthump.

Her thoughts rushed, jumbled among her pounding heartbeats.

He's a god. I can't kill him. He's not an ordinary human. This isn't real, not real, not real, not real. He is not an ordinary being—

A gasp of pain from one of them. A soft cry from another. Pounding hearts, stumbling steps, choking breaths—she couldn't tell whose sound was whose, where it all started or where it all stopped.

Stop.

She just wanted to *stop*.

But it was already too late.

Her focus crashed back to the present, to the sight of her sword impaled in her brother's heart, of his divine blood spilling over the dark blade, steaming in the cold air.

And the entire world began to shake.

CHAPTER 35

At first, Cas could not tell where the shaking was truly coming from.

Herself? Her sword? The ground beneath her?

Nothing felt stable. Nothing felt solid or real except the warm handle clenched in her fist and the drops of blood congealing upon her skin.

She withdrew her sword from Varen's chest. Let it fall to the earth. A web of cracks shot out from the point of its impact. The blood coating it simmered and burned, and even more cracks appeared in the ground all around it.

Cas could focus on nothing aside from her brother's face. On his eyes losing their ability to focus. On his lips trembling, taking in one last inhale before he collapsed against her.

She caught him and dropped to her knees, right in the center of the broken ground. It could have broken completely apart and swallowed them whole in that moment, and she would not have cared.

Currents of pale blue energy surrounded Varen's body,

spilling haphazardly out along with his blood, wrapping him up in one last violent display of magic. As the magic sank over Cas, blinding her, she didn't feel the terrible cold that usually accompanied it. There was only a slight chill, a wind that seemed to blow both around and inside her chest, right through her heart that suddenly felt impossibly hollow.

As the magic slipped away, her eyes fell on her sword.

The blood on its blade had burned completely away, leaving behind only clean steel, glistening as though freshly polished.

And Cas felt...*nothing.* Nothing else cracked, nothing else moved. She felt neither dark nor light energy, whether within herself, her sword, or her brother.

For what seemed like hours, she was suspended in a horrifying absence of color and sound and all sensation, unable to hear or feel anything beyond her own beating heart—and even that was faint.

As the disorienting nothingness slowly gave way to distant sounds and glimpses of dulled color, she gathered her brother's limp body more fully against her. He was strangely light, as though blood and magic had been the only things filling him, and now it was all gone.

Gone.

She hugged him tightly as she kept her eyes on her fallen sword. Fissures had appeared all along the blade. They glowed softly at first, but then began to brighten, rattling the steel as they did.

Cas curled herself more fully around her brother, shielding him from the break she sensed coming. And seconds later, it happened—Shadowslayer gave one last violent lurch and then shattered, its pieces flying in all directions.

A rush of dark energy spiraled up from where it had been resting, dispersing as it reached the sky, covering their surroundings in a thick black shroud. A great and terrible silence followed, but it didn't last long; Cas heard gasps and whispers building in the distance, followed soon by raised voices, anxious shouting.

Because things were already shifting.

She could sense it even through the grief numbing most of her body: the suffocating magic that accompanied the Dark God and his followers had been dealt a heavy blow, and the grip they'd clenched around this battle—this *world*—had started to weaken.

The dark shroud surrounding Cas became a thin veil of fog, still heavy but not impenetrable.

More power faded from the air—and from the dying god she held. The edges of Varen had started to blur, twisting into scant shadows that were thin and barely there, pulling away like spider-webs caught in the wind.

He was gone moments later, and Cas was left clawing her hands through the air and the dirt, trying and failing to catch the last of those shadows before they disappeared. Her throat was so dry she could barely swallow. Her head and her heart pounded as she stared at her empty, blood-stained hands, the sense of emptiness so immense it made it hard to move.

The sound of shouts and ringing steel drew her attention back to the world around her.

The battle was not over.

She wiped the tears from her eyes and staggered to her feet, gaze narrowed toward the sound of approaching voices and footsteps, preparing to keep fighting, knowing she had no choice.

Varen's sacrifice would not be in vain.

Then she realized she *recognized* some of those voices approaching her; they were calling her name. She froze, waiting, until one by one she saw them emerging from the fog, hurrying toward her—Laurent, followed swiftly by Nessa, and then Zev and Silverfoot.

They were carrying shards of her broken sword. The pieces glowed with a golden-white light, illuminating their tired faces.

Nessa reached her first, wrapping her in a tight embrace despite her obvious exhaustion. "Your sword…what happened?"

Laurent picked up what was left of Shadowslayer, looking it over, while Cas somehow found her voice and managed to quickly explain things.

"The air feels changed," Laurent commented once she was finished. "But has the power shifted enough in our favor to end things?"

Cas wasn't sure.

Frowning, Nessa circled the area, studying their surroundings. The unstable air and earth that had accompanied Varen's death had driven people away, scattered the battle in all directions, but it was clearly still raging in the distance.

Where was Elander?

What of their fortress and the rest of their allies?

Cas took a few steps back toward Laurent—toward her sword.

Zev was unusually quiet, absently scratching the ears of Silverfoot, who had perched on his shoulder. He was looking at Shadowslayer as well, his eyes glazing over. Wondering how much of Cas's power had gone with the sword when it shattered, maybe, and how much more she had left to lose.

Cas didn't know the answer to these questions, either.

But her friends were still holding on to the shattered pieces, and she *did* know that they would hold on to them—on to her—until the very end. And that was enough to keep her moving.

The sword's pommel had cracked, a line broken straight through the Heart of the Sun, dividing its already broken jewels. Only a jagged stump remained of the blade. Like those shards her friends held, its jagged tips were glowing with golden-white light.

Broken, but still bright.

The voice of the Sun Goddess was in her head, the words she'd spoken at their last meeting whispering through her thoughts, filling her up like a warm wind filling a ship's sails.

Hold tightly to it.

It's time to go back.

Cas had been tired and afraid to return to the battlefield that day; she still remembered the bone-deep weariness and fear. She'd gone back anyway. She'd kept fighting even after everyone—including herself—thought she was finished.

She had not been finished then, and she was not finished now.

She took her broken sword from Laurent and started to walk.

Far in the distance, she had spotted a section of sky that appeared darker than all the sky around it. She sensed him there—the God of Shades still sowing the seeds of his chaos, trying to sink his claws into the mortal realm and hold on to it, or else ruin it on his way out.

And suddenly she sensed another being fighting against the ruin.

Elander.

She didn't know what had become of her other allies, but this was where *he* was, she was certain: Holding the darkness at bay until she found the strength to rise once more, to pick up her sword and face that darkness alongside him.

She felt his magic and sent a wave of her own toward it, a signal she knew he would be able to feel, regardless of how much ruin and devastation stretched between them.

I'm still here.

His power answered a minute later, directed at her and sending shivers over her skin.

She picked up her pace, sprinting across the burned and cracked ground, her friends right behind her.

The dark patch of sky was soon directly above them.

To the left and right, the battle raged on, soldiers and monsters continuing to clash and rattle the earth. Cas caught a glimpse of the Goddess of Storms and her sister working their magic in the distance, aiding a group of soldiers as they overtook a host of their enemies.

Another group of their allies closed in from the other side —the numbers seemed to have shifted, at least in this section of the battlefield; their enemies no longer outnumbered them. Cas counted a half dozen banners bearing the Ethswen seal on the ground, muddied and flattened. Moreth banners were scattered among the fallen as well—and the Moreth soldiers aiding her had not carried such banners.

No more enemy banners flew within sight of where she stood.

The God of Fire was nowhere to be seen, either, nor was the Goddess of Time.

The sky appeared to be lightening, just the tiniest bit, a few stars fighting their way through the dark shroud.

And there, directly ahead, over a stretch of field littered

with blood and bodies and trampled white flowers, Cas finally caught sight of her king.

He was standing apart from the rest of their allies—the sole being standing between them and the Dark God. The two of them created a dramatic show of light and shadows against the backdrop of dark hills, their magic twisting and crashing together with increasingly frenzied energy.

Another group of their soldiers rose over one of those hills, and Malaphar's attention shifted their direction, a sword of shadows appearing in his grip.

Elander moved to protect the soldiers—

Cas lifted her hand and summoned lightning in the same breath, an entire storm of it that cracked violently across the field before her, shaking the ground and trees, drawing the Dark God's eyes to her.

She didn't flinch under his gaze. She stood tall and kept summoning, calling forth a storm as bright and terrible as the worst of the tempests that once terrified her.

She had no fear in that moment—she *was* the terror, the storm, and she continued to summon more and more lightning into her command. To send flashes of it shooting into the air, making her location impossible to miss. Just as that god had done earlier, she was *beckoning*. Daring him to answer, to follow the trail of magic she was laying out for him. He would come to her this time, not the other way around.

And they would finish this.

It didn't take long for him to answer her call.

While Elander was distracted by the newly-arrived soldiers, black wings unfurled from Malaphar's back and propelled him across the field with only a few powerful beats.

He descended upon Cas in a flurry of dark energy and tumbling grass, limbs, dirt, and everything else that had been caught up in his whirlwind of energy.

Cas summoned a shield to knock the energy and debris aside.

He slammed more of it into the shield, sending her stumbling backward.

She regained her footing and met a swipe of his clawed hand with another surge of shielding magic.

Parrying him proved easier than before; he had been slowed by the shattering of the Point, and the shadows around him were more sluggish too, their darkness less solid—but he was still massive and terrifying, his very presence making the air feel heavier and harder to breathe, harder to move within.

He clawed for her once more, managing to rip a swath of her shield aside, swiftly following the disarming with a blow that sent her flying. She hit a small tree several feet away, knocking the breath from her lungs before she fell to the grass.

Malaphar approached her crumpled body with slow, deliberate steps, darkness rippling like a cloak around him. He was speaking, hisses of words under his breath—but nothing in anything resembling a human tongue.

The weight in the air grew even more oppressive, making Cas feel as though she was being pressed into the ground, singled out and left alone on an island with nothing except pain for company.

But someone waited in the dark ocean, beyond her spinning vision— they were calling her name, just as before.

She was not alone.

The god's followers had started to flee at the destruction of the Antaeum Point and the resulting shift of power. But Cas's had not. They were gathering, hurrying to help her even now. Following her to the very end, broken and beaten down but still fighting. She only had to look up to see the evidence for herself —her friends were right behind the Dark God, still holding the shards of her sword, which continued to radiate light.

She held up a hand to stop them from coming any closer to the dangerous shadows circling around her.

"Hold tightly to the pieces," she called out, as much to herself as to them, as she fought her way back to her feet.

When they adjusted their grip on those pieces, she could feel something rising—waves of magic that would protect them from whatever fallout was coming. *She hoped.*

And she would have sworn that the tighter they squeezed, the more power she felt radiating from the broken piece of sword that she herself held—as if they were protecting *her* as much as she was protecting them.

She could almost imagine them as the Vitali themselves, standing around her like the stone sentinels she'd encountered in Dawnskeep. Except they were alive and breathing, and they were actually answering her call for help.

The magic rising from each piece of her broken sword was soon undeniable, whether drawn out by her own power or something more complicated, more divine and ancient, she didn't know. But it was becoming blinding.

Golden light—and accompanying power—seemed to be coming from every direction.

The Dark God twisted within the light, furiously swiping at the various surges of power. Aimlessly swiping.

He's confused, Cas realized.

Her allies realized it as well, and they began to move in even more confusing patterns.

They were soon joined by the Sky and Storm Goddesses, who took up positions on opposite sides of the field, summoning light of their own, sending it in all directions to create a circle around the already-furious god—a circle of all different kinds of light growing ever brighter, ever more blinding.

It gave Cas the advantage she needed.

She didn't need to see; she could feel her way into the dark, could feel the places where the light gave way to Malaphar's shadows. She only needed to aim for those shadows.

So this was what she did.

She held tightly to her sword, and she let her instincts for magic guide her and pull her toward her target.

Malaphar saw her coming and clawed for her chest—

She ducked and spun, swiftly maneuvering over the broken, debris-littered ground until she was face to face with the god once more.

Her movements no longer seemed to be solely her own; she felt it as she had that day on the shores of the River Drow: as though she was not a mere human, but a vessel for the Goddess of Life to work through. Yet she was more aware than she had been at the riverside—more aware than perhaps she'd ever been of herself, of every hard-won breath she took, every powerful movement she made, every drop of magic she possessed.

Goddess and queen combined and charged forward, plunging Shadowslayer's broken blade into the very heart of the darkness looming over her, holding on as shadows spilled out of Malaphar and engulfed her.

Cold came with the shadows—the familiar, savagely

bitter chill that also accompanied Death magic. That cold made her think of her brother now, poking at the raw, newly-broken place in her heart and making her legs feel as if they might collapse beneath her at any moment.

But she stayed on her feet, holding on through the cold and the dark until, finally, she saw it breaking through—

Light.

It flooded toward her from all corners of the battlefield. From each of her friends, her followers, from the divine beings who had stood at her side. And just as she started to sink beneath the weight of all the combined power, Elander was suddenly right beside her, one arm wrapped around her waist while the other helped steady her sword. He held her through the waves of darkness that continued to threaten, until the light surrounding them became invincible, warmer and brighter than any threat trying to break its way in.

The brightest light the world had ever known.

When it finally began to settle, to fade, the shift made her dizzy. She blinked her eyes several times to adjust them, then took a shaky step out of Elander's embrace, lifting her head up, hoping for a glimpse of clear sky.

A sound like ripping cloth made her twist around.

It happened in the span of a breath—a portal of some kind opening, a gash ripped through the air, black clouds swirling up between her and Elander.

And the Dark God was somehow still *there*, his eyes burning like wild torches in the midst of the black clouds, his claws bloodied and beckoning for her. His mouth did not move, but still she heard his voice in her head, terrible hisses of that inhuman language he'd used earlier.

Then a single sentence, clear and roaring between her ears—

If I am banished from this realm, you are coming with me.

She readied her sword but could do nothing with it; the pressure seizing her muscles was too great. It felt as if the very world was crumpling, the god's disappearance creating a vortex that pulled and pulled until she could no longer resist it without risking being snapped in half. She let go—not of her sword but of her power, no longer fighting against the shadows but allowing them to overtake her and pull her in.

They did so in no time at all, completely and utterly.

She didn't know where she was being dragged to, but she felt as if she had been pulled out of her body, her soul transcending and floating, veering wildly and battering about before finally sinking back and bringing some kind of awareness with it.

There were dark clouds on either side of her. Grey ground underneath her. Nothing above her that she could make out. She still felt as if she was in danger of being pulled into pieces, her skin crawling as though trying to escape her body.

Was this one of their world's hells?

It was not a place for living humans. She was instantly certain of this. But she could still *see* the living through the portal that had yet to fully close, and this was what she focused on—the other side. The battlefield. The sky. The clouds clearing, revealing the faintest trace of daylight.

The dawn was breaking in the world she'd left behind.

But it was so far away.

The only things close to her were those dark clouds and reaching shadows, black tendrils clawing at the edges of the portal as if trying to get past, as though Malaphar was attempting to leave some mark on that mortal world he'd dragged her away from.

A guiding mark so he could find his way back?

Cas knelt and stabbed her broken sword into the ground. It made cracks in the grey, lines that bled golden power which rose into a wall on either side of her, sealing off the portal and preventing the darkness around her from spilling through. As long as she could keep fighting, it would not reach that world or all the people she loved.

She thought only of those people as she bowed her head and focused.

A love strong enough to put it back together.

The cold, black clouds around her had retreated when she lifted her head again.

She exhaled—the weary but peaceful last breath of a life lived to its purpose. Her body slumped. She had no energy left to inhale again. Her grip slipped from her sword.

The blade pulsed with one last brilliant show of light before shattering completely, and then she was tumbling down, drowning in endless waves of gold.

CHAPTER 36

When the world stilled and the magic faded, Elander found himself kneeling among broken ground, his heart racing and lungs aching. The residue from the explosion of energy he'd endured was clearing. The strange portal that had ripped through the air had closed. Everything had an indescribable feeling of *after*. They had reached it—or something close to it—and he was somehow still alive.

But his wife was gone.

How?

She had been right there. They had been on the edge of victory, he'd felt it—the Dark God's power slipping away, the very world itself shifting. Casia had still been standing after the first of those shifts. She'd moved away to catch her breath, to look to the sky, he'd let her go, and then...

He replayed those final moments over in his head until he found the strength to get to his feet. He circled the area, squinting through air that was hazy from a combination of smoke and early morning fog.

Voices, muffled in the gloom, rose around him.

People were moving nearby. Battles resuming, arguments breaking out, confused orders being shouted.

He readied his sword, unsure of what to expect as he continued to move through the murkiness. His grip on the sword was half-hearted; he didn't *want* to keep fighting. The world felt strange, distant and…finished. No battle felt worth it if she was truly gone.

She couldn't truly be gone.

He walked over the cracked ground, winding his way through still bodies, discarded weapons, fallen banners. He should have been numb to the destruction by this point, but instead he was reliving every walk he'd made through similar battlefields. All the things they'd fought their way through, all the blood spilled and losses they'd endured, just to reach the ending without her…

This can't be right.

He spotted Soryn. As soon as she caught sight of him, she quickly finished the conversation she was having with one of her soldiers and rushed to his side.

"That light minutes ago…" she began, voice wavering slightly and eyes searching their surroundings before finally fixing on him. "Where is the queen?"

The question was nearly his undoing.

There is nowhere you could go that I can't find you.

It had been the answer for so long that he'd taken it for granted. But now he *couldn't* find her, couldn't sense her life or her magic, no matter how hard he tried. So he could only shake his head at Soryn's question.

I don't know.

His grip on Caden's sword loosened further as more of their allies caught up to them. Everyone had seen—and most of them had felt—the light pouring toward Casia and her sword. Most of them had seen the portal opening too, the way it had violently slashed the world apart, and the strange darkness that had reached out and pulled her in.

No one had seen her since what they believed was that last, desperate strike of the Dark God's existence.

One by one they looked to Elander, silently questioning him as Soryn had.

Over and over he had to explain that he could no longer feel Casia or her power. That his own magic felt dulled. Still there, buried beneath layers of grief, but pointless. No matter how many times he summoned it, hers didn't answer.

The others joined him in searching, picking their way through the battlefield, breaking up the last of the clashing soldiers, circling around and attempting to find balance under the weight of what had happened. The grief Elander felt was soon reflected on all their faces. All around them, the battle was coming to a close, but the cost of that closure was becoming harder and harder to deny.

They gathered together and continued to move through the aftermath as one united group—Elander, Laurent, Zev, Nessa, and Soryn. Silverfoot bounced from one lifeless body to another, sniffing and whining. More soldiers joined them as they walked, trying to sort through the wreckage, trying to decide where to go from here.

Soryn paused on a crest of hill overlooking a large swath of still-smoldering field—evidence that the Fire God and his beasts had ravaged it only a short time ago.

"So many beasts, just...*disappeared* along with the Rook God and his magic," Soryn said, her tone equal parts wonder and concern. "And my magic feels changed. Not gone, but altered. Dulled, as Elander said. And the magic-users I've spoken with have all said the same thing. It's the reason so many have retreated, I think...they're unsettled, unsure."

"Because who knows what happens next," Nessa said, stumbling a bit as her gaze caught on a group of soldiers still fighting in the distance. Laurent put an arm around her shoulder and they all continued to walk, still searching for answers as they went.

The search yielded no sign of Casia. No gods or goddesses either. The battlefield had been reduced to a wasteland of unstable energies and scattered, confused mortals.

A familiar fear gripped Elander—the fear that she had actually transcended this plane long ago. That her fate had become intertwined too tightly with the gods, with the divine blade and the task the Sun Goddess had given her. Now that task seemed to be over, and so this world had let her go.

And all he could think about in that moment was how he wished he'd been taken with her.

But he was still here, and the world had not stopped, even though it felt like it should have. So he was still walking, though he was no longer paying much attention to where he was going—not until Laurent drew to a stop and the rest of their group followed his lead.

"The majority of our enemies seem to have chosen retreat for the moment," said Laurent.

"They could regroup and return at any time," Soryn pointed out. "We still have plenty to worry about, and things are far from resolved."

There was a murmur of agreement.

Soryn swept a gaze around at everyone, calculating, hesitating the longest on Elander as she added, "Wherever Casia is, she would want us to keep moving until things were more settled."

Elander could not deny this.

But while Soryn and the soldiers around them dispersed, Elander kept still. Laurent, Nessa, and Zev stayed by his side for several minutes, but eventually they too carried on, off to continue to search, to grieve, to work through this devastation in whatever way they could.

Once they had all gone, Elander lifted his hand and tried one last time to summon magic that Casia might be able to feel.

He felt a faint flicker of warmth a moment later.

He turned toward the direction it had come from. He hesitated, terrified of what he might find if he followed it, but ultimately unable to keep himself from moving. If there was any chance…

When he reached the source of the warmth, he didn't find Casia, but he did stumble upon something familiar: Her sword had somehow come back without her—though only parts of it. Pieces of it that were different from the broken ones her friends had gathered; these were newly shattered, the remains of the handle and jagged steel she'd stabbed into Malaphar. He knelt and felt his way through the cold dirt, trying to gather all of the pieces.

It was in so many fragments it was hardly recognizable, and he only remained certain of what it was because he could sense the faint warmth emanating from it…and because the Heart of the Sun, the once-centerpiece of the fragmented pommel, was also resting in the dirt nearby.

He crawled toward the Heart and picked it up. Ran his fingers over the shattered jewels, the cracked face. Closed it in his fist and let its sharp, broken edges press into the mark the Savnas blade had burned into his palm. It pulsed one final time before its beat faded away completely.

He settled back on his heels, still holding tightly to the Heart.

The clouds were clearing, and the smoke and the fog were finally lifting, revealing a dawn sky splashed with every shade of red and orange imaginable. It had truly arrived, as bright and brilliant as they'd hoped for.

He looked at his palm, at the symbol upon it, remembering the vows they'd spoken. The Heart resting against that symbol still did not beat. But his search was not over. He had sworn he would find her again, regardless of what separated them.

And no matter how long it took him, that was what he was going to do.

CHAPTER 37

Cas could not open her eyes. Not for a very long time—not until she felt a hand brushing against her cheek and heard a voice that sounded vaguely familiar. Warmth swirled through her at the sound of this voice, and her eyes fluttered open long enough to see herself floating in what seemed to be a vast expanse of night sky, showers of shimmering gold and silver starlight cascading down around her.

She looked down, but saw no ground.

She reached a hand up to her face, intending to try and pinch herself awake, but her fingers felt nothing solid to close around.

It all made no sense to her exhausted mind, so she curled tightly into herself and went back to sleep.

When she finally managed to wake from her strange dream, she was alone, resting in a patch of soft grass.

A shard of her sword was clenched in her fist, digging in so tightly that it had caused a cut in the center of her palm. Dried blood covered the wedding symbol she shared with Elander. It covered the broken steel as well, and she didn't know where the rest of the sword had gone.

She didn't know where *she* had gone, for that matter.

Something moved behind her.

She fought against her weariness, lifting her head and twisting around.

A woman stood waiting for her, wrapped in robes of white and gold. Her dark skin shimmered like the night sky and falling light from Cas's dream. Ivory wings were folded against her back, their delicate feathers fluttering in the warm breeze she herself seemed to be creating.

The name left Cas on a soft, reverent breath. "Solatis."

The goddess smiled.

Cas took in more of her surroundings, fearing—as she had the last time she'd come face-to-face with this awe-inspiring being—that she was dead.

But if this was an afterlife of some sort, it was remarkably plain; nothing but green grass and pale blue sky stretched as far as she could see.

"What is this place?" she asked.

"*Galathdiel.*" Solatis's voice was pure and bright, like early-morning birdsong chasing away the last thoughts of sleep. "A gateway into the upper-heavens. A place for gods, not mortals."

Cas sat up more fully, pressing her fingers to her temple and shaking her head. "I am not a god."

Solatis laughed softly, her golden eyes shining as though Cas had just given her an answer to a question she'd spent an eternity pondering. "No, you aren't. I've brought you here as a temporary respite. A split decision, forced by the final, desperate act of the God of Shades… He tried very hard to pull you into the hellish realm you pushed him into, and had he succeeded…" She breathed in deep. Smiled again. "But he didn't. You resisted him one last time—and then I intervened. You are here because it was easier to bring you to this place on short notice, as opposed to sending you back to the mortal realm."

"Easier?"

"The veil between this realm and the one Malaphar now moves within is weaker than the one between here and the mortal realm. Especially now, after what you've done to protect that mortal realm."

What had she done?

Cas couldn't remember all of it. She only knew that she felt exhausted and pulled apart, restless even here in this peaceful place, as though parts of her had been left elsewhere.

Solatis offered her hand. "Let's take a walk, shall we?"

Cas let the goddess pull her to her feet. She followed her through the soft grass, her strength bolstered by that warm air surrounding the goddess. Solatis didn't speak for several minutes, as if giving Cas a chance to fully soak up the warmth and regain her energy.

"Do you know why I truly saved you at the end of your past life?" the goddess eventually asked. "Or rather, why I *allowed* you to be saved? Why I didn't interfere when Elander's guardian powers resurfaced and pulled your soul back into the mortal realm?"

Cas had several answers she thought she could give, but the goddess didn't seem to truly be asking for any of them.

"Because I could have interfered," Solatis continued. "It

was unprecedented, a controversial point among the divine courts, to say the least. Humans only live one life for a reason. And for his magic to guide you into one of the royal families of Kethra, and all the complicated things that might have followed...I knew it would be a risk. I could have stopped it."

Cas squeezed the sword fragment in her hand more tightly, thinking of how truly *complicated* things had been.

"But I didn't stop it because I had a feeling about you," said the goddess. "And you have proven me right several times over now. You held to the light even in the darkest of moments, and you passed my final test by going back to the past and fighting for the future of your world and yourself, even with all its complications and uncertainties."

Cas stared at the sky as they walked. She had not been thinking about passing any tests when she made that decision. But she was still glad she had made it, regardless of what had become of her now. Because now her world had a chance at a future not shaped by a mad god.

"You have proven yourself to be so very *human,* in this lifetime and every other," said Solatis, "and I think you understand now that this is not the weakness you once thought it was."

They came to a stop at the edge of a small lake, its surface as peaceful as everything else around them.

"It is a strength—and one that you will need going forward," continued the goddess. "Because the time of the gods in the mortal realm is coming to an end."

The statement sent a shiver of uncertainty through Cas.

The goddess's voice remained soft and reassuring. "I saw it long ago. So did my fellow Moraki. Which, of course, was what started Malaphar down the path that led to...well, *everything*. He was not ready to give up his influence in that realm."

Cas considered this. "So he's not dead. Just gone from the mortal realm."

"No, not dead." Solatis reached a hand over the water. A drop of light fell from it, turning the entire lake to a pale shade of gold. "Nor am I. *Dead* is not the right word when it comes to beings like us. His power is, however, sealed away from the realm you call home. He no longer has a Point—Antaeum or otherwise—that will allow him back into that world."

"So he's gone…but so are you…" Cas studied the goddess's reflection, the way her golden eyes and the shimmering designs upon her skin melded with the newly-transformed lake. "Or *are* you? Because I thought you were gone before, but I felt you alongside me several times over the past weeks. Did I imagine that?"

The goddess shook her head, her smile turning a bit somber. "I was with you in the River Drow, and I was with you in the final moments when you stabbed your sword into our enemy. All I had left—the thin bit of power I managed to keep in your realm—I saved it for the moments when you most needed it. But now it's truly used up, I'm afraid. And so we've reached the place where we must part ways for good."

Cas looked away from their reflections and gazed upon the goddess's true face, trying to imagine never seeing it again. She couldn't.

"Your world will need a mortal queen more than it needs any goddess," said Solatis. "And a king alongside her."

Her heart skipped several beats at the mention of Elander, and the goddess's smile brightened once more.

"A king who has proven worthy of standing by your side,

I think," Solatis continued. "For even as a god, he retained a mortal-like heart. He thought it a weakness in the beginning, much like you—but he's grown as you have. All the more reason I believe the two of you were destined for each other, and for the rule of a throne that will carry such an important role in your world's history."

"And our magic..."

"Will fade eventually, along with the magic throughout the so-called Marrland Empires. Another few generations, and the true age of pure humans will begin. Until then, I trust you'll continue to use your magic for good. My court has granted you the last of what they can give to this mortal world—enough to help you rule with power and light."

"So don't say I never gave you anything," came a familiar, candid voice.

Cas turned and saw the Goddess of Storms striding toward them, followed by her sister. They were both beyond radiant in this realm, their skin and hair shining brightly and sparks of lightning and wisps of clouds following in their wakes.

She met Nephele's eyes as she approached. They were an even more arresting shade of purple than usual, glittering like polished amethysts. Cas was too overcome to speak right away. Their history—the good, the bad, the *complicated*—played through her mind in rapid succession. The goddess started to speak several times, only to stop each time, as though she was sorting through that history and struggling to put it into words as well.

Nephele found her voice first. "You still have the mark I granted you in Stormhaven, don't you?"

Cas nodded.

"I told you to bear the mark and its magic well when I

gave it to you—the charge still stands, Queen. Along with one more."

"One more?"

Nephele's smile had a touch of her usual smugness in it. "Keep that idiot out of trouble for me."

Cas smiled back. "I'll try."

Nephele's expression became more genuine. She regarded Cas with a long look that came very close to tender before she gave a nod of her head and turned away.

Her sister started to follow, but paused long enough to meet Cas's gaze a final time as she said, "I underestimated you, it seems. Keep proving me wrong, won't you?"

Cas agreed, and thanked her, and then both of the Marr were gone as quickly as they'd arrived, their divine forms melting into the air in a way that Cas could only describe as graceful.

Cas lifted her right hand. The mark the Storm Goddess had placed on her wrist was in fact still there, jagged and bold against her skin. On her opposite wrist she now carried two more marks, side-by-side. One was the Sky Goddess's, but the other was unexpected—a star.

"Cepheid…"

"She saw this ending we've reached before the others did, as is her power," Solatis explained. "She left her blessing for me to pass to you, along with some of her magic."

Cas studied the marks for a moment longer, then lifted her eyes to the spot where the two goddesses had disappeared, unable to put into words how she felt in their absence. All the questions she still had for them… She could have spent a lifetime trying to understand and fully connect with them, and though they might not have been *dying*, part of her still ached at the thought of them going their separate ways.

"There is nothing left for them in the mortal world," Solatis assured her. "They gave the last of their power in it to you—willingly so—but they have other places to be now. So don't shed too many tears for them."

Cas nodded; she hadn't even realized the tears were forming until the goddess mentioned them. She tried to blink them away, but another familiar voice reached her before she could truly collect herself.

"We'll still be with you in a way, even if you can no longer visit us."

She turned to see the Goddess of the Moon standing on the shore in the distance, the silver light surrounding her a stunning contrast to the golden water.

Cas no longer tried to keep her tears from falling; they ran freely down her face as she went to the goddess and wrapped her arms around her.

The goddess's usual warmth enveloped Cas as she hugged her back. It had always made Cas feel a bit sleepy but safe. Now it struck her as a feeling of finding the way home, of being found after being certain you were irreversibly lost.

"We'll take different paths now," the goddess whispered before pulling away, "but that doesn't change the roads we've already walked together, does it?" Her hand brushed the crescent-shaped mark along Cas's jaw. It tingled, and though she couldn't see it changing, Cas suspected it was shifting to something that more closely resembled her other marks—another permanent symbol she would carry until the end of her days.

The goddess planted a kiss on the top of her head, then went to stand at Solatis's side. Together, they reached toward the lake. The golden waves parted, creating a path that led farther than Cas could see.

She didn't have to ask where it led. She knew it was a road back to the mortal realm. Back to her empire. Her friends. Her husband.

To everything after.

The Moon Goddess encouraged her toward it with a nod.

Cas hesitated. She was almost too overwhelmed to move, too afraid to take the first step into a future that seemed so big and so full of possibility.

But she was well-practiced at doing things in spite of her fear, so she clutched the broken shard of her sword and managed to put one foot after the other until she was at the beginning of the path.

"One last thing before you go," said Solatis.

Cas turned and found the goddess's hand outstretched, her eyes on the piece of sword Cas had clenched in her hand. As Cas handed it over it began to glow, its edges softening and expanding.

Once it was in the goddess's hand, it melted completely, twisting into a shapeless form that rose above her outstretched palm.

Solatis used her other hand to conjure up threads of gold, which she wrapped around the melted sword piece. The threads twisted and spun, creating a churning mass of energy around it. A *tinging* like hammering upon metal echoed from the mass. The goddess simply watched it all for a moment, letting it shift and tumble until, just as before, she pulled a solid shape from the chaos—two shapes, this time.

Two crowns.

The golden face of one was engraved with a half-circle, like a sun rising over the horizon, while multiple jewel-tipped spires rose like shooting rays around it. The other was more simple but equally beautiful, a circlet of twisting gold with five white jewels spread across it, the one in the center larger than the two on either side of it.

"A fair trade, I think," said Solatis. "A sword for a pair of crowns." She offered them to Cas, who took them without any hesitation.

They were unexpectedly light, just as Shadowslayer had been.

"Hold tightly to them," the goddess said, taking a step back, her shining gaze sweeping over Cas one final time. "And now, I think you're ready to go home."

CAS OPENED her eyes to the sight of the fully risen sun.

She was on her back, and it was directly above her, high and bright. Its beams were relentless, bouncing off the crowns Solatis had given her, making the jewels on them shine so brilliantly they nearly blinded her.

She clenched the crowns tighter, took a deep breath, and sat up.

As her vision adjusted, the battlefield came into sharp focus all around her—all the dead and burned things laid out before her a chilling contrast to the heavenly gateway she'd just left behind.

So much brokenness.

Cas got to her feet and made her way to the first patch of unburned, unstained grass she could find, kneeling among its softness and trying to get back to the peace she'd felt at Solatis's side.

She didn't doubt her purpose any longer, and yet the

questions started to sneak into her thoughts, quiet but relentless: *How do I put this world back together?*

Where do I even start?

She heard footsteps moments later—almost as if in answer to these unasked questions.

She turned around and there they were, rushing to her side just as they had in the battle earlier.

Zev saw her first. He paused, looking around as though he thought her appearance might have been a prank of some sort. Then he was rushing toward her, wrapping her up, and squeezing her so tightly she thought she might actually burst.

She placed the crowns Solatis had given her on the ground so she could wrap her arms more completely around him. Tears streamed down her face, and for once he didn't tease her about them—though he did lean back to wipe them away as he shook his head. "You look terrible," he informed her.

She laughed through more tears. "Better than you, at least."

Rhea and Silverfoot arrived soon after, the fox bounding ahead and leaping into Cas's arms, licking the remaining tears from her face. His eyes shimmered with magic as he looked her over. Cas didn't know how long that magic would last in this new world they were creating, but for now it was bright and clear enough that Rhea let out a relieved sigh at the vision the fox sent her.

She still took Cas's hands and squeezed them, let her fingers travel along Cas's arms and up to her face, feeling for herself that she was safe before she leaned in and pressed their foreheads together. She drew away nearly a full minute later, and only at the sound of Nessa's excited squeal.

Nessa somehow managed to crush her more tightly than

Zev had, pressing both more tears and more breath from her and making her somewhat relieved at Laurent's more subdued greeting. The half-elf was right behind Nessa, and he was the one who eventually rescued Cas from the rib-threatening hug, pulling her away into a quick, light embrace before placing his hands on her shoulders and looking her over.

"Still in one piece, then?" he inquired.

"Still in one piece," she assured him.

"Good."

They shared a small smile, and as the others all gathered around her, their chatter solemn yet hopeful, Cas realized she already knew the answer to those questions that had tried to overwhelm her.

She would start at the same place she had started so many other seemingly impossible tasks—with her friends beside her.

Her friends, and her king.

She had just started to ask where that king was when she spotted him in the distance, and her words left her along with her thoughts. Her friends were still talking, still moving around her, but she wasn't truly aware of anything they were saying or doing. No sound reached her aside from the restless fluttering of her own heart.

Elander's eyes met hers, and he stopped. Stared. He was holding something in his hand. The shattered jewels on it caught a bit of the bright daylight, and even though she no longer felt its power, she knew what it was—the Heart of the Sun—and she knew he had been carrying it, searching for her since the moment she'd disappeared, and that he would have kept on searching until his last breath.

She managed a few steps, clumsy at first, before finding

her footing and starting to walk, and then to run, sprinting so fast by the time she reached him that he only just managed to catch her and steady them both.

She'd thought she had no more tears left. She was wrong. They fell more rapidly than ever, overwhelming Elander's attempts to brush and kiss them away. Eventually he stopped trying, and they simply melted together in a whirl of tears and laughter and kisses, neither of them able to fully breathe or speak for several moments.

Finally, he stilled with his face pressed against her hair, his arms locked tightly around her, and he managed to whisper a coherent sentence. "What happened? Where were you?"

She leaned away and studied him, unsure where to start, and still too breathless to speak anyway.

Her friends had drawn closer once more. Nessa had picked up the crowns and carried them along; Cas took one of them, offering it to Elander as she finally caught her breath.

"I was off collecting a belated wedding gift from the Goddess of the Sun," she told him.

He took the crown, slowly turning it over and over, his fingers carefully tracing the twisting metal. And then he threw it aside so he could take her face in his hands and kiss her again.

They were lost to the rest of the world for several more minutes, until Zev loudly cleared his throat. "We have a few other things to do, I believe."

Slowly, they pulled apart and followed the others as they made their way back toward the fortress and their allies who had gathered there, discussing those allies—and what the future held for them all—as they walked.

"No more Fading Sickness. No more gods meddling, creating such things… It can only lead to good things," said Laurent.

"And magic, at least as we know it, will be gone eventually, as well," added Cas.

"But not all at once?" Nessa asked.

Cas shook her head. "It will be a gradual disappearance as it's used up, according to what Solatis told me. Which will make it easier to navigate, but the world is going to change—irreversibly. We'll have a lot of work to do."

She made a list of this work as they went, counting tasks off as she named them, tapping her fingers against her hand in that old, soothing rhythm of hers. Her step slowed as her thoughts raced. Her friends kept up their pace, pulling slightly ahead of her, but Elander stayed right by her side, listening intently even as her ordered listing gave way to less confident ramblings.

"We'll need to establish some sort of relationship with the leaders of Alnor, to coax them more completely from the shadows of their fallen lands," she said. "A more formal alliance with the southern empire as well, and perhaps more distant kingdoms…" She trailed off, thinking.

"And there's also a palace in the mountains that needs building," Elander reminded her.

Her thoughts grew still. She slowed to a stop and looked over at him, smiling—*truly* smiling—as a feeling of peace and promise overtook her, like the feeling that came from glimpsing the sun after weeks of rain.

The rest of her friends had stopped as well. Soon they were calling for her, eager to keep moving and get to work on all the plans and possibilities that lay before them.

Thick clouds had stretched across the sky, but Cas could

still feel the sunlight through them, warmer than it had felt in a very long time.

"That palace could take awhile," she told Elander. "We should hurry and get started."

He nodded, smiling back as he took her hand, and together they walked on toward everything after.

EPILOGUE

Eighteen Months Later

Cas stood on a balcony overlooking the mountains she and Elander now called home, inhaling the crisp, dewy scent of early morning.

Eighteen months had passed since their final battle with the gods—almost to the day—and the air was finally beginning to feel less heavy, easier to breathe. She had stopped bracing herself for disaster around every corner. She slept through the night more often than not, and though the days were still hard, filled with the endless tasks and challenges that came with ruling, she rose each morning with a renewed spirit, eager and grateful for a chance to work toward an increasingly brighter future.

She was *living* each of her days now, rather than simply surviving them—and so were her friends.

Rhea and Zev had taken up residence in Ciridan, working as her official representatives to help rebuild that city that had stood as a hub of politics and commerce for so long.

Laurent had gone to Moreth, along with a small army, to finish washing away the last of Sarith's filth. Months after he'd arrived there, as things had started to settle down, he'd sent word to Cas, asking her to send a consul on her behalf—an ambassador who would be familiar with her rule, who could help strengthen the ties between her kingdom and the elven realm.

He didn't name anyone in particular.

He simply described the ideal candidate so blatantly that anyone who had spent more than five minutes with Nessa would have known who he was talking about.

Nessa—who had been staying with Cas until this point—agreed to go before she'd even finished reading Laurent's letter.

I'll be back in a few weeks, Nessa had promised.

Cas had sent her along with her blessing. A few weeks turned into six months, then a year, and Cas happily assumed it was a permanent arrangement at this point.

Meanwhile, the construction of Cas and Elander's home had gone on, and now it was nearing completion. A forever home in the mountains, as planned—one closer to the Kingdom of Alnor, which was useful as they attempted to reestablish ties with that kingdom along with the rest of the empire.

Her and her friends' paths had diverged over these past months, and would continue to twist and turn throughout their lives, but she wasn't worried. It was as the Goddess of the Moon had said: *We'll take different paths now, but that doesn't change the roads we've already walked together.*

And they would always find their way back to one another, she was certain. That was happening *soon,* in fact—because her friends would be honored guests at her official coronation taking place in the coming week, and they were all scheduled to arrive at some point this very day.

The thought of seeing them all again made her feel like bouncing. She wandered inside, trying to settle her excitement. It wouldn't be *just* her friends attending the ceremony, but countless officials from across the empires; she probably needed to make an *attempt* at maintaining a dignified and royal appearance.

She walked the halls of her palace, breathing in the scent of wood and other fresh building materials. These halls were far from the extravagant ones she'd once walked in Ciridan; the dwelling had been built for comfort. Not grand and imposing, but cozy, warm, and welcoming.

Without really thinking about it, she ended up in her office. She sat at her desk for the next hour, restlessly leafing through the notes she'd made for the upcoming ceremony until a servant interrupted, presenting her with the crowns Solatis had given her, informing her that they were newly polished and ready.

As she studied those crowns, her thoughts shifted—as they so often had over the past months—toward what it would truly mean to have them officially placed upon her and Elander's heads. To the rule they would be fully embracing, and to all the rulers who had worn crowns before them…

And then to one ruler in particular.

Her heart clenched. She managed a polite thank you before dismissing the servant. Then she rose from her desk, hesitantly crossing to the smaller room attached to her office —a space used mainly for storage.

In the center of this space was an ornate trunk. It was battered and broken in places, its painted wood chipped and its gilded latches tarnished, but it was still beautiful. It had been discovered among the wreckage of the Ciridan Palace; one of the former head servants had recovered it and made certain it found its way into Cas's possession.

It had come from Varen's room.

Within the trunk, Cas had found a bundle of letters. According to the servant who delivered it, these letters were more than a decade old, penned by Varen with the expectation that his father would see them delivered to his sister, wherever she was.

They'd never been sent to her.

Their father had kept them, hiding them away, letting Varen believe he'd been sending them all along. When Varen discovered the truth, the fight that had commenced had apparently been the talk of the palace for weeks.

He'd burned some of the letters in his rage.

But not all.

No less than a dozen remained, buried in this trunk along with other childhood heirlooms—a stuffed tiger, a few dog-eared storybooks, crumpled drawings with both their names signed to them.

Cas hadn't been able to bring herself to read any of the letters for months after she received them.

But curiosity had eventually gotten the better of her, and she'd been reading them one at a time. Rationing them, both for the sake of her heart and because she didn't like the idea of *finishing*.

As long as she still had letters to read, it almost felt as if he was still here and able to talk to her.

Today was one of those days when she found herself wishing desperately that he was still *physically* here, regardless of all the complicated thoughts and feelings that would come with it. That he could have sat across from her desk and offered her counsel about the days to come. That they might have faced those days together, even, supporting and leaning on one another.

The longing for such things made her reach for the tarnished latch of the trunk. Her hands shook slightly, but she managed to get it open and dig through the contents until she had pulled one of the yellowed letters free. Heart pounding, she unfolded it and began to read rambling words, penned in the slightly-messy scrawl of a young boy still learning to write with confidence.

Dear Sister,

It's beginning to seem like a pointless endeavor, writing after all these years, but nevertheless I find myself picking up the pen, hoping against all evidence that you might someday read these words and respond. It's something to do at least—something to distract me from the strangeness I wrote about in my last letter. The air in the palace has only gotten stranger since that letter. I don't know precisely what is troubling

Father, but he grows more and more distant as the days pass.

I try not to think about the reasons behind it.

It's spring here, but it feels more like winter —I can't help but wonder if the Goddess of Ice has developed some sort of grudge against us. It wouldn't surprise me. The trees are still bare. The frost creeps deep into the palace, no matter how the servants work to warm it. More strangeness, as I said.

Do you remember the last spring we spent together? The trouble we got into for breaking the limbs off that flowering tree and stabbing everyone with them? That tree is gone, now—Father said its roots threatened to spread and break up the stone paths, so he had it cut down. I avoid the area where it grew. Foolish, don't you think? It was only a tree, and the fragile swords it provided us left much to be desired, anyway.

Wherever you are, I hope you've found a better sword to protect yourself with. And I hope it's spring, and that the warmth of the season has reached you in earnest...

THE LETTER WENT on for several pages, the handwriting growing increasingly messy. She could almost picture him bent over his desk, his pen scribbling more frantically as the time passed, needing to get the words out before they festered too long and caused lasting damage to his insides.

She understood it. More than once she had picked up a pen of her own and started to write back to him. Even knowing the letter would never reach him, it was still comforting, the thought of shifting the pain to words, transferring it somewhere other than her chest.

She sat with her pain for some time, numbed to everything else, before she managed to make herself move, to return the letter to its hidden place.

As she latched the trunk shut once more, she looked up and found Elander hesitating in the doorway, quietly watching her. She brushed away tears as he stepped closer.

"Another letter?" he guessed.

She nodded, bracing herself against the trunk, her fingers tracing the swirling carvings along its lid. "I...I feel as though I'll forever be unraveling him, trying to make sense of things."

Elander offered his hand and pulled her to her feet, gathering her against his chest.

There were still dozens of tasks they needed to do to prepare for the coming days, but Elander didn't mention any of them. And as long as he held her like this, she felt as if those tasks were further off, less imposing somehow. This was one thing that hadn't changed in the months since their battles—he protected her now as he always had, making space for her moments of doubt and uncertainty until she found the strength to carry on.

After a few minutes she lifted her head from his chest, tucking a strand of hair behind her ear as she composed herself. "As long as I'm reading those letters, it feels like he's still present, still breathing with every new word I read. That's not the worst thing, I suppose."

"No, it isn't," Elander agreed.

She inhaled deeply, leaning away, gathering herself a little more completely.

"And if it helps you feel better," he added, "I came to find you because we have company that I think you'll be eager to greet."

"They're here?" Happiness bubbled up inside her, chasing away the last of her lingering tears.

She didn't wait for Elander to reply—his smile said enough. She picked up her skirts and hurried to the foyer, where she spotted Zev first, lounging on a bench, already making himself comfortable as though he had been there for hours.

"You know," he said, sitting up and stretching, "I expected more of a welcoming parade—as your honored guest and all."

She grabbed his arm and pulled him to his feet before wrapping him in a crushing hug.

"But this will do, I guess," he said, chuckling softly as he hugged her back. Elander caught up moments later, and Zev's gaze darted between him and Cas. "He's still treating you the way you deserve, right?"

"Of course he is," Cas said, rolling her eyes as she smiled.

Zev let her go and turned to Elander. As they shook hands, the pitter-patter of paws upon the wooden floors caught Cas's attention.

She turned to see Silverfoot scampering toward her just before he took a flying leap into her arms. As she nuzzled the soft fur between his ears, Rhea entered the room, her staff tapping rapidly against the floor as she hurried to Cas and wrapped her in a gentle embrace, squeezing the fox between them. Silverfoot wiggled free, but Rhea continued to hold her just as she had when Cas was younger—patient and gentle, never in a rush to be the first to let go. Cas rose and fell against her chest as Rhea breathed in deep and exhaled a relieved sigh.

"I've missed you, love."

"I've missed you, too," said Cas.

"You've been eating?"

"Well enough."

"Sleeping?"

"Better than ever."

"You sound tired. Anything stressful happen since I last saw you?"

Cas smiled. "You mean aside from becoming queen? No, nothing else."

"It feels strange to not check in with you every day, that's all."

Cas laughed, reminding her that it had only been a little over a month since the last time she'd visited her in Ciridan.

"Seems like it was much longer," Rhea said with a shrug.

"True," Cas agreed. And Zev had not been there during that last visit—he'd been off on a diplomatic visit to Sadira—so it had been even longer since her last meeting with him.

This felt more like a proper reunion already. And she had scarcely managed to catch her breath and settle her excited pulse when more visitors were announced—a group of riders from the Realm of Moreth was making its way up the path to the palace gates.

She raced Zev to the front doors, bursting through them just in time to see Laurent helping Nessa down from the stunningly white horse she rode. They were accompanied by no less than twenty elves, each somehow more beautiful than the last, the group of them curving in a half-circle around Nessa and Laurent.

Laurent looked less human than Cas remembered, as if his time spent in Moreth had already started changing him, molding him into the king he was meant to be. There had been no ceremony for him yet—Cas wasn't even entirely certain what such ceremonies looked like in that elven realm, and she made a note to ask him about it later. Though it hardly mattered whether he wore a crown or not; there was no question that he was the ruler of the group following him.

And Cas couldn't help thinking that Nessa looked equally regal at his side. Clearly a human among the ethereal beings that surrounded her, yet those beings followed her as they dismounted, gravitating toward her as if she was one of their own. She looked changed by the airs of Moreth, too. Older, somehow, dressed in elegant riding clothes that looked distinctly elven with their flowing sleeves and intricate embroidered symbols. Her hair was braided neatly back, a delicate circlet of silver resting against it.

She looks like a queen, Cas thought, now beaming from ear to ear.

Nessa's regal look shifted somewhat as she caught sight of Cas and let out a squeal, pulling so abruptly from Laurent's hand that he nearly lost his balance. He didn't scowl at this as he once might have—there was instead a softness in his eyes as he watched Nessa racing across the yard, and it stayed even as his gaze lifted and met Cas's. He nodded hello; this was the only exchange they had time for before Nessa collided with her.

The force of Nessa's hug sent Cas stumbling back against the palace doors. Their laughter echoed through the space, along with their heaving attempts to catch their breath. Nessa caught hers and managed to speak first, but her words were so rapid, so excited that Cas couldn't understand most of what she said.

Cas couldn't speak herself. She tried, but she could only think the same thing over and over as her happiness kept building, filling every part of her and making her throat too tight to get the words out.

You're here.

I'm so glad you're all here.

HOURS LATER, the group of them sat around a table in the garden, still laughing and catching up with one another after an evening of dinner and drinks.

Cas reclined in her chair, her cheeks sore from smiling, her eyes drifting occasionally to the beautiful sunset painting its way across the sky. Silverfoot had curled up in her lap some time ago, demanding pets, and he was still there, nudging her hand every time she dared to stop.

"So it will be official in three days," Rhea said, smiling proudly at her.

Zev yawned. "I hope you don't expect us to start bowing or curtsying to you or whatever now."

"I only expect it of you," Cas informed him, drawing more laughter from the circle around her.

"So you should probably start practicing now," Laurent said, leaning back in his chair.

"And get it right," Elander added, "because I won't have anyone failing to show my wife the proper respect."

Nessa hopped to her feet, eager to help as always. "I can show you how to properly curtsy if you'd like."

Zev had already had enough to drink to accept this proposition with good-natured enthusiasm. He leapt to his feet as well, indicating for Nessa to lead the way, and the two of them were off, practicing all manner of official gestures, from salutes to bows and curtsies, laughing and waltzing their way around the yard.

"That's what you get for encouraging him to practice," said Cas.

The four of them watched as Nessa and Zev's *practice* became increasingly ridiculous. Rhea shook her head with a quiet chuckle. Cas felt as if she might never stop smiling.

"Idiot," said both Elander and Laurent, almost in unison, as they watched Zev take down one of the banners hanging beside the palace door, wrap it around himself, and use it as a pretend dress to practice his curtsy.

Cas laughed, her gaze sliding toward Rhea. "I *did* think he might start to take things more seriously, after all the official business you two have accomplished in Ciridan."

"He remains a lost cause in many ways, I'm afraid," Rhea said.

The antics and laughter continued for nearly another hour, until a wave of sleepiness overtook Cas. Though she was reluctant to leave her friends, she dismissed herself and went to dress for bed. They would still be there in the morning, she told herself—and the next, and the next after that, and she couldn't think of a better thought to fall asleep to.

Elander followed a short time later, carrying some of the glasses and bottles of wine from their garden party. While he readied himself for bed as well, she had a servant bring a carafe of water, and she poured herself a glass before moving to watch the last of the sunset.

The far wall of their room was made almost entirely of

windows, a few of which were cracked open and allowing sounds to drift in from the yard below. She could still hear her friends' laughter in the distance. She wrapped a robe around her nightdress and moved closer to the windows, more warmth flooding through her with every happy note that reached her.

Elander emerged a few minutes later. She heard him pouring a drink, and in the reflection of the darkening windows, she saw him drifting closer, watching her.

She tilted her head toward him, sighing happily. "I've missed them."

He mirrored her content smile as he moved closer, slipping an arm around her waist. She sank into his embrace, her head against his chest, briefly closing her eyes and focusing on the beating of his heart.

After a few minutes, she said, "I'm thinking of building more permanent accommodations on the palace grounds—proper guest houses—so they can be more comfortable when they come to stay with us for extended periods of time."

"Oh?" He stepped away and leaned a shoulder against the window, brow creasing in thought as he studied the yard before looking over to her. "Even for Zev?"

"Even for Zev."

"Are we certain about this? Maybe an apartment in a neighboring town would suffice."

She aimed a playful punch at his arm, which he easily avoided.

"A *nice* apartment," he amended with a grin. "And closer to us than Ciridan. Just not *too* close. I'm thinking twenty miles away, at minimum."

Cas couldn't help returning the grin. "You aren't fooling

me, you know. You two have grown fond of each other, whether you admit it or not."

He scoffed.

Cas shook her head, still grinning. "Also? He can be useful when he wants to be." She took a sip from her glass, swirling its contents as she leaned her back against the windows. "And we might need an extra set of hands around the palace in the coming year, that's all."

He placed his own glass on a nearby desk and moved back to her, letting his hands come to rest on her hips. "You think so?"

"I do." She gazed up at him, her expression drawing him closer, tempting him into a kiss. Her smile remained even as he pulled his lips from hers—she still couldn't stop. There were too many good things inside of her, still bubbling up; smiling was the *least* of what she wanted to do.

Suspicion dawned on Elander's face, a corner of his mouth inching up.

"Why are you looking at me like that?"

"Because you look like you're hiding something."

"Do I?"

He studied her, the combination of admiration and curiosity in his gaze making her cheeks warm. "Any specific *reason* we might need extra hands around here in the near future?"

She only took another sip from her wine glass.

"You're terrible at keeping secrets."

"I am not."

He arched a brow. "You are. And it's only a matter of time before the truth comes out."

"Oh, I think I have *at least* a few months before the truth starts to show."

to, always ready to chat and give advice. To Amanda Steele and the entire team at BOMM—thank you for your boundless enthusiasm and cheerleading. To my Shadowslayers—the greatest, most supportive street team I could have dreamed up. To all the publishers across the world who have picked this little indie book up and brought it to readers in more faraway places and foreign languages than I dared to hope for. To all the artists who have helped countless readers visualize what was once only in my head, through painted scenes, character portraits, book covers, or otherwise. To every reader who has reviewed, shared, and shouted about this series from the rooftops... I wish I could name you all personally, but that would take another book. To friends and family—Mom, Grant, Evie, Karla, Vanessa, Val, Rachel, Jenn, and countless others who deal with my erratic writer tendencies and are still ready and waiting to celebrate with me when it's all said and done...thank you, thank you, and thank you again.

To anyone I missed, know that it wasn't on purpose. I'm astounded every day by how wonderfully vast and warm the book community is, and I'm so glad that me and my characters get to be a part of it.

And now, I guess, we finally and truly come to the end. I'm sad to say goodbye to these characters and their story, and yet it feels like we're only just beginning—and I can't wait for everything that's coming after.

Until our next adventure,
S. M. Gaither

S. M. Gaither is the author of multiple bestselling romantic epic fantasy books. And while she's happiest writing stories filled with magic and spice, she's also done everything from working on a chicken farm to running a small business, with a lot of really odd jobs in between. She currently makes her home in the beautiful foothills of North Carolina with her husband, their daughter and one very spoiled dog. You can visit her online at www.smgaitherbooks.com

His suspicion melted slowly into realization. He eyed the glass in her hand. Took it from her. Tasted it. "Casia…"

"Hm?"

"This is water, not wine."

Her voice came out soft, thick with a sudden rush of emotion. "So it is."

He started to reply several times, but he seemed to lose the words over and over again. He set her glass beside his. His hands moved back to her hips and then hesitantly, almost reverently, up to her stomach, lingering there for a moment before he wrapped his arms around her and pulled her more completely against him.

She buried her face in his chest. Her head stayed against him, and her voice was slightly muffled as she said, "I think our people will be pleased at how seriously we've taken the matter of heirs."

He agreed with a breathless laugh before leaning back so he could meet her gaze. His eyes were shining, their pale blue somehow even more mesmerizing than usual.

She'd had a dream of eyes like this, just days ago—perfect blue eyes in the small, round face of a perfect little boy. It had woken her up, made her tremble as she looked at the star-shaped mark on her wrist. Her dreams had proven prophetic in the past. She didn't know if that would be the case this time. They would have to wait and see.

They would get to wait and see.

The thought sent another rush of emotion through her, and tears spilled from her eyes before she could stop them.

Elander wiped them away and pressed his lips to hers, and she tasted lifetimes in his kiss, the salt and tears of all they'd been through, all they'd survived, and the promise of all they still had left to do. To *see.* And her restless heart—her broken but beautiful human heart—felt as if it was finally home, beating in the place it was meant to beat, guiding her onward toward a tomorrow filled with hope and possibility.

The sun had nearly finished setting. They stayed by the windows, watching it, wrapped in each other's arms until long after the last of its rays had disappeared behind the mountains. Another day gone, another peaceful night closing in around them.

And she could not wait to see what awaited her on the other side of it.

AFTERWORD

We made it to the other side! Thank you for going on this journey with me. What an incredible few years it's been, bringing this world to life and getting to watch more and more readers become a part of it.

Though this story ultimately ended in light, it was born in a somewhat dark place, during a period when I came very close to putting down the writing pen for good. After years of pursuing publication, with some successes and plenty of failures, *The Song of the Marked* was the first story that I truly wrote for myself, without much thought about whether I might sell it to anyone else.

It began as a love letter to a much younger me, who grew up lost in dreams of dragons, faraway and fantastical places, and heroines capable of picking up their own swords and fighting their own battles. I'd wanted to write about a badass warrior queen for a very long time, but doubt and anxiety held me back for far longer than I care to admit.

Casia was not exactly the character I had in mind when I started. I tried to make her invincible, but she kept coming out anxious, flawed, and full of doubts (it seems I took the advice of 'write what you know' to heart)—and yet, somewhere along the way, I realized that she was strong not because of a lack of these things, but because of her ability to pick up her sword and crown in spite of them.

She was not the queen I necessarily wanted, but I believe she was precisely the one I *needed.* And, judging by the countless messages I've received, I think a lot of readers needed her too. Casia and her friends have been embraced in ways I could never have imagined; it's been such a privilege and an honor to hear from those of you who have related to these characters, who speak of them as if they were family. It's reminded me of why stories matter so much—because of the way we find ourselves in them, even when they're full of darkness and messy, imperfect, unpredictable things. Or maybe *especially* when they're full of these things.

Some of those messier, more vulnerable scenes were hard to write, but I hope I've done them justice. At any rate, making my way through them with you (pressing on to the other side, as Cas and company would say) has pushed me to grow, and given me the courage to keep putting words down and sharing them with the world, and for that I'll be forever grateful.

Speaking of gratitude, this series has had a lot of champions throughout its existence, and I would be remiss if I didn't mention some of them while I have this chance.

So, to Rachel Cass, PA extraordinaire—thank you for meeting me in cabins and coffeehouses and wherever else I roam